HOOKER
AVENUE

HOOKER AVENUE

A Queen City Crimes Novel

Jodé Millman

LeVel
BEST BOOKS

DISCLAIMER

This is a work of fiction. While I have mentioned actual places and locations in the story, they are merely to introduce the reader to the beautiful setting of the Hudson Valley and to set the scene for my narrative. Readers familiar with the area landmarks will note that I have taken artistic license by relocating certain locations to accommodate the plot, and to allow my characters to do their jobs. All of the characters and events in my story are the product of my imagination, and any resemblance to actual people, living or dead, or actual events is coincidental.

First edition

ISBN: 978-1-68512-082-5

Cover art by Level Best Designs

This book was professionally typeset on Reedsy.
Find out more at reedsy.com

To my mother, Ellin, and my grandson, Wade, for their unconditional love and the joy they bring to my life.

Praise for the Queen City Crimes

"So many skeletons are banging on the closet doors to be set free, in this heady mix of sizzle, punch, and danger. And, even more intriguing, it's all based on a true crime."—Steve Berry, International and *New York Times* bestselling author of *The Omega Factor*

"Jode Millman's *Hooker Avenue* is a terrific follow-up to her first novel. With her intimate knowledge of the law and her meticulous eye for detail, Millman creates an immersive and unexpected story. If you love police procedurals, you'll devour this book!" —Karen Dionne, *USA Today* and #1 International Bestselling Author of *The Marsh King's Daughter*

"Dark, dangerous and deviously suspenseful, *Hooker Avenue* kept me turning pages late into the night. I adored the fascinating cast of characters and the rich Hudson Valley setting. A truly terrific book!" —Alison Gaylin, *USA Today* Bestselling, and Edgar Award-winning author of *The Collective*

"Seemingly disparate storylines converge and surprise in Millman's second Jessie Martin novel. This outstanding exploration of the legal system and those it leaves behind is also jam-packed with enough suspense and to keep you turning pages well into the night." —Edwin Hill, author of *The Secrets We Keep*

"*Hooker Avenue* is a satisfying and twisty tale of estranged female friends, one a lawyer and one a cop, who are forced to collaborate when a serial killer menaces their community. Jodé Millman atmospherically weaves a tale of two cities: today's down-on-its-luck Poughkeepsie filled with bottom-rung prostitutes and their clients, and the grand boulevards and mansions of its former Dutch and French settlers. Crime fiction at its best!" —Deborah Goodrich Royce, author of *Ruby Falls*

"There's a lot of action in *Hooker Avenue*, and Millman does a fabulous job of keeping the pace going while educating the reader on police procedures, what's ethical, borderline, and crossing into unethical territory. I highly recommend *Hooker Avenue* to anyone interested in a spellbinding and thrilling read." —Linda Thompson, host of *The Author Show* podcast.

"Great sequel! Another fast-paced and entertaining procedural by Millman who is adept at creating beautifully flawed characters you want to root for despite their failings. Reading about the continuing journeys of Jesse, Hal, and Ebony was like visiting old friends. Can't wait for the next book in the series!" —Jerri Williams, Retired FBI Agent, Author and Host of the *"FBI Retired Case Review"* Podcast

Chapter One

There was no doubt about it. Jessie Martin felt a storm brewing. Without warning, the blue sky darkened to an ominous purplish gray. A blade of lightning sliced open the sky, releasing a sudden downpour, and illuminating the Hudson Valley landscape as though it were a grainy black-and-white photograph. Seconds later, a crack of thunder shook her car.

Staring ahead through the blurry windshield, Jessie gripped the leather steering wheel as her heart mimicked the rhythm of the windshield wipers battling the deluge. It felt as though the world was ending, and all she wanted to do was get home to her boyfriend, Hal Samuels, and her baby, Lily.

The shrill ringing of her cellphone made her swerve toward the oncoming traffic on the slick roadway. Jessie righted her Jeep, and reflexively tapped the button on her steering wheel, activating the Bluetooth connection to her cellphone. The act was second nature and offered a brief respite from the hazards demanding her attention.

"Hal?" she asked, believing he was checking in. "I'm on my way home from Adams Market and I'm caught up in a pop-up storm. I should be home in a few minutes, unless there are road closures because of accidents." There was a long silence and unease curled in her midsection. "Hello, Hal? Are you there?"

"Jessica, that's extremely interesting, but why aren't you taking my calls?" The low, raspy voice of her former mentor, Terrence Butterfield, resonated throughout the interior of the car. "How rude, my dear. After all we've meant to each other. And the secrets we've shared." He paused.

His menacing tone turned her skin to gooseflesh, and before he could speak again, she smashed the phone button with her fist, disconnecting the call.

"What the—" she screamed, stopping before an expletive slipped out. Like an idiot, she'd let her guard down. She should have known that even after she'd helped put him away for murder, Terrence wouldn't let her go.

Terrence had always been possessive of her, even when she'd been his student at Poughkeepsie High School over a decade ago. But something deeper, more disturbing, lurked beneath the surface. Last summer, he'd lured her teenage friend, Ryan Paige, into his home with drugs and booze. Ryan, who had been like a younger brother to her, was never seen alive again. And after the cops discovered his dismembered body in Terrence's basement, Terrence was charged with his murder.

It still alarmed her that Terrence, her father's best friend and one of the most popular faculty members at the school where her father was principal, was a psychotic, cold-blooded butcher. And as unreasonable as it may be, she felt responsible for Ryan's death because she'd been blind to Terrence's true nature, the monster hiding behind the charming mask.

Minutes ago on the phone, his voice had sounded so crisp and clear that he'd seemed to be sitting next to her in the passenger's seat, his icy breath whispering in her ear. With Terrence's vampiric presence lingering inside her car, Jessie's eyes cut to the rearview mirror. Only the pitch-blackness of the stormy night reflected at her. Then, out of habit, her eyes whipped to the car seat buckled in the back seat. It was empty. Thankfully, nine-month-old Lily had stayed at home with Jessie's mother while she'd made the quick trip to the grocery store.

The storm, the traffic, and the groceries rattling around in the hatchback had monopolized Jessie's thoughts, as they should have; she'd been too focused on them to expect that Terrence would call her. Again. It had been two days since Terrence's last call, and the problem was he never contacted her from the same number. He was a sneaky bastard. Sometimes he'd call her house and sometimes her cellphone, but he always phoned when he assumed she was alone.

It was unbelievable that a murderer, albeit a murderer acquitted on the grounds of criminal insanity and institutionalized in a state-run psychiatric center, could contact her. Or as she viewed it, stalk her. Jessie wasn't sleeping. She wasn't eating. She flinched whenever the doorbell or the phone rang, even if it was her parents, or Lily's father, Kyle Emory, or Hal. She'd kept Terrence's calls a secret from everyone, but Jessie felt like she was about to snap.

Another downpour engulfed the Jeep, and Jessie's gaze darted back to the highway. She hadn't thought it could rain any harder, but in an instant, Mother Nature had unleashed a tantrum.

Squinting to see through the misty sheets of rain, Jessie's grip on the steering wheel tightened. Her fingernails sliced into her palms and her arms trembled as she fought to steady the Jeep on the slippery roadway.

She needed to pull off the road. She needed to get it together.

Jessie switched on her turn signal and then flipped on the emergency flashers. She coasted off the highway onto the narrow shoulder, parking a safe distance from the road on a grassy patch enclosing a strip mall parking lot, and exhaled a deep breath. As the storm swirled around her, she wondered why her life was so damn complicated.

For years, Terrence had been her friend, her teacher, and her mentor, even her confidante. Then, he'd become her greatest betrayer. To get the murder charges against him dismissed, he'd accused her of violating his attorney-client privilege, jeopardizing her law license. He'd alleged that she'd informed the cops about Ryan's murder after he'd confided in her about the killing. But she hadn't talked. Kyle had called the cops and had only admitted it under oath at the pre-trial hearing to dismiss the charges. Although Jessie had been exonerated of all wrongdoing, Terrence's unfounded accusations had caused her irreparable damage. She'd lost her prestigious job, her fiancé Kyle, and almost her life and child.

"Don't be stupid," Jessie mumbled under her breath, battling the aftershock of Terrence's call. "He's been locked up for nine months and won't be released, ever." While the thought reassured her, Terrence had been harassing her since his commitment, and she hadn't done a damn thing to stop him. She'd believed she was rid of him. But her inaction, her passivity, was allowing him to ruin her new life with Lily and Hal.

The nagging tightness in her shoulders relaxed as she decided, there and then, to seize control. Resolving the Terrence crisis was on her, not him. She'd hatch a plan, and if necessary, seek Hal's help. After all, he was the District Attorney who'd prosecuted Terrence.

The rain was letting up and her yellow emergency signals pulsated in an eerie disco beat over the shimmering landscape. She switched them off and flicked on the high beams as she wiped away the condensation blanketing the inside of her windshield.

As her eyes adjusted, her vision followed the muted light of her Jeep's headlights deep into the rain-drenched darkness. A car length or two ahead, the lights reflected off a glittering object lying in a shallow puddle. For a second, the lights twinkling like tiny snowflakes mesmerized her. Then her sight expanded, focusing on what appeared to be a bulky, glistening mass.

At first glance, it appeared to be the size and shape of a small child. But it couldn't be. Logic told her that the object was probably a bouquet of deflated Mylar balloons, a pile of white garbage bags, or a golf umbrella blown off to the side of the road. Her eyes, and imagination, had to be screwing with her because any reasonable person would have taken shelter in the storm.

Jessie's thoughts flickered back to Lily, and the news stories about toddlers wandering out of their homes and into the woods. Her paranoia might be farfetched, but the shiny rolling waves looked more like the curve of a shoulder than deflated balloons. Another glance at the toddler-shaped mass confirmed that it was too human to ignore.

She needed a closer look.

Jessie opened her car door and stepped outside into the rain, a cold shower so fine and intense that the drops perforated her clothing like needles. She shivered. Her damp skinny jeans and silk blouse clung to her like a second skin.

The amber glare of the parking lot's lights shimmered along a narrow ditch lining the edge of the lot, and the beams of her headlights shone like a spotlight across the grassy roadside. Never veering from the path of light, Jessie inched closer to the slippery ridge of the ditch.

In a flash, the landscape became bathed in a blinding white light and then faded back to black. A sudden clap of thunder made her start and, losing her footing, Jessie tumbled forward onto the slick, rain-soaked earth. Her hands and knees sunk into the mud as she caught her breath and collected her wits. Water dripped into her eyes, and she blinked it away to regain sight.

Her eyes searched frantically through the storm for whatever she believed she'd seen.

Scrambling to her feet, Jessie crept toward the trench. The gully was about five feet deep, shoulder height for her, and was collecting runoff from the storm.

She sucked in her breath as realization dawned. She had not been mistaken. There, in the darkness, she spied the sole of a bare foot, pale and pink against the murky water. A sudden coldness seized her core as her eyes traveled up what appeared to be a leg toward a body partially submerged in the puddle. The person wore a silver sequined bomber jacket and jeans smeared with dirt and brush, which had camouflaged it, preventing easy detection. It had been pure luck that her headlights had reflected off the jacket at just the right angle to attract her attention.

From where Jessie stood, it was difficult to say whether it was a man or woman, dead or alive, but there was definitely a body lying in the mud curled up in the fetal position. The person's face was hidden beneath a mass of long, straggly hair that floated like a halo in the black water accumulating around it.

She thought she heard a moan, but the pulse throbbing in her ears and the rain pulverizing the ground muffled all other sounds.

"Hey," Jessie yelled. "Hey, can you hear me?"

She received no answer.

Jessie shouted again. This time, an arm and leg twitched in apparent response to her call. Those minute movements signaled she was staring

5

down at a person who was still alive, still breathing, at least for the moment. From the volume of water streaming into the trench, every minute, every second counted.

Juiced by adrenaline, her thoughts bounced between whether to climb down into the gully or call for help. The retaining walls of the ditch were already crumbling and sliding down into the bottom of the trench, making them steep and dangerous. If she climbed down, it might be impossible to scale back up the muddy slopes, and then they'd both be stuck in the ditch. Or worse, they could both drown.

And she'd left her phone in the car.

"I'm going to get help," she shouted. The whipping wind blew the words back into her face. "I don't know if you can hear me, but hang on. I'm calling for help."

Jessie's legs grew weak as she turned and dashed back to the car, her feet skating through the grass and mud. Breathless, Jessie slid inside, rummaged through her bag, and dialed 9-1-1.

"Dutchess 911. What is the address of the emergency?" the dispatcher asked.

"Hello, operator? I need your help," Jessie said, her voice ragged with terror. "There's a person lying in a ditch and we need an ambulance right away."

"Ma'am, please slow down. What's your location?"

"What? I've got a dying person here. I need your help."

"Ma'am, first we need to pinpoint your location in case we're disconnected. Now, what's the intersection or landmark closest to you?"

Jessie sighed in frustration and slowly repeated her plea for help. "I'm in the City of Poughkeepsie on Dutchess Turnpike, right across from Adams Farm Stand, near the Starbucks. There's an injured person trapped in a storm drain. The water is rising fast, and I can't get to them."

"Okay," the operator said. "What is your phone number and your name?"

"Jessie Martin," she replied, and provided her cell number.

"Thank you, Jessie. Can you tell me if the person is still breathing?"

"Yes, they appear to be, but not for long if they don't get help." Panicked, she'd been rushing through her responses and paused to compose herself. "He or she appears to be semiconscious. I don't know how they ended up there or how long they've been there, but the rainwater is collecting in the ditch and they're going to drown if you don't send help. Please, please send someone right away."

The dispatcher repeated the facts to her—injured person, storm drain, rising water, Dutchess Turnpike—and asked Jessie to confirm, which she did. "Thank you, Jessie. Are you in any danger?"

The operator's robotic, monotone inquiries made her question her involving the authorities. Recently, she'd learned that contacting them wasn't always the best course of action. Before Ryan's murder, she'd trusted the criminal justice system wholeheartedly. But that was before she'd almost lost everything she cherished. She couldn't face another attack on her integrity and professionalism without imperiling the fragile sanity she clung to like a life preserver. Yet, here she was repeating the same stupid mistake.

"No, I'm fine. I'm in my car, but there's a person outside whose life is in immediate danger." The dispatcher had asked her so many damn questions without providing one iota of help that Jessie felt like screaming. She took a deep breath, forcing herself to calm down and keep her emotions in check.

"Yes, I understand. I want you to remain in your car, and I'd like to keep you on the line until emergency services arrive. Someone will be on the scene shortly."

Shortly was a subjective, if not relative term, which could mean anytime between ten and twenty minutes. In this rainstorm, maybe even longer. Hopefully, the person would survive that long.

Screw this, Jessie thought, scanning the interior of the car for her first aid kit and anything that could serve as a lifeline.

As the line went dead, a flash of white light caught her eye. In the rearview mirror, Jessie detected headlights careening toward the rear of her Jeep. Right toward her.

Chapter Two

Although Hal Samuels had been Dutchess County District Attorney for the past six months, his new office felt strange. He couldn't quite put his finger on it. Maybe it was the lingering scent of his predecessor's Chanel No. 5. The heavy perfume refused to quit; even after cracking the heavy wooden windows open all winter.

Or perhaps it was the turmoil that his predecessor, Lauren Hollenbeck, had left behind. An office so understaffed, overworked, and beleaguered by a spike in gang wars, assaults with illegal handguns, and home invasions that he felt like he was dog-paddling to keep up.

While he'd been Chief Assistant DA, he'd paid little attention to the bureaucratic demands upon his boss. He'd been bureau chief of the Major Crimes Division, prosecuting violent felony offenders and career criminals. The grand jury annex and the courtroom had been his second home, where he'd ensured that justice had been served.

Now, not only was he in charge of everything—narcotics, DWI, justice court, appeals, and the special victims abuse unit—he was drowning in the tsunami of paperwork that accompanied them. And he missed the nitty-gritty of trial work. He was too damn busy pushing papers around to be a real lawyer, a prosecutor. The edges of his litigation knives grew duller and more rusted with each passing day.

As Hal sat behind the government-issue desk commandeered from his old office down the hall, he shivered. The ghosts of Lauren's twelve-year tenure haunted him, suffocating him and reminding him he was an intruder in her territory. She'd offered him the position of chief of staff in her State

Senate office, but he'd declined.

"Call me if you change your mind. We could have such fun together in Albany," Lauren had said, goosing him as she bid him adieu. His face had warmed at her touch, not out of embarrassment, but out of anger at her gall. Thank God the witch had finally flown away. Nobody would miss her.

Hal certainly didn't, and he'd vowed to establish a new regime based upon kindness, not threats. On cooperation, not intimidation. Although he could improve the culture within his office, he couldn't rectify the austerity budget and hiring freeze he'd inherited. During the upcoming budget hearings, he'd make his case to the county government for more money, but no one knew whether the legislature would grant his request for a budget increase. These were tough times all the way around.

Streamlining the office procedures would take time, but his management team, led by his Chief ADA Cindie Tarrico, wouldn't let him down. Together, they'd make the office run smoothly. He had no choice. If he wanted re-election in November, he had to succeed.

Cindie sat across from him during their end of the day review of the new murders, rapes, domestic violence, and drug busts stretching their limited resources. She paused and swiped her hand through her short silver hair. Hal knew the sign. She was saving the worst crisis for last.

"With Parkland and Newtown, school security is a hot button issue. We've received a report that a teen is missing from the Poughkeepsie High School." Hal felt his shoulders tighten at the breakneck speed of her presentation. "Chief, I don't have the details yet, but we're waiting for confirmation from Principal Martin."

"I don't want to send our investigators over there until we hear from Ed. If anything occurred, I'm sure the city police are on top of it and we'll hear from them, too. Until all the facts are in, we need to make sure that the school administration and the kid's family remain on media lockdown. Agreed? We can't have a widespread panic in the school system." Hal clenched his teeth, trying to suppress the yawn rising to the surface. "Anything else?" He surrendered to the reflex, extending his arms out wide.

"Am I boring you or is there trouble in paradise?" Cindie asked slyly.

Hal ignored her prying into his relationship with Jessie Martin, Ed Martin's daughter, and she launched into an update of two troublesome cases pending in their office - *People vs. Manheim*, the art fraud case, and *People vs. Watson*, where a woman had falsely accused a priest of sexual assault.

"And both Watson and Manheim are represented by—" Cindie stopped when his hand flew up in surrender.

"Let me guess... Jeremy Kaplan." He winced at the name of the adversary who had outwitted him in *People vs. Terrence Butterfield*. "He's not involved in the PHS case, is he?"

"Not yet."

"He's been awfully quiet lately. You would think he'd be dragging us into court every chance he got," he said.

"Yeah, it's out of character for him, but the rumor is he's had a heart attack."

"I'd heard that, too, but I really don't give a crap after the way he tortured Jessie. It hasn't been easy for her, almost losing everything because of—" He paused, recalling how Kaplan had tried to free Butterfield by claiming that Jessie had breached Butterfield's attorney-client confidence. While the court had dismissed the allegations of impropriety, Jessie had suffered irrevocable damage. He hated the bastard not only for his sleazy legal machinations but also for ipso facto ending Jessie's legal career and endangering Jessie and Lily's lives. Kaplan deserved the full force of his wrath, but he restrained himself. "I'm sorry to hear that."

"Are you really?" Cindie asked, a smirk curling the corners of her mouth.

"Yes, I am." He shifted his gaze to the window and the geese flying by, and then he yawned again.

* * *

The sound of rain pelting the window like pebbles caused Hal to glance up from the pile of correspondence deposited on his desk. The sky had turned purplish-black. Lightning flashed, and his thoughts shifted to Jessie. He felt relieved that she and Lily were home safe and not out in the storm.

The intercom buzzed. "Principal Martin's on the line for you," his secretary said.

He picked up the handset and cradled it against his ear with his shoulder. "Hey, Ed. I was just about to call you."

"Sorry to bother you, son, but have you spoken to Jess this afternoon?" Ed Martin asked. His voice had a deep, authoritative tone that could freeze a teenager in their tracks. It was no surprise that Ed, Jessie's dedicated father, would ask about her before settling down to business.

"No, but I'll see Jess when I get home later." He flipped through the pile of correspondence, scrawling his signature next to the red "Sign Here" stickers as he continued. "I'm sitting here with Cindie, and we're discussing the incident at your school. Can you fill me in?" When he reached the bottom of the pile, he slipped the documents into a folder and slid it across the desk to Cindie. "If anything's happened, we'd like to round up a list of eyewitnesses. Students, faculty, and staff. Okay?"

He paused, interrupted by the appearance of an assistant DA from the traffic safety division fidgeting in his doorway. The young man's furrowed brow reminded him of a boxer concentrating on the right moment to throw the first punch, and something warned him to prepare for a sucker punch in the gut. "Ed, hold on a sec."

Hal pressed the mute button and transferred the phone to his hand, covering the microphone end. His prosecutor's innate curiosity trumped his annoyance at the interruption. "Marcus?"

"Chief, the sheriff phoned in a multi-car crash on the arterial highway, but they're not sure about fatalities yet. A minivan and a Jeep Cherokee. They're running the VIN numbers and plates for identification. And there was a kid in one car."

The blow landed dead-on in the center of Hal's belly. Fatal automobile accidents, though rare in the county, always struck him hard, but again, his mind returned to Jessie. She and Lily wouldn't be out in this storm. These days Jessie rarely left the house, but with her, you never knew. They were just starting their long-delayed life together and should anything happen to her or Lily, he wouldn't be able to live with himself.

Hal returned to the phone call, disguising the tremor in his voice with cheer. "Ed, I'll call you back."

Better to keep news of the accident to himself for the moment. There was no reason to worry Ed unnecessarily.

Chapter Three

Detective Ebony Jones' left hip ached like a son-of-a-bitch. Rainy days were killers, tweaking her old gunshot wound, and today's thunderstorm was no exception. She squirmed in the passenger's seat of the unmarked SUV, trying to conceal her discomfort from her partner, Zander Pulaski. She glanced at him. Fortunately, he hadn't noticed her wince. Zander was staring out the windshield, gripping the steering wheel with brute force determination. So perhaps she was safe. He was a ballbuster, and Ebony wasn't giving him any reason to diss her, or to feel he couldn't rely on her when the bullets flew.

After a year, she thought the pain would've subsided, but it hadn't. She'd learned to live with it, manage it. Use it to make her a better cop. At thirty-two, with a long career ahead of her, there was no way she'd let a quarter-sized, crescent-shaped scar on the ridge of her thigh define her.

Ebony shifted her attention back to the blurry windshield. What a bastard of a night to be out in the storm. They should've been heading home, where Drew, a hot bath before steamy sex and a glass of Merlot with her name on it waited, but the call had come in at the last minute. She hoped Drew wasn't pissed about another postponed dinner, but he was a big boy. As a firefighter, he'd known what he was getting into when he'd started dating a cop. Hopefully, he'd remember to feed and walk her shepherd, Wrangler.

So, here she and Zander were, careening down the highway in a monster rainstorm toward a body. A body in a storm drain.

"How the hell does anyone fall into a storm drain?" Ebony asked.

"Just add another one to our crazy list," Zander replied.

"You mean the one with the college student getting his head stuck in the dorm banister and the drunken Zamboni driver at the skating rink?"

Zander scoffed as the car hydroplaned and fishtailed. "Whoa, hold on."

She clutched the door handle, every muscle tensing. He brought the car back under control and she relaxed. However, his cavalier attitude annoyed her. This call was different. There was nothing funny about death.

After almost a decade on the force, Zander should know better; they'd caught a fatality before. The gray, waxy sheen of death coating the skin. The body so limp it was hard to imagine it had ever been alive. The dull, unseeing eyes staring into an unearthly realm. Tonight would be the second.

"Well, this is what we signed up for, so let's get there safely, buckaroo," she said.

Outside the window, it was dark as midnight. The road shimmered like a mirage, and the rear lights of the Poughkeepsie Fire Department Rescue Squad's ambulance parked on the shoulder flashed red, blue, and yellow. The gale-force winds rocked their car, telling her that shortly angry gusts would be bitch-slapping her as she searched for the body lying somewhere across the street from the farm stand.

She would have to remain alert in the rain, the mud, or whatever else climate change would hurl at her. There was no time for her pain or Zander's cynicism.

Zander pulled up parallel to the ambulance, beeped, and rolled down Ebony's window.

"Z, what are you doing?" Ebony said, wiping the spray from her face as the ambulance window lowered. "I'm getting soaked over here."

"You're not going to melt like the Wicked Witch of the West, so pipe down."

What's eating *him*, she wondered, turning toward the EMT? "Nice night, huh, Rowley? We received a 10-54. What's the story?"

"Dunno. We just arrived and the ladder trucks are tied up," Rowley replied, looking around at the storm. The wrinkles around his eyes and mouth deepened, matching the craggy voice that revealed too many cigarettes and too much whisky. "We received a call that a body's trapped in a storm drain.

14

We were just about to investigate when you showed up."

"Where? Over there?" Zander asked. He jutted his chin toward a trench beyond the grassy strip separating the highway from a strip mall where a Starbucks mermaid presided. "That's not a storm drain, it's a ditch or swale."

"Doesn't make much difference what it is. We're here to investigate somebody stuck in it, so let's not quibble about technicalities. Who called it in?" Ebony asked.

"The person in that Jeep." Rowley gestured toward a dark Jeep parked up on the grass with its hazard lights flashing. "Dispatch told them to remain inside their car until we came to speak with them. We'll do that while you investigate." He smirked.

She recognized his gloat. He was volleying the dirty work back into their court. Just you wait, she thought. We'll see who ends up in mud up to their chins.

"Sounds good, and we'll signal if we find anyone. Tell the witness we'll need a statement later. Come on Eb, let's go."

"All right, let me change my shoes and grab my jacket and a flashlight." Ebony shrugged on her yellow rain parka, tugged on the hiking boots she'd stowed in the back seat, and joined Zander outside the car. The wind whipped her face, pelting it with rain, and stinging her exposed skin as if it were sleet.

"I can't imagine anyone surviving exposure to this storm for very long. We'd better book," Ebony said.

She tightened her hood around her face and trod head-on into the wind. Her boots sank into the thick muck as she slogged toward the edge of a deep trench. The howling wind lashed at her anorak as her flashlight swept along the swale, searching for evidence of life. The trench appeared to run a hundred yards along the edge of the parking lot and was shoulder deep, approximately five feet deep, and four feet wide. A curtain of fog engulfing both ends blocked her view of its full length, and a swift current of runoff rushed by in the section beneath her feet.

There was something sinister about the ditch.

15

"Look, the walls have started to collapse into the bottom and the water's rising. And the weather's probably washed away any clues suggesting a downward tumble," Ebony said, leaning over the ditch for a closer inspection. "We'd better find our victim fast before—"

"Watch out!" Zander yelled, grabbing her arm and yanking her backward. At that moment, the earth shifted beneath her feet as the rim of the trench crumbled and slid away.

"Damn, that was close." The whooshing of Ebony's pulse throbbed in her ears as she stumbled backward. "Thanks, you almost had two people to rescue."

"Hey, just be careful," he said. She must've looked startled because he followed up with a timid, "You okay?"

Ebony wiped away the water dripping into her eyes and nodded. Fortunately, the darkness would mask the flush of embarrassment creeping across her cheeks. "Yeah, I'm good. But there's nothing here. Let's split up. I'll move toward the eastern end, and you head west. We'll see what we find." She trained her beam on his waterlogged Italian loafers, now caked in mud. "Be careful. It's slippery. Especially in those fancy kicks."

He ignored her as he trod away, leaving her to move on. She flicked her beam into the trench and inched her boots along its muddy lip. The close call had set off an alarm in her head—one false step and she'd be trapped with the victim in the watery trench below, so she proceeded with care. She could be impulsive, but never reckless.

Ebony squinted at the blinding reflection of her light on the water's surface and scanned the scarred walls of mud. In this section of the trench, almost a foot of water had collected. It wasn't deep enough to cover a body, but it could serve as a grave for a drowning victim.

Her cellphone buzzed in her pocket, and shielding it with her body, she glanced at Zander's text. *Find anything?* She texted the thumbs-down emoji and returned the phone to her anorak.

With each step, the rushing sound intensified. About ten yards ahead, a security lamp overhung the parking lot, casting a wide circle of amber light on the rain-soaked ground. Toward the perimeter of the glowing ring, something caught her eye. A sparkling mound glistened from within the depths of the ditch. From her location, it was impossible to determine its identity, but the mass appeared to be sucked into a violent whirlpool circling the drain beneath the overpass leading to the parking lot.

A fight-or-flight rush of adrenaline seized Ebony, thrusting her toward the glittering object. Her feet skidded across the slick grass, unable to gain traction, as her mind switched to rescue mode. The distractions of the cold, the rain, and the danger had vanished like the mist rising into the raw air. Every fiber of her being focused on one goal—saving a life.

Her mind flashed through the rescue and recovery protocols she'd learned at the academy—identify the victim, safely reach the victim, remove objects trapping them, assess their condition and leave the extraction to the experts. Neither she nor Zander were certified in trench rescues, and thankfully, Rowley and his partner, Lulu, were there to do the heavy lifting.

Reaching the edge, Ebony dropped to her knees and fixed her beam into the trench. A body lay half-submerged in the swirling current. The person lay on their side facing away from her, their arms and legs bobbing in the soupy water like buoys in a turbulent sea. Their gender was indeterminate because of the darkness, the diffused lighting, and the current.

"Hey, can you hear me?" Ebony shouted. She hoped she wasn't too late. She didn't want anyone dying on her watch tonight.

There was no reply.

Ebony flopped onto her stomach, digging her boot's toes into the earth. She dangled over the edge of the culvert, extending her hands toward the lifeless body. She strained to reach them, but they were too far away.

"Sir. Madam. Help is here. Can you hear me?"

She thought she heard a low, guttural groan, but it could've been the wind or the downpour or her imagination. Then she heard it again, more clearly this time, and a leg twitched.

Oh my god, Ebony thought. Not dead. They're alive.

"Hold on. Help will be right there. Hold on!"

Jumping to her feet, Ebony waved her arms and her light at Zander and the paramedics to get their attention.

"Over here!"

As Zander and the rescue squad approached, Ebony retreated from the rim, aiming her light at the victim. Zander arrived first. He huffed, catching his breath, and his eyes traced her beam to the bottom of the trench.

"Down there, see 'em?" she asked.

The EMTs arrived on Zander's heels, laden down with gear unfamiliar to her, yet obviously necessary for the extraction.

"How are they?" Rowley asked as he and Lulu unloaded the first aid kit, oxygen tank, ladders, planks, pulleys, and ropes from the litter basket onto the ground. They peered into the culvert, accessing the hazards before returning their attention to Ebony.

"Looks like not good. But I heard a groan, and they moved, so I think they're alive. The water's accumulating pretty quickly, so we've got to get down there. They could be sucked down into the grate."

"There's no time to call for backup, so we need your help. Are you ready?" Rowley asked.

Zander and Ebony nodded in unison.

"Because of the size of the trench and water flow, we can't pump the water out," Rowley said, tightening the strap of his beat-up white hardhat beneath his chin. He selected a car-length plank and handed one end to Zander. "We need to secure the perimeter before we enter. Let's lay this panel down along the lip, so we'll have a stable working surface. Lu, you and Ebony install the cross planks."

Lulu grabbed two six-foot planks, which were not much taller than Ebony, and she and Ebony placed them perpendicular to the long board. Lulu stomped on one end, sinking it into the soil, and used it as a bridge to cross to the opposite side of the culvert.

"Hand me one end of the other longer panel. Then carefully cross over to help me lay it down on this side," Lulu said.

The brisk and unruly winds kicked up, jostling Ebony as she stepped onto the plank. She trained her eyes on Lulu. Her fingers turned clammy as she desperately clung to the wet board tethering her to solid ground. Her heart knocked against her ribs with each shuffle of her boots across the muddy wood. Don't look down. Keep moving. Don't look down, she repeated to herself, trying to steady her nerves and her footing, and not topple into the pit below.

"You're a natural," Lulu said, guiding her along.

On reaching the far side, Ebony exhaled in relief, and glanced at Zander, hoping he'd witnessed her feat of bravery. He hadn't, though. He and Rowley had unraveled the thick orange ropes and pulleys, arranged them on the ground, and were lowering a tall aluminum ladder into the trench. Zander jiggled the ladder, securing it into the watery bottom so that it wouldn't kick out during the rescue. They swung the second ladder over to Lulu and Ebony, allowing entry into the belly of the beast from both sides.

"Return to the other side, and Rowley will show you how to use the ropes to extract the victim once we secure them," Lulu said.

With greater confidence, Ebony scurried across the plank and waited for further instructions. The more she observed the paramedics, the more impressed she became at the way they worked in tandem. In a few brief moments, they'd created a sturdy support system to protect against the trench's eroding soil and to allow bilateral access into the storm drain, organized their equipment, and prepared for action.

She wondered whether she and Zander, who'd been her partner since their promotion to detective, appeared as in synch to observers. Maybe not, but cops were all about reading their partner's mind and reacting in the moment, often on the run. Besides, their felony collars had the highest conviction rate in the department, and that was enough for her.

Silently, Rowley and Lulu descended into the dark pit below. They prodded the victim, who moaned loud enough for Ebony to hear. As Rowley and Lulu gently lifted the victim into a sitting position, Ebony could discern that the victim was female.

She appeared to be unconscious. Her head lolled forward like a rag doll. The shadows and her long straggly hair hid her face. She wore a silver sequined jacket, her pants were ripped at the knees, and one of her feet was bare.

"Zander, clip the ropes, as I showed you, and lower the basket to me, slowly," Rowley shouted. Balancing on the side panel, Zander attached the rope's top carabiner to the highest rung of the ladder and the other carabiner to the aluminum stow basket.

"Now, lean the litter against the ladder and lower it down," Rowley ordered.

Ebony wrapped her arms around the icy side rails of the ladder to stabilize it as Zander lowered the basket.

"Give me some slack on the rope," Rowley ordered.

Ebony crouched over the edge, observing the EMTs carefully package the inert woman into the basket. They strapped her inside and tugged on the rope, signaling for them to haul her up.

"She's good to go. Bring her up," he shouted.

"She looks tiny, but the basket weighs a ton," Ebony said, as she and Zander tugged on the rope. The metal-on-metal scraping grated her ears, but it was proof of the victim's release from the watery trap. When the basket reached the top rung, they stopped.

"Hold on," Zander said, as the wind and rain kicked up again, tossing the litter from side to side.

Rowley and Lulu raced up the far ladder and dashed over to tip the top rung of the litter's ladder onto the ground. Ebony nestled between them as she and Zander helped drag the ladder away from the trench. The EMTs slipped an oxygen mask over the unconscious woman's face and covered her with a thermal Mylar blanket, even shinier than the woman's jacket.

"Thanks, well done," Rowley said. "We'll take it from here and see you at the hospital."

Ebony collapsed onto the ground, sprawling out in the mud. She closed her eyes, embracing the afterglow of exhaustion. The patter of rain and the rapid footsteps of the paramedics transporting the victim to the ambulance filled her ears. In spite of her exhaustion, she'd never felt more alive.

This is why I became a public servant, she thought. Solving crimes and catching scumbags are cool, but saving a life's the best.

But something about this victim nagged at her like a splinter in her finger.

Would a reasonable person wear a sequined jacket in a rainstorm? And how would a reasonable person end up in a ditch? Who was this mystery woman? What the hell was going on?

"Hey, Eb, you're going to need more than rain to wash off the mud, so let's go," Zander said, interrupting her musings. "We're off the clock, so let's return to the station and log out."

"Doesn't anything seem off about this situation? Aren't you the least curious about our vic?" she asked, sitting up.

He shrugged. "No. Not really. It can wait until tomorrow. I've got a hot date and I don't want to be late."

"That's no excuse. You've always got some girl on the line." Ebony extended her hand, and he hauled her to her feet. She shook off the excess water in a shiver. "You can drop me at the hospital on your way back. I'd like to do a little more digging before I write this day off."

"Suit yourself. I'll go tell the witness we'll call them tomorrow to set up an appointment for a statement."

"I've got it. I don't want you to totally destroy your shoes before your *hot* date."

Ebony slogged across the grassy area toward the Jeep and noticed that its hazards were still flashing after the forty-five minutes it had taken for the rescue. She had to give the Good Samaritan credit for making the initial call and sticking it out through the storm. The cops could always use more help from the public.

Ebony detached her shield from her belt, tapped on the driver's window, and flashed her badge as the steamy window rolled down.

Inside was the last person she'd expected to see.

Chapter Four

"Oh," Ebony said flatly. "It's you."

Jessie stared blankly at Ebony as though she didn't recognize her.

Drenched from head-to-toe and covered in mud, Jessie was a mess. Mascara streaked her flushed cheeks. Her rain-soaked brunette curls formed a rat's nest, and although wrapped in a bright red fleece blanket, she shivered uncontrollably.

The passenger seat of Jessie's Jeep was empty, and just a baby seat was strapped into the back.

"Jessie?"

"Yup. It's me." Jessie's voice trembled. Her pupils were so dilated she looked batty, ready to jump out of her skin. "It's been a while."

They'd last crossed paths nine months ago at the police station. Jessie had been pregnant, ready to pop, and smeared with blood when she'd come to speak to Terrence Butterfield about the murder of Ryan Paige. Back in the day when he'd been their high school history teacher, he'd been one crazy mother. Then he'd finally snapped and become a killer. She'd warned Jessie against getting in too deep with him, but had she listened? No. And everything had gone to hell after that.

Thanks to Jessie, Butterfield had been acquitted of the murder charge and had been shipped off to the loony bin, rather than to a maximum-security prison where the scumbag should've spent the rest of his miserable life.

Jessie had screwed up the Poughkeepsie PD's biggest case in fifty years, and just Ebony's luck, she was about to screw up this investigation. Sure,

Jessie had been a Good Samaritan phoning in her discovery, but more than anything else, Jessie was a lawyer and Ebony was a cop. They represented opposing views of the law. Jessie protected the sleazeballs and Ebony prosecuted them. If she probed further, she'd probably discover that they clashed over other things she'd never noticed before. Minute differences she'd overlooked when they were best friends, that now would create a gulf between them.

At the moment, with Jessie's guard down, she was easy pickings. Ebony could draw as much as possible out of Jessie before she clammed up.

Ebony casually propped her elbow on the car window's ledge, toning down her irritation and turning up the charm. "Jessie, you look like you need help. Anything I can do? Should we take you to the hospital?"

"I'm okay, just a little freaked out." Jessie paused. "What's up with the person in the ditch? I saw the EMTs go down with the stretcher."

"The person you saw in the trench is alive, but unconscious. So far, we know little, so maybe you can tell me something." Ebony swiped the rain out of her eyes. "How did you find them?"

Jessie's eyes welled up, and she tugged the blanket tighter. "It was pitch dark, and seeing them was like a miracle or something. I'd hate to think what would have happened if…." She rattled on about the rising water, waving her hands. "I got to the edge of the trench and the bank was crumbling. I couldn't get to them without falling in, so I called 911." She sneezed and blew her nose.

Ebony interrogated folks for a living, and she smelled a lie a mile away. Jessie was hiding something. But what? And why? Clearly, the victim was found too far from the highway for Jessie to have hit the woman, so was she ambulance chasing? Had she seen dollar signs in the rushing water? Was Jessie faking being upset, or was she really a reluctant hero? Why was her SUV pulled off the road at this weird angle?

"Let's go through this again, slower," Ebony said. "Start with why you pulled off the road."

Jessie forced a long, slow breath. "It was raining hard, so I pulled over to wait for the downpour to subside. My headlights flashed on a large sparkly mound over there." She pointed toward the trench. "When I saw the shiny jacket, I thought it could be a kid, so I got out and ran over to the ditch. I saw it wasn't a child. It was an adult caught in the current. The water was rising fast, and I couldn't reach them, so I called 911. Dispatch told me to stay in my car. And here I am."

"That's it? You didn't see anyone or anything at the scene? A car, maybe? Or another person? Did anyone else stop to help?"

Jessie's eyes narrowed and her shoulders went rigid, as though defending an attack. "No, why would they?"

Ebony sensed that Jessie was lawyering up and entering lockdown mode. Soon she'd be no help at all. Before that happened, she needed to pinpoint what Jessie had observed in the trench. Then she'd be making some headway. "So, while you were observing the person in the ditch, did you notice any movement showing that the person was conscious?"

"I told 911 I saw a foot twitch, but that's it." Jessie's head swiveled and she stared out the misty windshield.

Zander leaned on the horn, and Ebony scowled at him and flashed him the finger. She was done here anyway.

"Well, that gives me enough for now. I've got to swing by the hospital, so we'll grab your statement tomorrow. You'll be available, won't you?"

"I'm home all the time," Jessie said, sounding bored at the prospect. "Do you need me to come to the hospital now?"

"No, that's unnecessary. But if you think of anything, jot it down."

Jessie turned back to her. "You know who you're talking to, right?" With her ruined makeup and frizzy hair, she looked more like a clown than a legal eagle, but her glare hinted at the condescension percolating beneath the surface.

Lawyers thought they knew everything.

"Sure do. Good seeing you again, Jessie. We'll be in touch."

"Yeah, good seeing you, too." Jessie's bag started ringing, and she reached into it. "Sorry, Eb, I'd better take this. It's my mother. I left Lily with her hours ago and have to get going. I'll call you and set something up. Maybe you can stop by the house?"

Ebony smiled, watched Jessie answer the phone, and the window roll up. Jessie's phone call would never come. She'd have to hound her. Even when they were in college, she at Marist and Jessie at Syracuse, it was always Ebony who called Jessie. Jessie would only text back.

She raised her hand to shield her eyes because Zander had flicked on the headlights. He revved the engine as she walked down the wet roadway toward him. Growing up, she and Jessie had been inseparable until they'd gone off to college, and even then, they'd hung out during vacations and summers. But since graduation, their paths rarely crossed. They were two Metro-North trains operating on parallel tracks, with opposing destinations at the end of the line. Ebony's track led to the police academy, the Poughkeepsie PD, and Drew. Jessie's led to law school, Hal, a fancy law firm, Kyle, Lily, and back to Hal.

In the distance, a train whistle moaned, and Ebony jogged the last five yards to the car. Zander already had the door open.

* * *

Jessie hung up the phone and tossed it back into her bag. Her mother wouldn't worry now, but Jessie would because she'd lied. She abhorred lying, but that's exactly what she'd done. She'd told her mother the market had been jammed, delaying her return home. However, the truth about Terrence's phone calls remained locked inside Jessie, and it twisted her gut as violently as her morning sickness had.

And she'd lied to Ebony. The untruth gnawed at her almost as much as Ebony's aloofness. She'd been flooded with relief when Ebony appeared at the car window, but Ebony had been all business, probing and demanding answers. The silent accusations had made her feel like she was being interrogated. Like she'd done something wrong.

She hadn't. All she'd done was find a half-dead person in the trench, and report it to 911. It made no difference why she'd pulled over, because it was nobody's business about Terrence's calls. Not Hal's. Not even Ebony the cop's or Ebony her friend's.

Once again, Jessie had attempted to do the right thing, the lawful thing, but it seemed to have backfired. At least with Ebony.

And Ebony hadn't even asked about Lily.

Come to think of it, Ebony had dodged all of her questions. All Jessie knew was that the victim was alive. Not even if they were a man or a woman. Or whether they were injured. Clearly, Ebony was playing the part of "bad cop," keeping information close to her bulletproof vest. Why was Ebony stonewalling her? What was she hiding?

Jessie had risked her safety, and she was entitled to some answers.

Checking the rear-view mirror, she watched Ebony's SUV make a wide arc and swing out onto the highway in the hospital's direction. Jessie glimpsed her reflection in the mirror and gasped. She looked like the person the paramedics had dragged from the ditch. She'd mussed her hair, her makeup had run, and mud covered her ruined clothing. Chalk up another lie to her mother when she arrived home.

Her eyes drifted to the dashboard clock. It was almost dinnertime, and she really wanted to be home to feed Lily. However, a trip to the ER could fill in the blanks.

The wind kicked up again, rocking the car, and the deluge had resumed. As the windshield wipers frantically slapped away the rain, Jess realized there was one place she was meant to be.

She put the car in gear and drove home. She'd contact the hospital later.

* * *

"Z, can you wait for me, please?" Ebony pleaded as she jumped out of the car at the Emergency Room entrance at the Vassar Brother Medical Center. "I'll only be five minutes, ten at the most. I swear."

"You're going to nag me until I say yes, so okay. Ten minutes max, and I'm coming inside with you to make sure that's all," Zander said. "I told you I've got plans."

"You're the best partner." She smiled to herself, knowing that personal plans were a fluid proposition when you were a cop.

"Yeah, yeah. Let's go find our mystery woman."

For the third time this week, Ebony and Zander were back at the ER. Hospital visits were always a pain in the neck; the shortage of parking spaces, the territorial medical staff interfering with their investigations, and the biting stench of ammonia that permeated the halls in a toxic cloud. Oh, god, how she hated the antiseptic burn in her nostrils that reminded her of death, disease, and her own disability.

During their previous trips, the arrestees had pissed her off. They'd escorted rowdy drunk drivers to the lab for blood alcohol testing as required by police procedure. She'd recognized the perps as big shots around the Hudson Valley, so she'd been able to predict how the deal would go down. Their fancy-suited lawyers would assert any technicality as grounds that she and Zander had screwed up. The shysters would say anything or do anything to get their skeevy clients off, but with DWIs, she and Zander played it by the book.

What a waste of time. She and Zander should have been out chasing drug lords, gang leaders, gunrunners, smugglers, and arsonists. Not irresponsible idiots in dire need of rehab, who'd only receive a slap on the wrist for endangering public safety.

Today's hospital visit was much more intriguing. She needed to know the identity of the woman in the culvert and how she got there.

"Ten minutes, huh? It looks like we beat the ambulance here and who knows how long we'll be stuck here twiddling our thumbs," Zander said, tugging on the damp cuffs of his British double-breasted raincoat. "Come on, Eb, I'll buy you a cup of coffee." He dipped his head. "Oh, sorry, chai."

They'd risen together in the department's ranks, had been plainclothes partners for the last five years, and yet sometimes he still didn't get her. She and Zander were different, as different as black and white. Ebony chuckled at the thought that their skin color was the least of their differences.

Alekzander Pulaski was a bit of a hipster, with his dark hair cut long, floppy on the top, and shaved short on the sides. He had a penchant for designer suits, which she knew he always bought at the outlets. She was a little more rock-and-roll, preferring jeans and the black Napa leather

27

motorcycle jacket that had cost her a month's salary. He liked Nine Inch Nails and Thai food, while she preferred Coldplay and burgers. She liked him, though. They complemented each other, and she respected his quirks because she couldn't eat burgers or listen to Coldplay three hundred and sixty-five days a year.

"You go ahead. I'm going to check my emails. I'll be over there." Ebony pointed toward a wooden chair facing the semi-circular nurses' station. Her partner disappeared down the hallway, and she readjusted the gun holstered at her waist before settling into the designated spot, right in the middle of the tumult.

Ebony ignored the suspicious glances being cast her way by the nursing staff. She'd grown used to that. Her tawny complexion, tall frame, dusky blue eyes, and wild, blonde Afro had given pause to onlookers throughout her entire life. Except on the basketball court, where her speed and shooting had eclipsed her exotic appearance. And at the police academy, where her smarts and marksmanship had propelled her to the top of her class.

She glanced up from her phone as Rowley and Lulu appeared, rolling a loud, agitated patient into the unit. They must have revived the woman during the trip because, at her last sighting, she'd been out cold, on the brink of death.

"Get me off this fucking thing. I didn't ask you to bring me here. I've got rights, you know," screamed the young woman strapped to the stretcher. An orange collar immobilized her head, while thick black belts secured her shoulders, chest, and legs in place. One arm was in a sling; the other had an IV drip. The woman furiously flutter-kicked her feet, attempting to free herself from the gurney being guided into the cubicle next to Ebony's chair. "There's nothing wrong with me, so let me go."

"Just calm down, Ms. Sexton. You know we found you unconscious in a roadside ditch. We just want to make sure you're safe and have no serious injuries," Lulu said. "The sooner you cooperate, the sooner they'll discharge you." From her strained tone, it was apparent that the antsy patient had been dancing on Lulu's last nerve.

"I'm fine and I ain't answering any questions," the woman said. "Get me a doctor so I can get outta here. Where's the doctor?"

A nurse rushed into the room, greeting the EMTs. "Hey, Rowley, what've you got here? A psych case? Alcohol? Drugs?" They seemed to speak in shorthand, exchanging information about the patient assessment, IV insertion, vital signs, and chief complaints.

Ebony leaned forward in her chair, straining to eavesdrop on the conversation. She and Zander would have to interview the woman, but they'd have to wait until after the hospital intake and testing. The delay would irritate Zander, but in the meantime, she'd gather whatever evidence she overheard.

"Miss, are you experiencing any pain? Have you ingested any substances we should know about? Do you have any allergies? Is there anyone you'd like us to call?" The nurse rolled the blood pressure monitor to the bedside and slipped on her stethoscope. "I'm going to take your vitals and then, after we get you out of your wet clothes and into a hospital gown, you can see the doctor."

Ebony scooted to the edge of her chair and peeked into the room. Since it had been dark when they'd rescued the victim from the culvert, this was her first opportunity to get a good look at her. She estimated that the patient, a Caucasian woman who appeared starved to the point of emaciation, was approximately thirty-five years old. Mud caked the woman's face, her long dark stringy hair, and shredded clothing. One foot was bare and on the other she wore a filthy high-top sneaker.

"Stop!" the patient shouted, her eyes wild. "Don't touch me. I didn't do nothing wrong, so don't call the cops. Let me go. I need to go home." She bucked the gurney as though she was riding a bronco, startling the nurse, who jumped backward. A white plastic shopping bag that had been resting on the woman's protruding ribs plummeted to the floor.

The nurse, Rowley, and Lulu exchanged looks of annoyance and retreated out of the cubicle's doorway and stopped next to Ebony. "We'd better give her a few minutes to calm down before we transfer her to a bed and perform the intake. Do you have any information on her so I can log her into our system? A name? Address? Next of kin? Medical insurance?"

"Here's the chart," Rowley replied, unhooking the clipboard from the gurney and handing it to her. "According to her New York State driver's license, her name is Elisabeth Sexton of the City of Poughkeepsie. There's no insurance card inside the wallet we found with her things lying next to her in the water."

"Water?" the nurse asked. "Where did you find her?"

"In a storm drain on Route 44 near Starbucks. Between the storm and the mud, we had some job getting her out of there. Look at us, we're filthy." Rowley waved his hands over his body, emphasizing the muck coating his rain slicker and boots. "When we found her, she was lying on her side in a surge of run-off."

For the first time, Ebony examined her own clothing. She, too, looked like she'd survived a mud-wrestling contest.

"She's pretty beat up and not just from the weather," the nurse said, skimming the chart and shaking her head. "The doc should see her stat, and I really need to get her into dry clothing. If that doesn't happen soon, we risk adding pneumonia to the list."

"Her wounds seem mostly superficial. However, you'll know better once you get her cleaned up. My impression is that she'll need x-rays for any potential fractures in her neck, ribs and right arm, and a few stitches on her scalp," he said, taking out a handkerchief and wiping his foggy glasses. "Something about this smells of domestic violence, so you might consider informing the authorities." He turned and walked toward the ER counter to deliver the rest of his paperwork to the clerk.

"Thanks. We'll make an assessment after her exam," the nurse called after him.

"Good luck with that," he said over the sound of the patient wailing in the background.

The woman's situation fascinated Ebony. Her detective's mind spun a narrative of rape and assault and a woman left to die by the side of the road. Unless someone had thrown her from a vehicle? Or had she jumped from a speeding car? Who could have done this to her? Her husband? Her lover? Her pimp? Was this a drug deal gone sour? Or was she a robbery victim?

Rising to gain a better view, Ebony came to face-to-face with the nurse. "May I help you?" the nurse asked curtly.

Ebony scanned the name on the hospital ID hanging around the nurse's neck. *Patricia Whitlock.* She smiled and flashed the silver shield attached to her belt. "Patricia, can I be of any help?"

"No, thank you," Nurse Whitlock replied and stomped away in a huff.

At that moment, Zander returned, balancing two steaming paper cups in his hands. He handed the one marked with the letter E to Ebony. She took a sip, feeling the intense tingle of caffeine jolting her body. "Ah, thanks. That's good. I needed that."

"Any news about our victim?" Zander asked. He drank from his cup and pursed his lips at the apparent bitterness of the frothy liquid.

"She's a bit excited right now and needs to see the doc. It's going to be a while before we can interview her, so let's stop back tomorrow to check on her. She's not going anywhere."

Zander shrugged in agreement.

When whines from Elisabeth's room erupted again, Ebony glanced around, wondering whether she'd been the only person who'd heard the cries. She discovered she was.

"Zander, I've got to hit the restroom before we leave. So, I'll meet you in the car."

Her partner turned and strutted away, presenting Ebony with the opportunity to peek into Elisabeth's room. Discovering her alone, she slipped inside. The woman lay quiet, but her body twitched in its battle against the aftermath of shock. Ebony drew closer and leaned over the gurney.

Rowley had been correct. This woman had been on the receiving end of a vicious beating. Beneath the thin layer of mud encrusting Elisabeth's body, deep purple bruises were rising around her throat in the shape of fingerprints. Blood oozed from the deep gashes on her scalp and her swollen lower lip, which had split open. Beneath her cheap, gaudy clothing, the scratches and scrapes on her arms and legs looked as if she'd sprinted through a forest. The shards of glass embedded in her appendages sparkled in the overhead lighting like diamonds.

Ebony watched Elisabeth's chest steadily rise and fall, and a dense wheeze rattled from inside the woman's lungs. Pity swelled within her as she watched Elisabeth's bare foot, coated with a sticky mixture of tar, cinders, and clotted black blood, dance uncontrollably. Although a macabre mask obscured the patient's features, she seemed familiar. However, Ebony couldn't put her finger on where, when, or if the two had ever met before.

Elisabeth's eyes were closed. Her swollen left eye was turning black. The uninjured eye, brown and bloodshot, fluttered open and met Ebony's. Torn lips strained to mouth inaudible words. Then grubby fingers grabbed Ebony's and tugged, forcing her closer. Bending over, Ebony listened to the phlegmy whisper.

"Help me," Elisabeth whimpered. "Help me, please."

Chapter Five

J essie sat in her kitchen, swaddled in her fluffy bathrobe, trying to shake off the afternoon's chill. She loved her kitchen. It had been the first room she and Kyle had renovated after buying the house three years ago. With its butcher-block island, crisp white granite countertops, and gleaming stainless appliances, it felt like the heart of her home.

Especially with Lily there, wriggling in the highchair next to her. Jessie dipped the spoon into the jar of baby applesauce and fed it to her eager child, whose mouth hung open in anticipation.

"Mmm," Lily purred as she gobbled it down.

Jessie absentmindedly repeated the task as her mind drifted to the strange events of the day. Terrence's call, the unexpected storm, the person in the ditch, the encounter with Ebony and the barrage of lies she'd told along the way simmered in her mind. Her mother had bought her lies, but Ebony apparently hadn't. The spark of hostility in Ebony's eyes had been the tipoff. It wasn't her best friend Ebony she'd met at the scene. It had been Detective Ebony "just the facts, ma'am" Jones.

It was natural that Lily's arrival had quashed Jessie's social life, and perhaps Jessie's preoccupation with motherhood had miffed Ebony. But relationships were a two-way street. Jessie hadn't heard from Ebony since the night of Ryan's murder. Could her association with the killer, Terrence, be the reason for Ebony's deep freeze?

Lily squawked and kicked her feet, interrupting Jessie's musings. Jessie glanced down at the empty jar.

"What a good girl. You ate the whole thing," Jessie said, swiping a damp towel across her daughter's sticky face. Lily's hands were too quick, and she smeared her gooey fingers in her hair and over her face. "I guess we're ready for a bath, right Lilybean? Then, how about some sleepy time?"

Her daughter's gummy smile debuted her middle top and bottom teeth amidst a river of saliva streaming down her chin. For the past month, Lily had been fussy and drooling like a Saint Bernard, so neither Jessie nor Hal had slept in weeks. Finally, last night after tending to Lily around midnight, Jessie had heard the front door click shut. Hal had fled. She hadn't tried to stop him. The poor guy needed his sleep to battle evil in the Queen City.

"Oh, boy. Bath time. Looks like you already took one. After Lily, am I next on your list?" Hal asked, wiggling his eyebrows as he entered the kitchen through the backdoor. He deposited his briefcase on the countertop, removed his raincoat and hung it up in the mudroom closet. He kissed Lily's crown and Jessie's lips. "I'm awfully dirty from slinging mud today."

"You certainly are a filthy old man, aren't you? We'll see what we can do to remedy that, but I don't think you'll fit into Lily's tub."

Jessie handed her daughter a teething biscuit while she gave Hal a proper homecoming. His hands encircled her waist, and he pulled her close. "I'm sorry about last night," he whispered, nuzzling her nape before he softly kissed the spot. His lips trailed up her throat and found their way to her mouth with a deep, penetrating kiss. His hands traveled south, cupped her buttocks, and squeezed. As his kisses continued, she felt his ardent appreciation of her growing as he pressed against her belly.

Lily dropped her cookie on the floor and squealed. Jessie withdrew from Hal, playfully swatting his hands away from her rear end. "Mr. District Attorney, you're going to have to wait your turn. So let's get Lily ready for bed, have a nice supper, and continue where we left off."

"Works for me." Hal scooped Lily from her high chair and lifted her over his head. "Wanna fly in space, Lilybean? Here you go." He brought her back down, kissed her moist cheek, and followed Jessie upstairs.

* * *

A half-hour later, Jessie's house was quiet except for the soft bubbling of dinner in the stovetop skillet. The Baby Sleep app on Jessie's phone showed Lily asleep upstairs in the nursery, and the rattling of the water pipes had stopped, signaling the end of Hal's shower.

Jessie set out her crystal, bone china, and sparkling silverware for their meal, and dimmed the kitchen lights. In the center of the kitchen table, the flickering candles cast golden warmth around the room. The sweet aroma of the onion, tomatoes, wine, and oregano stewing in the chicken cacciatore stirred her sexual desires, and she plotted her seduction. *Dinner. Wine. The two of them.* Hal wasn't fleeing to his condo tonight.

She'd even styled her hair and slipped on a figure-enhancing cornflower blue dress, wondering if he'd notice her efforts.

"I'm ravenous and you look good enough to eat, Ms. Martin." Hal's skin was flushed and his hair wet. He grabbed a plate from her hand and kissed her. "I'm sorry about last night. There's a lot going on at the office and I was exhausted. Later, I'll prove to you the benefits of my good night's rest."

"You know how to charm a girl, Mr. Samuels." Jessie pulled away from him, winked, and continued serving the meal. "I'm thinking of asking my parents to take Lily tomorrow night, so we can have a date night, and sleep in Sunday morning. But, I don't know if that would be fair to them. She's been quite a psycho-baby lately. Sweet one minute, a crazed lunatic the next. I can't blame her. I'd be cranky too with that teething pain." She set her steaming plate on the table and took a seat. "What do you think?"

"They're tough. They handled you and your brother, so I'm sure they can handle her."

Hal wrestled with a stubborn bottle of Pinot Noir, and winning the match, he poured them each a glass. He sat down across from her, and venturing a sip, he ran his tongue along his bottom lip capturing every drop. Every movement reeked of unbridled sensuality, as though he was making passionate love to the wine.

Captivated, Jessie's eyes were riveted to his mouth. Heat stirred in her belly as desire blossomed into hunger. She craved his wine-flavored mouth kissing her, his tongue licking every inch of her body.

He glanced up and caught her staring at him. "Who needs a bath...or a cold shower?" He chuckled.

Jessie's cheeks grew warm, and she cast her eyes downward, giggling in embarrassment. He was laughing with her, not at her, and the warmth of his smile put her at ease. Just like he always did.

She didn't want to kill their romantic mood, but their conviviality seemed the perfect gateway for sharing the news of her day.

"There's something I need to tell you." She immediately regretted her words and hesitated, considering how to spin Terrence's call, discovering the woman roadside and the run-in with Ebony. While the events had been alarming, she'd survived. She'd wait. There was other news. "I received a call from Townsend and Nash about the law associate's position."

"Good news, I hope."

"Nope. They felt I had too much experience, or that was their excuse. They're looking for a recent grad, not someone like me with five or six years' experience. Since when is having knowledge a bad thing?" she asked, not waiting for an answer. "That's the tenth firm in the Hudson Valley to reject me, and I refuse to take an entry-level position at Steinberg's foreclosure factory in Newburgh. I'm running out of options, and I'm in no position to commute to White Plains, Manhattan or Albany." A single tear rolled down her cheek, and she wiped it away with the back of her hand. "Because of my involvement with Terrence, no local firm will touch me. I did nothing wrong, so I can't understand why I'm the pariah of Poughkeepsie."

Sadly, she was. They both knew it.

"Jess, give it time. People will forget and move on. And if they don't screw them."

"You're right. Screw them." She didn't know why she was letting this rejection get her down. She had her law license, a supportive family, and a little money tucked aside. She could make her own opportunity.

"That's the right attitude, and as I've mentioned before, there's a vacancy in the Special Victims Bureau prosecuting domestic violence and child abuse. Our office is desperate for someone like you. A lawyer who's strong-willed, persistent, and sharp. You don't have any frontline criminal experience, but you'd learn quickly. You should consider it. There'd be no favoritism because I'll recuse myself and let the hiring committee decide." He leaned closer to her and placed his hand on top of hers, releasing the butterflies in her stomach. "It might be nice to work together like at NYU. Look how that turned out." Hal's voice was smooth, seductive.

She let the bittersweet law school reference slide by without comment. At NYU, he'd been her research and writing teacher, and from the start, there had been an undeniable attraction between them. Their relationship had developed from one of mutual respect into flirtation, and then they turned hot and heavy as lust blossomed into love. After almost two years together, he'd blindsided Jessie by marrying the daughter of his father's business partner.

Part of her wanted to accept his offer. The part that wanted to protect women who'd suffered battery and abuse, like she'd suffered at the hands of Ryan's older brother, Robbie. Robbie had been her first love and when she'd broken off with him, he'd taken his revenge against her body in a drunken rage. Believing no one would prosecute the son of a prominent businessman for rape, she'd kept her mouth shut. Except she'd naively confided in Terrence, who'd threatened to reveal her secret if she refused to help him beat the murder charges.

However, the other part of her craved a fresh start on her own terms.

"Thanks. Let me mull it over a bit longer. Besides, I'm not sure I'd like being bossed around by you all day. I get enough of that here at home, so wipe that silly smirk off of your face, Mr. Samuels." She playfully pitched her napkin at his face. "I've got my Curtis and McMann severance package, plus, Kyle's been helping support Lily and the house, so I can afford to take my time."

Jessie hoped she'd sounded convincing because Kyle had been unreliable with his payments. She was at her wit's end, but didn't want to burden Hal with her troubles. He had enough on his mind.

"Are you sure you're *ready* to go back to work? What about Lily?" he asked. Concern wrinkled his forehead.

"Yes, I'm *sure*." Her voice lilted cheerfully, disguising her annoyance at his remark. Hal clearly pitied her. He believed she wasn't stable enough, even though her doctors had given her the green light. Except for when Terrence called her, the night terrors were less frequent and, although she'd initially resisted taking anti-anxiety meds, they appeared to be working. She withdrew her hand from his to hide the slight tremor.

"I'm only agreeing that you take your time. There's no hurry. I'm here for you and as I've told you before, I'd love to be here with you all the time."

She wanted to reply, "Yes, let's move in together," but something held her back. Maybe it was their history; she'd once made a commitment to Hal, and he'd dumped her. As hard as she tried, her trust issues lingered. Or was it Kyle emotionally holding her hostage?

"I love you, you know that. But Kyle's been dragging his feet over a final settlement. He seems to derive sadistic pleasure from keeping me in limbo. Besides, it's easier for you to move forward. You're divorced and you have joint custody of Tyler. I'm nowhere near that stage, and I need to settle things with Kyle before we take the next step. You understand, right?"

A vertical wrinkle formed between his brows when he nodded, and then he took another sip of wine.

Jessie glanced at the crisp linen tablecloth, the sparkling crystal brimming with wine, the exquisite meal, and the golden candlelight reflecting in Hal's eyes. She regretted starting the job conversation, which had detoured to Kyle, but perhaps she could salvage the evening.

She shimmied her shoulders like a stripper, teasing him with a peek at her bountiful cleavage. "Come on, let's eat because I'm ready for dessert. I've made fresh whipped cream."

Chapter Six

The next morning, Jessie drew aside the bedroom curtains and peered outside. Although yesterday's storm had blown through, another tempest brewed. Soon, her ex, Kyle Emory, would arrive for his visitation with Lily, which always spelled trouble.

Precisely at nine, the doorbell rang, and she tensed up at its hollow sound.

She opened the front door to find Kyle jiggling the white wooden porch railing, testing the integrity of their mutual investment. His biceps strained against the sleeves of his windbreaker as though he'd bulked up from weight training with the New York Nets.

A slight breeze ruffled his wavy black hair, and the angle of the morning's sun striking his face caused him to squint at her. "Hey, babe. How's my princess? Is she ready?"

Jessie cringed. The terms of endearment rankled her, and he knew it. They bothered her almost as much as his canceling his visits with Lily at the last minute, and his late support and house payments. To keep the peace, she'd let him slide on all accounts, but her patience wore thin. She hated being such a wimp, and his taking advantage of her good nature weighed her down like a hundred-pound barbell.

Silently, she counted to ten before replying. "Lily's teeth are coming in, so I've packed some frozen chewing rings that seem to help. Also, there are bottles and snacks, and baby Tylenol if she gets cranky. You know, the usual, diapers, wipes. I don't think I've forgotten anything. Do you guys have big plans?"

"I might take Lily over to see the ducks at Sunset Pond or out to the

Trevor Zoo in Millbrook since she loves the ring-tailed lemurs." Kyle smiled, cocksure. "Your mother offered me the use of their house for Lily's naptime, so no worries."

"Well, it sounds like you've got it all covered." Jessie held out a peppermint green diaper bag, the spare one stocked for his visits. When he grasped its strap to take it from her, she held on tight, reluctant to let go. Kyle tugged and Jessie relented because she had no real choice. He was Lily's father. And despite him being a jerk to her, she believed he loved his daughter and would ensure that no harm came to her.

From down the hallway, Hal approached, cradling Lily, who clung to one of his ears as she sucked on her binky. She'd dressed the baby for the chilly spring day in a pink hoodie with bunny ears and matching corduroy pants. Bright red Nike sneakers completed her outfit.

The tension mounted with each of Hal's approaching steps. Hal was a man of honor, and a man of action, and he loathed Kyle for many reasons, especially his abandoning Jessie when she was seven months pregnant. If Hal learned about Kyle's financial irresponsibility, she shuddered to think about his reaction. Only her silence preserved the peace between her past and her present.

The men exchanged last name greetings with half-sneers.

"Your mother mentioned you were looking for a job," Kyle said, his eyes narrowing at her. "I thought we agreed you'd stay home with Lily until she's a year old in September. Then she'll be old enough to stay with me in Brooklyn, or go to daycare." She didn't need a reminder he'd accepted a big VP job at the Barclay's Center behind her back, and when she refused to move with him, he'd dumped her.

His words confirmed her suspicions. Her mother, Lena, preferred Kyle to Hal, but breaching Jessie's confidence was going too far.

Kyle slung the diaper bag over his shoulder, and with an air of disgust turned toward Hal. "I bet you're behind this."

"I don't appreciate your tone, Kyle," Jessie said, tempted to slam the door in his face. "Hal has nothing to do with this, and I don't recall any agreement of the kind. In fact, I'm having difficulty remembering anything we've agreed on." She trembled with anger. Kyle knew exactly how to push her buttons and wheedle his way under her skin. She couldn't help it. Hal's hand squeezed her shoulder, steadying her and reminding her of the futility of fighting with Kyle again. Jessie exhaled slowly, checking her anger. "My mother misled you." She'd have plenty to say to her mother about her constant meddling.

"Where do you get off making such an important decision without consulting me?"

The sun slid behind a cloud. The sky darkened, reflecting the blind fury boiling within her and rendering her speechless.

"Listen, Emory, let's be reasonable. Why don't we sit down and discuss things rationally?" Hal asked, standing his ground next to Jessie. Lily reached over, tugged at his nose, and gurgled. The baby's mossy eyes sparkled when the sunlight returned.

"This is between Jessie and me, and concerns our daughter," Kyle growled through his gritted teeth. He snatched Lily from Hal's arms, jouncing her. Lily's chin quivered and tears streamed down her cheeks. The pink binky popped from her mouth and fell to the ground as whimpers filled the air.

"Kyle, maybe it's not a good idea for you to take Lily today. We're both upset and this fighting isn't good for either us or Lily," she said, trying to quell the uneasiness entwining her heart. "Nothing ever gets resolved between us. So, before we say more things we'll regret, let's finalize custody and support once and for all. Our issues have dragged on long enough."

Her ex-fiancé didn't respond immediately. Grasping Lily, he stomped toward the rusty BMW parked in the driveway, opened the rear door, and deposited their baby in a car seat. "I'll see you at five. Be home, because I'm not calling," Kyle yelled as he slid in behind the wheel and slammed his door.

"Hey wait," Jessie yelled as he backed out of the driveway and sped down the street. "You forgot the stroller." She paused and turned to Hal. "I honestly believed Lily's birth would change him. No such luck. I'm done with Kyle's games. It's time to get a lawyer and get on with our lives once and for all."

41

It was time to nip Kyle Emory in the bud.

Chapter Seven

At the station, Ebony reached inside the top drawer of her desk and withdrew an orange prescription bottle of meloxicam. She shook the empty container, and seeing there were no refills left, she swore and chucked it into the trash. It was going to be a banner day. Burnt out by the Saturday dawn patrol, an angry sciatic nerve, and the lack of caffeine, her dwindling patience compounded her misery.

This morning, she'd bypassed the department's bulletin board plastered with posters of the Most Wanted, terrorists, sex offenders, missing animals, departmental memos, civil service job openings, foreclosure notices, and missing persons. With each previous pass, her chest had tightened as the haunting eyes of the missing women peered down at her. Their ragged photos had yellowed with age, and their cases had been deemed beyond cold, arctic, and unworthy of investigation.

If they'd been social influencers or the wives of bankers, lawyers, doctors, or ministers, no expense would have been spared to bring them home alive. But they weren't. These women were hookers. Women with limited choices, who were forced to sell their bodies to survive. And because the authorities considered them to be lower than dirt, their missing bones rotted to dust.

She'd studied them so often she knew their faces and names. Camila Cordoba. Sharone Standly. Justine Harp. They were someone's mother, sister, granddaughter, aunt, or friend. They had lives, and they mattered.

But they'd been forgotten by the establishment, but not by Ebony.

She'd tried to pursue their cases, however, the chief had ordered her to concentrate on the active cases of robbery, assault, and vandalism. So today, she'd avoided their probing eyes and frozen stares by answering emails and completing the overdue incident reports.

Long ago, her Aunt Alicia had been one of them. She'd been thirteen when Alicia had disappeared, and the sting of emptiness had only intensified over time. The pain sharpened its teeth whenever she saw her aunt's smiling face and inquisitive eyes in the photos at her parents' home. Ebony often wondered whether one of those precious family moments had been stolen for use on Alicia's missing person's poster, like the ones pinned on the station's bulletin board.

Fingering the emerald charm on her gold necklace, Ebony peeked through the one-way window out into the public lobby. Friday night's leftovers waited in single-file as though at the deli counter. The desk sergeant bellowed her surname and pointed at the beginning of the stalled parade of complainants. Six Advils and seven hours later, she'd finessed a grab bag of beefs; a stolen carbon fiber racing bike worth two grand, a noise complaint about a late-night college keg party, graffiti desecrating the abandoned Woolworth building, and a woman claiming to have been roughed up after having sex.

She blamed the cases on May's full moon, but questioned why they'd been dumped on her. And where the hell was Zander?

"Hey, Eb, how's your day?" Zander asked, plunking down on the edge of her desk during a momentary lull. "You've got to love being stuck inside all day when we should be out on the streets."

His perkiness annoyed her, so she grunted in response. She rose and stretched the stiffness from her back, hoping he didn't notice her flinching at the prickly pain shooting down her leg.

"You've really got to take care of that hip."

"I've told you a hundred times, I've got it under control." Zander could be such a nag. Worse than her folks. She knew he felt responsible for her injury, but his overprotectiveness was getting on her nerves. It hadn't been Zander's fault that a drug bust on the city's north side had suddenly gone south. The situation had been a perfect storm of the suspect with

44

a concealed semi-automatic weapon getting off a lucky shot at her while they were in hot pursuit. The pitch darkness and the unfamiliar back alleys hadn't helped either. "Don't go beating yourself up about it. You caught the asshole, and that's what matters most. Besides, there's nothing you could've done, short of throwing yourself in the bullet's path. And that would've been damn stupid."

Zander snorted a dismissive laugh.

To distract him, she mentioned Ms. Sexton. "Is there any news about our injured vic?"

"The hospital said that since she was banged up pretty good, they're holding her for observation over the weekend. There's no rush. Monday's soon enough." He glanced at his smartwatch. "I'm clocking out soon, so, Monday it is?"

"Sure, but I'm sticking around for a while. See you Monday and have a nice evening," she said sarcastically. Zander was a player, so whatever his plans were, they were more exciting than hers - walking her dog and doing laundry. It would be only four o'clock when she finished her casework, so she could swing by her apartment, feed and walk Wrangler, and head to the movies. Drew would be done with his shift at the firehouse, and if he wasn't too exhausted, he should be good to meet her at the mall. The laundry could wait.

* * *

A few hours remained before sunset, and Ebony felt a pleasant glow from spring's lengthening daylight and the triple dose of Advil she'd taken when she'd arrived home. She'd attended to Wrangler and had withstood the magnetic pull of the couch, which often attacked after a day on the beat. Ebony itched to go out and do something. The evening was young.

On her way out of the door, she texted Drew. *Going to the 6:20 of Timekeepers at the Galleria. Hope 2 C U.* Fingers crossed emoji.

Ebony hopped into her banana yellow VW Bug and drove south on Route 9 toward the Galleria Mall. The Vassar Brothers Medical Center, a bluish concrete and glass state-of-the-art medical campus, sparkled like a sapphire on the hilltop overlooking the city's waterfront. The dashboard clock read 5:50 p.m., and she figured, considering the coming attractions, the movie wouldn't actually begin until 6:35 p.m. It was still visiting hours, which left plenty of time to check on Ms. Sexton before the show.

She parked in the hospital lot and strolled through the sliding glass doors into the main lobby. The sleek leather couches, the polished floor-to-ceiling Carrera marble, and the gleaming crystal chandeliers reminded her more of a luxury hotel than a hospital. The lobby's grandeur still impressed her because her investigations customarily occurred in the ER or the less grandiose back passages of the hospital.

A white-haired volunteer manning the admissions desk glanced up from his monitor. "May I help you?"

"I'm looking for Elisabeth Sexton," Ebony replied, showing her badge.

The gentleman checked the computer and handed her a yellow visitor's slip. "Miss Sexton is on the second floor, Room 213."

Flashing the pass at the security officer guarding the elevators, she tapped the UP button. Her old friend, the antiseptic odor, greeted her when she exited the elevator onto the second floor. The floor was silent except for the hum of white noise. Smiling at the nurses busy in their station, Ebony followed the long semi-circular hallway until she located Room 213 at the end of the hall.

Loud, overexcited voices drifted out into the corridor and Ebony glanced inside. The room was bright and cheery, with its sage green walls and blinds that were open to reveal a breathtaking view of the Catskills. She spied Elisabeth lying in the bed, propped up by pillows. A portable tray table, holding a bouquet of daisies in a plastic water pitcher, a drinking glass, and an untouched dinner, covered her lap.

Elisabeth's disfigured face was black and blue. Her left eye was swollen shut, and her right arm was cradled in a soft cast. Half of her straggly, over-dyed black locks had been shaved with a white bandage covering her scalp.

Electricity charged the air, as Elisabeth appeared to be facing off with two visitors, a man and a woman. Ebony pegged the unwelcome guests as Elisabeth's parents.

"Damn, nurse. She had no right to go through my stuff," Elisabeth shouted.

"Lissie, she had every right to call us. We're your family and should be here with you," a frail, birdlike woman said, clutching her purse to her belly. Beside her, a burly man in a slate grey New York State Trooper's uniform fidgeted with the visor of his Smokey Bear Stetson. The two silver bars pinned to his collar indicated the rank of captain.

"You didn't tell Luke nothing, did you?" Elisabeth asked. Her voice was urgent, fearful.

"What am I going to tell him? His momma's in the hospital again. I'm not telling that boy anything. You've put him through enough," the trooper yelled back. The man, with long crevices running down the sides of his face, rubbed his silver buzz cut and paced the floor. "We shouldn't even be here after what you've done, but your mama...."

"Clint," the mother said, shaking her head at him. "This isn't the way to treat your daughter."

"Some daughter. We haven't heard from her in months. Not since she checked herself out of that fancy rehab center. And who got stuck with the bill? You know who," Clint said, stabbing his thumb into his barrel chest. His face reddened, and one large vein bulged on his forehead when he raised his voice to respond. "And where's that moron boyfriend of yours? He's never around when you're in trouble. Or was he the one who put you in here?"

"Leave Kurt out of this. He's got nothing to do with it." Elisabeth's tone became belligerent and protective.

"Damn it, Lissie. Stop defending that loser."

"Keep your voices down, we're in a hospital," the mother whispered.

"Ella, I know where we goddamn are. Look at you, Lissie. You're a mess again. Sometimes, I wish... I wish...." Clint's fist punched the crown of his cap so hard that Ebony thought he might puncture it.

"What? That I had OD'd? Is that what you want?"

Clint Sexton's taunting was bitter and hurtful, but Ebony understood the strain of living with an addict. Her Aunt Alicia had battled drug addiction. Ebony had been too young to understand the late-night phone calls, the hospital visits, and the police at her door. But the terrible, drawn-out fights had scared her the most; Alicia screaming at her parents and her grandparents, and her parents bickering with each other. The memory of the damp, dark closet where she'd hidden with her younger sister, Carly, to escape the commotion sent a shiver up Ebony's spine.

"Well, this time, it wasn't my fault. After work, I was crossing the road to get to the bus stop when somebody sideswiped me…ah, ah, a white van. It was dark and rainy out and I didn't see 'em coming. I swear. They drove off and left me for dead in a ditch. A hit and run, Dad. A hit and run."

Her father's suspicious eyes narrowed. "A white van in the dark, huh? Hit and run, my ass. I'm a cop and I can smell a lie a mile away, especially from you. That's what you do best, girl, lie, and it's about time you learned to tell the truth. It would go a long way in allowing you to see Luke. Keep lying and you'll never see him." He waited for a response, but Lissie simply glared at him, as though she wanted to strangle him with his purple necktie. "Knowing you, you were probably high and meandered across the highway in your own world, not giving a crap about anybody or anything. I give up on you, Lissie. Are you happy now? Is that what you want?"

It had taken Ebony a long time to admit that her aunt had been a selfish liar, like Lissie, making promises she couldn't fulfill. Saying anything, doing anything, to hide the truth about her addiction. Not caring who she hurt. It still tore at her heart to think about those horrible times; Alicia disappearing from the Mall food court, leaving a ten-year-old Ebony behind alone, Alicia stealing, and maxing out, her mother's credit cards, and Alicia's lying to everyone at their Thanksgiving dinner about her phenomenal progress in rehab, when she'd been expelled from the facility.

Alicia had disappointed her family so often that the incidents blended together, except for the last time. That one had hit Ebony especially hard. To celebrate Ebony's thirteenth birthday, an allegedly sober Alicia had promised to join Ebony, Carly, and their mother on a girl's trip to New

York City. However, Alicia had never shown up, or even called. This had been on the heels of discovering her grandmother's heirloom pearl-and-diamond ring and matching earrings missing from her jewelry box. Ebony had cherished the heirloom as much as her aunt, and they'd both disappeared without a trace.

"I didn't ask ya to come here, and if you don't believe me, then get out and leave me alone," Lissie said, shooing her parents toward the door.

Ebony caught Lissie's eye and held it for a split second, recognizing the humiliation, loneliness, and fear concealed behind the stony mask. Those emotions reached out to her and penetrated her, filling her with guilt over eavesdropping on such an intimate moment. And over her own inability to save someone she'd desperately loved.

Their connection quickly severed when Lissie swiveled her head back toward her father. "I can take care of myself," she said bitterly.

"Don't pay him any attention, sweetheart. He's under a lot of stress right now. You just concentrate on getting better. Don't worry, your baby won't know nothing about this." Ella spoke softly, reassuringly, as she wiped the flyaway strands of hair from her daughter's battered face.

With an icy glare, Clint stormed out of the room, bumping into Ebony's shoulder as he passed. "Excuse me, miss," he barked.

"Up yours, Daddy-O."

There was a pause; the room felt like a vacuum had sucked the air out of it. Then, in a sudden, violent rage, Lissie swiped her cast across the tray table, flinging the food, pitcher, and glass to the floor with a crash.

Ella stumbled backward as the overturned pitcher dowsed her with water. "Darling, I'd better go find your father. Get some rest and I'll call you tomorrow."

Lissie's eyes welled, and she looked away from her mother toward the window. Ella pecked her daughter's flushed cheek, and flew from the room, dabbing her wet blouse with her handkerchief.

Retreating from the doorway, Ebony flattened her spine against the wall as Ella raced by, searching for her husband. The woman found him slumped against the wall by the elevators, his head buried in his hands. Ella hugged him, but Clint straightened up and shrugged her off, practically shoving her away. He stabbed the elevator button, and the two stood apart, as if strangers, waiting for its arrival.

She'd been right. Lissie Sexton was no ordinary victim who'd fallen into a ditch. She had secrets. And Ebony had questions.

Lissie didn't look high now, but addicts could disguise their cravings. What type of drugs was Lissie addicted to? Had she almost overdosed once, twice, or more than that? What was her deal with rehab? What else had caused the estrangement from her parents? Had she been stoned last night? How had Lissie gotten the busted arm and bruised face? What had she been doing out in last night's rainstorm, and most importantly, how had she ended up in the ditch?

Ebony withdrew her phone from her pocket and was jotting down notes when it buzzed. A text from Drew.

I'm here at the movies. Where R U?

Chapter Eight

Saturday had started out chaotic, but Jessie believed better things were in store. It was soccer day and Hal was in a huff. His lips barely brushed Jessie's cheek as he rushed toward the kitchen door, juggling a duffle crammed with soccer balls, and a pair of cooler bags bursting with enough snacks to feed his hungry team of eight-year-olds. His kiss had been rough, rushed, not like the usual kisses that made her toes curl.

"Hal?" she called. "Can you meet me in front of your office at three o'clock? We can take Tyler out for a bite before dropping him at Erin's."

He didn't stop to answer, but waved in reply. Hal tossed the gear in the back seat of his Volvo, slammed the door, slid inside, and sped away.

Jessie was half-convinced he'd gotten the message. If he hadn't, she'd call him later. Right now, she was still shaking off the shadow Kyle had cast over the morning. Not only had they quarreled, he'd made Hal late for his son's game, and he'd derailed a life-changing discussion with Hal. A surprise her mother's loose lips had almost spoiled.

Earlier in the week, she'd made the mistake of confiding in her mother about going office hunting. She should have guessed her secret would find its way back to Kyle.

Her realtor friend Bellamy had shown her and Lily offices meeting Jessie's strict criteria; rent of six hundred dollars per month (including utilities), a five minutes car ride from home, an office large enough to accommodate a porta-crib, off-street parking, in a safe neighborhood and in an attorney-occupied building with a shared library. Poughkeepsie was littered with

51

empty rental space, and Bellamy had whittled the options down to an even dozen.

Jessie had narrowed the field to three possibilities: the Church Building, the Barrie Building, and the Bardavon Building. The Church Building was a squat two-story mid-twentieth century building across the street from Hal's office and the courthouse on Market Street. The Bardavon Building, also on Market Street, was a magnificent structure constructed over a historic opera house with a three-story illuminated marquee. And the Barrie Building was a former brick residence located one block from the courthouse, which had been converted into offices with a common waiting room, secretarial area, library, kitchen, and restrooms.

Each location presented pros and cons, but she was eager to start this new chapter of her life and hoped Hal would share in her excitement.

She walked over to the stove and turned on the kettle to make a cup of tea. While she waited for the water to boil, she checked her phone for new notifications about last night's accident. There were none, so she googled "storm rescue Poughkeepsie." A link to a brief *Poughkeepsie Journal* article, accompanied by a stock photo of an ambulance, appeared.

STORM INCIDENT SENDS WOMAN TO HOSPITAL AFTER NEAR DROWNING

At approximately 5 p.m. last night, two City of Poughkeepsie Detectives and the Rescue Services extracted a woman from a culvert along Route 44. The victim sustained minor injuries and was taken to VBMC for treatment. The police are seeking witnesses and encourage anyone having information to contact the Police Department immediately.

The victim was a woman, and she was alive. Thank goodness. But no name had been mentioned.

Hal could probably snag the info with one phone call, but that would open a can of worms about Terrence's harassing her. Relying on Hal was a nonstarter.

Ebony was the only person who could give her the woman's name, but since it was an active investigation, odds were she wouldn't share it. Despite yesterday's weirdness, their friendship had once meant something, so it was worth the shot.

Jessie typed out a text. Sweet, simple, and to the point:

Just following up. Available to make my statement anytime. Any info about the woman? I'd like to visit her.

She hit send, and the shrill whistle of the kettle sounded.

* * *

As the downtown church bells chimed three o'clock, two smiling faces greeted Jessie at the appointed place.

"Hey Tyler," Jessie said to the youngster bouncing a soccer ball on his knee. He'd sprouted up an inch since she'd seen him two weeks ago, and shedding his baby fat, he looked like his gorgeous blonde mother. "Did you have fun at your game? I hope your coach wasn't too rough on you."

"I scored the winning goal, and we kicked their butts," Tyler said. His amber eyes sparkled like his father's. "It was cooool."

"Jess," Hal said, "I know you have something up your sleeve. Are we looking at office space?"

"Maybe," she replied coyly. She twirled a strand of her hair around her index finger and stopped before her tell gave it away. Her cheeks flared with heat.

"You'd make a terrible poker player," he said and laughed. "Come on, show me what you've got." He turned to Tyler. "You don't mind helping Jess pick out her new office, do you? Maybe we could go for some ice cream afterwards. What do you think, Bud?"

The youngster's face lit up, and Hal grinned.

"Will baby Lily work there, too?"

"Sometimes." Jessie bit her lip to keep a straight face. "Come on, the sooner we finish, the sooner we get—"

"Ice cream!" Tyler yelled eagerly.

The three of them held hands as they crossed the street, met the broker at the Church Building, and toured the first two sites. Tyler remarked that the Church building was spooky and smelled like old people and cabbage. She agreed it did.

"This place looks rickety," Tyler said innocently, staring at the massive Bardavon marquee overhead.

Stepping off the elevator on the fifth floor, Hal grabbed her arm when her heel caught on the tattered hallway carpet. "Look, your office windows look directly into mine across the street. But as convenient as that is, the old wooden sills and sashes are rotten, and you'll freeze in the winter and stew in the summer. Even if utilities are included, you and your clients want to be comfortable."

Jessie felt the air fizzle out of her balloon as she analyzed the buildings through his objective eyes. In her mind, she'd arranged the new oak desk, laid the oriental carpets, and installed the window curtains. Her excitement had blinded her to the chipped paint, uneven floorboards, cracked plaster, and dim overhead lighting. These rental spaces were not even diamonds in the rough. They were lumps of sooty, black coal.

"There's one more," Jessie said hesitantly.

They walked one block up the Main Mall and cut across to the arterial highway.

"Here it is," Bellamy said. The group stopped in front of the Barrie Building, a former mansion with bright yellow and green trim that contrasted with the red brick facade. The cars and trucks whizzed by, exceeding the thirty-mile-per-hour speed limit and kicking winter's dust into their eyes. "You can't hear the traffic once you're inside."

Out of the corner of Jessie's eye, she noticed Hal grimace at the thundering rumble of a sanitation truck and a school bus as they passed.

Bellamy hurried ahead to unlock the door and disengage the security alarm as she and Hal crossed the wrap-around porch. Tyler, eyeing the wooden porch swing swaying in the breeze, scampered over and jumped aboard.

"Come on, Bud," Hal called, and the trio entered the building.

Jessie had intentionally saved her favorite option for last. Although her mind was set, she wanted Hal's blessing. "What do you think?" she asked.

The Samuels boys gazed at the polished mahogany banisters of the grand foyer staircase before them. To their left, the landlords had converted the parlor with a marble fireplace into a secretarial and waiting area, and to their right, the formal dining room served as the conference room and library. The conference table looked minuscule inside the cavernous room, which could've easily accommodated a banquet table set for twenty. Floor-to-ceiling bookshelves stocked with leather-bound treatises and casebooks flanked the library's fireplace. Sunlight streamed in through the delicate stained-glass windows that stretched the length of each room. Above their heads, the crystal chandelier captured the sun's rays and refracted them on the walls in hundreds of tiny rainbows.

"Wow," Tyler said, craning his little neck to view the light show.

"You should've led with this one," Hal said, his voice echoing in the empty room. "You're not planning on living here, are you?"

Bellamy ushered them upstairs to the room that would be Jessie's office. Situated over the library/dining room, the former master bedroom had also retained the original polished woodwork and flooring. Two bay windows overlooked the highway and huddled in between was a window seat. A cedar walk-in closet occupied the wall opposite the brick fireplace.

"If you like, you can arrange for coverage with the staff secretary. When I receive the signed lease and security deposit, I'll email you a security code so you could move in at your convenience." Bellamy handed her the lease. "I'll need a decision soon, Jessie. This is a prime location and there's someone else who's viewing the space next week."

Jessie knew she wasn't being hustled; it was the truth. This space was incredible.

For five years, she'd slaved for Curtis and McMann because they'd dangled a partnership before her like a lottery jackpot. She'd lost vacations, holidays, and weekends to line their pockets, and they'd screwed her. It was time to hang her shingle on this front door and show the world, and herself, she could make it on her own.

"Who's ready to celebrate?" Hal asked.

Chapter Nine

Striding toward the courthouse elevator, the sound of Hal's loafers echoed like thunder across the lobby's marble floor. The elevator doors slid open, and the agonizing memory of the day Jessie had hemorrhaged on the Grand Jury's witness stand pierced his heart. He'd been running the Butterfield case, but against his wishes, his boss had subpoenaed Jessie to testify about her relationship with Butterfield. Mistakenly, the DA had asserted that Jessie had been the killer's accomplice, and the stress had triggered Jessie's medical emergency. The stretcher had been too bulky for the compact lift, so they'd evacuated her down the rickety, iron emergency staircase. Fortunately, Jessie had been fine, but the episode had flipped his life upside down. Amid the chaos, he'd fallen in love with her again.

It was strange having the bittersweet memory percolate to the surface today, but he shook it off, entered the elevator, and jabbed the button. He rode up to his fifth-floor suite that offered panoramic views over the Hudson. From his summit, he could see as far north as the Walkway Over the Hudson, and southward, just beyond the Mid-Hudson Bridge to the Shadows Marina. He'd often interrupted his former boss, Lauren Hollenbeck, gazing out of these windows deep in thought. The spectacular views of the Hudson, its bridges, and the Catskills invited it.

The struggling Mid-Hudson Civic Center across the street did not. The black letters on the marquee reminded him about how Kyle Emory's tenure as the civic center's manager had ushered the place into bankruptcy. He'd done as much with Jessie's life.

Since Hal's own domestic issues with his ex-wife, Erin, were mostly settled, he itched for Jessie's being resolved as well, so they could begin their long-postponed life together. Live together, or better yet, get married. Perhaps, sell her home and buy a new one of their very own. Have a kid together. That would make three kids between them, which would be a lot, but nothing unmanageable.

A light tap on the door interrupted his reverie, and he turned to find Cindie Tarrico standing in the doorway. The silver in her coarse dark hair hinted that she was more than a decade his senior, and the crinkles in the corners of her eyes bespoke her kindness as a former physician's assistant. "We're still waiting for the police investigation on the high school incident," she said, entering his office. "Sometimes they move slower than dial-up."

"Dial-up? Do you remember the cassette player, the Model-T, or, maybe, the Brontosaurus?"

"No, but I remember when a loaf of bread cost fifty cents," Cindie said, closing the door behind her and settling into the seat across from him.

He maintained a strict open-door policy, so he eyed her suspiciously. "Something on your mind?"

"Have you given any thought to your re-election campaign?" She whispered, as though the room was bugged.

"No." He'd been too busy getting up to speed with his DA duties to consider the elections that were six months away. "It hadn't even crossed my mind."

"You'd better get going. It's May 1st already. You need to secure your party's nomination, additional party line endorsements, and your petitions. And you've got to think about fundraising, selecting your campaign staff, and appearing at events. If you want to remain in office, you're running out of time."

Hal leaned back in his chair. They had a comfortable working relationship, but she was speaking gibberish to him. Her political jargon was way off his radar, unlike murder, grand larceny, and rape.

"I'm a lawyer, Cin, plain and simple. I'm an un-enrolled voter because I've never had to deal with getting elected." He knitted his fingers together and rested his chin on his knuckles. "Isn't the Governor's appointment the

57

Rotten Tomatoes "Certified Fresh" Seal of Approval for my re-election? Lauren never seemed to pay any attention, and she was re-elected three times."

"Lauren's party controls the State, but there's been a shift. People are unhappy. They're going to seek a change across the board, Hal. You'd better figure out your side of the political bed and make a decision. Soon." Cindie leaned forward and rested her hands on her knees. "There are plenty of attorneys who'd love to make a hundred and sixty grand a year plus state perks to run this department. None of them would do it as well as you, but there's been gossip."

"Oh...gossip." He nodded his head in agreement. At first, Cindie's comments had confused him, but then he understood. As prosecutor, he'd made enemies eager to sabotage his campaign by exposing his personal baggage. There was his divorce from Erin, his relationship with Jessie, and his rift with his robber baron father. "How do you know so much about this?"

"My husband, Paul, served as a county legislator years ago and had to endure the vetting process. It's unbelievable how petty and competitive small-town politics can be."

"How am I supposed to run this office and run for election simultane-ously? Something's, everything's, going to suffer." He tugged at his shirt collar and opened the top button, relieving the imaginary constriction of his airway.

"Ah, democracy. Ain't it beautiful? Just be glad we live in a country where these problems exist," Cindie said. "Let me know what you decide, and I'll put you in touch with people who can help." She stood up to leave and paused with her hand on the doorknob. "I'd really like to see you re-elected. You're a smart guy and a great boss."

"Thanks. I appreciate the tipoff."

"Just making my boss look good." Cindie smiled, and he swiveled his chair back to face the window. The soft click of the lock told him he was alone.

It hadn't been long ago that he'd made DA Lauren Hollenbeck appear flawless in the eyes of the community. He'd drafted her speeches, prosecuted her most problematic cases, and had been her confidante, at the expense of his marriage. Mercifully, those days were over. With his promotion, he'd passed the torch to Cindie, and her unwavering loyalty proved he'd made the correct decision.

The intercom buzzed, and his secretary said that State Senator Hollenbeck wanted to speak with him. His chest tightened. "Please tell her I'm in a meeting and I'll call her back."

Content that he'd bought himself a few minutes of peace and quiet, Hal propped his feet up on the sill and returned to the geese sailing through the sky. If only his life was as fearless and carefree as theirs. The door hinge squeaked, and he whirled around to find State Senator Lauren Hollenbeck sauntering into his office.

"I can see that you're far too busy to take my calls."

Chapter Ten

Ebony could hear the caterwaul echoing off the cinderblock walls and into the break room at the far end of the police station. She was grabbing her second cup of chai of the morning because her brain craved more caffeine after the blissful, sleepless night with Drew. Sometimes she wondered if it was a base animal attraction that aroused their ardent, nocturnal lovemaking. Or was it his rugged cowboy good looks combined with his Tom Sawyer impishness? Or maybe they were simply blowing off steam after long, hard days as first responders. Whatever reason, she really didn't care. Drew was hot. He loved her, and his sweet southern drawl made her knees weak.

Curious, she grabbed her mug, and detouring on the way back to her desk, she peered into the reception area. In the lobby, a woman flapped her sling like a chicken wing at the duty sergeant inside his reception booth, causing Ebony to spit boiling liquid all over her white shirt. It had been less than twenty-four hours since she'd seen Lissie Sexton at the hospital, and here she was. Loud, offensive, and demanding. How could the hospital have discharged her so soon? There must be more to that story. First, though, she had to discover what the hell was going on.

"Ma'am, I've already told you three times. You walk outside, turn left and go upstairs. City Court is right there." Through the microphone, the stone-faced sergeant explained the procedure. "If you're seeking monetary reimbursement from someone, you need to file a small claims action in City Court. Or if it's a domestic squabble, you could get an order of protection. Either form of relief is available upstairs, not here in the police station."

"Look what he did to me." Lissie plastered a hospital invoice against the glass for the officer to read. "Where'm I gonna get twenty-five hundred bucks? That's what the hospital charged me. That fat bastard's got to pay for these bills. This is his fault, not mine. And I've already told you I don't know who he is. You're the cops, can't you find him for me?"

Ebony entered the booth and whispered into the sergeant's ear.

"Ma'am, please go over to the glass door on the right. Someone will meet you," he said.

The lock on the door buzzed. The door swung open to admit Ebony's guest, and she signaled for Zander to join them inside a small interrogation room situated off the central bullpen. She'd found that the best tactic for eliciting information from a frantic interviewee was to make them feel comfortable, away from the bustling energy of the other cops. Establish trust. Let the interview occur organically rather than as a fact-gathering exercise. Most important of all, to listen without passing judgment.

Lissie looked worse than she had during the previous evening. The bruises on her face had blossomed into a monstrous map of fuschia and green continents dotted with tiny scab encrusted islands. The left eye, blackened and nubby as a ripe avocado, was swollen shut. Half of her hair had been shaved away, clearing a space for a dingy bandage covering the other half. A frayed bandana circled her throat, presumably hiding the scars of the perpetrator's violence.

Once again, Ebony sensed that they'd met prior to the emergency room—somewhere on the beat. She was usually a whiz at facial recognition, but Lissie's grossly distorted features stumped her. It was like having an itch in her brain that she couldn't scratch.

Lissie swiveled her neck, inspecting the small windowless room. "Are you busting me?" A thin line of droplets formed across her puffy purple upper lip that was sutured with a Steri-Strip. "I didn't do nothing wrong. I'm within my rights to work, you know. That guy hurt me so I can't make no money. And I got bills to pay. I'm trying to get what's due me, that's all."

That's it, she thought. That's why this woman seemed so familiar.

Last year, Poughkeepsie Mayor Meriden had complained to the chief about the sex workers trolling for patrons outside of City Hall, the county offices, and the shops along the Main Street business district. Ebony had been assigned to the special detail designed to discourage the unwanted solicitations. Her beat had been uneventful until a belligerent woman had refused to vacate the white granite steps of the Post Office.

The prostitute had taunted Ebony, shouting obscenities. "Hey, Miss Pussy Cop. I'm within my Constitutional right to earn a living, and you can't arrest me. I'm on federal property." Lissie had chained herself to the Post Office railing and had refused to leave, even though it was raining. After an hour-long protest in the downpour, Lissie had stomped away, spewing vulgarities that would make a longshoreman blush.

Lissie Sexton had been the Post Office girl, all right. The one who'd called her a "black bitch." Any rational person would now tell Lissie to go to hell or to fight her own battles, but Ebony was not any rational person. She was a cop. It was her sworn duty to suppress her prejudices and hard feelings, and protect and serve the public. And clearly, this woman desperately needed protecting from someone.

"Miss Sexton, I'm Detective Jones and this is Detective Pulaski. We'd like to help you, so why don't you start from the beginning? Do you remember what happened to you last Friday? Take your time, there's no hurry."

Lissie twirled her peacock feather earrings, eyeing her distrustfully.

Experience had taught her that victimized women, such as Lissie, only sought the police as a last resort. They'd arrive at the station with a hidden agenda, one often unapparent to themselves, until they'd opened up. They'd complain about being evicted when their true motive was to report a sexual assault by their landlord. Underlying a gripe about stolen money was a squabble with their drug dealer. The list was endless.

Hopefully soon, the state legislature would decriminalize prostitution and assist women who wanted to exit the sex trade. However, until then, it was a detective's job to uncover the reason behind their visits and the victimization dwelling beneath the dark surface.

"How d'ya know my name?" Lissie asked.

Ebony softly repeated the request for Lissie's story; one she suspected was the product of complicated life choices. "Please, we need information so we can help you get your money."

"Well," Lissie said, pausing as her uninjured eye darted back and forth between Ebony and Zander.

"Ms. Sexton," Zander said, "we know this is difficult, but sometimes talking about things can make you feel better. What d'ya say?"

A long moment of silence followed. The woman massaged the soft cast cradled in the sling and squinted as she made a soft humming noise in the back of her throat. "It happened last Friday in the late afternoon. I was walking along the highway, minding my own business. Then Bam!" Lissie clapped her hands, seeming to startle at the volume of the noise. "Some guy in a black car smacked into me and mowed me down. I didn't see him coming or nothing," she said, wiping her runny nose on her sleeve.

Ebony and Zander exchanged glances in tacit recognition of the symptoms. The red rheumy eyes. The runny nose. The jitters. This chick was high on speed, maybe crack. It was possible they'd hear the truth or some junkie's fantasy, but since they had a job to do, Ebony kept her skepticism in check and listened.

"Are you sure about the color?" Zander asked flippantly.

Ebony cast him a sharp look of warning, reminding him that they'd get nowhere with Lissie if he used his bad cop routine. He repeated the question more respectfully this time, and she nodded in approval.

"What's the matter? You don't believe me?" The hooker's voice was bitter and determined. "Wait, maybe it was a grey...no...white. Yeah, it was a white van. It was dark and rainy so it was hard to see." She sniffled and wiped her nose again. "He hit me right in front of the plaza where the ambulance got me. My boyfriend said that guy should pay, not me." She rubbed the mottled eggplant skin beneath the neckerchief.

Something wasn't sitting right with Ebony. This woman didn't appear to be an easy mark, and neither was she.

"Miss Sexton, may I call you Lissie? We can check the security videos in the plaza, if you prefer," Ebony said, watching terror creep across Lissie's mangled face. "Or we can start from scratch and you can tell us what really happened. You're the victim here and we're not going to punish you. We need your help to locate the person who hurt you."

Lissie licked her scaly lips and, with a grin directed at Zander, asked, "May I have a glass of water, please?" Taking the hint, Zander left them alone in the interrogation room.

"I know this isn't easy, but you can trust me," Ebony said. Lissie's pupils dilated and her shoulders fell away from her ears. "I've been in your shoes, had someone hurt me. I badly wanted my revenge, but I couldn't have done it alone. I needed to trust others to help me."

Her left hip ached at the mention of the .38 bullet, which had penetrated deep into her femur during a drug bust. She hadn't been lying about believing in people, either. When a fleeing suspect had gunned her down in the dirt of a desolate backstreet, pain had left her paralyzed. As Ebony lay hemorrhaging on the pavement, she'd begged Zander to leave her, to apprehend the gunman. He hadn't wanted to leave her, but they'd both known it might be their only chance for an arrest. She'd relied on him to call an ambulance on the fly, which he'd done while chasing and capturing the felon.

The perp received a life sentence for drug trafficking and the attempted murder of a cop. Regardless, he'd altered her life forever. The wound plagued her, but her partner's valor and loyalty helped ease the pain.

Lissie slumped back in her chair and let out a deep exhale. As the minutes passed, Ebony sensed the barrier between them disintegrating, being replaced by connection, a sisterhood.

"Someone has perpetrated a terrible crime on you and should be prosecuted. You don't want this to happen to anyone else, do you?" Ebony asked.

The woman meekly shook her head, and a tear trickled down her cheek. Her trembling hands reached out for Ebony's. Lissie's icy skin felt as rough as sandpaper, but Ebony sat still, allowing her to draw upon her strength and courage.

"I knew you'd understand." A slow half-smile revealed Lissie's chipped front tooth.

The doorknob jiggled, and Lissie slipped her hands into her lap. Zander entered and set the water bottle on the table. Ebony's eyes remained glued on Lissie, and she prayed their connection had survived the interruption. Relief flooded her when Lissie spoke.

"Kurt'd kill me if he knew I was squealing to you. All he cares about is the bread." Lissie unscrewed the top and guzzled the water. A thin stream of liquid dribbled from the corner of her mouth down the bandanna around her neck.

"Don't worry. We'll get you the assistance you need," Zander said, with uncharacteristic empathy. "We can refer you to a shelter, doctor, or mental health professional, if need be."

Lissie placed the water bottle on the table and explained that on Friday afternoon, she'd been with the man she referred to as "Doc." "I call him that 'cos he always wears scrubs and I thought he was a doctor. He never gave me his real name, and I never asked 'cos it don't matter so long as his money's green." Her voice was phlegmy, and she took another drink. "We sorta got a regular thing every other Friday 'round three. Doc picks me up at the northwest corner of Reservoir Square Park."

Ebony knew the spot. There was a marble statue of a Union soldier with a black iron cannon at his feet to honor the county's Civil War infantry volunteers. The cops had ironically nicknamed it "Hooker Avenue" even though the actual street named after Union General Joseph Hooker was located three blocks away. "Fighting Joe" had the reputation of being a hard partier, a ladies' man, and a magnet to a league of prostitutes who followed him around the countryside. The pseudonym just seemed to fit because the postage-stamp-sized park was a notorious landmark for working girls lingering and hustling the drivers passing by. She'd clocked endless rookie hours chasing the pros away from the commuters and arresting the more persistent girls who'd defied her warnings.

"He's a big guy, with a small dick," Lissie said, her confidence returning, "but I know better than to tease a man about those things, especially if I want to be his regular girl." Her anxiety seemed to ease, and she talked animatedly with her hands. "I been doing Doc for about three months and he's generous with me. I don't mean that he takes me to motels or nothing like that, but he tips me, big time. I never tell my boyfriend Kurt about the extra because he'd want me to fork it over. No way, José. It's my dough." Lissie's face was set with indignation. "Anyway, Doc has favorite spots where he takes me, like behind the deserted supermarket on Route 44, the train yard down by the river, or the bridge underpass. He says the vibration of the cars passing overhead makes him come quicker, which is okay by me. Sometimes he's a little rough, but he never hurt me. Not like this." She tugged at the neckerchief and displayed the purple finger marks around her neck.

Ebony surreptitiously slipped her phone from her jacket pocket and snapped a quick photo of the bruise.

In response, Lissie's hands flew up to hide the welts. "Hey, what're you doing? I don't want my picture on Facebook or Instagram."

"Don't worry. Please continue," Ebony said, setting the phone on the table.

"This time, Doc drove me to a house behind Adams' greenhouses. I didn't think nothing of it 'cos I figured he'd pay me no matter where we was. He parked inside the garage, and even with the windows up, the place reeked of piss so bad I wanted to puke. Anyway, we got it on in the back seat of his car, and he wanted to go again without paying me. I said, 'No way, mister, I got to get paid or you get nuthin' and he said 'oh, yeah?'"

Lissie's bloodshot eye glazed over and her voice trailed off, as though considering whether to continue. Then her expression settled into determination. "The next thing I felt were his thumbs crushing my windpipe. I could barely breathe. I couldn't free his hands from my throat, but somehow, I bit one of his fat fingers. Doc yelled 'you ungrateful bitch' and he let go of me." She paused. "I tried to scramble away, but he was too quick. He punched my face so hard I toppled backward out of the open car door. It felt like my head cracked open when it smacked on the concrete floor, and my arm snapped when I landed on it." She shuddered as if remembering the shattering of her bone. "I got up and, even though I was seeing stars, I stumbled around looking for a way out. But I was trapped inside that garage. Doc tried to grab me, but he slipped in a puddle. That gave me time to climb out through a broken window." She massaged her shoulder and winced. "He must've been too big, because he didn't follow me."

Lissie explained that once outside, she didn't know where she was or which way to escape. The darkness and thunderstorm had disoriented her. She remembered muddy yards and bushes. Dogs on run-lines barking at her. Blood mixed with rain dripping into her eyes, making it impossible to see. There had been bright lights ahead, and she trudged toward them through the driving rain. Then she'd stumbled, wandering onto a busy road, desperately trying to flag a car down for help. But no one stopped. After that, everything went dark.

"The last thing I remember is hearing sirens and waking up in the ambulance." Lissie examined them as though expecting applause. "Now, I got bills I can't pay 'cos of Doc. I can't work 'cos of Doc. I need you to find the dirtbag and make him pay for what he done to me."

Ebony tried to make sense of the story, but she suspected it wasn't the whole truth. There were too many gaps in the account and the timeline, and Lissie's injuries didn't jibe with her description of the events. Also, there were too many unanswered questions.

Ebony could usually tell when she was being conned, but Lissie Sexton was a bit of mystery, a mixture of fact and fiction. At least Lissie had opened up, unless she'd concocted this load of crap to get her hospital bill paid.

Zander had risen and leaned against the wall, digging crud out from beneath his nails with a paperclip, as was his habit during interrogations. While he pretended he wasn't listening, he absorbed every word. As was their routine, she was the good cop, making the preliminary introductions and cajoling the interviewee into cooperation. Afterward, Zander jumped in with the tough questions. The specifics. The who, what, when, where, and how. However in this situation, this witness demanded greater finesse.

Before she could stop Zander, he'd leaned over the table and began pummeling Lissie with questions about Doc's age, physical description, personal hygiene, sexual preferences, their previous hook-ups, and his vehicle. "Did he ever mention where he worked? Was this his garage? Do you know any other girls he's been with?"

"Hey, just a sec, cowboy," Lissie said. "Jonesy, you brought me in here, so why's this dumb ass asking all the questions. I'll tell you anything you want to know, but not him. He's creepy. And I've gotta pee."

"Zander, let's take five," Ebony said. "Come on, I'll show you to the restroom. We'll be right back," she shot over her shoulder at Zander.

Escorting her witness down the corridor, Lissie's story replayed in Ebony's mind. The facts, as outrageous as they sounded, rang remarkably familiar. She stopped outside the restroom door and held it open for Lissie to enter. "I've got to get something from my desk, so I'll be back in a minute. Need anything?" Lissie shook her head, and Ebony walked down the hallway through the bullpen to her desk.

Rummaging through the paperwork, empty coffee mugs, Snickers wrappers, and loose-leaf binders on her credenza, Ebony found what she'd been seeking—an incident report from one of Saturday's cases.

Chapter Eleven

The yoga session began at nine o'clock, and Jessie had pleaded with her mother, Lena, to arrive at eight-fifteen to babysit. This would be her first class in more than a year, and she didn't want to be late. However, Lena being on Lena time, she appeared at the door as the grandfather clock struck eight fifty-five.

"Darling, sorry I'm late, but Kyle called. He wanted to buy new shoes for Lily and forgot her size. So, we had a pleasant chat. He really misses you... but anyway, where's my precious little pumpkin?" Lena approached her granddaughter, who was bouncing in a sling rocker and teething on a silicone elephant, and scooped the baby up in her arms. "Here's my Lilybean."

She'd heard the same old story repeatedly from her mother. Kyle was sorry. Kyle loved her. Kyle wanted to reconcile. She was sick to death of hearing about Kyle. Her mother refused to accept that she was in love with Hal. Always had been and always would be. Her dad, Ed, understood and had embraced Hal, but her mother remained defiant.

While Lena babbled on about Kyle's virtues, Jessie hurriedly grabbed her mat, bag, and jacket, kissed Lily, and scooted out of the door. Her irritation mounted when she had to park three blocks away from the Namaste Yoga Studio. The class had already begun when she slinked inside the studio and crept into the back row next to a flexible, fortyish brunette who was clearly no stranger to yoga. She scanned the supple bodies dressed in the trendy yoga garb and pretended to be unfazed about the shapeless red sweatpants and tee-shirt, which couldn't disguise her flabby, post-baby body or her

69

inability to touch her toes.

In unison, the class assumed the warrior pose, lunging and pointing their fingertips toward the sky. Jessie struck the stance, and her muscles quivered in revolt. She'd forgotten how demanding the poses were. Part of yoga was becoming attuned to your body, and hers begged her to flee straightaway. Who was she kidding? She should be home with Lily, not attempting fancy, pain-inducing contortions.

"Shit," she grunted as the group sat on their floor mats, bent their knees, and pulled their soles together into the cobbler's pose.

The well-toned brunette giggled.

"Hurts like hell, right?" Jessie whispered, ignoring her classmates' sneers.

"Let's assume the downward dog," the instructor said.

A half-hour later, the final segue from the cat-cow stretch into the praying child arrived. Jessie groaned gratefully, and a bit too loudly, as the students rose to their bare feet, bowed, and chanted "Namaste."

"Are you all right?" the brunette asked as she rolled up her mat, shrugged on her jacket, and took a long draw from her water bottle. "I feel your pain because I haven't been here for a while either."

"I'm trying to get back into it after having a baby, but this is awfully tough."

"Don't let one class shake you. You'll catch on, just give it time."

Jessie zipped up her jacket and extended her hand. "My name's Jessie Martin."

"Nice to meet you. I'm Gayle." A beat passed. "...Morrison. Do you want to grab a coffee at the café around the corner?"

With no word from Ebony, she'd planned on researching the rescue victim, but it could wait. It would be a treat to kibitz with another adult on topics other than diapers or baby food. "Sure, I'll call my mother and ask her to watch my daughter a bit longer."

She and Gayle strolled around the corner to The Krafted Cup Café, which was empty except for a few telecommuters exploiting the free Wi-Fi. They ordered tea and scones from a scruffy guy in a wool beanie and walked upstairs to the art gallery. Being across the street from the Vassar College campus, the café encouraged the college's art students to display their work on its exposed brick walls. Part of the café's charm was its ever-changing vibe, and this week's exhibit featured bold graffiti upon wall-size canvases. They selected a table beneath a modern interpretation of the characters from *Alice in Wonderland*.

Feeling as nervous as if she was on a first date, Jessie fidgeted with her tea bag and let Gayle take the lead.

"You mentioned you have a daughter? What's her name?" Gayle asked.

"Lily," Jessie replied, and the rest of the conversation flowed easily. Apparently, Gayle was a doer, improving her community by donating time to the library, the SPCA, the domestic violence shelter, and her twins' soccer league. And she carried herself with an air of sophistication and class.

As they chatted, the dead weight of Jessie's past lifted from her shoulders. The nightmares of Terrence's phone calls and Jeremy Kaplan's courtroom attacks vanished. She envisioned Gayle becoming her friend, especially after discovering they were both Syracuse University alumnae.

"The Newhouse School of Public Communications," Gayle said, jingling her SU key chain like it was a dinner bell.

"Maxwell School of Citizenship and Public Affairs." Jessie pulled her SU water bottle from her yoga bag and shook it. "We're pathetic. Aren't we?" Her laugh emerged a bit too loud, but she caught herself before it became awkward. There was no need to impress Gayle. This was only coffee, not a job interview.

"I was editor of *The Daily Orange,* and where did it get me? *Good Housekeeping Magazine.*"

"From the *Orange* to the Big Apple. That's another thing we have in common. I lived in the city when I attended NYU."

"Law School?"

She glanced at Gayle suspiciously. "What made you say that?"

Gayle hesitated for a second, as if caught off guard. "I assumed, because of Maxwell. It has the reputation for launching its top students into the best law schools, such as Yale and NYU."

"Oh, yeah." Jessie tensed at the response that didn't ring authentic to her.

Maxwell was a leader in public policy and international relations education, but not necessarily a farm club for law schools. "Well, you're right, but I'm taking a break to raise my daughter. Though lately, I've been thinking about going back to work. Lily's almost a year old now."

"My twins are thirteen, and every autumn I consider going back to work, but here I am. Taking yoga and having coffee. Not a bad life."

"Not bad at all," she said, sizing up the three-carat diamond ring on her new friend's finger and the gold watch on her slender wrist. If you can afford it. While they shared a special camaraderie, one thing was obvious. Gayle didn't have to work out of necessity.

The clinking of coffee mugs, plates, and cutlery swelled around them, and Jessie noticed that the café's tables were filling up. She checked her watch. It was noon, and they'd been talking for two hours.

"Time flies. We'll have to do this again," Gayle said, pulling a five-dollar bill out of her designer wallet to leave as a tip.

"I'd really like that," Jessie said, refusing to let her paranoia ruin the respite from her humdrum life.

"Here, put your number in my phone."

Jessie and Gayle exchanged phone numbers and bid farewell outside of the café. It was still chilly out, but the wind had died down after scattering pink cherry-blossom petals along the sidewalk. Warm with the excitement of an unexpected new friendship, Jessie hummed *Baby Shark* as she strolled toward her Jeep. Despite the morning's rocky start, the yoga class had been worthwhile. She'd made a new acquaintance, and she'd bid adieu to the past. Today might not be such a miserable day after all.

Chapter Twelve

Hal straightened up in his chair and flattened his tie as his former boss, Lauren Hollenbeck, sauntered into his office and gave it the once over. He'd been relieved when she'd resigned to assume her senate seat in Albany, only calling occasionally to bitch about her new staff, the state bureaucracy, and the arctic north winds. But those winds had blown the witch back into his office. She sniffed the air as though testing whether her perfume still lingered.

He remained seated behind the battered desk that bore the brass nameplate "HAROLD SAMUELS III, Dutchess County District Attorney."

"I see you haven't disposed of my old law journals." Lauren flicked her jet-black hair as though brushing lint from her shoulder. She shoved aside the dusty stacks accumulated during her regime and collapsed on her old leather couch. Her navy and white Chanel blazer was unbuttoned to reveal a deep V-neck lace-trimmed shell, which inappropriately exposed too much of the New York State Senator's creamy décolletage. "So, have your princely charm and good looks banished all the crime in the kingdom yet? And how are the princess and former princess? Just splendid, I suppose?"

He was in no mood for her coquettishness, and he refused to be baited by her cheap shots. "Lauren, is this a stop on your goodwill tour or is there a purpose for your visit?"

"No. I have time to kill before my lunch with County Executive Ketchum, so I thought I'd pop by."

She extracted her compact and lipstick from her matching Chanel purse, admired herself in her mirror, and applied a fresh coat of bright red to her lips. She wiped a smudge from the corner of her mouth with her fingertip and smiled at him, a radiant, deadly smile. "That's better, now. Isn't it?"

He studied her. Lauren could charm the skin off of a snake and he pitied those she'd bitten. Fortunately, he'd become immune to her venom, but he wondered about her true motives for meeting with his boss, Dan Ketchum. There was nothing overtly sinister about their luncheon, considering her position as the conduit to the state coffers. No doubt Ketchum sought funding for infrastructure, the jail expansion, economic and agribusiness development, and coaxing IBM to remain in Dutchess County.

But she wanted something from Hal. He sensed it. Information. Loyalty. Sympathy. Sex. As her Chief ADA, he'd willingly provided everything but the latter, though she'd spread her legs before him at every opportunity. Yet, he sensed she was toying with him, in the same way a cat bats around a mouse before pouncing.

"Looks as though we'll both have campaigns to run this autumn," Lauren said. The topic of elections seemed to pop up too frequently for him to ignore. "I'm fortunate where that's concerned. Our session ends in June, which gives me plenty of time to campaign until the November elections. But you'll be fighting crime full time and managing your harem and brood. How will you survive?"

His stomach clenched, but he'd never reveal that her jibes were rankling him. She knew too much about his past, and he'd be damned if she meddled in his future. "I wouldn't worry about me if I were you. I'd concentrate on your re-election campaign. You're as much of a novice as I am, and you know it."

"Yes, but I'm well-connected after my first term. I have PACs and supporters. My team's in place and ready to go, and our polling starts in two weeks. I hope you've been taking advantage of your opportunities."

"Thanks for your concern, but everything's under control," Hal replied, trying to convince her as well as himself.

"Well, I'm pleased to hear that. You know that I only wish you success, but I can't help thinking about how successful we would've been if we'd joined forces in Albany." She sighed. "Some things aren't meant to be."

Lauren rose and flattened the wrinkles in her skirt and stockings. "Well, Mr. Ketchum awaits."

"As usual, Lauren, it's been a pleasure," he said sarcastically.

"You know, this office will always be my home." She walked to the door, stopped in the portal, and glanced back at him over her shoulder. Lauren sashayed out of the door, passing Cindie without even acknowledging her.

"Brr! It's chilly in here," Cindie said, stepping into the office. "I can almost see my breath."

Lauren's parting shot had caught Hal off guard, but her veiled threats about campaigns and Ketchum had hit the bulls-eye. She might have made a big splash in Albany, but she was gunning for his job. She was plotting to challenge him in the November elections. His eyes shifted toward Cindie, who was staring at him, wrinkling her nose. "I'm sorry. Did you say something?"

"What did she want? Your blood? Your first-born child?"

"I have my suspicions, but there's a guy who'll know for sure." Hal picked up the phone handset and cradled it against his shoulder. He dialed and gestured for Cindie to close the door and grab a seat in his office. When he heard a voice on the other end of the line, he said, "Hello, I'd like to speak to Attorney General Hutchins, please. Tell Steve, its Hal Samuels. Yes, I'll wait."

Cindie's eyes widened at the mention of the Attorney General for the State of New York. She had no way of knowing that he and Steve Hutchins had worked together at New York City's Law Department. Hutchins, ten years his senior, had mentored Hal during his internship, and when he'd joined the staff after graduating from law school. In fact, it had been Hutchins who had suggested that Hal apply for the opening in the DA's office in Poughkeepsie. He'd insisted that it presented a unique opportunity, and his old pal hadn't steered him wrong. It had never crossed his mind that his old love, Jessie Martin, would live there, too. And in reality, their paths hadn't crossed until late last summer when *The People vs. Butterfield* had turned his life upside down.

"Stevo, Hal Samuels here. I'm placing you on speakerphone." He depressed the button.

"This is a surprise. Are you finally calling about the round of golf at Wingfoot that you owe me?" Hutchins asked.

"Better to owe you than cheat you out of it." Hal loved busting Steve's chops because he was gullible. They both knew he'd pay up, eventually.

"Come on, Samuels, you're killing me. You're the only guy I know whose family belongs, and I'm not letting you off the hook. So, if you're not calling to make good on your debt, why are you bothering me?"

"I have some questions about Lauren Hollenbeck."

"Senator Hollenbeck, huh?" A static silence crackled over the line. "What's taken you so long?"

* * *

Emboldened by the file tucked beneath her arm, Ebony returned to the ladies' room to collect Lissie.

"Lissie?" she called. The sound of her voice reverberated off the white tile walls.

She ducked to peek beneath the three stalls, and finding nothing, she swung open each door. The stalls were empty. Her heart pounded as she dashed back to the interrogation room, hoping to find Lissie waiting for her there. The metal door stood wide open, and the room was vacant, as were the other rooms.

"Hey," Ebony shouted above the din of the bullpen. "Has anyone seen Pulaski or the woman we were interviewing?" Half of her colleagues shook their heads while the others ignored her. "Shit. Shit."

She'd let her guard down, and within two minutes, Lissie had given her the slip. Zander would never let her live this down. Worse yet, Lissie's comments had steered Ebony's attention toward a similar incident, and now she'd never know whether there was any connection between the complaints.

"Where were you?" Zander asked, sneaking up behind her. "And where's Sexton?"

She whipped around to face him. "Where were you? Have you seen Lissie Sexton?"

"What do you mean? I thought she was with you."

"Come on, we have to go look for her." The adrenaline coursing through her veins made her feet dance in place and her mouth go dry.

"Eb, forget about it. She's long gone by now." A small muscle twitched at the corner of Zander's mouth like it did when he was processing the evidence of a crime. "Who is Lissie Sexton and what's going on here?"

She motioned toward Interrogation Room One, and he followed her inside. Zander closed the door behind them, and they took seats at the metal table in the center of the room. Ebony set an incident report from a woman named Kiara Taylor on the surface between them. She explained that Ms. Taylor, a cheery woman about the same age and slight physical build as Lissie, had been her last complainant on the Saturday shift. At first, she had given little weight to Kiara's allegations because "john" complaints were usually about money. However, something in the woman's quiet, polite demeanor had made her accusations seem credible.

"You know the routine," Ebony said. "I gave him a…you fill in the blank… blow job, hand job, had sex…and he didn't pay me." They'd heard the story a zillion times, and like most cops, they were jaded where prostitutes were concerned. Not that the girls were lying, but the police department wasn't a collection agency for sex workers.

"But, similar to Lissie, Kiara was different," she continued. "Ms. Taylor had refused the second time for free. The man yanked her hair, twisted her arm behind her back, and threw her to the ground. Then, he mounted her doggy-style and assaulted her. The bastard had gotten his freebie, anyway. Kiara hadn't been as brutalized as Lissie, but she'd suffered a dislocated shoulder, sprained wrist, and scraped bruised knees. The alleged attack occurred around two a.m. in the parking lot behind the deserted Parker Avenue diner. That's less than a mile from where Doc had picked up Lissie at Reservoir Square Park."

Ebony tapped her pen on the physical description of the perpetrator, "John Doe," and opened the folder. "I've also pulled Kiara's RAP sheet. She's clean, only a few petty arrests for shoplifting and trespass when she was a teen."

She'd done her homework. The RAP sheet included Kiara Taylor's arrest records, arrest locations, court docket numbers, and dispositions of the cases. According to the social worker and probation reports, Kiara had been orphaned at seven and had bounced around among relatives until she split when she was fifteen. Kiara had kept herself free of drug and prostitution charges, which was a mighty accomplishment, considering she'd been living on the streets.

Ebony didn't mention Kiara's rough past because, unlike Ebony, empathy didn't sway Zander. He viewed everyone as a liar, a suspect, or a killer.

Zander picked up the incident report and read the description aloud. "Taylor described him as approximately *six foot two. African American. Mid-thirties. Two hundred fifty pounds. Black stringy hair.* There's no mention of hospital scrubs or any distinguishing marks, so what makes you think it's the same guy?"

"I know there's not much to go on, but it feels as if it's the same dude. Same modus operandi. A hooker. A deserted location. Smacking her around when he doesn't get his way. When Lissie began her story, an alarm sounded."

"Do you know how many of these complaints we receive? Dozens. As horrible as it is, I don't see any connection between the two incidents," Zander said. "Not without more evidence."

Her eyes met his, seeking reassurance that she wasn't totally crazy. He knew she'd only pursue a case if the facts supported an investigation.

"I'd planned to pry more out of Lissie, but since she's bolted, we've got to track her down. I told you I've got a feeling that Lissie and Kiara's attackers are the same perp." Ebony rose and paced the tight cubicle. The gears in her mind clicked, cog-by-cog, trying to piece together the puzzle of the two victims who'd suffered the same fate.

"I don't know. We're not officially assigned to Sexton's case, and you can't make a case out of thin air, especially one claiming there's a serial rapist on the loose." For a hipster, Zander was sure acting like a fuddy-duddy by-the-book cop.

She leaned against the wall and scratched an itch behind her ear. No wonder he wasn't on board. Zander didn't know about her visiting Lissie yesterday at the medical center. Sometimes, she assumed that being partners, he could read her mind. Other times, she assumed that she'd apprised him of events, when in fact she hadn't. He must've been thinking she was as loony as Lissie Sexton.

"Just give me a few minutes and everything I'm saying will make sense."

Zander listened as she brought him up to speed. "So, Lissie's father's a Captain?"

"That's your takeaway?" At first, Ebony was piqued, but quickly realized he was mocking her.

"Please, indulge me. Let's see if we can drum up Lissie's address from the hospital's records department. If we can, we'll go speak with her and see if she confirms Taylor's description. We've got nothing to lose."

Zander glanced around the room uneasily, and she could see he was waffling. Even if he didn't agree, she would follow-up on this lead herself.

"Okay, you win," he said, finally. "Let's locate your missing ho."

Chapter Thirteen

Flashing her badge hadn't worked. Neither had asking nicely. But Ebony noticed that in response to her inquiry, tiny beads of perspiration dotted the upper lip of the Vassar Brothers Hospital medical documents clerk. She'd assumed control of the inquiry because she felt as though this was her case, her investigation, and Zander was along for the ride. Her intuition had led them to the hospital, and if necessary, she was prepared to beat Lissie's details out of the obstinate bureaucrat.

"Without a court order, I'm not revealing any information about our patient named Elisabeth Sexton," the millennial snipped.

"And I'm telling you again that Ms. Sexton's a material witness to a crime and it's imperative that we locate her. All we need is her address and phone number. Under the HIPPA rules, we're entitled to this information without her permission, and I'll gladly cite the provisions." Her stare remained frigid, hard, and undeterred.

The clerk pushed his shoulders back, standing his ground.

"Sir, don't get my partner started. She'll cite you statutes 'til your head spins. So, for expediency's sake, we'd like to speak with your supervisor. If they're available." Zander flashed an optic white smile.

"I don't see what good that'll do, but I'll check to see if he's free," the clerk replied in a sharp tone. He disappeared into a back office and returned shortly, accompanied by an older gentleman with a spare tire straining his shirt buttons.

The administrator listened to Zander's explanation, while Ebony feigned anger, and then he shot his younger colleague a reprimanding look. "Why

80

don't you give me the witness's name and I'll see what we have. You understand that this can only be a limited disclosure."

They repeated Lissie's name as the older man entered it into the computer.

"Here she is, Elisabeth Sexton, DOB 3/4/87. Admitted on April 30th and discharged against doctor's orders on May 1st. The address listed is 375 Smith Street, Apartment 2B, Poughkeepsie. The only phone number listed is an emergency contact, Kurt Hendricks. Is that what you're looking for?"

Ebony typed the information into her phone, restraining herself from lobbing a sarcastic retort at the clerk. They thanked him and returned to their vehicle parked with its hazard lights flashing in the "No Parking" zone outside the entrance.

They drove across town toward Smith Street and cruised through the once-thriving neighborhood infected with the cancer of abandoned warehouses, dilapidated apartments, and boarded-up zombie buildings. It had become a battleground, where drug dealers and old-timers clashed over the soul of the street. Sadly, the druggies were winning the war.

Lissie's address was a three-story brick apartment house where satellite dishes sprouted from its ramshackle roof like mushrooms. They parked at the curb and exited the car.

"Suppose Sexton's not here? What then, Sherlock?" Zander asked as they strode up the uneven sidewalk toward the house.

Peals of laughter drew Ebony's interest toward the elementary school diagonally across the street. On the playground, children attacked the monkey bars, walloped a kickball, and chased each other around the large asphalt playground inside a chain-link fence. The students' innocent delight in the spring sunshine didn't escape her, sparking her longing for simpler, happier days.

She tripped and Zander grabbed her arm, yanking her away from a gap in the cement walkway leading to the front porch.

"Watch your step, will you? Come on," he shouted.

They climbed the steps toward a colony of rusty mailboxes littering the doorjamb. Nestled among them was a green one with the name "Hendricks" scribbled in pencil on a piece of masking tape. Zander rang the doorbell for Apartment 2B and waited. Moments passed and there was no answer, so he jabbed the bell again.

Ebony hated waiting even more than Zander did. It made her feel edgy and out of control, and as a detective, she was used to being the one calling the shots.

"Hey, you ring my bell?" a man's voice hollered from above. She and Zander stepped off the porch and peered up at an unshaven man leaning out the second-story window. "What d'ya want?"

"You Kurt Hendricks?" Ebony shouted.

"Who wants ta know?" The man inhaled on a vape and blew the smoke into the fresh air.

Zander flashed his badge. Its shiny metal caught the afternoon sun, causing the man to squint and shield his eyes from the glare. "Mr. Hendricks, please come down. We want to speak with you. We're looking for Elisabeth Sexton."

"All right. I'll be right down," Hendricks said, disappearing from view.

Moments later, a storm door slammed. The sound of heavy boots sprinting across the gravel driveway on the right side of the house grabbed their attention. Without missing a beat, Ebony and Zander reached for their sidearms and raced toward the noise. Rounding the side of the house, they glimpsed a compact, muscular man in a white wife-beater undershirt dashing toward an opening in the backyard's wooden fence.

"Stop," Ebony shouted. "Police, stop."

Hendricks ignored them as he tried to escape.

Ebony's heart pounded in unison with the slamming of her boots across the rocky surface of the driveway. With each step, an electric charge zinged from her hip to her knee and down into her ankle. Absorbing the pain, she bulldozed ahead, reducing the distance to Hendricks. As the yards shrank to feet, Zander darted past her, propelling his long body into the air and diving toward the escapee. With an outstretched arm, Zander seized Hendricks' pant leg as the man tried to squeeze through a narrow gap in the fence. Bodies colliding, the two men tumbled to the ground, landing upon the broken beer bottles, dried leaves and branches strewn along the property line.

Beneath the weight of Zander's body, Hendricks squirmed face down in the debris, struggling to break free. Finally acknowledging his predicament, the man's lanky body grew limp, and he moaned.

Seconds later, Ebony hovered over the men, doubled over and clasping her knees, winded. She cursed herself for being out of shape and Hendricks for making them chase him down. The mention of Lissie's name had triggered his flight, and she hoped Lissie's disappearance hadn't been the cause. All along she'd believed Lissie was unharmed, but now she wasn't so sure.

Ebony let out a deep breath, drew herself upright, and aimed her weapon at Hendricks. "Don't move until we tell you to or I'll shoot you, you slimy bastard."

Zander rose, grabbed Hendricks by the scruff of his neck, and pulled him to his feet. "Hands behind your head. Now," he ordered, patting him down. Finding no weapons, he handcuffed the suspect and then dusted the dirt and debris from his clothing.

Hendricks thrashed about, cussing and kicking the gravel up into a gritty cloud. While Hendricks didn't match the description of Doc, it was clear to Ebony that he was deceptively muscular and strong enough to squeeze the life out of Lissie. Maybe Lissie lied about the attack. Doc, the money, and his car could have been a ploy to shield Hendricks and throw the cops off his scent.

Apparently, Zander was having the same thought. "Mr. Hendricks," he said, "before we take you in for questioning, we have a few questions about your relationship with Lissie Sexton."

"Hendricks. Upstairs, please," Ebony said, returning her gun to its holster. "Let's see where you've buried the bodies and why you're so eager to bolt."

"Come on, move it." Zander prodded Hendricks toward the back entrance of the house and dragged him up the narrow side stairs leading to Apartment 2B.

He ushered Hendricks through the kitchen into the living room and pushed him onto a moth-eaten chenille sofa. The Jersey shore bass of a

Bon Jovi video blared from a ninety-inch flat screen, making Ebony's ears ache and her chest thrum. She snatched the remote from the dining room table and flicked off the television. As a welcome silence flooded the room, she spied the source of Hendricks' distress. A mound of plastic Baggies, almost as tall as her shoulder, buried the dining room table. They contained white pills of various shapes and sizes. Beside them, a glass punch bowl overflowed with a rainbow mixture of capsules and tablets.

"Z, check out the party platters over here. Take some photos, will you, while I scope out the other rooms to see if Lissie's here," she said.

Ebony snapped on her blue latex gloves and followed the skinny hallway to the large bedroom in the front of the railroad-style apartment. The front window was open, letting in a breeze that fluttered the stained flowered quilt haphazardly strewn on the mattress set on the floor. Clothes flowed lava-like from the dresser's open drawers and the closet tucked into the corner of the room. Her toe nudged aside the discarded socks, jeans, undershirts, boxers, and tee-shirts littering the tattered carpet. Lissie was nowhere to be found, but the glittery bras, panties, stilettos, and counterfeit designer bags buried among the junk showed a female lived there.

Disgusted, Ebony peeked inside the bathroom off the kitchen. A layer of furry green mold grew on the tile walls, and bloodstained towels filled the trashcan, spilling onto the floor. It looked as though their missing person's case may have escalated into an assault, battery, or even murder.

"We'd better call this in," Ebony said, upon returning to Zander and their suspect. "I found bloody debris in the bathroom. Forensics and Narcotics will have to sift through this garbage. Let's take Hendricks in on the narcotics charges for now, and we'll see what forensics finds after they scour the place."

"Those pills aren't mine, man. I'm holding them for a friend," Hendricks shouted as he wiggled to free himself from the handcuffs. His bloodshot eyes contradicted his assertions, as did the black and blue veins in his sinewy arms.

"Simmer down. Before we take you in, where's Lissie Sexton?" Ebony leaned close to Hendricks and she wrinkled her nose at the herby smell of cannabis and alcohol on his breath. "We know she lives here, so give it up. What did you do to Lissie?"

"I didn't do nothing. What do you want with her, anyway? She done something wrong?"

"Mr. Hendricks, just answer the question. Where is she?" While Ebony still wasn't convinced that he hadn't harmed Lissie, she was convinced that he knew her whereabouts.

"You didn't answer me. Has Lissie done something wrong?"

"Sir, we're involved in an investigation and need to speak with her. Does Elisabeth Sexton live here?" Zander repeated.

"I don't keep her on a leash, if that's what you're asking. She comes and goes as she pleases." Hendricks scanned Ebony from head to toe, pausing a second too long on her breasts. "You're too hot to be a cop, lady. If you ever want to ditch Mr. Suit here, call me." He smiled a gummy smile, lonesome for his lower incisors. "She went out yesterday morning, early, and I don't know when she's coming back."

If that was true, the fresh blood in the bathroom couldn't belong to Lissie. Forensics would confirm it, but right now, they were no closer to finding her.

She swiveled her hips, reflecting the sunlight off her badge into Hendricks' eyes. "Would you like to reconsider your answer?"

He squinted and then spit on the floor at her feet. "Screw you."

"That's it. We're done here. Eb, let's contact HQ to send over the drug task force and the K-9 unit," Zander said. "Kurt Hendricks, you're under arrest for possession of controlled substances...." He recited the Miranda warnings as he'd done a thousand times before.

Hendricks sneered at Zander and leered at her again.

"I think you have an admirer," Zander whispered to her.

"Lucky me."

* * *

For months, Hal had heard the rumors, and he'd followed the news. Tired of the racketeering, bribery, and fraud allegations levied against the state legislature, Governor Amelia Serrano had clamped down on the corruption by enacting a comprehensive ethics reform bill. In the future, they would require all legislators and public officials to report outside income, verify per diem requests, and comply with a complex scheme of campaign finance reform checks and balances.

"Albany looks like a sequel to *Goodfellas*," Attorney General Steve Hutchins complained to Hal. "We're lawyers, not babysitters for every elected official in the state."

Hal had followed the controversy with mild interest, and was surprised when Steve mentioned that the new rules applied to him, as District Attorney and a candidate for public office.

"It's not so bad for you local guys," Steve said. "Unless you're an insomniac, you're too busy to hold down another gig. For the State Legislators, like your friend Lauren Hollenbeck, it's a different animal. They're in session for six months out of the year, and rely upon outside income and opportunities that flow from the job." He hesitated and cleared the smoker's rasp from his voice. "That's who Serrano was aiming for, the legislators with million-dollar consulting clients. But for candidates, the reporting requirements are going to be a nightmare."

There was that word again. Candidate. At thirty-seven, Hal identified himself as father, lawyer, boss, ex-husband, lover, friend, brother, and son. If he was to keep his position as DA, he was going to have to add "candidate" to the list.

"As far as Lauren Hollenbeck is concerned, she's exhibited remarkable leadership potential up here in Albany and has scored appointments to the Finance and Criminal Justice Committees. She seems to be following in her grandfather's footsteps." Steve took another drag. "It'd be a shame if this ethics business dissuades her from seeking a full term in November."

He'd been pleased to hear about Lauren's success in Albany, but Steve's comments reinforced his suspicions. Lauren was weighing her options and considering a return to her old stomping grounds inside this building. He selfishly hoped she stayed put upstate.

Hal couldn't deny that the election references by Cindie, Steve, and Lauren had left him feeling overwhelmed and late getting out of the gate. It was the first week of May, and he had less than a month to prepare his designating petitions.

His mind raced. Time was of the essence, and with only six months until Election Day, he needed to know where he stood.

He needed someone to manage his campaign, the political parties, meetings, deadlines, and contributors. Cindie was the natural candidate. He chuckled at his choice of words. But, no. It would be unethical for the ADA to manage her boss's campaign. He required someone reliable and familiar with the law. Someone who loved a challenge and had time for the task.

Only one person's name immediately sprang to mind.

Chapter Fourteen

On the drive back to the station, Ebony's eyes dropped to the gaping hole in the knee of Zander's new trousers.

"Come on, Z, don't be such a baby. It's only a minor scratch, and they're only pants. You can get new ones at Macy's at the Mall. I saw they're having a big sale."

He snarled in response and gripped the steering wheel with rage, which oozed from him like the blood from the nasty scrape on his knee.

Suggesting that he shopped at the Mall, rather than trendy boutiques, was as excruciating as pouring salt into his open wound. Ebony playfully nudged his elbow, but his concentration remained glued to the road.

"Hey, why are you pissed at me? I'm not the one you tackled. It's the jackass in the back who's responsible."

In the back seat, Kurt Hendricks rested his head against the door with his eyes closed, pretending to sleep. His lips curled into a smirk.

Zander ignored her and kept on driving.

When they arrived at the station, they processed an unexpectedly cooperative Hendricks. Then they locked him in a holding cell.

"You ain't seen the last of me, foxy lady," Hendricks said, cocking his finger at Ebony and blowing her a kiss as the cell door slammed.

"Mr. Hendricks, you're a real charmer. You'd impress me even more if you told me where Lissie is."

"Don't I get a phone call?" he shouted as she strutted away, exaggerating the sway of her hips.

"Talk to him." She pointed toward the deskbound officer guarding the cellblock. "I've got nothing to say to you until you tell me about Lissie."

Ebony pulled up Hendricks' RAP sheet on her desktop computer. The results didn't surprise her. As a teen, he'd been in juvenile detention for larceny, car theft, possession and sale of pot, all non-violent felonies. And as an adult, he'd upped his game to assault, disorderly conduct, speeding, and DWI convictions. Without a doubt, Hendricks was a small fry, a street-level distributor for a bigger fish. Certainly, he wasn't the brains or the bucks behind the drug operation discovered in his crib.

With Hendricks off the street, it was up to drug enforcement and the DA to make him sing about his supplier. Unfortunately, he wasn't singing about Lissie.

Ebony wondered about Lissie's role in the venture and what her next move might be. She speculated that since the cops were swarming Smith Street, Lissie wouldn't be returning to their apartment soon. Absent a miracle, their search for Lissie had reached a dead end. She'd probably vanished like the other girls on the bulletin board. Like Aunt Alicia.

"Hey Jones, the Chief wants to see you and Pulaski. Pronto," a fellow plainclothes detective yelled. Ebony grabbed a few files and joined Zander outside the Chief's private suite. Zander continued glaring at her, presumably now angry about the summoning. She couldn't win with him today.

"Come on in. Take a seat," Chief Shepardson said, returning to his worn leather chair. The wall behind him displayed three decades' worth of commendations and awards, and his Naval Bronze Star hovered above his head in a crown.

Those citations reflected his tough, no-nonsense leadership, which Ebony admired but which had occasionally clashed with her creative police work. More than once, he'd summarily dismissed her theories, which ultimately had proven correct.

Sometimes, she felt the chief had it out for her. Maybe it was because she represented two minorities on the Poughkeepsie force; she was female, and she was black. And she was the only female detective on the force. She didn't believe the chief was a misogynist or a racist, but he ran her harder and demanded more from her than anyone else, even Zander.

Chief Shepardson's cold, flinty eyes implied she wasn't in his good graces at the moment. She wiped her sweaty palms on her jeans as she took a seat, carefully balancing the short stack of files on her lap.

The chief cleared his throat. "I want to commend you both on your excellent job of apprehending Kurt Hendricks. The county drug task force and our guys discovered an additional fifty bags of marijuana hidden in the floorboards of the apartment. Hendricks was totally off our radar, but it's shaping up to be a major bust. Upwards of a half-million in street value. You did an outstanding job, however," he paused for effect, "I still can't figure out what led you to him. We have no tips or pending cases on his operations. Who'd like to explain?"

She opened her mouth to speak, but Zander beat her to it. "Sir," he said bitterly. She held her breath, waiting for him to throw her under the bus. "I believe Detective Jones deserves the credit for this collar."

Ebony stared at him in surprise.

"Is that correct?"

"Detective Pulaski is being modest, sir. It was a team effort." She summarized the rescue of Lissie Sexton, the abuse complaints of Kiara Taylor and Lissie, and the hospital records that led them to Smith Street. "Zander backed my hunch about Lissie, so I can't take sole credit for the bust."

Chief Shepardson glanced around, as if looking for a response. "Jones, I appreciate your perseverance and loyalty, but I'm concerned about your taking matters into your own hands. I can't have my officers impulsively placing themselves and their partners at risk. There are procedures to follow. If every officer ignored those rules, there'd be chaos. I'm alarmed by your irresponsible actions, Detective."

She needed to hustle. Her badge and gun were on the line.

"Sir, I believe there's a relationship between Ms. Sexton and Ms. Taylor's attacks because they had several things in common." Ebony leaned forward, eager to make her point. "They'd both been solicited on Hooker Avenue at Reservoir Square, and they'd both been brutally beaten by a large, thirtyish black man after having sex with him. There are too many similarities to ignore. We may be dealing with a serial rapist."

"Understood. You may be correct, but you can't go off on a wild goose chase, dragging your partner along for the ride." He narrowed his eyes at her. "Give me the reports and the information you've collected, and I'll take a deeper look. I'll get back to you after I've reviewed them."

Lissie Sexton and Kiara Taylor had escaped the attempts on their lives, but what about next time? She felt a moral and professional responsibility to help them, protect them.

"These attacks weren't random, and sir, I believe that time is of the essence. We can't stand by and let them join the missing, and presumably, dead souls up on our bulletin board." She handed him the folders, realizing that her assertiveness straddled the fine line between advocacy and insubordination. "We've got a predator out there."

"All right." Chief Shepardson raised his hand to stop her. Slowly, he opened the first folder and reviewed the dossier. He extracted the photo of Lissie, her face marred by purple and green bruises, and her neck encircled with fingermarks. Next, he examined a photo of Kiara with her arm in a soft cast sling, and her knees swollen to the size of grapefruits. "I see you've done your homework, Detective Jones." He paused, turning the photos repeatedly, toying with her. Ebony sucked in her breath as though she were waiting for the doctor's test results. Finally, the chief slid the stack back to her. "Continue with your investigation, but don't stray off the reservation again or you'll face the consequences. Remember that this isn't your only case, and I want a report by next week."

"Thanks, Chief." Her shoulders relaxed.

Zander nodded in agreement.

"Again, good job. But stay the course."

Ebony tucked the files beneath her arm and pursed her lips to smother a smile.

Chapter Fifteen

The tile of the kitchen floor felt chilly on Jessie's bare feet. She dangled her pumps from her fingers as she tiptoed toward a seat at the table to slip them on. It had been a while since she'd worn heels, let alone her camelhair blazer, navy skirt, and silk blouse. Luckily, she'd lost most of her baby weight, but her clothing still felt snug.

"Wow. Look at you. Nice outfit. You got a date?" Hal asked.

"I'm taking Lily over to my mother's," she replied. "My yoga buddy Gayle Morrison and I are doing lunch at American Bounty Restaurant at the Culinary Institute."

"The CIA? Pretty fancy company you're keeping. It's great that you're getting out of the house and being a lady who lunches."

"I know. I couldn't believe it when Gayle called this morning with the invitation. You usually have to book tables months in advance." Reservations were no small feat at the famous farm-to-table restaurant, and it impressed Jessie that her new friend had scored a table on such short notice. "I'm going to revel in every second of this afternoon because I've got to let Bellamy know about the Barrie Building tomorrow. So let's review the lease tonight, please?" She slipped her arms around his neck and kissed him on the mouth. "But today is all about girl talk."

Jessie arrived at the Culinary Institute of America early, allowing time to enjoy the panoramic view from the cliff-top plaza of the former Saint Andrews-on-the Hudson Jesuit monastery. The springtime air was cool and crisp, and the brisk breeze sprinkled the refreshing mist from the plaza's fountains on her face. Below, the Hudson shimmered bluish-gray, and sailboats captured the wind to hitchhike southward to New York City. Across the river, the soft green of the Catskills stretched westward, fading into blue and purple off into the distance.

The shortened shadows of the plaza's twin porticos signified it was almost noon. The rendezvous time was swiftly approaching.

"Jessie." Her name floated in the air. She turned to see Gayle getting off the garage elevator and waving to her. They met on the broad steps of Roth Hall, a memorial to the school's co-founder Frances Roth, and entered through its massive oak doors. Their heels clicked along the marble corridor past the bustling Apple Pie Bakery, The Bocuse Restaurant, and toward the American Bounty Restaurant at the end of the hall.

Inside the restaurant, the maître d' escorted them to a quiet corner table overlooking the inner courtyard's herb garden. After presenting their menus, he disappeared.

"It's always a treat to come here. I love how they support local farmers with their menu options." Gayle said, peering at Jessie over her reading glasses.

"I'm thrilled that you suggested the Bounty. It's one of my favorite restaurants," Jessie said, shifting her eyes to the courtyard to avoid Gayle's probing gaze.

A lanky student server, dressed in a starched white shirt and black pants, set a breadbasket upon the table. The sweet aroma of homemade Parker House rolls beckoned Jessie toward the menu that featured seasonal and regional delicacies from New York State.

They both ordered the asparagus soup and salmon entrée, and unable to resist any longer, Jessie selected a pastry and bit into the buttery crust. It was absolute heaven.

"Good. That's out of the way." Gayle folded her reading glasses and turned them over in her slender fingers. A shadow crossed her attractive face and a vertical wrinkle appeared between her brows.

The mood shift inside the restaurant was palpable, as though the room was holding its breath. "Is everything all right? You look worried," Jessie said.

"I'm feeling guilty, because I've invited you here under false pretenses."

Jessie couldn't imagine what Gayle was talking about, but a sinking sensation gripped her as she read Gayle's mortified expression.

"My name is Gayle Kaplan, Jessie. Morrison is my maiden name."

"Jeremy Kaplan's wife?" Jessie gulped hard to keep down the pastry she'd just devoured.

Gayle nodded.

Not long ago, Jeremy Kaplan had done the unspeakable. To protect Terrence, his client, he'd falsely accused Jessie of ethical improprieties, costing her a job, a partnership and her fiancé, and jeopardizing her license to practice law. Although exonerated, she couldn't seem to dispel the lingering nightmares about the accusations and their aftermath.

"I'm sorry, but I can't stay," Jessie said, springing to her feet. Her muscles quivered with anger as she snatched her jacket and bag. She might forgive Jeremy for his transgressions against her, but not the stress that had nearly cost her Lily. As far as Jessie was concerned, Gayle was guilty by association.

"Please, don't go. Listen to me. He doesn't know that I'm here. Please, Jessie. I need your help." Gayle stood and Jessie had the creepy feeling Gayle might follow her if she tried to leave.

Jessie pinned her with an angry, disbelieving glare. "Are you crazy? You lured me here through trickery and you want me to help you?" The room grew silent, and Jessie looked around to see the diners from nearby tables staring at her. She realized she must have been shouting and softened her volume as she hissed through clenched teeth. "Do you have any idea how your husband destroyed my life?"

"Yes, I do. Jerry told me everything, but you're the only one who can help." The color drained from Gayle's face, turning her lips white. "Jessie, please sit down so we can discuss this rationally. If you hear me out, you'll understand my, our situation."

Jessie held up her hands to prevent Gayle from continuing. Initially, she'd liked Gayle. However, Gayle's deception had shattered any respect she'd held for her.

Whatever the crisis, it wasn't Jessie's problem. She had enough of her own. But Gayle must be desperate if she was turning to a stranger for help. And her hopelessness resonated deep within Jessie. Not so long ago, she'd been pregnant, alone, unemployed, and implicated in a murder. Handling her issues hadn't been easy, but at least she'd had the support of her family and Hal.

Though common sense urged her to run the hell away, empathy bid her otherwise. "Against my better judgment, I'll give you five minutes. That's it."

Gayle nodded.

Amidst the return of the room's hum, Jessie and Gayle returned to their seats.

* * *

Jessie listened as Gayle barreled ahead like a runaway freight train, ignoring the imposed five-minute deadline. Punctuating her monologue with gulps of red wine, Gayle described discovering Jeremy lifeless on the floor of his office about a month ago.

"I thought I was going to lose him. Jerry's breath was shallow, irregular, and his skin had the slick, clammy sheen of death. The paramedics saved him, but the ultimate diagnosis was life-shattering. Jerry needed a heart valve replacement, but first, he needed to recover from endocarditis, a bacterium that had settled in his heart." Gayle rambled on, getting tipsier and more loose-lipped by the sip.

"For months, he'd hidden the chest pains, sweats, and shortness of breath from me, as well as the bourbon, cigars, and coffee. Of course, I was furious with him. He'd treated his heart like crap, and the bastard wasn't thinking about me or the kids." Gayle paused, wringing her napkin into a long, white snake. "Jerry hasn't been able to go into the office for weeks. His secretary, Mo, has assumed the day-to-day office operations, but we're treading water. We are drowning in a case backlog, and neither Mo nor I can assist his clients."

Jeremy's health issues were horrifying, but for the life of her, Jessie couldn't make the connection between the Kaplans' tragedies and her part in the solution. Frankly, she didn't care. If her new "friend" wanted sympathy, she'd picked the wrong girl.

"That's why when I recognized you at yoga, it was serendipity. It was as if my prayers had been answered," Gayle said. "I know Jerry sabotaged your career. We've discussed it, and he feels terribly guilty about what he did to you."

"He could've apologized personally rather than sending his wife to do his bidding." Jessie tasted the bitterness of betrayal in the back of her throat.

"I told you Jerry doesn't know that I'm here."

"Honestly, I'm really missing the point. I'm sorry about your problems and I hope Jeremy feels better, but I've got to go." Once again, she rose to leave.

"Jessie, stop, please." Gayle reached out for Jessie's hand, but she snatched it away. "I'm sorry for misleading you and I'm sorry for what he did, but I intend to make it up to you. I know it will never compensate you for the losses you've suffered, but I want you to come work for us."

"You're offering me a job? Are you kidding?" Jessie stared at Gayle in disbelief. She couldn't believe that Gayle was asking Jessie to overlook that Jeremy had represented Terrence, and probably still did. Further, Gayle was deceiving her husband by propositioning the attorney he'd destroyed, nearly fatally. Either this woman possessed more chutzpah than Jessie imagined, or she was delusional.

On cue, a pair of servers appeared at their table bearing silver serving domes. In unison, and with a great flourish, they presented their lunches plated with artistic garnishes of peewee potatoes, bacon, and oyster mushrooms, and then bowed and disappeared.

"This isn't a pity offer," Gayle said. Her head spun toward the loud laughter at the next table and then back to Jessie. "You interned with Jerry when you were in high school, and he recognizes that you're smart and capable, and can handle anything thrown at you-" Gayle pushed her plate aside and knitting her fingers, she rested her elbows on the white linen. "Especially after, please don't make me spell it out again."

"You're going to have to because Jeremy and Terrence are interconnected, and for all I know, Jeremy still represents Terrence."

"I wouldn't be here if he did. Jerry hasn't heard from Terrence since the sentencing, and good riddance. He always made me uncomfortable when the twins were his students. There was something off about him, and now we know, don't we?"

Jessie didn't answer. She couldn't believe she was still listening to Gayle. She wanted to leave, but didn't want to appear rude. "Look, Gayle, this isn't going to happen."

"I disagree. I've thought this through and I know we can make the opportunity beneficial to both of us." She withdrew a folded piece of paper from her pocketbook and presented it to Jessie. "This is a proposed starting salary, but it's negotiable, and since Lily is your priority, we'd make our arrangement flexible. Part-time. On a trial basis to see how the situation progresses."

"Gayle, I appreciate your offer, but this is insane. I have no experience with criminal law," Jessie said, without opening the paper. "Besides, what's my incentive for joining Jeremy's firm? And how do you think he's going to react when he learns you've made me this offer behind his back?"

"You and I can work out the specifics, but I think this proposal shows that we'll make it worth your while. And let me worry about my husband. First, I need to know you're interested."

Gayle's blue-grey eyes bored into her. It was difficult to read whether they betrayed desperation or sincerity, however, the puffy blue rings of exhaustion were evident.

With her mind revving like a turbo-charged engine, Jessie found it difficult to understand the wacky job offer. She calmed herself, recalling the advice of her former boss, J.R. McMann. The king of negotiators had taught her to never accept the first offer, no matter how enticing it may appear. Play it cool. Take control. Mull over the options.

She folded the paper in half again and slipped it into her blazer pocket. "I appreciate your offer and candor, but I need time to consider it. I'll let you know." Mr. McMann had trained her to repeat these words, although not necessarily mean them.

Gayle Kaplan nodded.

Was she really considering crossing over to the dark side? To Jeremy Kaplan? The man who'd almost had her disbarred, who'd cost her the partnership at Curtis and McMann, her engagement to Kyle, and who'd threatened her life and Lily's? Was she out of her freaking mind?

Chapter Sixteen

I t was well after midnight and Jessie lay in bed wide-awake, while Hal slept soundly beside her. Her thoughts danced inside her head like the shadows of the windswept branches upon the ceiling. Should she work for Hal, open her own office or work for Jeremy Kaplan?

Hal snorted and rolled onto his side, facing her. The constant tension in his jaw had relaxed, and he looked peaceful, as though the pressures of being District Attorney didn't exist. His job offer had been a sweet, if misguided, Hal thing to do. There was no way could she work *for* Hal. It would tip the balance of power within their relationship in his favor and blur the lines between work and home. This wouldn't be healthy for either of them. Further, sleeping with her boss would be inappropriate and an HR nightmare.

Jessie fluffed her down pillow and mulled over opening her own law office. The move would be risky. It would demand time and financial commitments to develop a client base. Yet, the idea of being her own boss and defining her own future excited her. But it bore additional costs. She already relied too heavily upon Hal and her parents, and if she went solo, she'd become more dependent upon them for childcare and loans to tide her over. Balancing the dollars and common sense, the thought of losing this opportunity tore at her as she weighed her third opportunity.

In the darkness, her decision about Gayle's proposal became clear. The sum written on the tiny scrap of paper had made her head spin. She couldn't believe it. She'd blinked once, twice, and reread the words "Five Thousand Dollars per week–Part Time." That equaled over two hundred fifty thousand dollars a year, almost twice her associate's salary at Curtis and McMann. It was a hard offer to refuse. However, it entailed working for Jeremy Kaplan.

Despite his reputation as an opportunistic shyster, she'd admired Jeremy until he'd screwed her over. Had his betrayal been personal or professional? The rules of professional conduct required a lawyer to represent his or her client to the best of his or her ability and abide by the client's decisions. Would she have used any legal means to exonerate a client, even if it meant endangering another attorney's license?

Jessie feared her answer to the question. She was a litigator, a gladiator, like every other attorney. When representing her clients, she had done, and would do, everything legally permissible to protect them. Even if, like Jeremy, it meant catering to the whims of a madman.

And she wondered who'd devised the scheme. She smelled Terrence's handiwork. Did he hate her enough to want to steal her career, her life, and her child? Why did he refuse to let her go even now?

If she worked for Jeremy, she might discover a solution to stopping Terrence's harassment forever. She'd be on the inside, gaining access to Terrence's file and information she could use to her advantage. Plus, she'd be mentored by the best criminal defense mind in the Hudson Valley.

"Learn on someone else's nickel," her father had preached before her high school internship with Jeremy. Ironically, the words still rang true. Accepting Gayle's proposal might yield much more than nickels. It might present a chance for redemption and revenge.

* * *

After a few fitful hours of sleep, Jessie rose, bewitched. She'd intended to discuss the pros and cons of Gayle's offer with her parents and Hal before deciding. But a supernatural force had seized control, making her brave. Bold. Her old self.

Shortly after Hal left for work, she reached for her phone.

First, she called Bellamy to tell her she'd changed her mind. Then she

100

made another call.

"Gayle, I know your situation is extremely stressful and I appreciate your thinking of me," Jessie said, racing through her words. She hesitated, steadying the shakiness in her legs and knees. "I...I'm open to sitting down with Jeremy to see where he's coming from. Let's see if we can work something out."

The long silence from Gayle worried Jessie. Perhaps she'd changed her mind.

"Hello, Gayle? Are you there?"

"Why, yes? I'm here," Gayle said excitedly. "That's fantastic. Are you free this morning at eleven?"

"Sure, sounds great," she replied with surprise. "See you then."

Click. The call ended, but her knees still trembled.

For the first time in months, Jessie felt lighter, brighter. Her life had finally turned a corner.

Her excitement momentarily deflated at the thought of one enormous problem. Hal. He despised Jeremy Kaplan, and she heard him ranting inside her head, warning her.

She'd deal with him later, after the meeting, because there might be nothing to report. Why incite a battle if there was no war?

Jessie checked her phone. The time read 9:05 a.m. There was plenty of time to shower and get dressed. Turning toward the bathroom, she stopped in her tracks at a rustling noise emanating from the baby monitor on her nightstand. A soft gurgling escalated into a full-blown yowl that prickled the fine hairs on the back of her neck.

Crap. She'd forgotten about her plans to spend the entire day with Lily. The park. The library. The market.

There was only one solution to her problem, but her mother was lousy at keeping secrets.

Chapter Seventeen

Jessie climbed the marble front steps of the Kaplan's Federal-style mansion, which boasted four chimneys with a porch as wide as a trio of Jessie's houses stacked side-by-side. She recalled that as a teen, she'd viewed the house as being as monumental as FDR's Sunnyside, but not as intimidating. Inching toward the door, she rang the video doorbell, waved at the fisheye lens, and for good measure, double tapped the tarnished doorknocker.

The heavy oak door slowly opened. Through the crack in the door, an apparition of Jeremy Kaplan appeared. She'd last seen him in court when he'd defended Terrence Butterfield against murder charges. Last August, he'd been hale and hardy, flaunting a flamboyant flowered Hawaiian shirt, khakis, and topsiders.

Now, liver spots speckled his pale, almost transparent skin and his smooth, balding scalp. The gaunt, ashen man appearing before her in a navy blazer, baggy tan trousers, and loafers was the ghost of the sharp, renegade shark she remembered.

They stared at each other in mutual shock.

"Hello, Jeremy," Jessie said, pity surging through her for this once-rugged man.

"Jessie? I don't want to be rude, but I've got an office appointment in a few minutes. Would you mind speaking with my wife? Perhaps, she could assist you." The loose skin along his jawline swayed along with his slight tremor.

Gayle approached her husband and placed a gentle hand on his shoulder.

"Jessie, I'm sorry. I thought I mentioned coming to the side office entrance. Please come in, and we'll go downstairs." She beamed and gestured toward the foyer.

Jeremy's eyes flicked toward Jessie, and then back to Gayle in confusion.

"No worries, darling," Gayle said to him, and then to Jessie. "Please follow me."

Jessie strained to hear Gayle's words over the blood thrumming inside her ears. Something felt awry. She squinted, studying the couple standing on the threshold. Gayle appeared relaxed and confident while Jeremy wobbled on his feet, unaware of the spittle dribbling down the corner of his mouth to his chin.

Suddenly, a tiny voice inside her head whispered, *"Run!"*.

Gayle had played them both.

* * *

Once more, Gayle had painted Jessie into a corner and it stung to be duped by her again. Jessie turned to leave.

"No, Jessie. Wait a minute," Gayle pleaded. "Please come in and I'll explain everything."

Jessie stared at her, and allowing her curiosity to outweigh her anger, she followed the Kaplans into the cherry-paneled library off the foyer. Her eyes swept across the embellished plaster ceilings, the pastel Aubusson rug, and the French door overlooking a Koi fishpond. Gayle directed them to a pair of weathered leather wingback chairs facing the fireplace, where she paced across the hearthstone like a caged tigress. Her features tightened as tension filled the room.

"I know how this looks, but I didn't mean to deceive anyone," Gayle said.

"With all due respect, that's all you've been doing since we met the other day," Jessie replied.

"You two have met already?" Jeremy balled his fist and slammed it on the armrest. "Gayle, you conspired against me?"

"Jessie had nothing to do with this." Gayle explained her chance encounter with Jessie at the yoga studio, and how one omission had precipitated another, weaving a web of deception. "Jerry, for months, Mo and I have been nagging you to hire someone, but you've been too stubborn to listen. The pressure of running your practice under the current conditions is killing you. Mo and I know it, and deep down I believe you do, too. Somebody had to take charge, so I pursued Jessie. She's incredibly talented and I think you two would be good for each other. And honestly, you owe her...."

Jessie wriggled as an uncomfortable warmth flushed her body. She should've bolted when she'd had the chance, but now she'd become trapped in the cross fire of bickering spouses. Love, if that's what it was, certainly made people do crazy things. Lie. Cheat. Steal. Just look at the Kaplans.

"Honey, why weren't you honest with me about Jessie?" Jeremy asked.

"It was difficult enough to convince you to meet with anyone, and if I'd mentioned it was Jessie, all bets would've been off."

"You didn't know for certain, did you? And that wasn't fair to me, was it?" he asked quietly. "Or Jessie."

"I didn't think anyone would get hurt. I figured that once Jessie was here, the situation would work itself out, and it did. Didn't it?"

"I can't enter a relationship seeded with betrayal," Jessie said. She'd already suffered through enough duplicity for one lifetime. Kyle's lies. Terrence's refusal to let her go. Hal's dumping her for Erin. Her past refused to leave her in peace.

"Jessie, first, I owe you an apology. I don't know if Gayle told you, but I've regretted any harm I caused you or your family." Jeremy spoke slowly, in the paternal inflection reminiscent of her father. Gentle and caring, not the knife-sharp tone he'd used to impress the judge and jury. "I also apologize for being a coward and abetting Terrence's attacks, but practicing criminal law is complicated. You're a lawyer, so you understand the duties owed to our clients, and I needed to save Terrence's life. That was my job. I can tell you it wasn't personal, but for you, it was immensely personal. For that, I'm truly sorry."

He paused, seeming to gather his thoughts, and steadied his quivering hand. "My wife loves me deeply and knows that I can be obstinate when asking for help, especially from her. I can't justify the way Gayle brought us together, but her intentions were honorable." The wrinkles around Jeremy's eyes softened as he gazed at his wife. "I'll give her credit for that. She believes you're the right person for the position. I trust her choices. After all, she married me."

Jeremy's attention shifted back to her. "Jessie, we go way back, and you came here in good faith. I'm convinced that we owe it to ourselves to explore our options."

"Besides, if you don't talk, next week I'll parade in another victim who I've shanghaied off the street," Gayle said, trying to lighten the mood.

"Jessie, I much rather it be you. And you've got nothing to lose," he said.

Damn it. They were tag-teaming her.

While she was grateful for the apology, their melodrama was unsettling, especially with the questions nagging at her. Was Jeremy's acquiescence sincere or expedient? What else had Gayle neglected to reveal to her? Was a Supreme Court brief due tomorrow? Or a statute of limitations expiring? How ill was Jeremy?

She'd arrived planning to meet with Jeremy while he'd been completely in the dark. If anyone deserved outrage, it was he, not her. He was being a good sport, so she'd take the meeting with Jeremy for herself, for Lily. For their futures.

Jeremy's apology was a starting point. And he seemed willing to give her answers. All she had to do was ask.

Chapter Eighteen

With Hendricks in lockup and the Chief's consent obtained, Ebony and Zander returned to the bullpen to begin their formal investigation. Since more than a day had passed since Lissie Sexton had visited the police station, time was of the essence. She could be anywhere by now.

Ebony sat down at her desk and although Hendricks was in custody, she dialed the emergency contact number the hospital had provided. Maybe she'd get lucky and Lissie would answer phone. The number rang once and went to voice mail. She tried again with the same result. The metallic ring could signal more than a dead phone battery. Her jaded cop's mind drifted to seamier scenarios—abduction, mutilation, strangulation, and overdose.

Then she rang Lissie's mother. Sniffing back the tears, Mrs. Sexton reported that she'd been unable to reach her daughter, and she worried that Kurt Hendricks had hurt her. The strain in Mrs. Sexton's voice relaxed after Ebony reassured her that Kurt was, and would be, behind bars, indefinitely.

Beside her, Zander hummed a Bon Jovi tune as he logged into his computer terminal to pull up Lissie's RAP sheet. His mood had temporarily lightened, but it could swing back to black at any moment.

"Kurt Hendricks is a pill pusher, not a murderer," he said. "He doesn't have the balls." Ebony smiled; relieved he was speaking to her again. "Sexton was pocketing some of the coin she'd earned. Maybe Hendricks found out, got ticked off, and killed her. But, my gut says he's not our guy." A smirk spread across Zander's crooked mouth. "Or Lissie could've taken the money and split with Dr. Small Dick."

"Nothing's making any sense. She and Kiara couldn't have disappeared into thin air, but Doc is still out on the streets. And there's not enough for us to issue an APB. Let's pull some reports and see if we get any hits."

Being a detective had its perks. At the mention of her name, Detective Ebony Jones of the Poughkeepsie Police Department, expedited searches from telecom carriers, banks, AMTRAK, airlines, the FBI, New York DMV, and Homeland Security appeared in her inbox. They ran them all.

"From all indications, Elisabeth Sexton is a ghost," Ebony said. "No bank accounts or credit cards. No FBI or TSA records. Nothing except the NYS driver's license confirming the Smith Street address. Even Lissie's Social Security and Medicare accounts showed no deposits, ever. Apparently, she's never been on a payroll in her life. And as we know, her current business is cash only."

Lissie's RAP sheet provided the most information, but no clues to her whereabouts. Three months ago, she'd been arrested in the City of Poughkeepsie for prostitution. She'd paid a hundred dollar fine, served three days, and was released. A serial arrestee for hooking and minor misdemeanors, she'd stacked up a dozen convictions over the past two years. She'd simply paid her fine, done the time, and walked.

"Lookie here. The form lists Jeremy Kaplan as her attorney, so he's probably pled down the charges or gotten others dropped," Zander said. "It pays to have a shark like Kaplan on your side."

Ebony shook her head and scoffed. The New York Penal Law was a joke, categorizing the act of prostitution—soliciting sex for money—as a low-level Class B Misdemeanor, similar to fortune-telling, rent gouging, false impersonation, loitering, and unlawful assembly. Because hooking carried minimal jail time and fines, there was no incentive for the pros to stop their trade or get rehabilitation. On the upside, they'd enjoy a few nights of shelter, hot showers, and meals at the taxpayer's dime. On the downside, they'd lose income and spend their hard-earned cash on the bail bondsman and the lawyers to spring them from lock-up. Shysters such as Jeremy Kaplan, who probably gouged them.

"No drug arrests," she said, surprised. "That's weird because her mother mentioned a few stints in rehab."

"And that's relevant because?"

"No reason. The facilities probably wouldn't be much help, anyway."

She feared they'd reached another dead end.

* * *

Later that morning, Ebony and Zander stood before the vending machines in the office break room. Eyeing a prepackaged apple Danish, she inserted the coins, and against her better judgment, pressed the button. Something gnawed at her mind with the same intensity as the hunger pangs in her belly.

"Kurt Hendricks," she muttered, retrieving the snack from the machine.

"Huh?" Zander said, stuffing a slice of bagel into his mouth.

"Lissie's boyfriend/pimp. He's playing stupid, but he knows where she is." The guy was a con artist, if she'd ever seen one. But she was a cop. "Come on, let's go to the tomb."

"You're joking, right?"

She threw him a look. The look. The one that indicated he'd better not mess with her. She was on a mission and wouldn't be deterred.

As Zander crammed the rest of the bagel into his mouth, he and Ebony signed a requisition form to access to Hendricks' evidence stored in the property room, and they rode the elevator down into the damp sub-basement, three levels below the station.

"I really hate this place. I've got an iron stomach, but the mildew smell of decaying cardboard even makes me queasy," he said, snapping on his blue latex gloves.

"Nobody enjoys going to the tomb, so suck it up. CSI confiscated a ton of contraband from Hendricks' apartment and who knows what we'll find."

"Do you have any idea what you're looking for?" Zander asked as he examined the cartons stacked on the floor and tagged with *People versus Hendricks*. To maintain the chain of custody, the department had inventoried all evidence seized and logged it into the computer. Then they'd photographed, weighed, tested, and packed and sealed it into a dozen cardboard cartons marked Exhibit A-L.

"Lissie didn't have a phone in her name, so I'm betting that Kurt gave her one. If he synched the phone to one of the seized computers, we might be able to track Lissie's phone by GPS." The property locker was as cold as the unsolved cases rotting there, and the damp settled into Ebony's bones as she studied the inventory prepared by the forensic team. "Try the carton marked Exhibit A."

Zander whipped out his Swiss Army penknife and carefully slit the seam of the carton. It was the party box packed with glassine bags containing colorful pills, and brown leaves and buds, each marked with the amount of substance and the sample amount transmitted to the crime lab for identification. He resealed the box and set it aside. From Exhibit B, he extracted a plastic bag and held it up for her to examine. It contained a dozen burner phones and one more expensive Android model. "Now what, Einstein?"

"Just set them aside. Are there any tablets or computers in there?"

"Nope," he replied.

For the next hour, they rummaged through the contents of the remaining cartons, uncovering enough stolen goods to populate a pawnshop. Dozens of used handguns, mostly Colts, scratched and worn from handling, antique Samurai swords, Rolex watches, diamond solitaire rings, and tennis bracelets, power drills, a Martin Acoustic guitar, a Tiffany silver tea set, Mont Blanc pens, and ten thousand dollars in uncirculated hundred-dollar bills. One carton contained electric vibrators, dildos, and other sex toys.

"Ever use one of these do-hickeys? What about your boyfriend, Drew?" Zander asked, waggling the rubber penis in her face.

"Don't be a jerk. Put that back," she said, swiping the dildo away. Ebony hoisted another box onto the table and slit it open. She peeled back the bubble wrap and beneath it was a carton of unopened iPhones and Apple watches. "We're getting warmer."

"I've underestimated our friend, Mr. H. What a haul." Zander admired the latest 18-carat gold Apple watch, which made his low-end sport model look cheap in comparison. "This thing costs fifteen grand. More on the Asian market." He re-boxed it and heaved the last and largest box onto the table.

Ebony took the knife and sliced open the top of the box marked "Exhibit L-Fragile." She unfolded the flaps, and beneath the Play Stations and Xboxes, she spotted the treasure she'd been seeking. Three Mac laptop computers. Four iPhones. Still sealed in their original packing.

"Bingo," she said smugly. Perhaps one of these devices would lead them to Lissie.

Chapter Nineteen

E
bony flipped over the first computer box and discovered a stained manila envelope glued to its bottom. She peeled away the envelope and removed a stack of crumpled papers from inside. Cautiously, she flattened them out on the table.

"They're some type of ledger," Zander said, stamping his feet, and blowing into his palms. "Mr. Hendricks, you're full of surprises, aren't you?"

"You're not wimping out on me? It's not that cold." Ebony had worn sandals to work and wiggled her toes to fend off the freeze. She'd rather endure the chill than admit she was also losing feeling in her extremities. "This will put some heat in your chassis... look at this. They're for property, lots and lots of transactions."

The columns on the spreadsheets contained what appeared to be the stolen property's description, the date received, the supplier as coded by a series of initials, the item's disposal date, the amount received, and the purchaser, again coded by initials only. The volume of the transactions was astounding, tracking the movement of hundreds of goods at a time. Her fingers skimmed along the perforated edges where someone had torn the pages from a binder. "It looks like a large-scale operation carried out over the past couple of years. But there's possibly more."

"Is there any key for deciphering the suppliers and purchasers?" Zander asked.

She rifled through the papers and shook her head. However, the painstaking care invested in the project was evident. Page after page, precise rows filled the lines of the thick white vellum. The swirling numbers and script, written in indigo ink, were beautiful. It was a woman's hand, she thought. Presumably, transcribed using one of the stolen Mont Blanc pens.

The penmanship looked similar to the distinctive signature on Lissie Sexton's license and booking sheets. She'd dotted her *i* with a circle and the letter *s* had double slashes through it like a dollar sign. Those telltale symbols ran rampant throughout the sheets.

Ebony shivered as the chill settled into her bones, and Zander must have noticed the table tremble.

"Come on. Don't be an idiot. It's freaking freezing in here, so let's bring the evidence upstairs for a closer look." Without waiting for an answer, he grabbed a trolley and loaded up the computers, tablets, and phones. After signing the property log, he dragged the trolley behind him, leading Ebony into the elevator.

Clutching the inventory ledger to her chest, Ebony and Zander returned to ground level and warmth.

* * *

Another manila envelope marked "Urgent" waited on Ebony's desk chair. She noticed it, pitched it on her "to do" pile, and eased herself down with a groan. Furtively, she slid open her top desk drawer and grabbed her emergency prescription painkillers containing codeine. She examined the bottle. With only six left, she needed to make them last until she could renew her script next month. Ebony shouldn't have been popping them like candy, but the relentless throbbing stretched from her hip to her pelvis. The pain registered at level five, so she snapped a pill in half and let it dissolve into bitter sand on her tongue. She swallowed it dry and hard, and shoved the bottle back into her drawer, praying it would do the trick.

She rose stiffly, retrieved the "Urgent" envelope, and met up with Zander in Interrogation Room One, where they would encamp.

The printout contained the telecom company's billing statements for five cellphone lines registered to Kurt Hendricks. It also included the usage data for each line and the logs of all incoming and outgoing calls.

112

"We've got five phones. One Android and four iPhones," Zander said, arranging the phones across the metal table, reminiscent of dead bodies at the morgue. "If we have five bills and five phones, doesn't that mean that Sexton didn't have one of Hendricks' phones?"

"No, not necessarily," Ebony replied flatly. Sometimes, he infuriated her, jumping to conclusions because of his waning interest in a case. Zander fancied himself as a techie, with his smartwatch, smartphone, and smart car, but sometimes he could be really dense. She guessed she had to spell it out for him. "These phone bills may not belong to any of the phones we have in our possession. Our first step is to open the iPhones and lift the numbers off them. Next, we need to match the bills against those numbers and the one on the Android. We may get lucky and find Lissie's phone in the batch." She paused, gesturing toward the table. "Or these phones could be brand new ones or locked ones. If so, we're up shit's creek and we're back at ground zero. But the only way to know for sure is to fire them up and compare their numbers to the bills."

"So, assuming they're unlocked, we have four possibilities. One, the phones match the bills, but we don't have Lissie's phone data, so we can't track her calls or locate her through GPS. Two, her phone is on the list and we can track her. And three, some of the bills match the phones we have. Or the fourth possibility is that none of the bills match." Zander puffed out his cheeks and blew out an exaggerated breath, which made his lips vibrate. "Phew! This seems like tons of work, which may be for nothing."

"Any chance of finding Lissie means something, and we don't have time to spare. Z, I'm not the geek in the room, so we need you to figure this out. Pronto."

"Well, I'm betting the info for Sexton's phone is in this room, and that our friend Hendricks was too lazy to lock his phones. So let's get to it."

Zander flicked on the Android first. Its battery charge icon glowed green, so he checked its settings, retrieved its number, and rifled through the billing statements. "Here, this phone's on page two. That's one down, four to go."

"Maybe you're right about Hendricks," she said. "Since this one's unlocked, the others might be as well."

They held the four iPhone boxes up to the light to study them. The small, transparent plastic discs sealing each slick white box had been slit and resealed. Removing them from their packing, they discovered only one iPhone was charged and unlocked, but its number didn't appear on the bills. Exchanging worried glances, they plugged in the remaining three cellphones and waited.

Chapter Twenty

While the phones charged, Ebony remained content to relax. In contrast, Zander, a bundle of nervous energy, removed each computer from its carton and plugged it into the surge protectors he'd commandeered from their colleagues. One by one, the screens blinked to life, emitting the hum of endless possibilities.

Zander glanced up from the bank of computers and cellphones, his eyes glowing with excitement. "You were right, one iPhone wasn't activated, so it's not on the bill. There is another phone number listed in the paperwork, but that phone isn't part of the evidence seized. The call logs show it was last used on Wednesday morning at two a.m."

"Great, that's the day Lissie disappeared, so it could be hers. We should be able to GPS track it on one of the computers."

"If Hendricks stored his cloud email and password on one of these babies." Zander guided his finger across the square mouse pad of the first Mac laptop, attempting to log on. A tiny rainbow disc churned and then guided him to the setup page. The equipment was a virgin, untouched by human hands. The same proved true for the second laptop. "Crap," he grumbled.

She watched him rub his hands on his pant legs and repeat the sequence one last time on the remaining MacBook. He gave a short bark of laughter as the home screen opened to a scene of Yosemite National Park overlaid with icons for mail, photo, calendar, and other Mac applications. After he connected to the station's Wi-Fi, Zander navigated to the iCloud website where he could trace the missing phone, but it stopped him dead in his tracks.

"Damn, we can get into the computer, but not the Cloud. Hendricks didn't auto-save his cloud password." Zander slammed his fist on the table, banging his watch. He stroked its glass face as though soothing a child. "This computer won't be much help, unless he stored the password in his settings." After a few quick keystrokes, he shook his head.

"Z, I know you're a genius, but maybe it's time to call in IT to hack the cloud," Ebony said, twisting her lips to stifle a laugh. "Or we could get a warrant to have the service provider ping the cellphone through their towers to reveal its location."

Her partner rewarded her insult with a scowl. "No. Just hold off, will you? I'm sure I can solve this. Just give me a minute." Zander itched the two-day growth on his chin and squinted at the monitor.

Short of interrogating Hendricks again, the alternatives appeared limited. By now, he'd probably lawyered up, so any information he volunteered would come with a hefty price tag such as a plea bargain on the larceny and drug charges.

"Let's go through every step one more time, please," Ebony insisted, "for Lissie's sake."

Zander grunted in apparent frustration. They powered down the laptop, rebooted it, and once again, he hit a roadblock at the Cloud site.

Ebony selected the Android phone and balanced it within her palm. Hendricks' wallpaper displayed an old Bon Jovi album cover, *Slippery When Wet*, with its title splattered in black graffiti. How careless of a thief to leave his smartphone unlocked. It was as though Hendricks was tempting her to search its data and uncover his secrets. She fiddled with the phone, but found nothing.

"Think...think," she murmured. "Why would Hendricks have all these Apple products and only one Android? What makes this phone different from the others?" She paused. "I'll tell you why. Because this was his personal phone, the one he used to transact his business. Somewhere in here are the passwords to his kingdom."

Ebony's hands grew clammy, and she wiped them on her jeans before scrolling through the phone's alphabetical directory of his contacts again.

There were no obvious entries under Passwords, Kurt Hendricks, or Me, but there was something odd. He'd assigned the names of Bon Jovi hit singles to the letters in the directory. She recalled the rock video blasting over Hendricks' television in his apartment, and following her hunch, she checked for clues to his passwords in the first entry-"*It's My Life.*" Nothing. "*Livin' on a Prayer.*" Still nothing. She scrolled through each letter, each song title, past "*Wanted Dead or Alive*" to the last song, "*You Give Love a Bad Name.*"

Her skin tingled with anticipation and fear. If she were wrong, she didn't know where else to look. If she was right, they were finally on their way.

Ebony clicked on the entry, and her passport into Hendricks' digital life materialized before her eyes.

"This is an example of what *not* to do with your phone," she said, waggling it in Zander's face.

"What a dope," Zander said, chuckling at his pun. "And by the way, gloating doesn't suit you."

For his cloud password, Kurt had plagiarized another Bon Jovi reference. *Badmedicine88.*

Zander typed the password into the cloud website, selected the "Find my Phone" application, and reentered the password. A cartoonish map of the Northeastern U.S. popped up on the screen. A single green dot blinked at them from upstate New York.

He zoomed in and tracked the missing phone to a spot a few blocks away from Hendricks' apartment. "These maps can be sketchy, but one minute ago, the phone was in College Hill Park." He pointed at the map. "Thank goodness for GPS."

"No, thank goodness that Hendricks is such a hardcore Bon Jovi fan."

* * *

Ebony had always considered the Dudley Memorial Pavilion at College Hill Park an enigma. The Parthenon-like structure looked out of place, as though it had been transported from ancient Greece, and plopped down on the city's highest point for no good reason. She'd heard stories about a hotel, a college, and a reservoir having been located here, but no evidence of the past glory existed today. Though recently, a famous Broadway actor had reenacted Frederick Douglass' Emancipation Day speech on this very spot, where Douglass had delivered it over one hundred fifty years ago. The history of College Hill wasn't the only mystery lurking on this hilltop.

Time and time again, her uniformed colleagues had complained that patrolling the place had become a real pain in the ass. The landmark had deteriorated into an attractive nuisance as a haven for drug deals, sexual liaisons, or teenage beer parties. Now, she and Zander were there on the hunt for a cellphone or a dead body, or both.

From her vantage point in the parking lot, the portico's white paint was peeling with age, and its chipped plaster pillars, missing banisters and railings, were eyesores. Her eyes strayed to the surrounding tall, overgrown grass, and she reflected on her city's general state of disrepair.

She and Zander crossed the graveyard of broken glass and beer bottle tops toward a gang of teenage boys smoking a joint on the building's steps. They made little effort to hide their activities from the two strangers approaching them. Two boys jostled each other, rose, and chased one another in and out of the columns. Another boy, sporting a curly pompadour with wide sideburns, inhaled a long drag on the stub of the joint and held his breath.

"You guys seen a lady up here?" Ebony asked and flashed her badge. "White. Short. Skinny. Thirtyish. Beat up pretty good with a half-shaved head. Arm in a sling."

"What's it to you?" Pompadour Boy asked. Then he exhaled. "You looking for a dead body or something?"

"We could bust you for smoking weed in public, so drop the attitude and answer the question," Zander said.

"No, but I know who you're talking about," said a glassy-eyed black kid with a tattoo of Tupac on his neck. "She hangs with my brother. The other night, she stopped by our house and they said they were coming up here to party."

"About what time?" Ebony asked.

The boy shrugged and shook his head.

Ebony walked past them, up the granite steps into the shelter, and surveyed the landscape. The vast lawn encircling the structure was wide open with no visual obstructions, but then dropped dramatically downhill into the thick woods. Overnight the vegetation had blossomed into a dense, impervious barricade blocking her view down the hill, but she recalled the lay of the land. Beyond the trees to the west were the tennis courts, a play structure, and basketball courts, and directly due east beyond the golf course was Morgan Lake, green with algae.

College Hill contained over a hundred acres, and Lissie had been here. Ebony sensed it. Her cellphone was somewhere on this hilltop, and if they were lucky, Lissie might be here, too.

Zander returned to their car, opened Hendricks' computer, and connected it to his phone's Wi-Fi hotspot. He joined her and pointed to the GPS dot appearing within the park, as of a minute ago. This time he sent a location signal, a metallic ping, through to the missing phone.

"You guys looking for a girl or a cellphone?" Pompadour Boy asked. "Jez, if I'd known there was an iPhone around here, I woulda snagged it for myself." The other boys, thinking their leader's comment was hysterical, formed a stoner's chorus of laughter.

Ebony ignored them, concentrating on the signal. "Do it again?"

Zander transmitted another ping.

This time, she heard the sound.

A second later, Ebony sprinted eastward through the knee-high grass and down the slope toward the golf course and Morgan Lake. "Again," she yelled. Her feet navigated through the ruts and rocks hidden among the overgrown weeds. The soles of her sandals slid across a mossy outcropping and, unable to stabilize her footing, her left ankle twisted on the slimy surface. Flinching, she hesitated for a moment, and channeled her college basketball coach bellowing inside her head. He goaded her to continue sprinting despite the pain. To run it off. Ebony gritted her teeth and hobbled onward toward the woods, gathering speed.

"Again," she bellowed, her voice quavering.

Zander repeatedly tapped the button, transmitting fresh tones. The closer she came to the sound, the faster her heart beat. Up ahead, the earth disappeared into thin air and treetops took its place. She skidded to a dead stop at the edge of a ravine, her legs as heavy as concrete. Just in time, she reversed her course as the dry earth crumbled beneath her feet, sending dirt and stones plummeting into the precipice. Her ears pulsated with the drumming of her heart, and a hot pain shot up into her hip.

Ping.

She bent over to catch her breath and cursed herself for not taking the whole painkiller earlier. Her breath grew ragged as she battled the needles piercing her hip and the humid air squeezing her lungs. The pain had rocketed to level nine now, but she had no choice except to soldier through it, as she always did.

Peering down into the overgrowth of brambles, maple saplings, and pine trees, she scanned the dappled floor of the forest below. Nothing appeared vaguely human. Only the corroded handrails of an abandoned staircase and half-buried rusty chicken wire waited for her like booby traps. There was no sign of a body. No sign of Lissie.

In an instant, the sun slid behind a layer of black, broken clouds rolling in from the west. A sudden wind gust kicked up, rustling the tree canopy overhead into a deafening frenzied roar. The leafy pistachio underskirts warned her to proceed with caution. She might be horrified by what she discovered.

Ping.

She shut her eyes and listened, trying to detect the sound caught up in the storm.

Ping.

The ringing was close, maybe a hundred yards ahead on the far side of the gully. The gorge stretched for a half-mile or so, and there was no easy way across. To reach the opposite side, she'd have to scale down the rocky walls almost three stories high and then back up again. It would be painful, but not impossible, even in her current condition.

Ebony limped along, combing the cliff for a safe path down, one that would leave her unscathed by the thorns, jagged boulders, and barbed wire. But none was visible.

Behind her, heavy panting grew louder, startling her. Could it be Lissie? Or the pot smokers? She pivoted around to discover Zander approaching her, toting the laptop beneath his arm.

Ping.

"Listen," she said, bending down to massage her swollen ankle. "It's over there." She pointed due east. They exchanged worried glances at the chasm before them.

"Eb, the sound's not coming from the ravine, so let's get the car and see if we can trace it on the other side."

Chapter Twenty-One

Jessie rifled through her bedroom closet, considering what to wear on her first day of work after almost a year. Her white blouses had yellowed, the waistbands of her skirts and slacks pinched, and she'd worn the heels of her pumps down to nubs. Her wardrobe looked more like rags than current fashion, which, like her life, direly needed a makeover.

With bittersweetness, she glanced over at Lily playing on the bedroom carpet with a stack-and-roll toy, her favorite. Where had the time gone? It was only yesterday that Lily had been a scrawny three-pound and nine-ounce preemie, and now Jessie sensed that Lily's first steps were imminent. Although it would break her heart if she missed that milestone, she needed to feel productive again.

Lily giggled as Jessie flipped through the hangers, finally selecting a pair of cream slacks, a floral silk blouse, and navy blazer. She held it up for Lily's approval. "What do you think, Lilybean? Will this do?"

Her daughter responded by dropping the green ring, rolling over onto her knees, and crawling to Jessie's bare feet. She waved her arms in the air and grunted, her signal to be picked up and cuddled.

"Up? You want up?" Jessie stashed the clothing on a brass hook and gathered Lily up in her arms.

"Nice outfit. Going somewhere special?" a gentle voice asked.

Lily excitedly kicked her feet and extended her arms toward grandma Lena, who'd joined them in the bedroom.

"Give me my precious girl," Lena said. As usual, her mother looked elegant. Her freshly coiffed hair and the lilac cashmere sweater complimented her gold and green mismatched eyes, a trait shared by the three females in the room. "I stopped by to take you both to lunch at the Alumni House. They'll be closing after Vassar's graduation next weekend." She seized her granddaughter and planted a kiss on Jessie's cheek. "I thought it might be fun. Just us three Martin girls."

"Mom, since you asked, would you be interested in watching Lily for me on a more regular basis?" She swallowed hard. "I've accepted a job. It was quite sudden."

Lena perched on the edge of the bed and planted sloppy kisses on Lily's pink cheeks, prompting the baby to giggle with glee. "Who could resist her gorgeous face?" She buried her nose in Lily's curls and inhaled. "And that baby smell. If they could only bottle it."

"Mom, are you listening to me?" Jessie slammed a dresser drawer shut.

"Yes, darling, you've accepted a job. I assume you aren't going back to those monsters at Curtis and McMann, or becoming a dreary prosecutor for the DA."

She regretted confiding in her mother about Hal's offer, especially after Kyle's wrath over her returning to work had sideswiped her. However, bringing her on board now was necessary.

"It's with Jeremy Kaplan. He's suffering from serious cardiac issues and his wife, Gayle, contacted me to be his backup."

Lena froze and stared incredulously at her. "Jess-ica Grace Mar-tin!" She'd punctuated each syllable as a reprimand, shrinking Jessie into a teenager caught sneaking a beer from the fridge. "Are you out of your mind? How can you forgive that man? What about the anguish he caused us? Your father still hasn't recovered from the Terrence debacle." She paused, gathering more ammunition. "How can you forget you almost died...and my Lily along with you? How can you be so insensitive?"

Her mother was on a roll, and she waited for the inevitable, the speech where she acted as the head cheerleader for TEAM KYLE. Jessie cringed in anticipation of hearing his name, with Lena's over-exaggeration on the first syllable, *Ky-le.*

"*Kyle's* going to be livid. It will upset him, you're returning to work so soon after… Anyway, how are you two going to patch things up if you're working? Or was this what's his name's fakakta idea? That man is always lurking around here and cozying up to your father."

"You know perfectly well that his name is Hal Samuels, and he had nothing to do with my decision. He's been busy, so I haven't really discussed it with him, or Dad either." In truth, Hal was barely speaking to her since she'd broken the news last night. He'd gone to sleep early and had left for work at sunrise, presumably to avoid her. Jessie refused to give her mother another reason to berate Hal, and besides, they'd work it out, eventually.

"Well, maybe your father can talk some sense into you, if I can't." Lena rose from the bed, and with Lily in hand, she left the bedroom and called out. "I'll get Lily dressed. You make yourself presentable and we won't discuss this again."

"Maybe we won't discuss this again, but this is my life and I'm going to live it as I see fit. Everybody thinks they're smarter than me and know what's best for me, but they're wrong. All of them. I know what's best for Lily and me, and this is the path I've chosen. So, screw them all," she said to her reflection in the closet mirror. She examined the tangled mess of curls she'd pulled back in a headband, her baggy, oversized white tee-shirt and the distressed jeans shredded at the knees.

Her mother was correct in only one thing, her outfit was not presentable.

* * *

Hal had never seen Jessie's father, Ed, so haggard and distraught. The man squirmed in the chair across from Hal's desk and appeared as monochromatic as the obituary photos in the *Poughkeepsie Journal*. Even his dress shirt was the color of weathered barn wood.

"I tell you, Hal, I'm at my wit's end. Ever since my student's disappearance, the superintendent's been clamoring for my termination, but luckily the school board has held her at bay." Ed let out a deep, sorrowful sigh. "Along with the Butterfield disaster, I've lost the community's trust, and I feel helpless."

124

Over the past few weeks, Ed had confided in him about the state of affairs at the high school. He'd told him the parents and the faculty were nervous. It galled Hal that after three decades of Ed's faithful service to his students, the parents, his faculty, the school administration, and his community, he faced the threat of dismissal. It bothered him even more that he was about to compound Ed's problems.

"I understand," Hal said and hesitated, mustering the courage to tell Ed about Jessie's new job.

Starting tomorrow.

Tomorrow didn't give them much time to change her mind. Or to convince her to open a solo practice, or to manage his campaign, or to accept the position in the Domestic Violence unit, or to stay home with Lily a bit longer. If Jessie would listen to anyone, it would be Ed. He hoped.

Hal swallowed hard and continued, "Ed, Jessie's taken a job with Jeremy Kaplan. You know he's a sleaze-ball and we've got to stop her before she makes a terrible mistake." He waited for a ferocious response, but none came. Instead, the wrinkles on Ed's forehead relaxed and his shoulders drooped.

Hal was furious with Jessie and desperate to stop her. Since Jessie's actions were a personal affront to both men, it baffled him that Ed had remained calm.

He'd known Jessie for ten years, and since the first moment, he'd been as smitten as a lovesick teenager. He'd thought of her as flawless, immune to human foibles, and until now, she'd been just that—perfect. In the blink of an eye, she'd betrayed him, and ironically, as he had betrayed her by marrying Erin.

Finally, Ed spoke. "Son, you're right to tell me about Kaplan, but there's little we can do. I know you're upset, but you know Jess, the more you push her..." Ed's voice trailed off.

Ed was correct. Tenacity was one of Jessie's most endearing, and infuriating, qualities. It caused her to advocate ferociously for her clients, against all odds, as her father did for his students.

"Working for Kaplan might be the greatest opportunity she's ever had.

Only time will tell. And if you're smart, which you are, and if you love her, which you do, you'll let her figure that out for herself."

It had been a long time since anyone had lectured him about his love life. If it had come from someone other than Ed, he would have suggested they mind their own business. But oddly, he felt comfortable taking advice from Jessie's father.

Hal thought about what Jessie meant to him. He'd been stumbling around in a fog until she'd re-entered his life. He'd been trudging through the days absorbed in work and apathetic about his marriage to Erin. His son, Tyler, had been his only source of pure, true love until seeing Jessie reminded him about finding happiness with the right person. After seven years apart, he'd spotted her in the law library and he'd felt like a starving man hungering for nourishment. He couldn't live without her. She was his air, water, and fire. All of life's elements rolled into one. He was prepared to give himself completely to her, to be hers forever.

Half of his brain mulled over this revelation, while the other half conceded to Ed's advice. Jessie had chosen her own career path, and he should support her decision. While letting her fail might tear at him, he'd abide by Ed's advice, because he and Ed loved Jessie more than anyone else in the universe, and they both wanted the best for her. Still, his pulse quickened at the thought of Kaplan.

Hal returned his full focus to his guest and locked onto his eyes. The words he'd rehearsed were on the tip of his tongue. There certainly would be no better time than the present.

He took a deep breath and plowed ahead. "Ed, there's a question that I need to ask you. It concerns Jessie."

Chapter Twenty-Two

Zander pressed the gas pedal to the floor, making the tires on the SUV shriek with every steep hairpin turn down College Hill. Digging her nails into the dashboard for safety, Ebony wished she'd walked to the bottom instead. Finally, the car screeched to a halt halfway down the hill in the parking lot of the public golf course. Dead ahead sat a cream-colored building that housed the course's pro-shop, and to their right, a golfer tapped a ball into the putting green hole. Just past the putting green, a red and white "POSTED-KEEP OUT" sign alerted them of a utility road belonging to the City of Poughkeepsie.

"That sign doesn't mean us, you know," Ebony urged. "Go on, get moving."

Zander drifted into the posted zone, and parked at the bottom of the ravine next to the snowplows, retired for the season. They exited the car onto a wide, flat plateau, which had been hidden from their clifftop view by the thick foliage. Straight ahead stood a tractor-trailer-sized mountain of gravel. Felled trees and debris from past storms formed a massive pyramid next to the gravel.

With no time to waste, Zander balanced the computer in his hands and dispatched another signal.

Ebony listened. A moment later, the response rang out: *PING*. The sound echoed off the shale walls towering above them.

Zander drew closer to the gravel and transmitted again.

Ping.

The sound seemed to come from the mountain of timber. "Over here," Ebony shouted, running toward it.

Reaching the base of the pile, she squatted. There were three distinct sets of footprints; two pairs of men's work boots and one set of smaller tracks. Sneakers. They could belong to Lissie.

She grabbed her phone, snapped some photos, and then tracked the prints around to the backside of the log pyramid. The treads vanished, but discarded among the pebbles and dirt was a used condom.

Ebony found a stick and marked the spot. She'd return to gather this evidence later.

Before her, the haphazard timber stack soared approximately two stories high and looked as long as a fire truck. Dumped on the edge of a seventy-foot cliff, there was no fencing or railing enclosing the logs. It presented a dangerous situation for them and the golfers on the course below, but their only clue to Lissie could be hiding inside the stack.

A flash of light drew Ebony's eyes eastward, beyond the course. On the horizon, lighting crackled across the blue ridges of the Taconic Mountains and the drumming of thunder rolled toward her. Closer, white caps fractured the pewter surface of Morgan Lake. Out of nowhere, the air grew heavy, damp, and smelled of rain. They were running out of time.

Zander pinged the phone again. The signal had faded into the stiff breeze of the oncoming storm.

"Did you hear that? It's coming from the logs. Keep sending the signal and I'll climb toward the sound."

"Are you crazy, Eb? That pile is a disaster waiting to happen and a storm's coming."

"How else are we going to search the pile? We don't have time to bring in a forklift to search for a cellphone, and besides, the chief would think we're crazy if we requested one. We don't know how much longer the battery will last, and if we don't move now, we could be sunk," Ebony said, mounting the log pyramid. Rough bark tore at her palms as she scrambled up the ever-shifting tree trunks and branches. "Don't worry, I'll be fine. Again!"

"Take it slow, will you? One misstep and you'll be riding an avalanche onto the fairways. Just let me know if you need me to climb up there," Zander replied, transmitting another tone.

"I'm good."

Ebony crested the stack and as she was backtracking toward the ground, the toe of her sandal glided across the slick bark. Losing her footing, her body pitched backward toward the cliff's edge. Scuttling to stabilize her balance, her injured foot slipped into a deep crevice, trapping her ankle in the spiky branches. The flesh of her shins tore as her foot torqued sideways. Ebony clawed at a grey, worm-eaten log, clinging to it with all her strength.

She lay motionless, flattening her body against the wall of the timber pyramid. The rough bark scratched her cheek and the fine sawdust coated her tongue. She swallowed, listening to her heart pounding, afraid to breathe or move. A droplet of icy rain splattered on her face, and she closed her eyes. Her mind raced. How could she have been so stupid as to attempt such heroics? She and Zander should have strategized before she'd maniacally scaled the logs. Now she was like a snared rabbit waiting to die.

"Eb, I've got you. No worries," Zander whispered in her ear as he muscled up against her. "Take it easy. You're stuck in there pretty good and you don't want to break your leg." His hand squeezed hers. "Lean on me and ease it out. Don't make any sudden moves."

Ebony exhaled and breathed. Wedged against him, she wiggled her foot free from its capture, and trunk-by-trunk they descended the unstable logs to the bottom. Once again on solid ground, she collapsed onto the dirt, rubbing her swollen ankle.

"Thanks." Her cheeks warmed with embarrassment. Both her leg and her ego were going to turn twenty shades of purple by tomorrow.

"You okay? Do you need medical attention or should we call in backup?"

"Nah, I'm fine. Just a few scratches. We know the phone is in there, so let's do this. But first let me change my shoes." Ebony hobbled over to the car, tugged on the spare boots she'd stowed in the trunk, and returned to the woodpile.

"If we're going to tackle this beast, let's do this together, but take it slow. No arguments. Understand?" Zander didn't wait for her response and whipped off his belt. He buckled it and slipped the loop over his head so that it hung across his chest. Zander slid the open laptop beneath it and tightened the belt so that the device pressed against his chest. He tapped the key, transmitting new signals to the phone. *Ping-Ping-Ping.* "It's coming from the putting green side of the logs."

She nodded, brushed off the sawdust, and led Zander up the timber. The wind kicked up and trilled through the logs like a train whistle, rattling the surface beneath their feet. They climbed halfway to the top, sounded the alarm, and listened. *Ping-Ping-Ping.* The ringing emanated from inside the pyramid. They exchanged excited glances.

"Lissie!" Ebony's cop brain reassured her that Lissie couldn't be in the pile, but the plea escaped as they burrowed through the logs, branches and debris as rough as sandpaper. "Lissie, are you in there?"

Only their search signal replied.

"I see something," Zander said, rolling over a thick tree limb. "Help me with this one." He groaned as they heaved aside a century-old tree stump, judging from the diameter of the trunk. Ebony directed her phone's flashlight into the darkness. A strip of green neon tape reflected back. Zander squeezed his arm into the opening and reached into the well.

"Got it," he said, retrieving a florescent yellow hoodie. He pitched it to her.

"Good job."

They scrambled to the ground and Ebony snapped on her latex gloves to examine the hoodie. There were no rips or tears, but blood had dried on the garment's hem. The outside pockets, which were outlined with the reflective strips, were empty, but from within an interior hidden compartment she retrieved an iPhone, a set of house keys and a baggie containing tiny white pills. Ebony handed them to Zander for inventory, and he deposited them into plastic pouches and sealed them.

Zander removed his gloves, unfolded his handkerchief, wiped his hands and offered it to her. "All this for nothing. No Lissie."

"I wouldn't say that. There's blood, and maybe fingerprints and DNA. We'll send it off to the lab and see if there's a match with Lissie. And if there's a positive ID, that should warrant issuing an APB." Ebony was strategizing the next phase of their investigation out loud, more for herself than for him.

"There might be hair samples…and we'd better grab that condom…. We can contact a locksmith to trace the keys and the pills can go to the lab…."

"Or there may be nothing." Detective Skeptic, Zander's alter ego, had returned. "This exercise could be another waste of time."

"Hey, we've got more than we had before." Ebony approached the cliff's edge and surveyed the valley's panorama again. Below them, in the loose, rocky dirt and the freshly mowed fairways, there was no place to hide a dead body. They could check the gravel mound, but it appeared undisturbed and there were no footprints in the vicinity. However, the woods were still a possibility. Or was Zander correct that they'd reached the trail's end?

"FUCK!" she shouted into the wind that flung her curse back into her face. Another drop of rain grazed her cheek and the ear-piercing alarm of the lightning warning system on the golf course blared.

"Come on," Zander said, "let's get out of here before we're fried to a crisp."

To her dismay, the grizzly reality of the situation sunk in. Despite their best efforts, she'd be pinning Elisabeth Sexton's "Missing Persons" poster on the bulletin board back at the station.

Chapter Twenty-Three

For the twentieth time today, Hal traced the outline of the square box tucked away in the breast pocket of his blazer. He was about to ask for Ed's blessing, and despite his calm demeanor, he was freaking out. His damp armpits were proof of that.

He withdrew the robin's egg blue box from his pocket and slowly opened it. Nestled within the snowy silk lining sparkled a round two-carat diamond with a platinum band. Classic like Jessie, not over-the-top, dripping with pavé diamonds like the one Erin had insisted upon.

"Do I have your permission?"

Ed grabbed the box and examined the setting. "Tiffany's. Pretty fancy." The corners of his eyes crinkled. "I'm impressed that in this day and age you'd ask me. Of course, Hal, I couldn't be more pleased for the two of you. My daughter's suffered some hard knocks lately, and as strong as Jess pretends to be, she's a softie." He sniffled, retrieved his handkerchief, dabbed his eyes, and cleared his throat. "She needs a stand-up guy like you to keep her on track and on her toes. I hope she knows how lucky she is to have you."

Hal's father, Harold Samuels, Jr., would never have been so kind. Embroiled in litigation with Erin's father, his former real estate partner, Hal's father had blamed Hal's divorce for the disintegration of the Samuels family's international real estate empire. Once again, Hal had been disinherited, but he didn't care. In Hal's book, love triumphed over money, and he couldn't wait to start fresh with Jessie.

When their meeting ended, Ed extended his hand toward Hal, but then he appeared to change his mind. He gathered Hal up into a bear hug. "Welcome to the family, son."

"Thanks, Ed. I promise I'll take care of her. You can trust me." Hal felt a twinge of guilt making the promise. Years ago, he'd made the identical promise to Jessie. She'd placed her absolute trust in him, and he'd disappointed her. He believed this pledge to Ed more than he believed anything else in his life. He'd spend a lifetime fulfilling it.

"I do. Besides, I know where you live and work," Ed replied with a chuckle.

* * *

Jessie placed her iPad on the oak desk in her den and glanced at the video stream of Lily asleep in her crib. Her daughter looked angelic with her dark ringlets, chubby cheeks and her tiny thumb tucked in between her rosebud lips. She silently thanked Kyle for installing the baby-cam. It had been one of his rare contributions to the household, and despite her annoyance at him, she was grateful for this small favor.

The house was peaceful, and lulled by the hissing of the white noise, she could finally carve out a few minutes to research the New York Mental Health Law and its regulations pertaining to the harassment of an individual by an in-patient at a state-run psychiatric center.

And just in time, because Terrence was getting bolder. This morning, he'd left a disturbing, defiant voice mail.

"My dear Jessica, I've been playing nice at the spa and have requested my own cellphone. We'll be able to chat more frequently soon. Can't wait."

She shuddered, knowing her life would be hell if Terrence received a cellphone. It would give him free reign to badger her whenever he wanted. Fortunately, Jessie had taken steps to guard against his digital invasion of her privacy shortly after the phone calls had begun. She'd deleted her profiles from her Facebook, Instagram, LinkedIn, TikTok and Twitter, reasoning that if he'd finagled phone access, he'd probably wangled computer access, too. Unlike losing or destroying her phone, or changing her number, she'd insulated herself against the madman without raising Hal or her parents' suspicions.

With her new job and her renewed confidence, Jessie needed to stop acting like a doormat and take charge. What had been holding her back? Had it been the demands of parenthood? Her guilt over Ryan's death? Or just plain stupidity on her part? Whatever reason, there were no more excuses.

She booted up her computer and pulled up the statute to research whether the law provided her with any recourse to Terrence's actions. To her dismay, she discovered that every psychiatric patient possessed a "Bill of Rights," entitling them to unrestricted contact with the outside world, including personal phone calls once per week. However, recently Terrence's calls had increased to twice a week, so there had to be a reason for the uptick.

Terrence had always been cunning. If there were a way to manipulate a rule, Terrence would find it. He'd probably told the hospital staff that he was contacting her as his attorney, and they'd probably believe him. That would mean that even without a cellphone, Terrence could contact her as often as he wanted, and he wouldn't be breaking any laws. In fact, the law would shield him. Conversely, she'd be exposed, naked, without protection.

Disheartened, Jessie powered down her computer and crossed the room to open the window. The day was sunny, but a brisk breeze carried the damp scent of the earth into the room. Bright yellow forsythia flowers were in blossom, while the peonies that Ryan had helped her plant were poking up through the garden beds. On such a glorious day, Jessie was grateful to be alive, but Terrence's endless pursuit of her dampened her spirits.

She wondered whether Terrence was seeking the control over her he'd possessed when she'd been his student, or whether he was exerting control over his chaotic life inside the psychiatric hospital. Or was Terrence seeking retaliation against her for helping to put him away? Or had Kyle been correct; had she been too blind and loyal to recognize Terrence's obsession with her?

Nevertheless, Terrence had evaded his confinement to torture her. Perhaps, once again, he was more than she could handle alone. Or could her working for Jeremy lead her to a solution to her problem?

A wail rang out, and Jessie shut the window and bolted upstairs to the nursery.

Chapter Twenty-Four

That night, Jessie dreamed about Terrence. He was looming over her bed, staring at her with dead, cold eyes. Then he crouched down beside her, and she felt his fiery breath whispering her name in her ear. Jessie awoke with a start, gasping for air. She turned toward Hal, and although tempted to wake him, she let him sleep undisturbed. Instead, she lay still, waiting for her racing heart to slow. Waiting for morning to arrive.

As the night dissolved into day, Jessie listened to the soft, lamenting calls of the mourning doves. Their serenade only slightly eased her jitters. It was natural, she thought, to be nervous about the first day of work. She hadn't seen a client, written a brief, or appeared in court for ten months. Or had Terrence's phone call intensified her dread?

She checked the time on her cellphone. Six-thirty. Jessie quietly slipped from the bed, padded silently across the carpet into the bathroom, and closed the door. Collapsing onto the chilly tile floor, she wrapped her arms around her knees and willed herself not to cry. Tears wouldn't solve anything. To move forward, she'd have to dig deep to conquer her fears, and not let the past haunt her future. Otherwise, Terrence would win, and she'd never be free of him.

After showering, Jessie dressed in the outfit that she and Lily had selected, and admired her reflection in the closet mirror. She was going to impress the hell out of her new bosses, Gayle and Jeremy Kaplan.

The morning's routine of feeding and clothing Lily had made the time fly by. Before she knew it, she was standing in the kitchen, bidding goodbye to Hal and Lily. It proved harder than she'd expected when Lily pumped her little arms and legs and reached toward her.

"Maybe I should call Jeremy and postpone my starting date?" Jessie couldn't release her grip on Lily's plump feet.

"Don't worry, you've got this. I'll deliver Lily to your mother, scout's honor. Now go save the world." He kissed her goodbye and nudged her toward the back door. "By the way, you look professional and beautiful, as usual."

As they waved to her from the kitchen door, nagging pangs of guilt and insecurity intermingled with excitement. Adapting to the newfound freedom, with its unknown risks and rewards, would take some adjustment, as would her balancing work with motherhood. But she wasn't a superwoman. She needn't conquer her new world in one day or one week. Baby steps, she thought, baby steps.

Jessie slid into her Jeep and cast a last glance toward her family, but they'd vanished. She started the ignition and backed out of the driveway onto the street. The cellphone buzzed, and she checked the number. It was unknown to her, so she let it go to voicemail.

* * *

The threadbare stairs leading down to Jeremy Kaplan's law office creaked beneath Jessie's tentative steps. She entered the office and noted that it hadn't changed since she'd been in high school. It still had the same dark, dreary paneling, burnt orange carpet, and the smell of mildew. Jessie spied an older woman, presumably Jeremy's secretary, with the phone cradled against her ear, feverishly typing on her computer. In the corner, a copy machine clicked and churned, spitting out a document. The henna-haired secretary shifted her eyes to Jessie and flashed a harried smile.

"Morning. It's Maureen, right?" Jessie asked cheerfully.

"It's Mo." The woman sighed with dramatic exasperation and slammed down the phone receiver. Mo rose from her desk and snatched a foot-high pile of folders from the bench against the wall.

"Is Jeremy here? Or Gayle?"

"Follow me. For the time being, you'll work in the library. Ignore the cartons. We're going to put them in storage one of these days, so just navigate around them. We'll figure out something for your office soon." Without checking whether Jessie had followed suit, Mo plopped the files on the conference table. "I'm ecstatic you're here, but I'm under a litigation deadline and I really don't have the time to bring you up to speed. Please, review these and if you have questions, let me know. Welcome aboard."

"Shouldn't I meet with Gayle and Jeremy? Maybe they have a list of priorities for me."

"Gayle manages the office finances. I run the day-to-day operations, so if you have any issues, you can speak with me. But, please, not right now." The soft ringing of the telephone filled the air, and the buttons on the library's phone console lit up like a Christmas tree. Mo rolled her eyes.

"Weren't they expecting me today?" Jessie wondered what she'd gotten herself into, and how humiliating it was going to be to quit after her first hour.

"They were, but Mr. and Mrs. Kaplan have a lot on their minds with Jeremy's last-minute doctor's appointment in New York City. So, if you could pitch in this morning, I'd appreciate it. We'll try to figure things out later. I'm assuming that you know how to review a matrimonial case." Mo rested her hands on her hips and shifted her weight onto one leg.

Flustered, she replied, "Oh, yeah, sure."

"Just give it your best shot.... Coming, coming," Mo shouted, slamming the library door with the force of a prison guard locking down an inmate.

"Well, then. My best shot, whatever," Jessie said. This was clearly the beginning of a strange relationship with the Kaplan crew.

Jessie wandered around the library admiring Jeremy's dusty diplomas from Yale University and Yale Law School, and his certificate to practice before the United States Supreme Court, which were hanging on the dark walnut paneling. A series of faded photos also looked interesting, so she swiped her hand across their powdery surfaces. In them, a younger, robust Jeremy, posed arm-in-arm with one of her favorite bands, The Rolling

138

Stones. From the floppy haircuts, oversized shirts, and stage sets named *Steel Wheels* and *Voodoo Lounge*, they probably dated back to the 1990s.

"With Mick Jagger and Keith Richards as pals, you're really a rock star attorney, Jeremy Kaplan," she murmured.

Skirting around the stacks of white cartons, she moved on to the bookshelf. Opening its glass doors, she skimmed the spines of the New York and Federal Statutes, casebooks, legal treatises, and form books. The musty, leathery scent of the law reminded her of how long she'd wanted to be a lawyer, forever, and the two men responsible for her career.

Because of Terrence's mentoring, and her clerkship with Jeremy Kaplan, she'd chosen the path of justice, and those volumes had become her bibles. Terrence and Jeremy had provided the encouragement she'd needed to become the best lawyer possible until they'd betrayed her. Jeremy had apologized, and this job was proof of his remorse. Meanwhile, Terrence refused to release her.

Jessie glanced around at the worn furniture, tattered carpet, and nicked conference table. Everything about Jeremy's office was shabby compared to the polished chrome-and-glass offices, and the amenities she'd taken for granted at Curtis and McMann; the Espresso machine, windows overlooking the Hudson River, an elevator, and her own assistant. Sadly, this decrepit place reflected its owner and made her homesick for her former workplace. And, most of all, for Lily. But she'd vowed to remain positive; to give the job a try. To hell with Mo's tepid reception.

Determined to hunt for coffee before digging into the files, Jessie reached for the doorknob, and to her surprise, the door swung open.

"Jessie, welcome. I thought I'd find you in here. Let's get to work," Jeremy said. He smiled at her and sank into one of the faded orange chairs around the table. His eyes twinkled, revealing the superstar attorney who'd partied with the Stones.

His enthusiasm reminded her why she'd accepted the job, and she reprimanded herself for misjudging him and his offices. Jeremy Kaplan possessed one of the most ingenious criminal defense minds in the Hudson Valley, and she felt honored he'd selected her as his associate. His first associate. If she were smart, she'd listen and learn from him.

"Let's start with the Astor case," he said, professorially. "Our client, Margaret Morse Astor, is quite a bird, as you'll see."

There was a knock at the door, and Mo slipped into the library, closing the door behind her. "It's Mr. and Mrs. Douglas. They dropped by unannounced and insist on speaking with you. They said they'd wait as long as necessary." She shrugged.

"Sure, show them in," Jeremy said. A moment later, Jessie and Jeremy rose to greet the Douglases. "Henry, Rita, please come in. This is—"

"Jessie Martin, look at you. All grown up and a lawyer." Mr. Douglas, who was a contemporary of her father, stepped back to examine her from head to toe, not in a creepy way, but in a proud uncle's way. "You look just like your mother did at your age. For a moment, I thought you were Lena. How're your folks?"

Jessie tried to place the couple, but she hadn't a clue who they were.

"We haven't seen you since grade school," Henry Douglas said, vigorously pumping her hand. "Remember? You were in Mrs. DuBois's class with Rebecca? The fifth grade, wasn't it?"

A light bulb blinked on. Becky Douglas. Becky, Ebony, and Jessie had attended Clinton Elementary School through Poughkeepsie High School together. As kids, they'd been gymnastics, swim, and soccer teammates, but once they'd hit middle school, they'd gone their separate ways. By high school, Becky had gone Goth with dyed blue-black hair, lipstick and nails, and facial piercings. In the halls, they'd nod in acknowledgment of each other, but that's all.

"Right. How's Becky? I haven't seen her since graduation."

Rita Douglas sniffled, and her husband responded, turning to Jeremy. "That's why we're here. We haven't heard from her in over a week. We don't want to go to the police and thought you'd be able to help."

Mr. Douglas continued. "After high school, Becky attended Dutchess Community College for graphic design. She's become a tattoo artist, quite a good one, but that's not the profession either of us dreamed of for our little girl." He paused, examining Jessie as though comparing her with his

140

daughter. "Look at you, an attorney, but you were always so motivated." He shook his head and his blood-shot eyes filled with sadness.

"Becky's a tattoo artist? Locally?" Jessie asked.

"Yes, but over the past year, she's been using drugs. First prescription meds for a back injury, then recently we discovered she's been swept into the opioid epidemic. We've tried to get her help, but she's refused. Said she'd handle it on her own. That was a week ago and we haven't heard from her since. We've spoken to her boss and so-called friends, but no luck." Henry sighed deeply. "Despite our differences, Becky has never cut off communication, so we're worried something's happened to her."

"Has anyone contacted you for money?" Jeremy asked.

"No, there's been no ransom demand, so we're assuming it's not a kidnapping. We'd prefer to handle this privately and keep it out of the press because we don't want my insurance clients getting skittish. You know, it's a small community, and everybody knows everyone. I hope that you, Jeremy, had some contacts who might assist us."

"I'll do everything I can to help. Do you have her last address? A photo?"

Rita handed Jeremy a slender red envelope. "Here's all the information we have. And you should know she's changed her name. She goes by Epiphany Rivers." Her voice dropped off, and she wrinkled her nose. "No, she's not married or anything, she just assumed the alias."

Jeremy opened the package and handed Jessie a recent photo of Becky Douglas a/k/a Epiphany Rivers. After all this time, Becky's round apple cheeks and cute pug nose looked the same. She'd shaved her dark blackish-purple hair on the sides except for two long pigtails, making her look like a Japanese anime character.

Jessie couldn't help staring at Becky's skin. What she could only describe as the Sistine Chapel of tattoos, including a representation of Michelangelo's frescoes of Adam and Eve and the Last Judgment, covered almost every visible inch of her appendages. It was weirdly magnificent. From the broad grin on her face, Becky proudly owned her body art.

"Jessie, you were her friend, and Jeremy, you're our lawyer, so we'd appreciate anything you can do to help us." The Douglases rose to leave.

Mr. Douglas handed Jessie his card. "Please spare no expense. We want our daughter brought home safely."

Holy crap. This had been a day for the record books, and it wasn't even noon.

Chapter Twenty-Five

J essie checked her watch. It was 11:30 a.m. For over two hours, Supreme Court Justice Antonia Coppola had kept Jessie stewing on the hard wooden bench outside her chambers. During the entire time, the sound of laughter had filtered out through the frosted glass, causing Jessie to wonder whether her torment would ever end.

When she'd delivered Jeremy's Temporary Restraining Order to the judge's clerk, Jessie had said she'd wait for the documents to be signed, but apparently, Judge Coppola didn't care. The interminable wait was payback for Jessie's unforgivable sin of greeting the judge in chambers by her first name.

"Inside the courthouse, I'm not Toni. I'm *Judge* Coppola," Antonia Coppola had replied, sneering at Jessie over her half-moon glasses.

"Sorry, your honor. It won't happen again," Jessie had replied sincerely.

She'd thought the judge had accepted her apology, especially since the Martins and the Coppolas had been lifelong friends, but evidently, Judge Coppola hadn't.

Now, over a year later, Jessie's punishment for the faux pas was a public shaming. As Jessie warmed the bench, most of her former adversaries ignored her. Others expressed shock that "Jessie Martin, the Pariah of Poughkeepsie" had returned to the courthouse. More than once she'd considered that Mo had dispatched her on this fool's errand, just to be rid of her. There'd been something disturbing about the secretary's smirk when she'd relegated the menial task to Jessie.

Without warning, a young woman sporting a Yankee baseball cap charged around the corner at breakneck speed. Careening sideways, the woman skidded across the polished marble floor, her sneakers screeching like fingernails on a chalkboard. When her shoulder slammed against the wall, she released a sharp cry and collapsed to the floor, sliding to a stop at Jessie's feet.

The pink camouflage print hat had been a dead giveaway. Jessie's father had purchased the cap for Ebony when he'd taken them to Yankee Stadium a few years ago. While Ebony projected a tough veneer, Jessie believed that, deep down, Ebony was sentimental about certain people, places, and things. Just look at her ratty cap.

"In a hurry, are we?" Jessie asked, bending over to collect the loose papers that had escaped from Ebony's messenger bag.

"They should put up a caution sign in these hallways. I think I broke my ass." Without looking up, Ebony performed a quick check for any injuries.

"Don't be such a drama queen, but then you could never resist, could you? I've seen you make better blocks on the basketball court."

Ebony flipped up the cap that had toppled over her eyes and blinked rapidly. Her face tightened and then relaxed as Jessie hoisted her friend onto the bench beside her. "I should've known it was you by those fancy shoes."

"Like 'em? I haven't broken them in yet, so they're giving me blisters." Jessie twisted her ankles, admiring her new navy spectator pumps. "You all right? That was quite a tumble."

"We cops are tough, you know, almost as thick-skinned as you shysters," Ebony said, massaging her shoulder. "What brings you downtown? I didn't know you were back working with McMann."

"I'm not, and would it kill you to answer a text?"

Ebony winced as she held up her palms. Her tawny complexion glowed pink. "I have been meaning to call you, you know, for your statement, but shit happens. But seriously, how's my Lily doing?"

Jessie was tempted to remark that she'd know that too if she'd ever stopped by, but she resisted. Ebony had pissed her off, justifiably so. She treated her like crap. Not just the other day, but for a while now. They'd been inseparable from kindergarten through high school, but lately, life seemed to get in the way. Marist College, the basketball team, the police academy, the Poughkeepsie PD, and Drew had sent Ebony down one path. Syracuse University, NYU law school, Kyle, her legal career, Lily, and now Hal had nudged Jessie in another direction. Representing conflicting arms of the law, such as during Ryan's murder investigation, had created irreconcilable tension in their relationship.

She'd expected more from her oldest friend. All Jessie required was a tiny effort from Ebony once in a while. Just return a goddamn text.

"I'm working with Jeremy Kaplan and I've been waiting all morning for the judge to sign his injunction." Ebony smirked, but she gave Ebony one more shot before writing her off for good. "Hey, how about I tell Coppola's secretary that I'll stop back later, and we go grab some coffee at Alex's?"

Ebony glanced at her watch, then back at her. "Sure, let me gather these up. After I drop off my search warrant application, we'll grab a cup." Ebony rose and groaned dramatically. She brushed off her jeans, scooped up her papers, and limped into the judge's chambers.

* * *

In the bustling diner, Jessie and Ebony sipped their coffees, laughed, and caught up with each other's lives. Ebony still acted reserved, but it was a start. Half-hidden in a booth next to the cash register, Jessie spotted the former colleague at Curtis and McMann who'd snagged the junior partnership she'd forfeited because of Terrence's case. He politely kissed her cheek and promised to meet for lunch. Sometime soon.

"Sure," Jessie said, knowing the chances were slim. Her attention returned to Ebony. "Eb, I'm glad I bumped into you. I've got this situation."

"Is it about Kyle? I never trusted that guy." Ebony leaned in.

Jessie shifted on the sticky red vinyl seat, considering whether to mention Becky Douglas. The Douglases had requested keeping the matter confidential, but she was desperate. She didn't know how to locate a missing person or hire a PI. Ebony would surely know. It was her business to know.

She fiddled with a sugar packet and asked in a hushed voice, "This is strictly off the record, agreed?"

Ebony's eyes narrowed, then nodded. "Give me one minute, please." She hailed another cup of coffee from their server.

"Do you remember Becky Douglas? We were jealous of her. Hair down to her waist, and she performed those awesome backflips. Remember?" Ebony sipped her coffee thoughtfully. "She turned all Goth in high school and gave up gymnastics. She hung out with that heavy metal band, The Shrieking Banshees. You know who I'm talking about, right?"

Ebony scrunched her eyes as if mining her memories. "Vaguely. Why?"

Jessie paused for a second, but it was too late to stop the train. She reached into her briefcase, extracted their old high school yearbook, and opened it to the letter *D* of the *Senior's* section.

"Look, here's Becky Douglas." Jessie tapped her finger on the photo of a girl with a black shag hairdo and a gold ring piercing the nostril of her pug nose. Becky Douglas's kohl-rimmed eyes rolled upward in boredom, while her sneering purple lips broadcast her contempt to the camera. Jessie set the more recent photo on the Formica tabletop. "Becky now works as a tattoo artist at the Skin Gallery across from Marist College. She's changed her name, it's Epiphany Rivers."

"Wait, a sec. Becky, oh yeah. She was also in Butterfield's class. Remember, he called her the Princess of Darkness? What about her?"

"Well, her parents haven't heard from her in a while. The last time they spoke with her, they tried to convince her to enter rehab, but she blew them off. They're worried, naturally."

Ebony's pupils dilated. "She's missing? For how long?"

"Long enough for her parents to contact Jeremy to help find her. I really don't know where to begin this search. I considered using his PI Carey Wentworth, but if you have a better idea…"

"Jessie, exactly how long?" Ebony's voice sounded urgent.

"Over a week."

Ebony's eyes glazed over. She knitted her manicured fingers together, rolling her wrists in a circular motion. She grew quiet, letting her rotating hands speak.

Jessie recognized Ebony's tell. Ever since they were kids, Ebony telegraphed her anxiety through her twirling fingers. She suspected her friend was contemplating whether to share something troubling or keep it to herself.

"We're off the record, right?" Ebony whispered.

Jessie nodded.

"This past week, two women came into the station complaining about a guy beating them up. Now, they're both missing."

"And now Becky."

"Yeah. Remember the woman you saved during the storm? Lissie Sexton, she's one of them. Zander and I stopped by her house, but she wasn't there. We've arrested her boyfriend for fencing stolen property and drugs, but I don't think he's responsible for her disappearance. He claims he doesn't know where she is. That's why I was visiting the courthouse, to get search warrants for our investigation. And we're issuing APBs for Lissie and the other woman."

"This is too coincidental. Three women vanishing within days of each other." Jessie twisted Lily's sapphire birthstone ring on her finger, contemplating Becky's whereabouts. At first, Becky's opioid addiction had shocked her, but these days, Percocet seemed to ensnare the least likely people. Perhaps naively, she'd hoped that Becky had taken a spontaneous vacation, or fled after a lover's quarrel, or the fight with her folks. However, if her disappearance was sinister, then she'd made the right call by mentioning it to Ebony. "You probably can't answer this, but is there a pattern to the disappearances or any connection between the girls?"

Ebony remained silent, pensive. A deep vertical wrinkle appeared between her brows as she stared out the plate-glass window at the courthouse across Market Street. "We know that Lissie's had some addiction issues in the past, so she could just be off on a bender somewhere. We'll have a better idea after forensics examines the evidence we've gathered at her house, but honestly, we're stumped."

Jessie wondered what other terrifying theories were churning inside

Ebony's mind, and what she wasn't being told.

"Becky Douglas, huh? Let's hope that we can find her..." Ebony's voice trailed off as she pulled out her wallet. "Check please."

Chapter Twenty-Six

With Judge Coppola's signed Restraining Order finally in hand, Jessie slipped into her car in the courthouse parking lot and started the engine. The soft chiming of her phone's calendar reminded her of this afternoon's OBGYN appointment, which she had forgotten. After dropping the documents at Jeremy's, she raced to the doctor's office, arriving with minutes to spare.

Inside the sterile exam room, Jessie lay half-naked on the table and her arm ached from the vice-like squeeze of the blood pressure cuff. Generally, doctors made her vitals spike, but her gynecologist, Dr. Bakool Suryaprasal, was the exception. His gentle manner and touch always calmed her, and she felt indebted to the petite man for saving her life and Lily's.

Jessie would never forget collapsing and slipping into oblivion in the courthouse during the hearing to dismiss the murder charges against Terrence. She'd been told afterward that at the height of her eclampsia seizure clusters, Dr. S had administered anticonvulsants and safely delivered her premature baby. Thanks to Dr. S and the neo-natal unit at the hospital, three-pound Lily had been given a fighting chance.

Since then, he'd insisted on Jessie's undergoing quarterly exams. Until now, they'd been routine, which was what she'd expected today.

The cold steel of the stirrups chilled her bare feet, and she shivered when a draft of frigid air smacked her thighs. Distracting herself from Dr. S's exam, she revisited the morning's conversation with Ebony. Three women were missing; one of them, another old friend. It appeared that death hunted her like a bloodhound. First, Ryan. Now, Becky. Although they weren't the same degree of friendship with her, they were threads woven into the fabric of her life. Without them, the material snagged, weakening her structure and threatening to unravel her life.

Dr. S dispensed his trademark Jack-o'-Lantern smile, pulled off the latex gloves, and deposited them in the waste bin. "Jessica, please get dressed and I'll meet you in my office."

After rushing to dress, Jessie took a seat in Dr. S's office across the hall. He cleared his throat and flipped through her thick folder. "I won't sugarcoat this. Your blood pressure is elevated and requires monitoring. Given your history, I'm going to run some additional tests as a precaution." He typed a few strokes on his computer. "You're not pregnant now, but you may be in the future, and I don't want to take any chances. We see little Eclampsia, maybe five percent of all pregnancies worldwide, so you're at greater risk during any subsequent pregnancies. The good news is we can manage it."

Eclampsia. Jessie's temples throbbed at the mention of the rare disease that had masqueraded as gestational hypertension. The condition had nearly proven to be fatal for herself and Lily, and now appeared to be threatening any future family with Hal.

"Jessie?" the doctor asked, drawing her back from the gloom. He held her eyes captive, and she noticed the intense glacier-green color of his eyes. "And since you're here, I can squeeze you in for a sonogram today. Do you have the time?"

"Do I have a choice? I'd like to know about having more children in the future."

"Let's take it this one step at a time, so first let's get the tests done."

She nodded.

A half-hour later, Jessie lay on another exam table with a white sheet draped across her belly. The darkened room was lit by the amber glow of the ultrasound machine, which illuminated the back of a nurse busying herself at a computer on a desk in the corner, and a tech with a grotesquely square head that was too small for his monstrous body. His icy gloved hands ruthlessly poked a long, slender ultrasound wand inside her, and her muscles tensed at the searing pain inflicted by his pelvic exam.

150

"Hey, take it easy, will you?" Jessie blurted. "How much longer will this take?"

The nurse glanced over in Jessie's direction. "Is everything okay?" she asked.

"We're fine. We'll be done in a few minutes," the tech snapped, with a shadowy smirk on his glowing face.

Jessie opened her mouth to speak, but he narrowed his eyes and gave her a threatening jab with the wand. She squeezed her eyes shut as they grew watery.

"Good." The nurse returned her attention to the computer. "I've got work to do, so don't dawdle with the exam."

Evidently, the sonographer enjoyed Jessie's pain and was adroit at hiding his brutality from his chaperones. From the exam's beginning, he'd treated her like a slab of meat, not a patient or a woman in need. Other than confirming her name and birthdate, he'd remained aloof, making her wish it were gentle Dr. S, not this fiend and his accomplice, who was conducting the ultrasound.

Jessie wanted to scream for him to stop, but Dr. S had assured her that the procedure was a medical necessity. He wouldn't have ordered it otherwise. Later, she'd complain about this bastard and the inattentive nurse. Not only because they'd been rude, but because the tech had been rough and abusive. No woman should be violated this way.

She gritted her teeth, counting the machine's trills until he'd finished with her.

* * *

After dinner, Jessie stood crib side admiring her daughter, who was sleeping peacefully beneath a rotating projection of the Milky Way. The planets and constellations waltzed across the nursery's ceiling, and periodically, the cow jumped over the moon. Lily was the center of Jessie's universe, so it seemed only natural that she was the sun at the heart of the galactic light show.

Jessie gently brushed the soft, dark curls from Lily's face as the baby wrinkled her nose and stirred, rolling onto her back.

Out in the hallway, the floorboards creaked and Jessie's eyes shifted toward the door. Hal propped his shoulder against the jamb, a ghostly silhouette against the silvery moon glow. He was bare-chested, his boxers hanging from his solid hips.

Jessie leaned into the crib, lightly kissed Lily's forehead, and moved toward him, closing the door behind her.

Hal slipped his arms around her waist, pulling her close, and kissed her deeply. She tasted the salt from the pretzels he'd snacked on earlier.

"You look so..." he murmured.

"Beautiful?"

"I was going to say maternal."

From Hal, that was a compliment of the highest order. He was a man who valued his family above all else. Later, she'd obsess about Dr. S's bad omen. Right now, it was her and Hal.

He slipped a spaghetti strap of Jessie's nightgown from her shoulder and kissed the bare spot. Her skin turned to gooseflesh beneath his warm, soft lips. His hands ruffled the gown's hem and his cool fingers slid beneath, teasing her. She moaned with desire.

"...And beautiful," he whispered, releasing the other strap from its resting place.

Chapter Twenty-Seven

The next morning, Jessie juggled her tote bag and travel mug as she approached the entrance to Jeremy's office. She did a double-take at the sight before her eyes. Perched on the stoop was a young woman wearing a black patch over one eye. The girl extracted her right arm from the sling hanging loosely around her neck, raised a vape to her mouth, and inhaled. A horsefly buzzed about her head and she shooed it away, choking on the gray smoke escaping from her lips and nostril. As she flogged the air, her false eyelashes fluttered like feather dusters, and tendrils of her wiry hair sprang loose from her pink babushka.

What astonished Jessie the most was the woman's overdone makeup and funky outfit. Her denim cutoffs were so indecently short that the pocket linings poked out below the hem. With her bony legs crossed at the knee, and bouncing in rhythm to an imaginary beat, the woman revealed she was going commando. Her tank top was equally provocative. A black demi-bra peeked through the transparent fabric, leaving nothing to the imagination.

"May I help you?" Jessie asked, approaching the stranger.

"Naw. I'm not ready yet. I'm enjoying the sunshine."

"You know, this is a law office. Are you here to see Mr. Kaplan?"

"What's with all the questions?" The woman took another drag on the electronic cigarette and blew smoke out of her twisted lips. "It's a free country, ain't it?"

"All right," Jessie said, politely. "Have a nice day." Rather than descending the stairway to the office, she climbed the stairs into the Kaplans' kitchen. She discovered Gayle peeking out of the kitchen curtains, watching the visitor dive into her white vinyl tote for a cigarette refill and a sip of Diet Coke.

"I see you're checking out the show. Do you know who she is?" Jessie asked.

Gayle shook her head. "I've thought about contacting the police, but she seems harmless and she'll probably move on once the office opens."

Jeremy appeared out of nowhere and peered over his wife's shoulder. "I see we have a guest," he said, mildly interested. His sagging navy polo shirt exaggerated the translucence of his skin, and the veins throbbing in his arms.

"A friend of yours?" Gayle asked.

"As a matter of fact, yes." He craned his neck for a better view. "She's not *that* good a friend, but we've had a bit of history. I can't tell you her current pseudonym because I never know what it's going to be. Cherí Sunday, Wisteria Lane, Bayoncee, Princess Laya, Aurora Borealis." There was an impish note in his voice. "The poor kid's always broke or had a fight with her druggie boyfriend, and whenever she gets arrested, I don't have the heart to let her rot in jail. Plus, she offers to take her legal fees out in trade."

Gayle's eyebrows shot up, but she said nothing.

"My darling, you'll be pleased to know that I have never, ever engaged her services. But, she caused quite a spectacle when she tried to unzip my trousers in the City Court parking lot." He chuckled. "I'm lucky they didn't arrest me for solicitation."

At that moment, Mo drove into the parking lot, and Gayle raised her fist to rap on the pane in warning. But the stranger had vanished. Mo sprang from her BMW, dropped her satchel, and dashed toward the back of the house.

When shrieks and screams filled the air, Jessie and Gayle rushed outside toward the mayhem in the backyard. They shoved open the wooden privacy gate to encounter the woman helplessly floundering in the Kaplan's in-ground swimming pool. Jessie vaguely recalled when, as a teenager, the Kaplan's pool had been the talk of the town because not even wealthy people had them. Almost two decades later, it was hard to fathom that the envied family retreat had become the death trap before her.

"Help!" the woman bellowed, sinking below the roiling waves. A moment later, she burst upward, gasping for air. Her arms floundered around like useless fins. The contents of the tote—a bra, a soda can, a half-empty fifth of Bacardi, a bag of M&M's, a few stray dollars, a purple Chuck Taylor sneaker, a pink head wrap, and an eye patch—bobbed alongside her in the foam.

Balancing precariously on the end of the diving board, Mo extended the pool skimmer toward the hysterical victim and barked commands over the chaos. "Grab the pole, damn it. I'm not coming in after you. I just had my hair done. Do you hear me? Grab the goddamn handle."

With no flotation device in sight, Jessie kicked off her heels, stripped off her blazer, and dove into the pool. The shock of the frigid water was so numbing it felt like she'd plunged into a bath of ice cubes. The pressure of her wet clothing crushed her chest and limbs, and she struggled against the weight of gravity, dragging her downward toward the pool's dark bottom.

Breaking through the surface, Jessie blinked the chlorine from her eyes and spied Gayle in the shallow end of the pool. Gayle waved and called to her, "Are you all right?" Jessie waved back.

Long ago in lifesaving classes, Jessie had learned the dangers of saving a drowning person. If agitated, they might drag her down, drowning both of them. But she was determined to save this woman, and she and Gayle had no choice. Without their help, the woman would die.

"Let's grab her," Jessie yelled back. "Be careful!"

From opposite directions, they swam toward the woman thrashing about between them. She must have seen them approaching because she panicked and swatted her sharp nails at them as if they were flies. They backed off, waiting for the hysteria to subside.

Jessie knew it was impossible to negotiate with terror, so she kept her voice level and calm. "We're here to help you. Do you understand?" Her question went unanswered as shrieks and splashing swallowed her pleas. Slowly, Jessie inched closer, but a sharp heel jabbed her ribs, thrusting her backward and knocking the air out of her lungs. Catching her breath, she treaded water and planned her next move.

"Gayle," Jessie called out, "on the count of three, we'll grab her armpits from behind and drag her into shallower water. Watch out because she packs a mean punch."

"Got it. One... Two..." Gayle replied.

Unexpectedly, the woman quit thrashing. The pool grew still. Before their eyes, the stranger vanished beneath the dark waves, leaving a ring of tiny bubbles where she'd once been. If they didn't act fast, she might sink to the bottom and blend into the pool's surface, which was dyed the natural blue-grey color of a mountain lake. She'd be as invisible as a catfish on the muddy river floor.

Jessie filled her lungs with air and dove beneath the water. Through the murky water, she spied Gayle swimming toward her, motioning at the sinking woman. They seized the lifeless figure beneath her arms and hauled her out of the darkness and into the light. The chilly spring breeze seemed to revive her, and the woman began thrashing about, wrenching free from her saviors.

In one swift movement, Gayle swiped her hand backward and hurled it forward, striking the woman across the face. Her eyes and mouth shot open in alarm as Gayle smacked her face. To Jessie's relief, the victim stopped flailing, and surrendered as she and Gayle latched onto her slippery arms, dragged her into the shallow end of the pool, and deposited her on the stone steps. Pool water streamed from the woman's mouth and down her nose as she doubled over, racked with a violent cough. A hand-shaped welt rose on her cheek.

Clinging to the pool's edge, Jessie panted, catching her breath. It may have been a foolhardy lifesaving attempt, but the woman would have died if they hadn't jumped in after her. Deep inside, she glowed with the warmth of being a hero, but outwardly, Jessie was too cold and exhausted to dwell on the glory. From the crooked smile on Gayle's chattering lips, she sensed Gayle's agreement.

Without warning, Gayle's expression darkened. "What the hell were you doing? Trying to kill yourself? Or us?"

The woman coughed in reply, casting her eyes skyward.

"Ladies, it's a bit early in the season for a pool party, don't you think? I strongly urge you to get out of the water before you catch pneumonia," Jeremy said, hovering over them on the pool deck. He cradled a stack of striped beach towels, shaking his head. Mo waited beside him, gripping the skimmer in one hand. "Elisabeth, what's it been five months? It's a record for you. To what do I owe this pleasure?"

* * *

Swaddled in oversized pink-and-red striped towels, Jessie, Gayle, and Elisabeth huddled on a lounge chair, shivering. Jessie blew across the steaming mug of tea clasped in her shriveled fingers, wondering what the hell was going to happen next. Elisabeth, who'd bundled herself up into a mummy, seemed clueless to the trouble she'd caused. While Gayle appeared to be waiting for Jeremy to speak, he paced in front of them, pensive.

"Elisabeth, you're like a bad penny. Turning up in the most unusual circumstances." The coldness in Jeremy's eyes expressed his annoyance. No one was going anywhere until he had answers. "Can you kindly tell me what you're doing here?"

"Mr. Jay. Quit kidding me. You're always happy to see me. I promised you I'd be good, and I been." Elisabeth frowned and tugged her towel tighter. Her eyes flashed with fear and uncertainty, as though deciding whether to bolt or remain and take whatever Jeremy was about to dish out. "Haven't ya got anything stronger?"

Apparently, Jeremy sensed Elisabeth's skittishness, and moved closer, blocking her path to the gate. "I'm going to ask you again. What are you doing here and what were you doing in the pool?" His voice was stern, yet paternal.

Elisabeth's eyes flicked toward the white tote on the bottom of the pool, then returned to Jeremy. "I spilled some soda on my shirt and noticed the pool, so I came over here to wash it out." She affected a defiant tone, as though Jeremy was the crazy one. "The next thing I knew, splash. I was in the water."

"So you fell in? You weren't trying to hurt yourself?"

"No frickin' way. I came to see you because I gotta problem." Jeremy's curly white eyebrows furrowed, and his shoulders drooped in apparent disappointment. "No, it's not that kinda problem. I told you I been good."

"Elisabeth, it wasn't only cola in your can, was it? You promised me you'd lay off the booze. Don't lie to me." He snatched the skimmer from Mo, scooped up the Bacardi bottle bobbing in the water, and brandished the dripping net in Elisabeth's face.

Jeremy was right. Elisabeth reeked of a combination of chlorine, rum, and body odor. A stiff breeze ruffled the leafy canopy overhead, freeing Elisabeth's head and body from the shelter of the towel. Rays of sunlight bathed the scrapes and purplish-green blotches disfiguring her face, and the lacerations on her legs and arms.

"What the hell happened to your face and neck? And your arms and legs? It wasn't Kurt, was it? He didn't hit you again?" Jeremy demanded.

"No, it wasn't him. And in case you haven't checked the mirror lately, you ain't looking so great yourself." Elisabeth swaddled herself in the towel, tucking it tightly between her legs. "Stop acting like my pa, will you? I had an accident. That's all."

Jessie examined the pitiful creature sitting next to her. With her false eyelashes and caked-on makeup washed away, Elisabeth appeared more waifish than she had earlier. Her wet tee-shirt sagged on her emaciated, boyish frame, and she'd cinched the notorious short shorts at the waist with a man's black belt. At most, she was in her early thirties, but she'd driven hard miles on her tires.

What had caused the raw, sutured section of her scalp to fester with yellow pus? A beating? A fall? Had she smashed her head through a car windshield?

"Elisabeth, come on." Jeremy's voice pressed, trying to coax the truth. "Please tell me what's going on." His flinty gray eyes softened, turned gentle.

Elisabeth's body quivered, and she stared at him blankly as a tear rolled down her cheek. She flinched as Gayle embraced her trembling shoulders.

"Please, honey, come inside. Let's find you some dry clothes. Nobody's going to bite you," Gayle said.

Elisabeth stared at Jeremy inquisitively.

"My wife's right. She hasn't bitten me lately, and she's had plenty of opportunities."

The group rose as Gayle guided Elisabeth toward the office doorway, with Mo and Jessie trailing behind. Jeremy caught his wife's eye and smiled as she led the procession upstairs into the kitchen toward the smell of brewing coffee.

Chapter Twenty-Eight

More than ever, Jessie longed to go home. The near-drowning had sent her spiraling into melancholy, and the memories of Lily's sweet face, her lavender scent, and her weight snuggled against Jessie's chest twisted her up inside. She tried to shake it off, but she couldn't.

Risking her life for Jeremy's clumsy client, and practically swallowing half of his pool, had made her question whether she made a mistake by passing on the Barrie Building rental space. The Kaplan's toxic, complicated life wasn't worth sacrificing her life with Lily and Hal. It was time to bail and go home.

"Lissie, we're old pals, aren't we? We've faced jams worse than this, and we've always been straight with each other, so what's the problem?" Jeremy pleaded.

Hearing the unusual nickname for Elisabeth, Jessie's ears perked up.

Was this woman Lissie Sexton, the injured party from the trench and Ebony's missing person? It was a possibility, but not a strong one. Yet, Ebony had mentioned the woman's addiction issues and a bad news boyfriend, but these similarities might be purely coincidental. Until she heard more, there was no solid evidence identifying Elisabeth as Ebony's victim, or as the woman she'd saved before.

Sticking around a few minutes more couldn't hurt. Then she'd leave.

"Wait here," Gayle instructed before departing the kitchen, leaving Jessie and Elisabeth with Jeremy. "Jerry, offer the girls more tea or coffee, won't you?"

He followed the command and walked over to a marble counter stretching the length of the kitchen, and turned on the electric kettle. "Ladies, don't stand there dripping. Take a seat, please." He gestured toward the chairs around the kitchen table.

Jessie's feet were bare, and the iciness of the stone floor froze her in place. She tugged the towel tighter around her, marveling at the serene beauty of the room. Natural light streamed in through the wall of windows, reflecting off the floor-to-ceiling white subway tiles. Similarly, the cabinets stretched upward to meet the ten-foot ceiling and they'd painted them dove grey to enhance the veins in the countertops. A massive oiled butcher-block island, with gleaming copper pots dangling overhead, dominated the space, suggesting a gourmet chef in the house, presumably Gayle.

The kettle whistled as Gayle returned, wearing a change of clothing and carrying two bundles. She handed a bundle to each woman. "I'm sure these will do the trick. Elisabeth, please come with me, and honey, show Jessie where she can change." Gayle escorted Lissie down the hallway, and Jeremy led her to a hobbit-sized powder room tucked beneath the foyer's grand staircase.

"See you in a bit. In case you get lost, I've left a trail of breadcrumbs," he said, closing the door behind him.

* * *

Exchanging her sopping outfit for one of Gayle's comfy sweatsuits, Jessie considered what appeared to be a recurring theme in her life. If Lissie was the mystery victim, the conflicting arms of the law—criminal defense and the public interest—had trapped her once again. As Jeremy's associate, she had to act in Lissie's best interest and keep their conversations confidential. Conversely, Ebony had been frantically searching for Lissie and suspected she may be dead. Kiki and Becky were missing, and, if Ebony and Zander were correct, Lissie held the key to their safe return.

Jessie's mind whirled, dreading the descent of the black curtain of panic. A state so crippling she couldn't move or think straight. However, as the moments passed, her anxiety subsided. She needed to assist both Ebony and Lissie without violating the law. Each was relying upon her.

From experience, she'd learned that the rules of professional conduct were flexible, subject to interpretation. Certainly, the attorney-client privilege protected anything Lissie confided in Jeremy. So far, Lissie had revealed nothing; she'd shut up like a clam. Even if she had confided in Jeremy, there was an exception. The rules permitted the disclosure of private client conversations to prevent reasonably certain death or bodily harm. And since Lissie's assailant remained at large, Lissie remained in danger.

This theory justified her informing Ebony that Lissie was alive. But to circumvent the ethical quandary, she'd have to be careful.

First, she'd have to confirm her suspicions.

* * *

With her mind settled, Jessie returned to the kitchen. She joined the group ensconced in the breakfast nook and grabbed the spot next to Lissie, who was pleading her case to Jeremy.

"Mr. Jay, the cops... are after me. But, I didn't do nothing wrong. I swear." Lissie's blubbering and slurring her words made her response incomprehensible.

"Sweetie, don't worry, we believe you." Gayle grabbed tissues from the counter and handed them to Lissie. "Here, getting upset won't solve the situation. You need to take a breath and calm down."

Lissie smiled at her, blew her nose with a loud honk, and dried her eyes. "I don't know where to begin." She smacked her parched lips. "My mouth's awfully dry. Are you sure you don't have anything stronger?"

Jeremy scowled, filled a glass with tap water, and slammed it on the table in front of her. "Drink this."

Cradling the glass with fingers in desperate need of a manicure, Lissie told them about her rendezvous with Doc, his assault, her escape, and her trip by ambulance to the hospital. The full horror of Lissie's attack shook

Jessie, confirming her decision to inform Ebony about Lissie's return from the dead. She'd saved Lissie's life, not once but twice, and felt responsible for protecting her. With any luck, Ebony could track the maniac before he struck again. Next time, Lissie might not be so lucky.

"Kurt didn't even come to see me when I was laid up. So, when I got home, I gave him a piece of my mind. I'm fed up with his fuckin' games. He steals all my money, and I have to beg him to get it back. It's my property. I know my rights. My dad's a cop." As Lissie became more agitated, her voice rose in volume and speed. "He said, 'I'm not giving you jack-shit so you can pay those rich doctors. They don't need your dough, baby.' Baby, huh." Lissie snorted and gulped the water down in one swallow. "I told him, 'I pay my bills, so I'm going to find the prick who messed me up and get it from him.' And Kurt said, 'You'd better 'cos you're not getting it from me.'"

Lissie puckered her mouth as though tasting something sour. "So, screw him. I marched down to the station to ask the cops for help to get com-pen-sat-ion from Doc. And you know what? They asked me too many questions, so I split. Pretended I had to go pee. Pretty smart, huh? So, I dropped by Kiki's, figuring I could crash at her place. Mr. Jay, you know Kiki, right?"

Jeremy nodded.

"Her old man said she wasn't home. He hadn't seen her in days, so what was I supposed to do?" Lissie shrugged and scratched a scab on her head. "Kurt kept callin', all nice and sweet, but I was mad. I didn't feel like talking, so I ghosted him." Lissie surveyed the other women. "Ladies, you know what I'm talking about? Do I go home to that jerk or what?" She shook her head. "No way, damn right. Well, wrong. My stash was in our crib, so I had to go back. I waited in the schoolyard across the street until I saw Kurt leave. Then, I sneaked in, grabbed some of my stash, a baggie full of good pharma, a little insurance, and a gun."

At Curtis and McMann, Jessie's job had been staid and reliable, even boring. They'd chained her to her desk drafting documents, researching, talking on the phone or attending an occasional conference or court appearance. With Jeremy, she was an Alice tumbling down the rabbit hole into Wonderland. If Kyle got wind of Lissie's case, he'd be in court seeking custody faster than she could change Lily's diaper. This was the ammunition he'd been waiting for.

Lissie continued. "After all I been through, I said 'screw this.' I checked into the Springbrook Motel, watched cable, and ordered pizza and beer. Anybody got a cigarette?" Silence met her.

"I know I'm a jerk, but I missed Kurt something bad, so I went home. I'd make nice to him and we'd be square, but when I got home this morning there was yellow tape across the front door. Kurt's gotta be dead, and it's my fault.... The cops think I did it, that's why they're after me." She formed a nest on the table with her arms and laid her head inside, letting her tears resume. "Mr. Jay, I didn't know where else to go. And now, all my stuff's at the bottom of your pool. I got nothing."

"You did the right thing coming here. Jerry will make a few calls about Kurt, and I'm sure he's fine. There's probably been a big misunderstanding. And we'll fish your stuff out of the pool. Don't worry," Gayle said, gently stroking Lissie's shoulders.

"Lissie, you're safe with us," Jeremy said. "Nobody's going to get to you. Leave it to me."

"Lissie, is your last name Sexton?" Jessie asked. A great deal rested on the answer.

Lissie's head snapped up, and she glared at Jessie. "What's it to you? Do I know you or something?"

"No," Jessie lied, "but if it is, I know someone who's worried about you. She thinks you're dead."

"I ain't, though, am I?"

Chapter Twenty-Nine

As the day drew to a close, Jessie sat cross-legged on her bluestone patio, sipping a tall glass of peppermint-iced tea. The sun still hovered high in the sky, and she felt content, warmed by the sunlight stones beneath her.

Her tabby cat, Bono, lazily sunned himself on the nearby lawn, and when a robin hopped by, he pounced, but missed the bird. Unfazed, Bono plopped down on the grass and stretched out to resume his sunbathing.

Earlier, Jessie had texted Ebony. To her amazement, Ebony had shown up carrying a bottle of Rosé, and at the moment, she appeared to be relaxing in a teak rocker as Lily played at her feet. With each tap of Ebony's toes, anxiety squeezed Jessie's chest tighter as she weighed the ramifications of her intended action.

She spoke before she could change her mind. "I met Lissie Sexton today at Jeremy's. It's a very long story, but all I can tell you is that she's alive."

"Hold on," Ebony said, lurching forward in the chair. "You're telling me you met Lissie Sexton? Today? At Jeremy's? When? Did you talk to her? What did she say? Where is she now? How can I get in touch with her?"

"Wait a minute. I just wanted you to know she wasn't dead or missing. I'll get in trouble if I say anymore. So, I can't and I won't."

"Let me get this straight. You drop the bombshell that Lissie was in Poughkeepsie today, but you didn't call me immediately, even though you knew how important she is to my investigation." From the aggression in Ebony's voice, it was apparent that Jessie had misjudged Lissie's importance to Ebony's case. Ebony wouldn't let up now. She'd want more. Demand more. "Where can I find her now? I need to talk with her."

"I don't know where she is, but I wouldn't put out an APB just yet. She's awfully skittish, and you don't want to risk her running, do you?"

"That's irrelevant if I don't know where she is and can't speak with her." An ugliness pierced Ebony's voice, and her chilliness from the other night returned. "You're not withholding evidence from me because we have opposing interests here. You know...prosecution and defense?"

"Eb, come on. Give me a break, will you? I'm not jeopardizing my career again, especially when I don't know what the hell is going on." The sting of the attack caused Jessie to smash down her glass on the tray between them, making it tip over. To hide her anger, she quickly wiped up the mess before it attracted Lily's attention. "By now, you must have discovered that Jeremy has represented Lissie, so I suggest you contact him and maybe you'll get some answers." Clearly, Jeremy's instincts about protecting Lissie from everyone had been correct. Especially from cops like Ebony.

As she and Ebony glared at each other, Lily blissfully amused herself with a bright red plastic bucket with star, circle, square, cross, and triangle shapes cut out of its top. The baby clapped with delight after pushing the orange star block into the correct slot.

"Yeah, Lily," Jessie said, drawn in by her baby's carefree smile. Lily latched onto Jessie's arm, pulled herself up to a standing position, and released her grip. For a few fleeting moments, the baby balanced on her own feet. Then, as a slight breeze rose, Lily wobbled and fell onto her rump.

"Did you see that? She stood by herself."

Ebony stared off into the maple trees lining the back of the yard, oblivious to the child's accomplishment or Jessie's joy. Jessie squeezed Ebony's knee, jolting her friend from her daze.

"Are you sure you've told me everything? There's nothing you're forgetting?"

"Eb, I can't say any more, and I'm growing weary of your interrogation. The facts are the facts. No matter how many times I repeat them, they won't change." She paused. "I'm going out on a limb for you, so can you please tell me what's really going on?"

166

As before, their conversation had been a one-way street. She understood Ebony wore her detective's badge 24/7, but Ebony's remaining tight-lipped disturbed her. She was about to rail into her when a car door shut in the driveway.

"Have you told Hal about Lissie?" Ebony asked.

"Not yet." Hal was being a good sport about her position with Jeremy Kaplan, but she was leery about sharing too many details right away.

"Told me what?" With his briefcase tucked beneath his arm, Hal strolled up the path to join them. He'd loosened his tie and undone the top button of his shirt.

As he advanced, a kaleidoscope of butterflies fluttered inside Jessie's belly. She was thrilled to see him, but she wished she could be more honest with him about her new job.

"I'm not crazy about the looks of this. You both look awfully conspiratorial." Hal eyed them suspiciously over the top of his Ray-Bans and flashed a wry smile. "Are you plotting world domination or something of equal interest?"

"I was telling her how much I love you."

Hal raised an eyebrow in mock disbelief. Jessie tilted her head back and puckered her lips, inviting Hal's homecoming kiss.

Hal obliged and squatted beside Lily. He blew a raspberry beneath the baby's chin, making her giggle. "Hellooo, LilyBean. How's my girl doing today?"

"Hey there, handsome." Ebony raised her glass, rattling the ice cubes against the sides. "What's a girl got to do to score some vino around here? All your old lady offered me was iced tea."

"Off duty, Detective Jones?" Hal rose and strode toward the kitchen door. "Red or white?"

"Rosé. I wasn't sure if you stocked any, so I brought my own."

* * *

From across the patio, Jessie admired Hal as he approached them. His gait was long and confident, as if he ruled the world and challenged anyone to stop him. He carried the bottle of Rosé, three wine glasses, and a box of saltines, which he deposited on the slate coffee table next to Jessie. She distributed the goblets and poured the wine. At the sound of ripping cellophane, Lily again scaled Jessie's knees for a closer inspection. Jessie handed Lily a cracker, and the baby popped it into her mouth before greedily reaching for another.

"What a day." Hal let out a deep breath and discarded his loafers and socks. He slouched back in the Adirondack chair across from Jessie, stroking her ankles with his bare toes. "Just what I needed, the company of three lovely ladies and a tall drink." He sipped on his drink.

"Jessie's had quite a day as well." Ebony pursed her lips, but a sly grin broke through. "Haven't you, Jess?"

Jessie took a sip, and the wine tasted cool and spicy on her tongue. Hal turned toward her expectantly, but she gathered up Lily and cuddled her daughter in her lap. "Have you heard anything more about the student who disappeared from the high school? My Dad's doing his best to keep the school calm, but it's taking a toll on him."

"This is the first I'm hearing of this. Do you know who's working it from my department?" Ebony asked.

"I don't know. But we're waiting to hear from the chief before our investigators follow-up with interviewing witnesses, the teachers, the staff, and her friends. Ed mentioned that everyone says she is a happy, quiet girl." He nibbled on a saltine and washed it down with Rosé. "People simply don't vanish."

"Yeah, but I think there's more to the story. My dad mentioned that the girl's mother saw a post on Facebook. She suspects her daughter ran off with her boyfriend, who's on leave from the Marines. The student's a senior and eighteen, so there's not much anyone can do. But it reflects poorly on my dad, as school principal." She hadn't meant to divulge her father's confidences, but the wine was going to her head.

"When I get to the station, I'll check it out. But keep me in the loop, will you?" Ebony asked casually. "Maybe Zander and I can help."

CHAPTER TWENTY-NINE

"Sure, but nothing may come of it."

Ebony cleared her throat to catch Jessie's attention, and motioned her chin toward Hal. "Go on," she mouthed.

Jessie's ears grew warm. She fluffed her hair to hide them, but Hal caught her eye.

"More, please?" Ebony drained the last drop from her glass and held it out to Hal for a refill. "Don't either of you look at me that way. Drew can pick me up if I need a ride, or I can call a ride share." She snatched the bottle from the table, refilled her glass, and gulped down a generous mouthful. "Mr. DA, I have a dilemma and I'm hoping you can help me. Actually, *we* have a dilemma." She waved the glass at herself and Jessie.

Here it comes, Jessie thought.

"Is this off or on the record?" he asked.

"You decide after I tell you."

A deep horizontal crease appeared in Hal's forehead as Ebony explained about Kiki Taylor and Becky Douglas's disappearances and Jessie's encounters with Lissie Sexton. She flourished her hands as though she was tipsy, but she cogently expressed her frustration over Chief Shepardson's tight leash on the rape investigation and her suspicions about the possibility of more victims.

"Let me get this straight. You've confirmed that Kiki Taylor and Becky Douglas are missing?" Hal asked. "And there's no formal investigation tying the two together? However, you believe it's the same perpetrator."

Ebony nodded.

"And some guy beat Elisabeth Sexton to a pulp, and you believed she was missing, too, but Jessie knows where she is and won't say? And somehow she's linked to the same attacker."

"I don't know how to say this any clearer. I don't know where Lissie is, but even if I did, I couldn't say," Jessie interjected.

Hal wandered across the patio to a locust tree, where wind chimes hung from a low branch. He plucked at the metal tubes, making them tinkle, and then silenced them between his palms. "I have to agree with Shepardson, you need more evidence of a crime." He scratched his back against the tree trunk and continued. "If you want me to organize a county-wide manhunt, I need more than a hunch." He paused. "I don't need to tell you how to do your job, but you might check whether there are other reported incidents similar to Elisabeth's. And if you provide me with solid evidence like a name or a description, then my office can get involved. I'd hate to believe we've got a predator lurking in our backyard."

Until a few days ago, defending herself against Terrence had been the extent of Jessie's exposure to the criminal justice system. Then came the two encounters with Lissie, and the Douglases, and the mystery and intrigue of criminal law had sucked her in. It was no wonder that Hal and Jeremy craved the adrenaline rush of life and death. Murder, rape, and assault were much more exciting than negotiating a commercial lease for a mall. She craved the rush, too, and wanted to help find Becky.

Deep in conversation, Hal and Ebony discussed plausible theories and scenarios, acting as though Jessie wasn't even there. They seemed to forget that she was their connection to Lissie. It was damn insulting, and she felt she deserved better. Dejected, Jessie gathered the empty glasses on the table.

"I can't do this without Jessie. She's our only link to Lissie. Plus, whether or not you agree, Kaplan's reputation opens doors," Ebony insisted, looking straight at her. The fading sunlight illuminated her sapphire eyes, setting them ablaze. "Hal, Zander and I can't proceed without Jessie's help."

Hal pinched the bridge of his nose and tightly squeezed his eyes. The moment seemed to last forever until he returned to Jessie's side, slipped an arm around her waist, and raised his glass. "As DA, I'm warning you that there will be backlash. Nobody wants to admit there's a serial attacker, or rapist, or killer in their city. Personally, I hope you're wrong, but I wish your team good luck in proving he's out there. And as your friend, I'm warning you to be careful."

Finally. Redemption.

She'd prove to herself, Hal, Ebony, Jeremy, and the legal community that she had the right stuff to become a damn good criminal attorney.

Chapter Thirty

O n Monday morning, the police station was as dead as the morgue at midnight. Without the phones ringing off the hooks, the intercom blaring and the walkie-talkies crackling, Ebony barely recognized the place. It was as though crime had hopped on AMTRAK at Penn Station and by-passed Poughkeepsie on its way to Boston.

Usually, her post-weekend email inbox overflowed, but to her disappointment, it was empty. The biggest gamble of her career had failed miserably.

Drew had been on duty at the firehouse last night, so with Wrangler curled up at her feet, she'd worked doggedly until dawn pursuing her missing persons investigation. She'd theorized that there must be other Hudson Valley women who'd recently reported assaults or who'd been reported as missing. And she hoped to prove that one perpetrator was responsible. Not a serial rapist, but a serial killer.

She'd quickly discovered that with the valley lacking a centralized missing persons database, it was impossible to cross-reference similar incidents across the region. With each town operating in a vacuum, there would be no reason for any city, town, or village police department to communicate with their neighbors, unless a perpetrator crossed the invisible jurisdictional lines during a pursuit. Even the website for the New York State Police Missing Persons Division was outdated, the last entry being a decade ago. As a result, Ebony faced the daunting task of contacting every municipality up and down the Hudson in search of leads and evidence tying the crimes to one culprit.

While Kiki, Lissie, and Becky lived in Poughkeepsie, Ebony was convinced that her suspect was cunning, calculating, and mobile. Lissie had mentioned he had a vehicle, so it would be easy for him to hunt for prey throughout the valley. For the sake of these women, and the other unknown victims, she was committed to finding him, no matter the cost.

By early morning, with eyes dry and bleary from staring at her screen, Ebony had accomplished something no one else had. She'd created an Excel spreadsheet of the local police departments around the Hudson River Valley. From Highland, Beacon, Kingston, Newburgh, Hyde Park, Pleasant Valley, Millbrook, Town of Poughkeepsie, Fishkill, Rhinebeck to Hudson, she'd requested copies of complaints meeting the criteria of assaults perpetrated on women, and female disappearances over the past five years.

Her nightstand clock had read four o'clock when she'd collapsed into bed, unsure whether she'd wasted a good night's sleep. After a restless nap, Ebony had dressed and arrived at work by seven. She'd logged into her computer, hoping for replies, but there were none. Even her own department had failed to respond to her urgent request.

The morning dragged by, and she remained glued to the computer, jabbing the mailbox refresh button. Still nothing. With each try, she fought the feeling that her hunch had been wrong and the attacks on Lissie, Kiki, and Becky had been flukes.

"Hey, why are you taking your frustrations out on your keyboard?" Zander asked.

She told him about her gamble and her losses.

"Eb, give it time. Some of these record guys only work part-time and haven't seen your request yet. And if they have, they move as slow as snails. So hang in there. There has to be another victim out there."

"All we need is one hit. That's it. One more reported incident would bring Hal and the chief on board. Otherwise, we'll be back chasing drunks, druggies, and gas station robbers, while a killer remains at large."

"Don't be discouraged, it's not even noon, yet."

By late afternoon, two notifications flashed across her desktop. "Z, come here and check this out!" she shouted. "Pine Plains and Millbrook have finally responded. Can you grab the reports from the printer?"

Zander carried the reports into Interrogation Room One and set them on the table for them to study. He leaned over the reports and read the names aloud as Jessie entered the room. "Millbrook's victim was Eve Greenberg, and Pine Plains' was Vanessa Leone."

"Eve Greenberg hailed from Millbrook millionaires," he said. "Her family owned mansions in Palm Beach and Manhattan, but she and her siblings were raised on the family's rural horse farm. After flunking out of Dartmouth, she drained her trust fund and fell into a lifestyle of drugs, parties, and promiscuity."

From Eve's meticulous grooming and wardrobe, Ebony suspected she'd been a high-class escort. Rich women like Eve Greenberg didn't get busted for sex or drugs; they had expensive lawyers on speed dial.

Surprisingly, Eve's file contained a year-old dossier from PI Cary Wentworth reporting there had been no ransom demands or leads as to her location. With greasy hair and rotten teeth, Wentworth had an uncanny ability to blend in and extract secrets from unwitting sources. His information was reliable, and he knew better than to interfere with Ebony's cases, especially if he wanted any inside dirt from her.

Vanessa Leone hadn't enjoyed Eve's advantages in life. When Vanessa was four years old, her mother had dumped her, and her twin brother, on their alcoholic father. At fifteen, Vanessa had run away from home and at sixteen she'd given birth at a teen shelter. Allegations of child neglect had placed her one-year-old daughter in foster care. For the past dozen years, Vanessa had been in and out of emergency rooms for drug overdoses and the battered women's shelter, where she had last been seen eighteen months ago.

"How did you find these victims?" Jessie asked.

Zander brought her up to speed on Ebony's all-nighter, which had led to their latest hits.

"Looks like these ladies may have something in common with Lissie Sexton. Do they ring a bell?"

Ebony and Zander shook their heads in unison.

"Hmm," Ebony said, scanning the papers. "You see what's going on, don't you? They're saying it was the lack of leads and manpower that prevented them from taking further action on the cold case. But what's really going on is all about the victims' profiles. They didn't want to waste time or money on finding lost hookers."

"Sure looks like it," Jessie replied.

Zander busily constructed a Detective's Investigation Wall on the whiteboard at the front of the room. He'd already posted Lissie's, Kiki's and Becky's photos, and was taping up the pictures of the new victims. Jessie approached the board and thoughtfully tilted her head side-to-side, inspecting Zander's handiwork.

Ebony enjoyed using the evidence board. She found it easier to organize her thoughts when the file, charts, report, manual, or photos were visually in front of her. They reminded her of the colorful circles and arrows in her coach's basketball playbook, which plotted the defeat of an opponent. Over time, they'd add more pictures, maps, and notes to their wall, and hopefully, a common thread would develop from the information posted on the board.

"I have to give it to you, Eb," Zander said, attaching an avatar for their suspect, "you called it and you were right."

"It's not a matter of being right, it's a matter of justice for these victims. If you analyze the facts, you can't deny there's a pattern to the four missing women, and Lissie." Ebony leaned against the far wall, unconsciously massaging her left hip. "Jessie, don't you agree?"

Ebony still wasn't convinced that Jessie didn't know Lissie's whereabouts. Clearly, her badgering wasn't working, so she'd decided to let the "murder board" speak instead. The haunting eyes of Rebecca Douglas, Kiara Taylor, Lissie Sexton, and the latest victims, Eve Greenberg and Vanessa Leone, stared out at them. Beneath each photo, Zander had pinned a yellow index card with the woman's birthdate, height, weight, last known address, education, occupation, prior arrests, and the date and location of her last sighting. Jessie's knees visibly wobbled as she studied the wall, so perhaps the victim's tortured expressions were doing the trick.

"That's five victims over the past twenty-four months, and each story is sadder than the next," Jessie whispered.

"You have to wonder whether they knew it was the end when their attacker struck," Ebony replied.

"That's gruesome, but I guess morbidness comes with your territory." Jessie nervously twirled a lock of her hair around her pointer finger. "I can't help thinking about those poor girls...and their families. I couldn't live knowing that my sister or mother or daughter was lost. Could you?"

"We'll never know, will we?" Ebony had banked on Jessie being shocked by the photos, but Jessie's question had made her cringe. Was she implying that Ebony's family had forsaken Aunt Alicia? That they hadn't searched long enough or hard enough for Alicia or for the cause of her death? Or was she being overly sensitive?

"There's got to be some connection. There are too many similarities. Just look at them. Our suspect has a type." Zander shifted in his chair and tapped his pen against his cheek in thought. "They're all light-skinned with dark hair, in their late twenties or early thirties, and petite."

What he'd really meant, but left unsaid, was the real common denominator among them. The women were prostitutes, except Becky Douglas. It was a label that would forever identify them, and if Ebony was correct, would bind them to one man.

John Doe a/k/a Doc. The suspect's name was written in green block letters across the top of the board next to a faceless male image.

"Even though the crimes are separated by time and location, the victims' similarities have made you suspect a single perpetrator is responsible? You're talking about a serial killer?" Jessie asked.

"Yes. Initially, we suspected he was a serial rapist. You saw what he did to Lissie and Kiki," Ebony said. "However, the multiple disappearances suggest a different modus operandi. This person's a predator, a killer, though I believe his actions are sexually motivated. These women were easy targets because they'd willingly jump into a car with anyone. It's their job. Sadly, if they vanish, nobody takes note or reports it. Look at Lissie, Eve, and Vanessa. They were all estranged from their families. I'm sure that creep Kurt Hendricks wouldn't have reported Lissie missing."

"And considering Sexton's rap sheet, it would've been easy to assume that she'd been busted again or gone to rehab," Zander said. "That's the problem with sex workers and addicts. They can easily slip through society's cracks. And no one notices."

"The problem sounds more pervasive than these five women on our board," Jessie said. "It's troubling that local organizations and authorities have done nothing to protect the sex workers from danger, especially when everyone knows the perils they face. It's like the community is ignoring the issue and hoping the girls vanish." She paused and cocked her head. "Do you know whether the girls watch out for each other?"

"They do, but—" Ebony shrugged. "Even if the street informs our patrols when their cohorts aren't loitering at their usual spots, the patrols don't rush to issue any all-points bulletins on the reports."

"Until someone files a formal complaint, the victims float in purgatory," Zander added, "and only then will 'Missing Persons' posters be printed and low-priority investigations begun."

"That's awful," Jessie said. "What about Eve Greenberg? Her family had money, and they searched for her."

"The PI's report found nothing," Ebony said. "So, rich or poor, there's no police follow-up. That's why we have to."

Ebony remained silent for a long time, smelling the scent of crime, not the burnt coffee grounds or the waxy shoe polish residue that hung in the station's air. She smelled the blood, the damp, unearthed dirt, and the rotting corpses.

She wasn't giving up, not this time. She believed the women were waiting to be discovered somewhere in her city, her valley. It was their job—her's, Zander's, and Jessie's—to return them home and give their souls peace and their families closure.

Ebony didn't need to speak with the victim's families to understand that Eve, Kiki, Becky, and Vanessa were beloved as mothers, sisters, daughters, aunts, and granddaughters. She knew firsthand that despite their lifestyle choices, addictions, or difficulties, their families and friends still loved and missed them. It made no difference that their lives had slipped off the rails, and in fact, their flaws strengthened her resolve to bring the girls back home.

Her eyes shifted to the faceless avatar. Who was he? From the RAP sheets, interviews, and missing persons reports, it had been easy to develop the victims' profiles, but their predator remained a mystery.

"What's up, Doc?" Ebony murmured.

Jessie laughed nervously.

"That's not funny, Eb. We have little evidence to go on besides Sexton's vague description of the crime and perp. He's a six-foot-four African American who dresses in scrubs and has a puny penis. And he drives a late model white Toyota. What kind of woman can't describe a guy she's serviced a bunch of times?" Zander asked, smirking.

"One who's stoned or drunk most of the time. Or one who's screwed a lot of guys," Jessie replied dryly. "Not that I'd know anything about that."

Ebony chuckled at the jab at her own past indiscretions. While in college, she'd played it free and loose, but her promiscuity had ended with Drew. What had begun with a one-night stand had lasted for three years, a dog and the sale of his home on wheels, his beloved RV. If that didn't show his commitment, she didn't know what did.

"Lissie's been in the trade for a long time and since it's a cash business, I doubt she kept a journal of her Johns—A Johnal," Ebony snorted at her own joke. "But you never know."

She popped three Tylenol into her mouth and downed them with a diet cola. They fizzled on her tongue and she swigged again to rinse the chalky taste from her mouth. "Jessie, we need you to bring Lissie in to review the mug shots and meet with the sketch artist. She's a long shot, but she's all we've got." Ebony glowered at Jessie. "As a team, we have an obligation to pursue every angle of these crimes to bring justice to the victims. You need to weigh your misplaced loyalty to Jeremy against the safety of these women. If we don't find them, it's going to be all on you. Can you live with that?"

She hadn't meant to sound harsh, but the prick of Jessie's poke still lingered, intensified by her doubts about whether her family had exhausted

177

every resource to bring Aunt Alicia home safely.

* * *

Jessie's body stiffened at Ebony's latest censure. She felt like she was on a rollercoaster ride with her. One minute Ebony was her friend; the next, Ebony treated her as a suspect rather than a partner in the investigation. The one hundred-eighty-degree attitude flip frightened her, making her question whether she really knew Ebony at all.

All along, she'd been honest with Ebony and Zander. She hadn't a clue where Jeremy had stashed Lissie, except that it was a safe house somewhere in the Hudson Valley.

It was one thing to protect Lissie. She was alive. Hidden, but safe. It was another to hunt for an alleged killer. Ebony and Zander were detectives, and they'd been trained to wallow in blood, murder, and the seedier side of life.

Jessie was a lawyer. The deaths described in her law school casebooks had been published in black and white like a novel, not as high definition color photographs on a whiteboard. Her specialty, negotiating leases and real estate contracts, drafting corporate resolutions and bylaws, and zoning applications, had been squeaky-clean work. Ink had been the only substance staining her trembling hands.

Her cases may have kept her up at night, but they were frivolous compared to the soul-crushing suffering depicted in these victims' eyes.

"I've told you for the tenth time, I don't know where Lissie is," Jessie snapped, willing herself to push back against Ebony's bullying and to banish her insecurities.

"Find out from Jeremy. These ladies, particularly Lissie, and Doc's potential victims, are relying on you. I don't care how you do it, but I'm urging you to get it done," Ebony commanded, pointing her chin toward the whiteboard.

But Ebony was right. Lissie was real; flesh and blood, and her life was at stake.

Chapter Thirty-One

The fading daylight streamed in through the nursery windows, setting the framed letters spelling LILY aglow against the bright pink, white, and lime green striped wall behind the crib. The surrounding pale pink walls muted the energy of the room, setting the tone for Lily's bedtime.

Jessie cradled Lily in her arms, inhaling the sweetness of the freshly bathed babe, and looked out the window. Below, Hal swung his driver on the backyard lawn. He drew back the club in a slow, controlled motion, paused at the top of his swing, and throttled the imaginary ball in a perfect pendulum. After each swing, he repeated the exercise.

Feeling a heavy head pressing against her shoulder, Jessie tenderly transferred Lily into the crib and slipped out of the room.

"Getting ready for the Masters?" Jessie asked, joining Hal outside. One hand balanced a cup of tea and the other carried her cellphone open to the baby monitor app.

Spring's evening chill filled the air, turning her skin to gooseflesh. It reminded her about the four women lost somewhere in the night. If alive, they were scared and alone. If dead, they were as cold as the frosty earth in which they were buried.

Now, more than ever, Jessie needed Hal's advice about Jeremy. He'd know how to convince him to cooperate with the investigation. She was about to speak, but Hal struck his driving stance and addressed the blades of grass substituting for the golf ball.

"Do you know what I enjoy about golf? It's you against the course. Sure, the play changes with the weather and they shuffle the tees and pins around, but you know what to expect. For Christ's sake, they give you a map of the distances and the hazards." Hal swung forcefully and shaded his eyes, pretending to search the twilight for his ball. He twirled the driver's shaft in his fingers like a baton, and then he balanced its egg-shaped metal head in his palm. "And you know your equipment, the way it feels in your grip. You depend on that familiarity to conquer the course." He flung the driver up into the air and caught it by the grip upon its return to earth. "Some days you're good, and some days you suck. But one great shot and you feel like a million bucks."

"You're right, every game, every shot presents a new opportunity," she agreed. Hal wasn't discussing golf with her. It was more philosophical than that.

"How could I've missed it? Those women vanished under my watch. I was in charge of the Major Crimes Division. It's my fault." In one swift movement, he snapped the driver's shaft in half over his knee and hurled the broken metal bits to the ground. "Fuck."

"I know you're under pressure, but talk to me. Please, Hal. Tell me what's going on."

Hal snatched the pieces from the grass and stalked past her into the kitchen. The slamming of the screen door made her flinch, and fear crawled along her flesh. She'd never seen Hal so enraged, so withdrawn.

Jessie considered following him inside when he suddenly reappeared, shrugging on his leather jacket. "I'll be back in a while. I need to clear my head." Hal stormed past her, unlocked the Volvo's door, slid in, and sped away.

She stood paralyzed, listening to his screeching tires and watching the darkness arrive.

* * *

Hal was in no mood for talking. A dark, raging river of words was trapped inside his head with no escape. He needed time to think, to be alone and let the anger surge through him.

He had no notion of his destination. He couldn't think in his office where the books and files reminded him of the daily pressures; managing the staff, cases, and budgets, the election, the public, his duties, and his oath of office. Under no circumstances would he go over to Erin's. His former home was a brutal reminder of his failure as a husband and father.

Yet, he knew where he'd been. He'd taken his eye off the ball. There were no excuses. His callousness had endangered the community he'd sworn to serve. The disappearances, and whatever grew out of them, were his fault.

Driving south on Route 9, he pulled into the empty Casperkill Golf Club parking lot. The season hadn't peaked yet, but the clubhouse welcomed him home. It had always been a sanctuary of male camaraderie, where a nod was the only conversation necessary, either on or off the course. Where players found refuge by watching golf on television or playing poker.

Or where he was headed, in the "Nineteenth Hole."

Hal relaxed the instant he entered the cozy British-style pub that smelled of leather, grass, and aftershave. He took a stool at the mahogany bar and studied the beers on tap. His eyes were drawn to the 70-inch flat-screen mounted on the stacked stone fireplace. It was dedicated to Golf, the religion worshipped in this church.

The bartender, a clean-shaven young man sporting a man bun, polished the copper countertop. He set a coaster down along with a basket of tortilla chips. "Sir?"

"A bourbon neat, please, with an IPA chaser." Hal yearned for a strong libation to dull his senses, to make him forget. The pressures. The pain.

"Make that two," said a familiar voice. A hand clamped down on his shoulder, causing him to flinch. "I thought I'd find you here, son."

Chapter Thirty-Two

Bang! Bang! The sound of an insistent fist walloping Jessie's front door resonated throughout her house. Simultaneously, the doorbell buzzed as someone leaned on the ringer.

Crap, she thought. *Don't they know I've got a sleeping kid in the house?*

The tumult paused and then resumed as Jessie dashed downstairs and tugged the door open. It was dark outside, but the porch light illuminated the fidgety duo of Ebony and Zander.

"It took you long enough." Ebony brushed past her into the living room as if she owned the place. Zander trailed along on her heels.

Jessie flicked on the table lamps and walked over to the mantel as if guarding the antique English pastoral landscape mounted overhead. These days, they seldom used the living room, and the white bed sheets protecting her furniture from tiny handprints gave the room a ghostly air.

Ebony slapped a manila folder stamped with the City of Poughkeepsie medallion on the glass coffee table and paced the room. The room hummed with nervous energy as Zander rubbed his stubble, and Ebony fiddled with the badge dangling from her belt. Her eyes remained glued to the folder as though it contained a ticking time bomb.

Whatever followed would taint her home forever. But she was in too deep to turn back.

Opening the file, Jessie examined the growing collection of local cold cases spanning the past two years. Five more victims—Sharone Standly, Camila Cordoba, Jacqueline Randall, Angela Gibbons, and Justine Harp—had emerged. After digesting the grim accounts, Jessie snapped the folder shut and collapsed onto the dusty slipcover of a wingback armchair. "Five more women? Pleasant Valley. Highland. Beacon. Wappingers Falls. They look identical to the others. Do you think...?"

"You know what we think," Ebony snapped. "Over the past twenty-four months, we've found nine missing women. Same age, coloring, race, physique, addictions, and occupation. They've vanished off the planet and nobody has lifted a finger to find them or connect the dots."

"You don't know that, Eb," Zander said testily.

"You saw the files. The reports came in, and then nothing. No APBs, no investigations. The files sat around gathering dust."

"What about their relatives? Living all this time without knowing what happened? I'm surprised they didn't press their cases." Heart-wrenching sadness replaced Jessie's shock. How could their family, society, and the criminal justice system abandon these women? Who was accountable for this tragedy? The system? John Doe? Hal?

"For a while, everyone probably assumed they'd OD'd or moved away, so why bother to search," Zander said. "And there was no reason to link them. Until now."

"Shouldn't you report this to the chief?" Jessie wondered what would happen if she disappeared suddenly without explanation. What measures Hal, her parents, and Ebony would take to recover her? How persistent would they be?

"That's what I told her, but Ebony thinks we still don't have enough," Zander said.

"We don't. And we've got one shot to make our case. I'm not going to blow it by acting prematurely."

"What are you going to do?" Jessie asked.

Ebony approached her, and roughly grabbed her shoulder, almost shaking her. "No, Jessie. The question is, what are *you* going to do?" Ebony narrowed her eyes and her muscles twitched like a cat preparing to pounce. "I'm sure you're familiar with the terms 'habeas corpus' and 'obstructing the administration of justice,' aren't you?"

Jessie eyed Ebony. As a lawyer, her words had been her sharpest weapons, slicing her adversaries through the heart. Her hands never got dirty, and the only blood on them was from paper cuts. Conversely, Ebony clawed her way through the filth to ensure public safety. The discovery of these shocking, new disappearances seemed to have intensified Ebony's combativeness and deepened the gulf between them.

"We're both on the same side, aren't we? Do you seriously believe that threatening me is going to get your way?" Jessie drew back, out of reach.

* * *

In the kitchen, the door slammed, and Jessie heard Hal's footsteps approaching the living room.

He stopped in the archway and inspected the group assembled inside. "Detective Jones, exactly what do you think you're doing?"

Ebony guiltily eyed Jessie, but stayed silent. Zander, seeming surprised at the District Attorney's unexpected appearance, cast an inquisitive sideglance at Ebony as her cheeks flushed.

"You and your partner aren't employing coercive interrogation tactics in our home, are you?"

"Sir, if I may, I didn't know Jessie was...." Zander replied, sounding overly apologetic.

Hal raised his hand, cutting him off. "Relax, Detective Pulaski. This isn't about the serial rapist again, is it? Detective Jones, I thought I'd clarified that you need more evidence in order to proceed."

The scene unfolding in her living room only intensified the conflict, tearing at Jessie. Was helping apprehend an alleged serial killer more important than protecting her client's rights? By withholding Lissie's hideaway, was she responsible for any future disappearances?

There were no immediate answers to her quandaries, but it was best to present the latest evidence to Hal. He was the DA. It would be his call whether Ebony and Zander had compiled sufficient proof for a formal investigation. If so, then the next move would be hers.

"Honey," she said, resting a hand on Hal's clenched fists. "Here, you'd better read this folder."

Hal's jaw was tight but relaxed as he tore back the dusty sheet from a chair and sat down to study the contents. His face remained stoic, but a corner of his mouth twitched slightly. Only Jessie would notice the nervous tic predicting the brewing storm of his anger and outrage.

"These are besides to the three women I mentioned to you the other day," Ebony said, her voice cracking. "This situation is more complicated than we'd suspected. There may be other girls as well. We can't stand around doing nothing and wait until there's an even dozen."

When Hal finished, he glanced up at Ebony. "Are you still pestering Jessie about revealing Ms. Sexton's location?"

"They claim they're at a standstill and it's all my fault," Jessie said. "I've offered to speak with Jeremy, but apparently I'm not acting quickly enough." She hoped he recognized her ethical dilemma, but she needed to drive the point home again, if not for his sake, then for Ebony and Zander. "I've been down this road before, and I'll do everything I can to help, but I can't afford to jeopardize my license again. It's unreasonable to ask me to violate a client's confidence, so I'm drawing the line how far I'll go."

He'd heard her. His eyes sharpened and his Adam's apple pulsated slightly. He smacked the papers on his knee with a crack, making Zander jump. "Detective Jones, forward this information to my office first thing in the morning. While I agree that finding the perpetrator is a priority, you of all people should know that pressuring Jess will not improve your situation. The issue's not with her, it's with Kaplan." With the snap of his wrist, he pitched the file at her.

"Kaplan can be an asshole, and once he makes up his mind, he's unyielding. So, let Jess do what she's going to do. She understands the legal ramifications if we're forced to compel Kaplan's compliance. However, you should provide him with the same intel you're giving me." Hal paused, shifting his eyes between the two detectives. "If these cases are in front of him, he can't ignore them. He knows the game."

"Ebony, have we settled this crisis for the evening?" Jessie asked, buoyed by Hal's support. "Good. Then, kindly get the hell out of our house."

Zander tittered at the command, and he and Ebony started for the door. She stopped with her hand on the doorknob. "Wait a minute. What's your plan?"

"Honestly, I have no idea." One corner of Hal's mouth curled. "But, I'll think of something."

Chapter Thirty-Three

To welcome the fresh air into the stuffy library, Jessie cranked open one of the basement windows. Gayle entered, and catching Jessie pressing her nose against the window screen, she chuckled.

"We need to talk," Jessie said, withdrawing from the window, and swallowing the guilt lodged in the back of her throat like a fishbone. Then she explained the new discoveries and Lissie's importance to finding the missing women.

"You're telling me that the district attorney could prosecute you, Jerry, and Lissie for obstructing governmental administration if you don't cooperate with their investigation?"

"In a nutshell, yes." Jessie slid her legal research and Ebony's file across the table to Gayle. "Look, here it is, N.Y. Penal Code Article 195. The city and county could serve us with a Habeas Corpus petition to produce Lissie Sexton, and if we disobey, it's punishable as criminal contempt."

"They'd prosecute an ailing man like Jerry, and send him off to jail?" Gayle scoffed. "That's absurd."

"Detectives Jones and Pulaski are convinced that Lissie is crucial to their case and they won't let it drop. Their evidence suggests that the man who attacked Lissie may be a serial killer, and honestly, I agree with them." Jessie paused, waiting for a response, but Gayle remained silent. "Once you and Jeremy review the dossier, you'll understand why Jeremy's cooperation is imperative."

Jessie dealt out the photographs, rap sheets, and missing persons reports and summarized each woman's details, including the five new victims.

Jacqueline Randall had been missing for six months. Her mother had filed a missing persons report and had applied to the Dutchess County Family Court for the guardianship of Jacqueline's three pre-school children. Angela Gibbons' father was a minister in Hudson and he'd filed a report eighteen months ago, and Justine Harp was the same story—a college dropout missing for over a year with no police follow-up. Six months ago, the family of drifter Camila Cordoba had filed their report in Beacon, and finally, Sharone Standly, an addict and former police informant, had been missing the longest, almost two years.

"So, nine women have disappeared, including Rebecca Douglas? That's horrible," Gayle whispered, as though fighting tears.

"And the only person who can identify the prime suspect is Lissie. Gayle, I'm being pressured by the police and I need your help with Jeremy. He'll listen to you." Jessie poured her heart into her plea, praying it would do the trick.

* * *

"You recognize there's an attorney-client privilege protecting Lissie, right Jessie?" Jeremy's voice boomed like a cannon firing into Jessie's chest. Her head snapped around to discover Jeremy glaring at her from the doorway. His features hardened. "You must respect that rule. Otherwise, you'll be a lousy lawyer and no one will trust you. Not to mention you're being disbarred."

She smarted at his threats, but remained calm. She'd found a way to wiggle out from the friction between Ebony and Jeremy. "But there's an exception under the Ethics Rule 1.6 b, allowing a disclosure to prevent reasonably certain death or substantial bodily harm."

"I disagree that revealing Lissie's whereabouts meets the criteria."

"You wouldn't disagree if you read the files," Jessie said, jabbing at the photos. "Do you want to be responsible for a higher body count?"

"Why should I take the blame? It's the DA, Detective Jones, and her brothers-in-blue who've fallen down on the job. Give me one good reason why I should cover their asses?" Jeremy's cheeks reddened, and the indigo veins on his temples bulged.

"Honey, relax. You can't get so worked up." Gayle approached her husband and guided him to a chair at the table. She kissed the crown of his head and smoothed his downy hair. "I'm not taking sides, but you might want to review these cases. They're compelling. There are nine girls identical to Lissie, who weren't lucky enough to escape. Think about them and their families, and his future victims. You've got to do what's right for our community. It's bigger than just one person, especially if there's a killer stalking young women."

"I understand that. I may be ill, but I'm not addled. My answer remains no. Let them come after me. They've failed before and it won't stick this time either." His fingers mussed up his hair. "Lissie stays in hiding, and that's my final word."

"You're right, Jerry. You're not addled, you're goddamn stubborn," Gayle replied.

"Despite your low opinion of me, this is still my office, and I trust you follow my mandates."

This may be your office, Jessie thought, but there's more than one way to skin a lawyer.

Chapter Thirty-Four

Whores consumed Hal's thoughts.

He postured beside the video monitor in the Dutchess County Executive's conference room, prepared to make his case not to a jury, but to the politicos in attendance. Exhibiting various degrees of exhaustion, County Executive Dan Ketchum, Police Chief Matt Shepardson, Mayor Jason Meriden, Sheriff Skip Stone, and State Senator Lauren Hollenbeck flanked Ketchum at the oak table, chatting, and nibbling donuts, crullers, and bagels. He'd called this meeting to announce the establishment of the Missing Women's Task Force. Their support would be a political coup, a feather in his re-election cap, but he intended to proceed with or without them.

Although Dan Ketchum occupied the head of the table, Hal commanded the room. The silver flecks in Ketchum's temples foreshadowed middle age, but the man was a seasoned politician, joining the county legislature upon his college graduation. Hal viewed Ketchum as a friend, as well as his boss, and there was no reason to believe the present crisis would impact their relationship. Except they were dealing with a serial killer left unchecked by Hal's negligence.

Of the attendees, Hal was the least familiar with Mayor Meriden. The mayor was a crude, spoiled slacker, whose family's wealth had bought him the election, and who'd practically bankrupted Poughkeepsie with his incompetence.

In contrast, Chief Shepardson and Sheriff Stone had earned his respect, and were a study in opposites. Dressed in a dapper grey suit, Skip Stone, a

Quantico graduate, was the silent but deadly type. Hal never quite knew what the sheriff was thinking until he barked curt commands. Conversely, Shepardson was a man of the street. The chief's pressed blue uniform, decorated with medals, boasted his faithful public service for over three decades. The saddlebags beneath the chief's eyes, and the paunch straining his shirt buttons, were evidence of his tenure. Hal guessed both men were flirting with sixty-five, and that the retirement window was about to open for the chief. He'd be sad to see him go. Tall and robust, Stone pledged to serve until he lost an election or died, neither of which appeared to be imminent.

Last, there was Lauren. Clever, conniving, and contrary. His recent discovery of her Machiavellian maneuvers made him mindful of the venom of her rattlesnake fangs.

He observed the group's exchange of pleasantries, but it didn't fool him. Each was a political animal to the core, and with the November elections creeping up, Hal planned to emphasize the buzzwords necessary to make their ears ring. Despite the tragedy, he'd play up the positive spin to the story. The opportunity. He'd found the g-spot and planned to go all the way.

His laptop was ready and waiting. Hal clicked on the title slide of his PowerPoint, "A Murderer in our Midst: The Mystery of Nine Disappearances in Dutchess County." Collectively, the audience's jaws slackened. They'd taken his bait.

"Isn't the title a bit dramatic?" Lauren asked, arching her brows. Dressed in a curve-hugging camel pantsuit and a sheer chartreuse silk blouse, her attire, hair, and makeup were flawless. She swiveled toward Hal, rewarding him with a glimpse of the lacy bra beneath her gauzy blouse.

Hal clicked to the next slide, a photomontage of the victims. Their solemn faces faded from the screen as he eulogized them, walking the tightrope between compassion and melodrama.

"These women are mothers, daughters, sisters, aunts, friends, and neighbors. They shouldn't be judged by their life choices, their human failings, and addictions. They're flesh and blood like you and me. The simple fact is they are crime victims who cannot speak for themselves. Whether the outcome is positive or negative, these women and their families are entitled to closure."

Click. A close-up on Kiara, Rebecca, and Eve.

Hal was in the groove, so he continued.

"As public servants, we have a responsibility to their families and the community to expend every available resource to locate their loved ones, discover who's responsible for these heinous crimes, and render justice. That's our job, but we can't accomplish this goal alone. We must enlist state and federal agencies to deploy their expertise in our battle against an unknown enemy."

The group smiled and nodded along as he spoke.

Click. A close-up on Vanessa, Justine, and Sharone.

"Our citizens are deeply concerned about crime in their neighborhoods. They look to us to keep the peace. By our words and actions, we must assure them that their streets are safe and that their loved ones won't be snatched away and abandoned by the authorities designated to protect and serve them."

Shepardson coughed nervously and fidgeted in his seat. Stone frowned.

Click. A close-up on Jacqueline, Angela, and Camila.

"I guarantee that when this administration resolves this mystery, the return on our investment will reap benefits. Our neighbors will remember your success when they enter the polling booth in November and pull the lever."

Lauren offered an approving gaze, while the mayor fiddled with his wedding ring, avoiding eye contact.

Hal moved on to the next slide entitled: "The Dutchess County Task Force-OPERATION JUST CAUSE," which contained a mission statement and elaborated the roles of the local, county, state, and federal agencies to be involved in the task force. As he finished, he aimed his laser pointer at the bullet points of the slide.

"In conclusion, I propose the creation of a task force designed to investigate these disappearances, create a plan for identifying all leads, and find these girls and bring them home. This regional plan of action will involve all police departments within the valley, as well as the State police and the FBI. We can enlist their Bureau of Crime Investigation forensic crime labs, investigators, marine, canines, and aviation units. We want the public to know that we take this investigation seriously and we're being as comprehensive and transparent."

As with most juries, this group needed one final hard kick in the gut. The finale appeared on screen—a bulletin board plastered with the nine women's missing persons posters juxtaposed against images of their family photos.

Hal dropped his hands limply to his sides and bowed his head in a moment of silence, letting the images simmer. Slowly, he raised his chin. As was his custom during his jury summations, his eyes lit upon each member of the jury. Here, calling Meriden, Stone, Shepardson, Ketchum, and Hollenbeck to action.

A stunned silence exploded in the conference room. But their shocked expressions were riddled with the guilt of gross negligence in failing their oaths of office. They'd received Hal's message loud and clear. They'd lost the war against crime and shared the responsibility for the disappearances.

As if awakening from a nightmare, the politicos took aim at him. They bombarded him with questions faster than he could respond, but Jones, Pulaski, and Jessie had ensured he'd come armed.

"We didn't even know this problem existed. Hal, how was this discovered?" County Executive Ketchum asked.

"Do we have any suspects?" Sheriff Stone asked.

"Let's cut to the chase. You believe that this is the work of one person, this John Doe? Are you saying that we've got a serial killer in Poughkeepsie?" the naïve mayor asked. So far, his platform of tough criminal reforms had delivered nothing but a rise in gun violence and gang warfare.

Lauren remained suspiciously quiet.

"About a week ago, two detectives in my department brought several disappearances to my attention. However, we didn't know that the abductions were so widespread," Chief Shepardson said, unable to hide his distress.

"The other day, City Detectives Jones and Pulaski contacted me. They've been quite insistent about a connection between the Taylor, Douglas, and Sexton incidents here in the city, so I requested more evidence." Hal detailed the valley-wide search conducted by Jones and Pulaski. "Their discovery of the similar cold cases occurring over the past two years suggests a potential multiple murder situation. Without the commitment of resources, the predator could strike again soon."

Chief Shepardson furrowed his bushy brows, reflecting his colleagues' shared concerns. "Yes, my detectives have done an outstanding job. However, let's not jump the gun. We should first consider this as a search-and-rescue mission. It's possible that the perp is holding these women against their will. But I agree with Samuels. Until we get the task force up and running, we don't know what we are dealing with."

"The mission of OPERATION JUST CAUSE will be to examine all possibilities and leave no stone unturned," Hal said. "I'll need recommendations for the composition of the force, the loan of your field experts, and those from the other agencies."

"There's neither precedent for impanelling a criminal task force nor provision in our budget for this investigation. Where are we going to get the funding?" Mayor Meriden asked, dabbing the sweat from his brow with his handkerchief. "And once the media gets a hold of this, there'll be a firestorm from the community demanding answers."

"Maybe, if we had more cops and cars on the street, we wouldn't be having this conversation," Shepardson sniped, taking a shot at the mayor's recent defunding of the police department.

"Perhaps, if you didn't have so many cops abusing their disability leaves or on disciplinary suspensions..." the mayor retorted, narrowing his beady eyes.

"The way you run this city, it's no wonder there's a deficit and that the press has mocked us as the murder capital of New York." Shepardson leaned across the table accusingly, jabbing his finger at Meriden.

The mayor slammed his hand on the table, and his pudgy face turned beet red. "I've had enough of this." He rose to leave.

"That's your problem, Meriden. As soon as things get tough, you walk out," Shepardson yelled.

Lauren gave a slightly condescending shake of her head as she slipped off her pumps and wiggled her manicured toes on the carpet. Both Ketchum and Stone pressed back in their chairs out of the line of fire.

"Please, gentleman, enough. Let's put our personal grievances aside and concentrate on business," Hal said in a conciliatory tone. "Mayor, sit down. Please."

"Matt, Jason, let's not point fingers. That's unproductive. We must work together," Lauren said. Her brusqueness masked the panic, which appeared to be simmering beneath her polished veneer. The crime spree had begun during her watch as DA and, although Hal had supervised the felony prosecutions, she'd been in charge. Once the voters recognized this, her re-election campaign would be finished.

"Yes, of course," Ketchum said. "We'll bring public and community relations on board, and my communications staff will manage the flow and content of information released to the media." His reassurances seemed to diffuse the friction as the mayor and chief returned to their seats. "I'll request that Governor Assento mobilize the State police and I'll leave the feds to you, Hal and Skip." Ketchum swiveled his chair toward the scowling mayor. "Jason, I'm sure we can scrape up some funding. I'll get the Finance Commissioner working on it, and Chief, great job. We certainly owe your detectives a debt of gratitude."

"Or maybe not," Lauren said. The corners of her lips curled into a smirk. "Hal, you've got an awful lot on your plate. Are you sure you're equipped to manage this investigation?"

Hal ignored the barb and addressed Shepardson. "I'll wait for your recommendations, but I'd like Jones and Pulaski as point persons from your department. We wouldn't be here without their initiative." The chief nodded as Hal set his sights on Lauren. "I'll let you know what support we need from Albany. I'm sure you can handle that."

Ketchum rose and answered his cellphone, signaling the end of the session.

The others followed suit by gathering their possessions and walking toward the door.

The outcome of the meeting should have pleased him. However, Hal doubted whether the politicians had grasped the urgency and the gravity of the situation. Their petty comments had showed the priority of self-interest over the lives of the missing women.

There was no denying that whores surrounded him. Not just the women depicted on the flat-screen, but the political whores who'd attended his meeting. He replayed his own conciliatory words and wondered whether he was one as well.

Chapter Thirty-Five

The pendulum of Chief Shepardson's antique wall clock swung back and forth, drawing Ebony in, making her drowsy. She should've been concentrating on the chief's reprimand, but her mind drifted to Jessie, eager to hear about her meeting with Jeremy. If Jessie had bungled the job, she and Zander were screwed. They'd have to hatch another plan to find Lissie, but after interviewing Hendricks and Lissie's parents, she was running out of ideas.

At the sound of the chime, her attention shifted to the chief. He'd stopped lecturing, and the room fell quiet, except for the ticking clock.

"Detective Jones, am I boring you?" Shepardson's baritone voice reverberated through the office like an echo in a canyon. "Do you have somewhere more important to be?"

Her cheeks warmed at being caught daydreaming.

"As I was saying, Detective Jones, there are mandatory procedures to follow. Particularly, obtaining permission from your commanding officer to contact other municipalities. You know that. Our sister towns are asking why we need their assault records for the past two years. What was I supposed to tell them? Until my meeting this morning with the DA, I didn't know about the scope of your investigation."

He rose and walked around to the front of the desk. "I'm the goddamn chief around here and should be kept abreast of every move you make." The skin beneath his collar reddened, and he snorted deep breaths through his broad nostrils. "Jones, I smell your handiwork all over this, and I guarantee Pulaski didn't know about your stunt. You're a part of a team and should coordinate with your partner, not run around rogue. You're impacting his performance as well as your own. If I had any sense, I'd write you up on disciplinary charges." Shepardson paused. A worried expression flickered across his face, then vanished. "I understand you believe there's an imminent threat of a killer out there, but you need to abide by the rules, Detective. Remember that you'd be totally ineffective if you were on suspension."

Ebony had been reprimanded before, but her keen instincts had never failed her. This time, perhaps, she'd been too impetuous. She couldn't help it; she was hard-wired that way. While she hadn't meant to implicate Zander in her scheme, honestly, she hadn't considered him at all. Her impulsivity may make her a lousy partner, but it made her a good cop. And again, she'd been right on the mark.

"Sir, for the record, Jones discussed the emails with me before she sent them. We debated getting your permission, but it was after midnight and, considering the stakes, we wanted to speed up the process. Also, we've identified a potential witness and we're bringing them in for questioning."

"Pulaski, there are no excuses. You're damn lucky the DA requested you both on the task force, because if it were up to me, you'd be enjoying an extended vacation. You've been forewarned and I trust this won't happen again." He glowered at them. "It had better not because if it does, DA or not, you'll be surrendering your shields and guns."

A slight nod of the head thanked Zander for having her back. She wondered if the tables were turned, would she have done the same?

Chapter Thirty-Six

J essie resented being commanded not to do something. So, from the instant Jeremy had roared "No," her path had been set. She was going to find Lissie.

Her decision was unrelated to any sense of duty owed to Hal, Ebony, or Jeremy. She was driven by her conscience. Her conscience, and ingenuity, would lead her to Lissie.

To achieve her goal, Jessie needed to wait for the right opportunity. Being alone in the office was essential.

The workday was ending, and Jessie sat in the library watching the minutes tick by on the clock. She'd observed that Mo departed at exactly five o'clock, and at five minutes before the hour, Mo popped in. Her handbag hung from her shoulder as she jingled her car keys as though calling a dog for a car ride. "Ready?" Mo asked.

"I've got about another fifteen minutes, so would it be all right if I finished up?" Jessie replied, pretending to be deep in research in the treatises strewn around the table. "I'm on a roll."

"Sure. The door will lock behind you. Don't worry about the alarm. Jeremy always comes down to arm it before he goes to bed."

"Cool. See you tomorrow." Jessie's eyes returned to the page, hoping that Mo couldn't hear the pounding of her heart.

She listened for the click of the door's lock, and upon hearing it, she raced to the wall of dingy metal cabinets behind Mo's desk. The secretary's meticulous filing made easy work of locating Lissie's folder in the cabinet marked with the letter *S*. Jessie extracted the thick file, and thumbed through the stack of criminal complaints, court documents and RAP sheets, not once but twice, searching for a note, or an email, or any clue to Lissie's current location. There was none.

Damn, she thought. Jeremy had covered his tracks. She was about to shut the file when a yellow sticky note fluttered to the floor. Jessie retrieved it and examined it. The note could have fallen off Mo's desk or out of any file, but the notations caught Jessie's eye.

On the front, he'd written the initials *E.S.* inside a scratchy oval, almost like a headline. Below it, someone had scribbled *Hasbrouck* along with the doodle of a man wielding a stick. *E.S.* Elisabeth Sexton. It had to be Lissie. If so, what did *Hasbrouck* and the screwy stick figure mean?

The name sounded familiar, but it wasn't a place anywhere in the Hudson Valley. However, she believed there was a Hasbrouck, N.Y. on the southern edge of the Catskill Mountains near Monticello, about two hours away. The hamlet could be a safe haven, but she doubted whether Jeremy would stash Lissie so far away from him.

Hasbrouck was also a prominent family of early local settlers she'd learned about in Terrence's history class. They'd been French colonists, but she couldn't recall exactly where they'd settled in the area. Somewhere across the river, she thought. And Jeremy's doodle could be another clue to Lissie's whereabouts, but what did it mean?

She flipped the note over and discovered last Monday's date. The day she'd met Lissie at Jeremy's home. The day they'd been floundering in the pool. The day Lissie had gone into hiding.

"Hasbrouck, Hudson Valley," Jessie whispered, typing the names into her phone's web browser. A page appeared, dedicated to the stone houses constructed in the 1670s. "The Huguenot Street Historic District. This has to be it. Lissie's got to be in New Paltz."

Jessie captured a photo of the note and webpage on her phone, reinserted the note in the file, and returned it to the cabinet. Shutting off the office lights, she closed the door behind her with a lighter heart.

Tomorrow she'd drive the ten miles to New Paltz to search for Lissie. The excursion might cost her job or her law license, but she couldn't bear the loss of another life. This was a gamble she was willing to take.

* * *

The next morning, an apparition floated through the sun-dappled shadows along Huguenot Street in New Paltz, N.Y. Its ghostly gown billowed in the breeze. From Jessie's vantage point near the graveyard on North Front Street, the vision appeared headless. She squinted, then rubbed her eyes and chuckled at her silliness. She watched a woman dressed in a floral colonial costume enter one of the ancient stone houses down the street.

Jessie followed the bluestone sidewalk toward Fort DuBois. She entered the cheery yellow and fieldstone visitor's center and museum shop for the Huguenot Historic District and was surprised to hear Miles Davis tooting over the sound system. Shelves displaying Tattersall placemats, vintage patchwork quilts, beeswax candles, tee-shirts, mugs, and souvenir books about the Hudson Valley and the Huguenots lined the walls.

Behind the counter, a young woman smiled at her and reached for her tablet. The girl's red cardigan sweater, denim mini-skirt, and tall leather boots felt as anachronistic and unsettling as the jazz. The girl, whose nametag said *Yazmine*, brushed her long ash blond ringlets back over her shoulders and reduced the music's volume. She pointed toward the ceiling. "Ghosts," she said, with a visible shiver. "Sometimes I hear them walking around upstairs. It freaks me out, so I crank up the music so I won't hear them." She shrugged. "Would you like to take a guided tour? The next one's in fifteen minutes."

Jessie declined, stroking her own curls and regretting she'd cut hers to chin length. "But I have a few questions." She unfolded the map inside the visitor's guide that she'd taken from the counter. Two of the gabled stone houses bore the names Jean Hasbrouck and Abraham Hasbrouck, the latter being one of the original settlers. "I noticed they'd named these houses after the Hasbrouck family. Do any of their descendants live locally?"

"Maybe they're the ones banging around upstairs," Yazmine said with a giggle.

"There are tons of them in the area." A tall, silver-haired man doffed his black baseball cap with "Historic Huguenot Street" embroidered on the crown as he entered. The cowbell attached to the doorknob clanged as he pushed it closed behind him. "I can name twenty off the top of my head. Magdalen, Simon, Catherine, Andries, Benjamin? Can you be more specific?"

"I'm working on my Master's thesis," Jessie said. "Religious freedom and the Early Dutch and French Settlers of the Hudson Valley. So, I thought it would be helpful to speak with descendants of the original Huguenot families." Another easy lie slid off her tongue. "Can you assist me?"

"There's plenty of information at the Schoonmaker Library down the street, but you'll need an appointment to view the family archives." The man hesitated and scratched his head, thinking for a moment. "Go talk to old Abe Delamater. His mother was a Hasbrouck, and he's head of the family clan and maintains their website. He lives out in Gardiner on Bevier Road. You'll see his name on a purple mailbox with a coat of arms. You can't miss it."

Jessie's heart leaped at the thought of meeting the Hasbrouck patriarch. Abe Delameter could be her lead to Lissie, but he could also be a red herring designed by Jeremy to throw her off the scent. Jeremy was cunning, and knowing her persistence, he could've planted the note as a subterfuge.

She'd visit Mr. Delameter and see. She'd figure out what to do next if he was, in fact, a ruse.

Jessie thanked him and tucked the map into her pocket. The cowbell clanged as she shut the door.

* * *

At a remote intersection of cow pastures and cornfields, Jessie checked her car's navigation system. She was about five miles south of New Paltz, and she vaguely recognized the countryside from her pre-Lily days with Kyle. They'd spent a few lazy afternoons relaxing on the deck of the nearby Tuthilltown Spirits Distillery, enjoying oaky whisky and listening to the

Wallkill River rush by.

She followed the highway across the bridge, comparing her own life to the river's flow, swift and steady. She'd weathered obstacles—near death, loss, and betrayal—which were like the boulders protruding through the turbulent current. Those hurdles may have slowed her down, but they'd never beaten her.

What perils had Lissie encountered along her path? She seemed to have a caring family, and she had a son. So what had compelled her to abandon them and sell her body on the streets? And how could Jessie save her?

Ahead was the sign for Bevier Road, and she turned right to begin her quest for the purple mailbox. The road was a long and winding route hugging the banks of the Wallkill. Cottages and trailers dotted the riverbank, while across the street, vast livestock and crop fields separated the houses. She drove slowly along the roadway, eyes peeled for her prize.

After a mile or so, she spied an unusual mailbox, not quite as described to her. The mailbox was white, but beneath it hung a plaque painted with an ornate coat of arms. It displayed a purple shield with three gold torches separated by a gold chevron, and topped by a knight's silver helmet. Above the helmet, a Moor brandished an arrow overhead. Neither Hasbrouck nor Delamater appeared on the plaque or the mailbox, but recalling the squiggles on the yellow note, Jessie believed she'd found the right place.

She turned into the driveway and ascended a steep hill past a mare grazing in a field next to a white farmhouse trimmed in purple. Behind the house loomed a weathered red barn and a pair of half-full grain elevators. No people were in sight, but that didn't mean they weren't home or busy in the barn or the fields.

This isolated farm seemed to be the perfect spot for Jeremy to stash Lissie, but his connection to this place wasn't immediately apparent to her. Maybe the occupants could help solve the mystery, or better still, tell her where to find Lissie.

Jessie parked her Jeep and sprinted up the front steps of the farmhouse. She punched the doorbell and stared at the glossy purple door, willing it to open. But no one answered. She rang again. Still no reply. Impatiently, she rushed toward the barnyard behind the house. The yard was empty, except for a rusted tractor and a dusty Prius.

Dogs barked in response to the sound of stones crunching beneath her boots and within seconds, two German Shepherds darted through an opening in the barn doors, toward her.

She froze. The dogs bared their pointy teeth and snarled, halting a yard away from her. Her heart pounded as the canines inched closer, so close that she saw her reflection in the pupils of their golden eyes. The larger dog lunged, and Jessie staggered backward, catching her heel on a buried root and falling hard on her backside. Digging her heels into the dirt, she tried to push away from the shepherd nipping at her ankles. The dog growled low and lunged at her, sinking his teeth into her pant leg.

"Help," Jessie screamed as an acute pain seared her skin and a warm wetness spread across her ankle. "Help!"

The smaller dog continued to snarl, while the teeth of the other clamped tighter on her pants, not letting go. She futilely willed herself to relax and abate the scent of her fear.

"Help!"

"Remy, Bernard. Come here!" barked a voice from inside the barn.

At the sound of their master's voice, the large Shepherd released his grip, dropped his black nose to her boots, sniffed, and trotted back to the barn, followed by his companion. A ruddy-faced man who looked to be in his early seventies exited the barn flanked by the canine duo. She'd bet he'd been a bear of a man in his day, but age had weathered his broad frame, leaving him hunched and haggard. He wiped his forehead with his handkerchief and stuffed it into the pocket of his overalls.

"Don't worry about these two. They're afraid of their own shadow," the man said loudly, feeding them treats. "Aren't you, my boys?" He scratched behind their soft ears and their long pink tongues licked his gnarly hands.

Tentatively, Jessie rose and dusted the dirt from her clothing. She lifted her torn pant leg and examined a small, bloody gash on her ankle. The bite appeared superficial, but her ankle was swelling.

"Are you all right, Miss?" The farmer snapped his fingers for the dogs to sit and he approached her. Upon seeing her leg, he turned back to his pets. "Bad dogs. Remy. Bernard. Bad, bad dogs."

The Shepherds lowered their heads to the ground and whimpered.

"Mr. Delamater?" Jessie asked, unable to avert her eyes from the Shepherds. "Jeremy sent me."

Chapter Thirty-Seven

H al carefully studied the legal pad on his scarred wooden desk. The yellow sheet contained his "Dream Team" for the first task force in Dutchess County history: FBI, New York State Police, Dutchess Sheriff's Office, local police forces, Governor Gloria Assento, County Executive Dan Ketchum, Poughkeepsie Mayor Jason Meriden, Sheriff Skip Stone, Chief Matt Shephardson, and Detectives Jones and Pulaski. With so many moving parts, people and agencies, he'd be lucky to pull it off, but with the help of his assistant, Cindie, they'd get it done. If anyone could wrangle cats, it was Cindie.

So far, everyone was on board. Even the Feds. All he needed was confirmation from the Director of the FBI's Manhattan Violent Crimes Unit when they'd be arriving. By this time tomorrow, they would encamp the task force in the Grand Jury annex.

"Lauren Hollenbeck," he said. The name left a bitter taste on this tongue. Her odd behavior at the steering committee meeting had convinced him of her intention to seek re-election as DA. Her blaming him for the current crime wave, and her snide personal digs, had been designed to erode Ketchum's confidence in him. What a bitch. He had enough to worry about, and now Lauren had turned on him.

The committee, particularly Ketchum and Stone, had insisted that the task force's operation remain as secret as grand jury deliberations. Hal agreed, but in a world demanding transparency, it was going to be tricky. Moles and the media were everywhere, even where he least expected them.

"What do we know about John Doe?" he asked a pigeon pecking at a crumb on his windowsill. "Nothing, except he's a sex maniac who circulates among unsuspecting victims and who'll strike again unless stopped." These thoughts drained the blood from his body.

Seized by a sudden urge to hear Jessie's voice and confirm her safety, Hal snatched his cellphone from the desk. Her line rang and went directly to voicemail.

"Hi. It's me. Just wanted to check in. I'll talk to you later. Love you." As soon as he hung up, the private line on the phone console lit up. "Hey, Jess. I just tried calling you."

After a long silence, another woman's concerned voice answered. "Hal, this is Ebony. You can't get in touch with her either?"

"What do you mean?"

"I've left her a half-dozen messages, and she hasn't returned my calls. When did you last hear from her?" Ebony asked.

"I haven't all morning. Why, is there a problem?"

"Let's hope not."

Chapter Thirty-Eight

When Jeremy's name failed to register with Mr. Delameter, Jessie suspected Jeremy had duped her. She was ready to leave, but the slight flicking of his dull eyes toward the barn door changed her mind. His weather-beaten face remained expressionless, so she couldn't discern whether he was hiding something or testing her. Or whether he intended to sic the dogs on her again.

He reached into the kangaroo pocket on his faded overalls and cocked his head from side to side as he inserted the hearing aides he'd stored there. "Come again?"

"Jeremy Kaplan," she repeated.

"Who? What?" the bewildered man shouted over the high-pitched squeal emanating from his aides. He winced and adjusted the volume control on the earpieces. "Jeremy?"

"Abe, for cripe's sake, what's the racket?" another voice yelled.

A young woman, looking like she'd stepped from the pages of a farming magazine in her red plaid flannel shirt, jeans, and work boots, emerged carrying a pitchfork full of hay. The wide brim of a straw cowboy hat shaded her face, but Jessie recognized the acerbic tone.

Lissie's eyes met Jessie's, and she scowled. "What the hell are you doin' here?"

"Can we talk? Please?"

"I ain't got nothing to say to you." Lissie lowered the pitchfork and aimed its prongs at Jessie's heart. "How d'you find me, anyway?"

"Jeremy." She lied again. But was it truly a lie?

"Huh."

"I'm here because it's urgent. Please, Lissie, can we talk? I only need a few minutes." Jessie limped across the barnyard toward Lissie, dragging her lame leg across the gravel.

As Jessie edged closer, Lissie narrowed her eyes and pursed her lips, as if trying to predict Jessie's next move. Her hand trembled slightly as she tightened her grip on the wooden handle, keeping the metal tines pointed at Jessie's belly. Lissie would skewer her if provoked. But to challenge Lissie, Jessie needed to prove she wasn't afraid. She inched forward until the bladelike teeth grazed her jacket.

Time stood still as neither moved nor looked away. Then Jessie grabbed the prongs poking into her skin and slowly lowered them without resistance.

"Abe, what do you think? Should I talk to this bitch or should we boot her off the farm?"

"Hon, that's your call. I've told you I'm not interested in your business. It's healthier that way."

"You're no help, old man." Abe shrugged, turned, and led the dogs back into the barn, leaving Jessie alone in the yard with Lissie. "I guess I owe you two minutes, but that's all you got. Then, our score's settled. Understand?"

Jessie nodded. "First, I have to be honest with you. Jeremy didn't send me. But before you toss me out of here, let me explain. I've deceived him and probably will lose my job over this, but I needed to speak with you. I needed to do what was right." She launched into the tale of the disappearances before Lissie could interrupt her. "You're the only person who can identify Doc because you escaped from him. And if you don't help, he'll remain free and go unpunished for his crimes."

The pitchfork slid from Lissie's hands and hit the ground with a clang. Her hands flew to her throat and she massaged the faint bruises encircling her neck. "You think Doc's responsible for those girls? For Eve, Sharone, and my girl, Kiki? You think he killed them?" Lissie paused and dabbed her eyes with her shirt's hem. "So, the cops want to talk about Doc, and not Kurt? He's not dead, is he? 'Cos I didn't have nothing to do with that."

"No, Kurt's in jail for drug trafficking and possession of stolen property."

"I don't know." Lissie hesitated. "What if Doc and Kurt hunt me down?"

"With your help, they'll go to prison for a long time. I know this is a hard decision. If you want advice from Abe or Jeremy before you decide, go ahead. I'd at least like to tell the DA and Detectives Jones and Pulaski that you're thinking about helping us. I give you my word I won't tell anyone where you are, even if you decide to stay put." Jessie pulled out her phone. There was one service bar. "Take a few minutes while I try to call home to check on my daughter. You won't run, will you?"

Lissie smirked and disappeared into the barn.

It had probably been a tactical error to let Lissie out of her sight, but Jessie wanted to show Lissie she trusted her, had been truthful about Jeremy, and would keep her whereabouts a secret. She'd deal with the fallout from Hal, Ebony, and Jeremy later, but right now Jessie felt she'd acted with integrity.

The smell of fresh-cut hay and manure washed over Jessie as her cellphone's illusive service bar vanished as quickly as it had appeared. She shook the frustration from her shoulders and shoved the phone into her pocket as Lissie returned.

"I appreciate your being straight with me, but why should I help Jones? She acts like she's better than me 'cos she's got a badge and a gun. Big f-ing deal. I know tons of people who got guns and they don't act like a-holes." Lissie paused and thrust her hands into her overalls. "You're nice and all, and you did me a solid, but I'm not going back. I like it here with Abe. It's quiet. And nobody's gonna bother me." Lissie paused. "Sure, it sucks that Kiki got mixed up with Doc, but if she's dead, there ain't nothing I can do for her. You understand, right? And we still got a deal, right? You're not gonna snitch on me?"

For a moment, Jessie had believed she'd persuaded Lissie to return with her. But after all, Lissie was selfish, indignant, and disloyal to even her best friend, Kiki. She'd probably even betray Jeremy under the right circumstances.

"No, Lissie, I don't understand. How can you turn your back on Kiki? Don't you want Doc to pay for abusing you and for his crimes against those

210

girls? Has your life been so shitty that everyone is expendable unless you profit from him or her? No wonder your parents took your kid away. You don't deserve him." Her last accusation was a low blow, and maybe she'd gone too far, but Lissie's belligerence warranted it. "You know, I can't believe I saved your life. What a waste of energy. I thought you were a fighter, not someone who'd hide in the barn with the sheep."

Lissie narrowed her eyes and spit on the ground. "Mr. Jay don't need to know about your visit, you know."

"I can live with my decisions. Can you? Tell Abe and those mongrels I said goodbye, and Lissie, your secret's safe with me." Jessie called back as she hobbled toward her Jeep on her sore ankle.

Once inside her car, Jessie examined the teeth marks rising on her shin. Since the first time she'd saved Lissie, there'd been nothing but trouble. There'd been the storm, the pool, the police threats, the ethical dilemma, and a pack of dogs. Apparently, her reward for being a Good Samaritan was the blood-encrusted wound on her ankle.

From the baby bag stowed in the backseat, she retrieved an antiseptic wipe, cleaned her skin, and angrily slapped a bandage over the gash. "That'll do until I get home."

Jessie switched on the ignition, checked the dashboard camera, and made a wide U-turn in Abe's driveway. A sudden thump made her slam on the brakes. What now, she wondered, checking the camera again. There was nothing behind her. Figuring she'd backed over a twig, she shifted into drive and heard the sound again as Lissie's face pressed against the passenger window. Jessie's heart jumped.

"Man," Jessie said, lowering the window, "you scared me to death. What do you want?"

"Quit whining and let me in." Lissie tilted the cowboy hat back from her forehead, presumably as she'd seen in the movies. Her chipped teeth peeked out from her crooked grin. "You saved my life, so I'd be a real jerk to let you face the cops by yourself. Wouldn't I?"

Chapter Thirty-Nine

J essie drove her Jeep past the pastures, orchards, and hamlets dotting the route back to Poughkeepsie. Just past Modena, six yellow school buses pulled in front of her, sweeping her into the convoy discharging school children along the way. Tots and teens sluggishly disembarked in every driveway, apparently oblivious to the snake of traffic congesting the road. She cursed herself for taking this route, but it was the only two-lane highway between Gardiner and the Mid-Hudson Bridge, and usually the fastest route home.

Silently, she also cursed Lissie. In a bout of hyperactivity, her passenger fiddled with the car's radio. One second The Weeknd thrummed inside the car, then Billy Eilish, Pink, Drake, Ed Sheeran, and Adele. Then, like a bored teenager, Lissie explored the car's thermostat, navigation system, and seat, telephone, and audio settings.

Jessie felt her last nerve hanging on by a thread, so she reached over and snapped off the radio. At last, silence filled the car as they idled in the middle of an apple orchard. Nothing but acres of McIntosh, Yellow, and Red Delicious trees in white blossoms surrounded them, locking them in.

"Can't you pass them?" Lissie whined, jutting her chin toward the buses. Without the distraction of the music, her legs pumped as though competing in the Tour De France. She nibbled on her fingernails, smearing her bleeding cuticles on Jessie's leather upholstery.

"There's nothing we can do, nowhere we can go, so chill out. Will you? Besides, what's your hurry? I thought you weren't interested in going back."

Directly behind Jessie's Jeep, a silver pickup with dark-tinted windows revved its engine and inched closer to her bumper. Finally, it nudged her bumper, rocking her car forward. She glanced in the rearview mirror, but only a black windshield reflected at her. The pickup nudged her Jeep again, harder this time.

"Hey, what the f—" Lissie shouted, as the car jounced.

Jessie leaned on her horn in frustration, but to no avail. The pickup tapped her bumper a third time as the tiny hairs on the back of her neck prickled. She sensed danger. Whoever was driving the truck had trapped her and Lissie, and clearly wanted them to be aware of that fact.

Lissie rolled down the window and screamed, "What the hell, asshole."

"Put the window back up, please. I'm sure it's nothing," Jessie said, her eyes glancing toward the rearview mirror. The pickup remained on her tail. "I can't call 911 if I wanted to. I still don't have any cell service. So, sit tight. We're almost home."

Jessie's eyes flicked back to the snaillike line of traffic ahead and gave thanks for the safety in numbers.

"It's your car and you're driving." Lissie rolled up the window and flipped on the radio, settling on a country music station. While Rascal Flatts crooned of life being a highway, the traffic congestion and Jessie's racing pulse eased up. Ahead, the bus parade veered off at a fork in the road, and Jessie traveled straight toward home. "About freakin' time."

As they traveled eastward, Jessie remained on high alert. Something felt off-kilter about the truck on their tail. In the distance, police sirens triggered vibrations inside her belly. They grew louder with each rotation of the tire along the highway. In her side mirror, she spied the silver pickup skidding off onto a side street, disappearing into a cloud of dust. Still suspicious about the encounter, she sighed in relief as she sped homeward.

Around the next bend, traffic hit at a standstill again. Three New York State Police cars had formed a blockade, intercepting vehicles at the intersection with the main highway leading to the Mid-Hudson Bridge. At first, it appeared to be a routine checkpoint for license, insurance, and registration inspections. However, a short distance beyond the blockade, a familiar dark Explorer, with its grill lights flashing, waited in the parking lot of a strip mall. Detective Ebony Jones casually leaned against the unmarked car, her mirrored sunglasses sparkling in the sun. With her eyes obscured by her shades, Ebony's fury was undetectable, yet Jessie sensed it was there. Ebony spied Jessie and crooked her finger at her.

"What the f—? Did you tip them off?" Lissie's hand cocked the door handle, and she crouched, ready to spring into action.

"What are you talking about? We've been together every second."

"But you don't got anything to lose, do you?"

"Calm down. There's nothing to worry about." Jessie's grip tightened on the leather steering wheel, considering the ramifications of ignoring the police escort. Certainly, their evasion would spell trouble. They'd be apprehended before they'd reached the bridge, and she'd face prosecution for interfering with a criminal investigation and witness tampering. The repercussions would be severe, especially with Hal. He'd orchestrated the task force, after all.

Besides, there was no reason to run. They'd committed no crime. And where would they go? The closest border was hours away in Canada.

Kyle's smug expression flashed through her mind. Since there was no custodial agreement for Lily, these were delicate times. If she bolted, he'd manipulate her escapade to his advantage. Despite being an unreliable parent, Kyle was wily enough to employ every advantage to expand his parental rights. She wouldn't jeopardize her custody of Lily, not even to protect Lissie Sexton and catch a killer.

"I thought you said everything was cool."

"It is." Jessie swallowed the lump in her throat and drove into the lot. "I think."

* * *

Jessie and Lissie exited the Jeep and walked toward Ebony and Zander. Jessie grabbed Lissie's wrist, thwarting any escape attempt, and to assure her she wasn't alone. "Hey, Eb, what's going on?"

Ebony flipped her shades up onto her head, revealing the rage roiling in her eyes. "What the hell were you thinking?"

A sinking feeling, somewhere between fear and nausea, stabbed Jessie's chest. "What are you talking about?"

"I've been texting...Hal's been calling...no response from you. Killer on the loose...key witness... Can't disappear like that...Can't take matters into your own hands. Not your job...you've got a family...Lily." Ebony's rapid-fire rant was barely comprehendible.

"Yo. Hold on a second," Lissie said, shaking off Jessie's hand. "She didn't do nothing but try to help your sorry ass."

"I'll get to you in a minute," Ebony shouted, before returning her attention to Jessie. "Come on, you're an attorney and you should've known better than to jeopardize the entire case. All you had to do was reveal Lissie's location and let us retrieve her. You've been irresponsible in so many ways."

While Ebony berated Jessie, Zander crept up behind Lissie. In one swift movement, he wrenched her arms behind her back, slapped on silver handcuffs, and seized her by the scruff of her flannel shirt.

"Hey, let me go, you prick," Lissie hissed, twitching about and snapping her teeth at him. Her straw cowboy hat slid onto the blacktop, revealing the raw wound on her scalp. "Shyster, were you in on this? Was this a setup? I never shoulda trusted you."

"You've got no grounds to detain her. Release her immediately," Jessie said. "Lissie voluntarily agreed to meet with you, so we were on our way back home. We're all good, so let her go."

The two detectives responded with piercing, icy glares.

"I'm afraid we can't. She's threatened a law enforcement officer, and we must restrain her for our protection and yours." As though proving Zander's point, Lissie thrashed about like an angry cat struggling against the vet's grasp. "You have the right to remain silent—"

"This is bull, and you know it," Lissie cried as Zander dragged her toward the back door of the police car and guided her into the back seat. "You're crazy if you think that I'm gonna help you now. Lemme go, jerk face."

Rather than make an ill-fated rush at Zander, Jessie called out to Lissie. "Stay calm. I'm right behind you. And for god's sake, don't say anything."

"Why should I trust you?" Lissie yelled back.

The Explorer's passenger door slammed, and Zander backed away from the vehicle.

Jessie swung around to confront Ebony, her hands balled into fists and her muscles tensed, ready for a fight. Not only had Ebony's rebuke been soul-crushing, Lissie believed Jessie had doubled-crossed her.

"You'd better be prepared for Lissie's false arrest, civil rights, and police brutality suits. Without body-cam recordings, it's going to be your word against hers and mine. Are you prepared for the pushback?"

"Jessie, I'm warning you. You'd better back off, unless you'd like to keep her company in lockup." Ebony's hand rested on her shiny holster in an unnecessary show of force.

Jessie's throat felt tight, her words tangling up somewhere between her mouth and her brain. She searched Ebony's face for warmth or friendship, but there was only a pit bull gnashing her teeth.

"You'll see your client at the station." Ebony relaxed her hand and slipped behind the wheel of her car.

"That's not all that'll happen when I get there."

"You're right. Maybe she'll have fired your incompetent ass by then."

They both knew the bitter exchange contained empty threats. Yet, the underlying animosity felt real to Jessie. It was as though they'd returned to high school, when at the last minute, Jessie had opted to attend Syracuse University, rather than rooming with Ebony at Marist College. She'd had good reason for her decision, the offer of a full pre-law scholarship and an internship at a prestigious law firm. The opportunities were too good to pass up, especially since Terrence had pulled strings for her. She'd believed that Ebony had forgiven her, but apparently, the decade-old grudge had compounded with new ones.

Leaving Jessie with Zander, Ebony's car sped out of the parking lot and maneuvered northbound toward the Mid-Hudson Bridge. From the rear window, Lissie's terrified eyes trained on Jessie, shooting a chill up her spine.

"You, Martin, you're coming with me. Hand over your keys. I'm driving your car back to the station." Zander extended his upturned palm.

"Why am I under arrest? Have you trumped up some charges against me, too?"

"Shut up and get in the car." He snatched the keys from her.

Jessie's feet felt cemented into the ground as she considered how monumentally her plan had backfired. She hadn't meant to harm anyone. She'd only wanted to prove to Hal and Ebony that she belonged on the team and she could reel in the big fish. Ebony might be right. Her foolishness had injured Hal, Ebony, Jeremy, and especially Lissie.

She needed to inform Jeremy about Lissie's arrest on the bogus charges. It was all her fault. She'd beg for his forgiveness, but apologies wouldn't sway a guy like Jeremy. He didn't suffer idiots. Doubtless, she'd be searching for another job, and would be lucky if Jeremy didn't pursue a malpractice complaint against her.

There'd be no way that either he or Lissie would forgive her. Could she forgive Ebony for betraying her, or vice versa? And could she forgive herself for endangering Lissie?

A gust of wind kicked up, catching Lissie's straw hat and sending it tumbling on its brim across the parking lot and into the bridge traffic. A bright red tractor-trailer carrying wholesale fruits and vegetables zoomed by, mangling the hat beneath its massive sixteen wheels.

Seized by that image, a horrifying doubt crushed the air from Jessie's lungs. Had Hal conspired against her, too?

There was only one way for her to find out.

"Martin, what are you waiting for? Let's go."

Inside her car, Jessie checked her phone. There were multiple messages from Hal and Ebony, and one from an unknown caller.

Chapter Forty

It was Detective Ebony Jones, not Jessie's best friend Ebony, who greeted Jessie from within the Poughkeepsie Police Department reception booth. Contempt seethed from every pore of Ebony's tawny skin, and the severe fluorescent lighting accentuated the fine lines and creases around Ebony's hollow eyes and lips, and the dark roots of her blonde hair. They were the same age, thirty-two, and born two months apart, but it appeared Ebony had aged overnight.

Ebony swiped her card key and opened the glass door to admit Jessie and Zander into the station's beehive. Only a friend would notice Ebony's favoring her left leg and her biting down on the inside of her cheek.

The acidic smell of stale coffee hung in the recycled air, and it surprised Jessie to discover Gayle Kaplan waiting in a wooden chair outside the Interrogation Rooms. Gayle's shoulders slumped with the weight of worry, and she, too, wore the mantle of death.

Death. Jeremy. Her brain summoned the image. Oh, no.

"Gayle, is Jeremy all right?" Jessie asked eagerly.

"Yes." Gayle's tone was ripe with blame, making Jessie ashamed of her treachery and her meddling in their business.

"In here," Ebony said flatly, swinging open the door to Interrogation Room One.

Gayle's accusatory eyes followed her into the darkened room, where Lissie sat at the metal table with her head bowed and her hands clasped in front of her. It was impossible to see whether they'd cuffed or beaten or abused the girl, but a slender spotlight reflected off her bald patch.

Jessie rushed to Lissie's side and patted her shoulder in reassurance, but the girl shrugged her away. "I'm sorry about all this. I never should've interfered. As soon as I figure out what's going on, I'll get you out of here."

"It's all right, kid," a man's voice replied.

Jessie jumped at the sound of the raspy voice, which seemed to materialize out of thin air. The shadowy ghosts of Hal and Jeremy, an unlikely duo, stepped out of the black corners of the room. Hal flipped on the lights, and she blinked rapidly to adjust her eyes.

"I told them I didn't do nothing and I'm not talking. They can go screw themselves, and you can, too, shyster." Lissie rose and massaged her wrists. "I'm gettin' out of here."

"You're not going anywhere, Sexton. We need some answers from you," Zander said, and gently pressed her back into the chair. "Both of you."

"Hal? What's happening?" Jessie asked. "Jeremy, you can't let them treat her this way. They've got to release her. She didn't threaten anyone. Come on, will somebody please explain what the problem is?"

"Isn't the shoe on the other foot, Jess? You disappeared, telling no one where you were going or what you were doing, so why don't you explain?" Hal demanded.

"So you're not in on this?" Lissie asked, surprised.

Jessie could explain about stealing information from Lissie's file to hunt her down, but she'd look like an insubordinate, meddlesome fool. It was best to turn the tables and push Hal for answers. "We could go around in circles all day, so I'm going to ask again nicely. Please tell me what's happening."

The others were hesitating, afraid to speak as though they shared a secret. Since neither she nor Lissie were restrained, they weren't under arrest, but something was amiss. It seemed like Hal, Ebony, and Zander were stalling to keep them from walking out the door. But no one was letting on. Jessie needed leverage to force their hand. "If you don't, Lissie and I are leaving. And you can't stop us." She thought she observed a glint of admiration on Lissie's face.

"You can't." Ebony's voice remained flat, but edged with spite.

Jessie cocked her head to the side in question. "Are we being detained?"

No one replied.

"You're joking, right?" Jessie asked.

An uncomfortable silence settled over the room. All eyes fell on the district attorney.

"Well, then we're free to go. Come on, Lissie."

"No, wait," Hal said. "Your lives were in danger."

Chapter Forty-One

"Danger? What are you talking about?" Jessie's chest tightened. The crowded interrogation room felt fraught with tension, and all eyes fell upon her. Some accused, while shock gripped the others.

"We received a tip that Kurt's squad, the cartel he fronted, was coming after you and they were closing in fast." Hal's voice cracked, and he tried to cover it by clearing his throat. She knew he could compartmentalize his work life from their one at home by parking the murderers, rapists, and thieves outside the kitchen door. Yet, his tortured expression exposed his present struggle to keep it together.

"You mean those men in the silver pickup? They appeared out of the blue and started tailing us outside of Modena. They nudged my bumper a few times, but we thought they were just assholes in a hurry," Jessie said. "Why were they looking for us?"

"They weren't looking for *you*." He gestured toward Lissie, and she jumped up, clenching her fists.

"That sonofabitch. I thought he loved me. He told me so," Lissie burst in. "I slaved for him. Gave him all my money and did whatever he asked me to do. I knew Kurt was mixed up with some bad dudes, but he promised he'd protect me. Guess not."

"Lissie, sit down. Your yelling won't get us anywhere," Jessie said.

Lissie huffed, crossed her arms over her chest, and plopped down into the molded plastic chair like a spoiled child. "Wait 'til I get my hands on him. He'll really be sorry then."

"Jess," Hal said. "You never should have gone after Lissie. That was our job. Risking your life was a rookie move."

"Come on, that's harsh. And I was doing my job by bringing Lissie back to help find the missing women. That's it."

"Well, it was reckless." As though lit from within, Ebony's royal blue eyes glowed with a white-hot fury that Jessie had never seen before. "You were supposed to speak with Jeremy and put him in touch with us. You should have left the detecting to us, instead of running off half-cocked. If anything bad had happened, where would that have left us? You and Lissie could've been killed, and our investigations would've been blown—"

Jessie thought she heard Ebony mutter "again" under her breath, but it could have been her imagination. Ebony had mentioned her safety and the investigations in the same breath, but she wondered which meant more to Ebony. The way she'd been acting lately, Jessie had her suspicions.

Lissie turned to Jeremy, who'd patted her arm and squeezed it reassuringly. "See, Mr. Jay, I told you he'd come after me."

Jeremy cringed at the silent accusation that he'd contributed to the screwup and should have listened to Jessie when she'd asked for help. "Since the police had arrested Kurt, I believed you were in the clear. You never mentioned his drug or smuggling operations, so all of this has stunned me. By hiding you at Abe's I was only trying to protect you, and I never meant to put your lives in danger."

"I don't understand how they found us," Jessie said.

"No offense, Jess, but if you located Lissie, don't you think professional goons could, too?" Hal's voice caught and rung with strain.

"I got her here, didn't I?" She could have heeded Jeremy and let Lissie remain hidden, but she reasoned, if not for her meddling, the assassins would have hunted Lissie down at Abe's and slaughtered them like pigs. Not even Hal was going to convince Jessie she shouldn't have retrieved Lissie. Especially since she'd saved Lissie's life for the third time. It was becoming a habit, but there were serious unanswered questions. Was Lissie playing her, too? "Lissie, why were they looking for you? What haven't you told us?"

Lissie shrugged.

She was lying. Jessie's skin prickled at the sudden electricity charging through the air. Apparently, Hal, Ebony, and Zander already knew why Lissie was being hunted. Had it been the money she'd stolen from Kurt? But that made little sense. Lissie's haul was small potatoes compared to the crop of contraband seized from his apartment. What did Lissie know about Kurt's operation, which would make Kurt want her dead?

"What the hell's going on?"

Hal, Ebony, and Zander remained quiet, exchanging conspiratorial glances.

"So what do we do now?" Zander asked. His sights trained on Lissie, who leaned back in her chair, kicking the leg of the table. He rolled up the sleeves of his shirt as though preparing for a fight, while Ebony paced, muttering obscenities under her breath.

"*You*," Hal directed at Jessie, "are not doing anything else. It's our job to protect you and Lissie and the community, and we appreciate you bringing Lissie in, but you've done enough."

"Whoa, everything's fine, right? So where's the attitude coming from? Maybe you don't need Lissie's help either." She stood to leave, but he roughly grabbed her arm and pulled her close.

"You can't blame us for wanting to keep you alive. But you're right. This crisis is over, Jess. And now you have two choices. We can move on from this situation or let it fester. The choice is yours." He paused. "Well?"

"Now's neither the time nor place for this discussion." Jessie's voice grew defiant as she shrugged him away. His caustic remarks felt like the brutal strike of a match on a piece of flint, sparking a fire. She was tired of taking his crap and Ebony's, too. Tired of letting them exert the upper hand when she held the royal flush. She felt Jeremy and Lissie's eyes burning into her, waiting for her to take the lead. "You have your priorities and I have a client to protect, so I need to know if she's safe from Kurt's men?"

"Of course, she's safe. The state police intercepted the assassins in a silver and black pickup across the river, but unfortunately, Hendricks' cell's only one tentacle of the octopus."

"I think we need to take a breather," Jessie said. "This doesn't seem like a hospitable atmosphere, so I believe it's time for Lissie and me to leave. Come on, Lissie, Jeremy, let's go."

Chaos erupted as Hal, Ebony, and Zander raised their voices, shouting demands about what Lissie should do next. A cacophony of voices roared, "No Wait!" "We need her!" and "Stop being ridiculous!"

"Shut up, all of you. I ain't got nothing to say to nobody. But if I did, I'd say it to Martin. She's the only one with a clear head," Lissie shrieked.

"This is insane. We don't have time for this. Either you're going to cooperate or we're going to bust your butt on so many counts of conspiracy, drug pushing, and weapons possession that you'll never see your kid again," Zander said.

Ebony silenced Zander's rant by placing a hand on his shoulder. "Lissie, would you like a minute alone with Jessie?"

"Yes. So all of you get out now. Even you, Mr. Jay, no offense." Jeremy rose, and magically the room emptied. Jessie slid into the adjacent chair, and exhaustion hit her like the flu, zapping her energy.

"Martin, twice you've put your life on the line for me. Once in the pool, and then at Abe's farm," Lissie said, slouching in her chair. Apparently, the day had left them both bone-weary. "Look, I love Mr. Jay. He's been good to me, better than my bastard of a father, but no one's ever done that for me before. Not Mr. Jay. Not Kurt. All he's done is stolen from me." Her blood-shot eyes drilled into Jessie's. "You must be nuts to do that for a stranger, especially somebody like me."

There had been another time. But Jessie let it slide.

"I'm sick of everybody getting away with murder. Doc screwed me and beat me up bad. Kurt used me." Lissie scoffed. "What decent guy pimps out his lady and forces her to do his dirty work? I was his slave. I made some dough, had some fun, and got high a lot. But where did it get me? Nowhere. I got nothing. No money. No home. No kid. Only the shitty clothes on my back. Other than Jeremy, no one's been nice to me like you have. Like I said, you threw down your life for me." Lissie paused, blinking back a tear. "Bottom line. I trust you. Tell me what to do and I'll do it." She placed a clammy hand over Jessie's, and realizing the slip, she recoiled. The street-savvy hustler returned. "You call the shots and I'm game."

In law school, Jessie had been taught a cardinal rule: a lawyer should never become emotionally involved with their clients. However, she found it impossible with Lissie. The misfit had gotten to her. Lissie pretended to be tough, but terror and loneliness lurked within her eyes. It was unusual for Lissie to open up, and she couldn't disrespect her trust. Nor could she deny the proverb that when you save someone's life, you're eternally responsible for that person.

She fished around inside her bag for a pad and pen to make notes. Unable to locate them, she tipped it upside down, dumping the contents onto the metal table. A pistol fell upon the metal table with a thud.

"You sly bitch," Lissie said, eyeing the pistol.

"Don't get any ideas. It's not loaded." Jessie found the paper and pen, gathered up her belongings, and shoved them back into the purse. "Here's what we should do."

Chapter Forty-Two

Interrogation Room One grew hot and stuffy. The sweat trickling down the back of Jessie's neck reminded her of being in a crowded New York City subway car during the dead heat of July; bodies crushed against each other in a subterranean swelter.

Chief Shepardson, the sketch artist, and a stenographer, had joined the group—Jessie, Jeremy, Hal, Lissie, Zander, and Ebony—in the compact room, intensifying the heat and sucking the oxygen out of the air.

Jessie fought off the fuzziness attacking her brain and dictated the demands she'd prepared. "In exchange for Lissie's cooperation, we want absolute immunity from any charges stemming from Kurt Hendricks' criminal activities, and any other charges related to Ms. Sexton's actions. And until you resolve Hendricks' case, she's going to need a security detail."

"That's a huge ask," Hal said. His glance quickly shifted to the chief.

"I'm not finished. We want all of her past arrest records expunged, and all fingerprints and mug shots returned. You'll consent to the motions for this relief, and for issuing Certificates of Relief or Good Standing to remove any barriers for her future employment or housing. Also, we'd like a copy of her RAP sheet, immediately, so perhaps you can pull it while we're talking."

"We already have it. It's on my desk," Ebony said.

Chief Shepardson whispered in the stenographer's ear, and she disappeared, presumably to retrieve the arrest abstract.

"What makes you think you're in the position to make these demands?" Zander asked. He unbuttoned his top shirt button and loosened the knot of his skinny tie.

"We wouldn't be having this conversation, and you wouldn't have hunted Lissie down, if she wasn't crucial to your investigation. She's willing to cooperate, but you must return the favor."

"If Hendricks' case goes before the grand jury, the judge can subpoena her testimony. Then she'll have to cooperate, won't she?" Zander asked glibly.

"But that doesn't help you catch John Doe, does it?" Jessie dared him with her eyes.

"Chief, Detectives, can we speak outside?" Hal combed his fingers through his hair and led the group from the room.

The air was suddenly breathable again.

* * *

Hal escorted the group into Chief Shepardson's office and shut the door behind him. As he gathered his thoughts, he studied the picture frames on the Chief's walls. Cornell. New York City Mayor Bloomberg. President George W. Bush. He'd heard rumors that Shepardson had been a first responder after 9/11, and the proof hung upon these walls alongside commendations from the FDNY, NYPD, battered women's shelter, SPCA, City of Poughkeepsie School District, local parishes, temples, and food pantries. Over the past three decades, the chief had selflessly dedicated his life to assisting others.

Hal felt inconsequential by comparison and annoyed at the ethical dilemma confronting him. Jessie had a habit of blurring the lines of the law. First with Terence Butterfield, and presently with Elisabeth Sexton. Last time, she'd been a passenger on a runaway train. This time, she was the conductor. Truthfully, he admired her chutzpah, but his position demanded impartiality. This case was too significant to delegate to a subordinate, so he'd negotiate with Jessie as he would with any other defense attorney. He'd give her a true taste of the criminal law.

His mind had drifted off, but he caught the chief remarking, "—you have to determine whether we have a case without Sexton. If she can describe

John Doe's face, his car, other details, we can nail him." The chief chewed on the inside of his cheek, as if considering his own conclusions.

"But, Chief, she's an unreliable source. What's preventing her from lying her pants off to receive the deal?" Zander asked.

"As it stands right now, until Sexton identifies John Doe, we're treading water. We've got no other leads to his victims or survivors," Ebony said. She hesitated and glanced at Hal, signaling that she, too, walked the slender tightrope of neutrality. "Sir, we have a disastrous situation here, the convergence of an alleged serial killer and a major drug and larceny ring. We can't let Sexton slip through our hands. If we arrest her, she'll be an uncooperative witness." She shifted her weight and winced. "From my knowledge of her, she's more valuable as an asset than an adversary."

Hal weighed the detectives' competing arguments, finding it incredible that such opposites could function as partners. He didn't envy the chief's job of managing the pair, but he knew that Ebony's obstinacy, more often than not, was a facade.

"I agree with Detective Jones," Hal said. "And the conspiracy or drug charges are minor compared to these missing women and the creation of a task force. By law, we're supposed to seal Sexton's records anyway, so let's review her RAP sheet to get the full picture. How bad can it be?"

Zander laughed. "I mean no disrespect, sir, but this woman's been a pest as long as I've been on the force. Repeated prostitution charges, and a bible full of other sins, mostly Class C misdemeanors."

"But she's killed nobody. Is that what I'm hearing?" Hal scanned the faces, seeking input. Their noncommittal expressions reflected it was his call. They'd abide by it, like it or not.

* * *

Finally alone with Jeremy and Lissie, Jessie exhaled deeply, wiped the thin line of perspiration from her lip, and relaxed into her chair. While she'd believed she held the prosecution by the short hairs, it wasn't until that moment that faith became reality. She felt giddy over her assertive, if not excessive, demands. The knit of Hal's brows made her worry about the repercussions of her actions, but screw it, she thought with satisfaction. She was duty-bound to act in the best interests of her client, and that's exactly what she'd done. Besides, even if he refused to expunge Lissie's record, he couldn't deny her prosecutorial immunity if he wanted Lissie's cooperation.

"Dude, what did you do?" Lissie asked. "I told you I wanted out of this ball game with Kurt. I don't give a crap about my record."

"Either you trust me, or you don't."

"You've made your pitch, so let's see how this plays out, and if they counteroffer," Jeremy said. Cataract dullness settled over his eyes, reminding her of the magician who finally realizes his apprentice has surpassed him.

"Counteroffer? This isn't a business deal. Mr. Jay, this is my life. I ain't doing any time for Kurt, get it? What do you think you're doing, Martin?"

"We're getting you out of trouble," Jessie replied. "Your creative bookkeeping makes you an accessory to Kurt's crimes—drug dealing, trafficking in stolen goods, larceny—the works. Do you understand that?" She glared at Lissie, whose gaze shifted downward. "Love makes you blind, not stupid, so don't play coy with me. You must have known about Kurt's activities and you need to be straight with us. Nothing will pass beyond these walls." Jessie paused and receiving no response, she continued, "I'm offering you the opportunity to wipe the slate clean. There will be no current charges pressed against you, and all your past convictions will disappear. This is your get out of jail free card."

"But I—"

"Stop and think about it. All of your fingerprints, photographs, and arrest records will be destroyed." Jessie couldn't believe she had to hard sell her proposal to Lissie. The girl couldn't be that dim-witted.

"Jessie's right. Your RAP sheet reads like a mafia indictment, with drug charges, prostitution charges, petit larceny, disorderly conduct, harassment, resisting arrest, and public lewdness. Lissie, this is a gift, so listen to Jessie and pray the DA goes for it."

Stifling a smile, Jessie recalled Lissie's outfit from the first time they'd met—high-cut shorts, peek-a-boo tee-shirt—so the public lewdness charges made perfect sense. Knowing Lissie, the backstory of this arrest promised to be interesting.

"Yeah, they said I was dancin' naked in Soldier's Fountain. Why would I be doin' that in the middle of January? Okay, maybe I'd had a little juice, but I wasn't too high. Besides, I never strip for free." Lissie's voice dropped to a whisper. "You think you're better than me? Don't you? I hear it in your voice, getting all judgy like that chick cop. I don't need to confess my sins to you. I owe you nothing. I'll handle this myself 'cos I got my insurance and nobody's going to take it away. You both can take a hike."

"I don't know what you think you've got, but the DA won't negotiate directly with you, and it's not in your best interests to do so," Jeremy said.

"Lissie, be reasonable. You're in way over your head." Jessie was as well, but it was too late to turn her back on her client.

"Oh, yeah?" Lissie reached through the front buttons of her flannel shirt into her bra and produced a sandwich baggie encrusted in mud, and dangled it to taunt them.

"What's that?"

"Are you deaf? I've already told you. My insurance." Lissie unzipped the packet and withdrew a paper wad about the size of a postcard. She lovingly flattened out the vellum to diminish the grid of sharp creases. The indigo ink had run, blurring the artfully drafted letters, but the precise columns remained legible. "This is my insurance."

Jessie half expected to see a bank draft, or a compromising photograph of a famous John, or literally, a life insurance policy, rather than the columns of initials, names, emails, and phone numbers.

"This is the only copy of the key code to Kurt's enterprises. See, here are the initials for his suppliers and purchasers, and their contact information. This guy Chow, he's smuggling designer knock-off bags from China, and this guy Valdez, his coke comes from Columbia." Lissie traced her finger back and forth, across the list and down the columns. Most of the area codes were from California, Colorado, Utah, Arizona, Texas, and Georgia, but there was a series of international codes that Jessie didn't recognize, but suspected were from Middle Eastern or Slavic regions. "When Kurt and I fought the other day, I pinched it from the general ledger. I knew it would piss him off and he'd have to play nice to get the list, and me, back. Plus, I wanted some insurance, just in case, because—," she paused for dramatic effect, "it's worth millions."

Jessie's breath hitched. At last, she realized why the goons had been in hot pursuit. And why Hal had commissioned the patrols.

"It's worthless if you're dead," Jessie said. In the corridor, Hal's voice grew louder as the group approached the interrogation room. "Quick, stash that away and don't take it out again until I tell you. Please."

To her surprise, Lissie nimbly tucked the papers back inside her shirt as the door squeaked open.

Chapter Forty-Three

U nbelievable, Hal thought, reviewing the Record of Arrest and Prosecution of Elisabeth Anne-Marie Sexton, DOB March 4, 1987:

Prostitution. Loitering for purposes of prostitution. Marijuana possession. Public Lewdness. Trespassing. Disorderly Conduct. Assault. Petit Larceny. Perjury. Resisting Arrest. Harassment.

Over the past five years, Lissie Sexton had been busy plying her wares to middle-schoolers craving a cheap high and retirees seeking sex under the Mid-Hudson Bridge. Hal was certain that Kaplan had pleaded down other felonies to misdemeanors, but he didn't have time to root out the complete record of her offenses.

Hal agreed with Pulaski. Anyone would have made a better witness than Elisabeth Sexton. Pulaski had argued it was possible that her accusations were a vendetta against a John who'd stiffed her. Or Hendricks. And he wondered whether a grand jury, judge, or jury would find Elisabeth credible.

Instead, he ignored the noise inside his head, relying on his instinct, experience, and Ebony Jones. He trusted her. The chief trusted her. Jessie had trusted her. And, unfortunately, Jones was right. Sexton was all they had. If her statements turned out to be phony, he could always charge her with falsely reporting an incident. It was a minor Class D felony, which would have Sexton wearing an orange jumpsuit for a few years. The punishment would be small consolation for undermining his task force, but it was the best he could do.

Hal's thoughts spun in a whirlpool, like the water being sucked down a

232

drain. It was imperative to strike a deal with Jessie quickly and lock down Sexton's testimony. Memories, like bruises and scars, faded with time. And stories about minnows became tales about whales.

If Jessie sought prosecutorial immunity and expungement, she was going to have to accept his terms. He was the DA. He called the shots. Not Jessie, Sexton, or Kaplan.

Interrogation Room One was silent when he returned with his contingent. His stomach knotted up at the thought of crushing Jessie; not her, exactly, but Lissie Sexton. The hooker. The liar. The thief. He was going to make her beg for his benevolence.

Easing himself into a chair facing Jessie, he watched her bite her lip. He averted his eyes from the luscious pink pillows that had given him indescribable pleasure. "What proof do we have that Doc exists?"

"Yeah, maybe he's a figment of your drugged-out imagination," Zander said. "How do we know you didn't dream him up to mess with us?"

"You want proof? How's this?" Lissie shouted, pointing at the scar island floating on the swollen bald spot. "Do you think I did that to myself? And what about these?" Her trembling fingers spread apart the collar of her flannel shirt to reveal purple fingerprints dotting her throat like an amethyst necklace.

"Maybe Hendricks attacked you and you're protecting him," Zander replied.

"You muther—" Lissie sprang to her feet.

Zander startled and keeled over backward in his chair, slamming his head against the wall. "Whoa!" he screamed.

"Lissie, calm down," Jessie said, gently tugging on the girl's arm.

"Both of you, enough," Hal shouted, and silently counted to ten before proceeding. "Pulaski, pull yourself together. Ms. Sexton. Why don't you start from the beginning? Tell us about Doc."

"Are you going to record me?" Lissie glanced toward the corner of the room where a Hispanic female officer was attaching a video camera to a tripod nearly as tall as she. The officer paused, waiting for a signal to proceed.

"Yes, we need a record of your testimony. And please be warned, you'll be under oath, so if you lie —"

"Yeah, I know, the drill. Been there, done that."

Hal remained stone-faced as he dictated his commands. "First, we'll start with your testimony. Then, you'll review the mug shots and work with Officer Mancuso on a sketch."

"Hold on a second. That's not—" Jessie said, raddled.

"Then, do I get my deal?" Lissie interrupted.

"We'll see whether your testimony assists our case and warrants immunity."

"That's not the deal," Jessie said, regaining control. "We want a guarantee of immunity first. Then, she'll talk."

"I'm afraid that Ms. Sexton may have nothing valuable to offer. First, let's hear what she has to say."

"Hal, I can't advise her to do that." Jessie rose to leave. Her eyes narrowed, and a vertical furrow appeared between her brows. "I'm assuming you've got no grounds to hold us, so we'll be going. Come on, Lissie. Jeremy."

Smart. Jessie was calling his bluff. Her fierce determination reminded him of the way she guarded Lily, like a lioness protecting her cub.

"To move forward with an offer, we need hard evidence, not just her testimony." The pride of lions would play by his rules, or the game would be over.

He felt Jessie's eyes burning into him, but he waited for a sign of defeat. He hadn't meant to appear smug, but he doubted whether Sexton possessed even a shred of vital information, and besides, forensics had already stripped Smith Street of all the pertinent evidence against Hendricks.

"I'll give you *hard* evidence." Lissie glanced over at Jessie, who rocked her head and mouthed the word "No." "I'll give you the location where Doc messed me up bad. It's in that housing development up on Brickyard Hill behind Adam's Farmstand. Inside a garage. He said the smell of gasoline turned him on, the sicko. I slashed him up real good, so there should be blood all over the place. You've got them lights that shows up stuff. I know how this works, I seen it on TV."

234

Hal observed Lissie, hiding his elation. She'd stepped into his trap and was shooting off her mouth without even making a deal.

"That big fat bastard attacked me, so you'll see blood and sperm, too. A real Doc stew. Also, my old man's a pig. Kurt don't cook, clean or do no laundry. I betcha the clothes from that night, or what's left of 'em, are probably on the floor somewhere."

Every spectator in the room, except Hal, gaped at Lissie's crude, uncensored remarks.

"Close your mouth, Martin," Lissie said, "You look like a fish catching flies."

"Why didn't you mention this before?" Ebony asked.

"Nobody asked me."

Chapter Forty-Four

J essie hated being caught off guard, especially by a client, but Lissie was no ordinary client. Twice, within seconds, Lissie had bolstered her importance to the DA's investigation. By accusing Doc of the violent crimes of assault, battery, reckless endangerment, sexual abuse, rape, and unlawful imprisonment, she'd paved the way to search and seize evidence from his home, and she'd potentially linked Doc to the missing girls.

Hal had lost his advantage, and the ball was now in their court. Her next move was as obvious as the one-way mirror installed on the wall behind her.

"I'd like to propose an arrangement. It's unorthodox, but it reflects the circumstances. If Lissie immediately gives testimony, I'll retain the tape for safekeeping." Jessie paused for a drink of water to wash away the cottony feeling in her mouth. Then she continued. "I'll lock it in Jeremy's safe. And if, after your due diligence, you locate admissible evidence, we will release the tape to you. If not, the tape gets destroyed."

"Clever girl," Jeremy whispered in her ear.

"How do we know you'll return the tape? That you won't doctor it or—" Zander asked.

Hal raised his hand to interrupt Zander. "So there's no misunderstanding, you propose Lissie testifies right now, and you'll hold the tape in escrow. If we verify the location of Doc's home and uncover evidence tying him to a crime against Ms. Sexton, we will honor all of your requests. Then you'll deliver the tape to us?"

Jessie nodded. "We both want to catch the perpetrator. However, my primary concern is my client." Her firm position wasn't personal. It was business. And she hoped he respected that. "You're going to have to trust me, and Lissie, on this."

Hal's mouth twisted as though he was considering his reply, and he shot Shepardson and Jones a questioning glance. "We've never made this kind of bargain before."

Zander opened his mouth to speak, but shut it at the chief's stony glare.

"We've never faced a serial killer," Ebony said.

"And you never met anyone like me before, have ya?" Lissie asked.

"No, I certainly haven't," Hal said, casting a warm smile at Lissie. "You're a very resourceful young lady. And lucky to be represented by two extremely persistent and creative lawyers." He winked at her, and her face blushed.

"So you agree to the terms?" Jessie asked.

Hal nodded. "All right. Testimony now. Tape in escrow. Verification of the suspect's address. Collection of physical evidence. Immunity and expunction of Lissie's record, as requested. Tape Returned. Does that cover everything?"

Jessie strained to hear Hal over the pulsing in her ears. She couldn't afford to relax until the agreement was finalized. "Yes. The stenographer is here, so let's place our agreement on the record."

"Roll the videotape," Hal instructed the videographer. The eye of the camera blinked green as Hal and Jessie dictated the customary legal introductions: name, date, time, location, the parties present, the voluntariness of the witness' statement, and the deal.

Jessie leaned back in her chair, her body tingling in excitement. While the formalities were over, it was time for Lissie to deliver.

* * *

On cue, Lissie stared into the camera lens and spoke. Her low, faraway voice was hypnotic, and Jessie squeezed her eyes to concentrate as Lissie's dark tale unfolded in her mind's eye.

"I remember it was the last day of April," Lissie said. "It'd been rainin,' but even though it'd stopped around rush hour, it was chilly. Me and Kurt had a fight 'cos I'd bought a really cool silver sequined jacket that cost a chunk a change. Man, was he pissed. He told me if I wanted to keep it, I'd better get my ass out to work to pay for it. I stormed outta the house, wearing my new jacket. I figured I'd head over to Reservoir Square to check out the action. I hung around for a while, keeping my eyes peeled for cop cars in case I needed to make a run for it."

At the mention of the cops, Zander clicked his tongue, and Ebony nudged him beneath the table. Lissie didn't seem to notice and kept speaking.

"After a half-hour, I recognized Doc's white Toyota. I knew he'd stop and pick me up when he was ready. He always did. I'd been doing Doc for about three or four weeks, so I was used to his dance. He wanted me to be desperate, and I was gonna play along. His money was good, and I didn't think he was a bad dude." Lissie glanced at Jessie and shrugged. "Besides, I thought he was a doctor 'cos he always wore scrubs, and he had plenty of green to spread around.

"I was really glad when Doc finally pulled over. I leaned into the open car window to get warm. He reached over and unzipped my jacket to peek at my lacy red bra. I guess it turned him on, 'cos he said, 'Get in, Coco.'" She explained Coco was her most recent street name. "'Let's take a ride,' Doc said. He's got this really squeaky Mickey Mouse voice, which is weird since he's ginormous. Then, he flexed his hips, showing off his big boner, like I was supposed to be impressed."

Jessie felt her cheeks grow warm with embarrassment at the reference to Doc's penis, but she pursed her lips, bracing herself for the more explicit language to come.

"I'd smoked a joint on my way to the park, so I was pretty buzzed. But I didn't want Doc to think I needed him more than he needed me. I slowly slid into the car, and before I knew it, he'd taken my hand and put it on his thigh. He made a crack about more rain comin', but he said it didn't make no difference 'cos we weren't gonna do it on the hood of his car. I sneaked my hand over to his hard crotch 'cos I thought he wanted me to, but he frowned and slapped it away."

Jessie wasn't sure what Hal thought of Lissie's long-winded commentary. She worried he was going to cut her off and rescind the deal, but he seemed to be listening patiently. He was tapping his pen on the table, with his eyes glued on Lissie. He was more attentive than Zander, who repeatedly checked his fancy smartwatch. Ebony and Chief Shepardson appeared as enthralled by the story as Hal.

"I really didn't like Doc's attitude so I snatched my stuff from the floor and told him to pull over. I pointed to the big stone church on Academy Street and said, 'Let me out here. I'm not feeling it today. You're mean and disrespectful.'" Lissie swatted at the air as though shooing Doc away.

"'You won't get any business from the Presbyterians, so just stick with me, will ya, Coco? You know you love your big chocolate candy man. I always give you extra for your trouble, don't I? Come on, Coco,' Doc pleaded. He reached over and pinched my nipple. I wanted to smack his fat hand away, but I needed the dough and wanted to get this over and done with."

Lissie's desperation flooded Jessie with pity as Lissie explained how they drove into a development of vinyl-clad split-level homes called "Brickyard Estates." It was a quiet neighborhood near the main road where she'd found Lissie in the drainage ditch.

Ebony threw her a look of exasperation, as though Jessie controlled the speed or content of Lissie's storytelling.

"I was surprised when Doc pulled into the driveway of a dumpy house 'cos he'd never brought me to a real building before. Before, we parked behind abandoned warehouses or in the tunnels beneath the train tracks, where nobody was gonna bother us. He opened the garage door with a remote and we drove in. Doc seemed like he was in a hurry, and said his family would be home in less than an hour. He wanted me gone long before then.

"Ya know, I thought the set-up was weird. Although nobody was home, he didn't take me inside. He told me he liked screwing inside the garage where it was dark, and it smelled of motor oil and gasoline. Whatever, I thought, but then I seen there was only two small windows and they was covered in yellow newspaper. The place was spooky, with all kinds of tools dangling

from the pegboard walls. There were hammers, and drills, and chainsaws…
all kinds of scary shit like in a horror movie. Broken lawn chairs were piled
in a corner next to boxes with rags and drop cloths. I wasn't feeling good
about this, 'cos he'd trapped me inside the smelly garage."

A shiver slithered down Jessie's spine, foreshadowing the grisly events to
come.

"He wanted to get down to business right away and told me to jump onto
the blanket he'd thrown on the back seat. It's not like I didn't trust him, or
nothing, but I told him cash up front and to take precautions. A girl's got
to be careful, ya know. I tossed him a condom from my bag, and he handed
me a roll of bills that I stuffed inside my bra. Then, I told him to move his
car seat forward so I wouldn't be all squished like last time."

"Can we move this along?" Zander asked, crossing his arms over his chest.
"Yeah, we know you had sex with him, but did he beat you up or not?"

"Excuse me," Lissie replied sarcastically. "You wanna to know the story
or not?"

"Ms. Sexton, you're doing fine. I'm sure Detective Pulaski didn't mean
any harm. Take your time. We want to make sure you tell your entire story,"
Hal said.

At the subtle tongue-lashing, Zander leaned back in his chair, avoiding
eye contact with everyone in the room.

"Thank you, sir. As I said, I scrambled into the back seat and took my
jeans off while Doc got ready, you know, rolled on the condom. I was in a
hurry 'cos it was cold in the garage and my teeth were chattering."

"Lissie, I hate to interrupt, but you really haven't described Doc. It would
be helpful if we knew what he looked like," Ebony said.

"Sorry, I shoulda mentioned that. He's over six feet tall and I wouldn't
call him fat, but his rolls of walrus fat are disgusting. I've done all kinds
of guys, but I gotta be careful with Doc, so he don't suffocate me. Look at
me, I'm small and he could easily crush me, but I put up with him for the
extra tips I hide from Kurt." She cupped her hand and whispered as though
revealing a secret. "They're my getaway stash. Someday, I wanna get away
from Kurt and take care of my kid. Whenever I drop to my knees or lay on

my back, I know it's so I can add dough to my kitty." She breathed deeply and blinked hard, as though fighting off tears, and then slumped down in her chair. "I ain't gonna allow Doc, Kurt, or anybody else to steal my dream of bein' with my kid. He's with my folks, which is the right place for him now. I know someday we'll be together again."

A sudden sadness washed over Jessie. She and Lissie had more in common than she'd ever considered. Since she'd met Lissie, she'd thought of her as a tough troublemaker who sold her body for the thrills. That was far from the truth. Her true motivation was her child. Like herself, Lissie was sacrificing for her child; scrimping, saving, and living the only way she knew in order to be reunited with her son.

Lissie continued, her voice almost a whisper. "I know I shouldn't say nothing, but that day is comin' soon. I've been skimming extra. It's in a safe place where he won't get his mitts on it. Kurt's stoned most of the time, and so far, he hasn't said nothin' about the shortfall or found my money." Jessie squeezed Lissie's hand in reassurance, after Lissie brushed a tear from her cheek.

Lissie glared at Zander. "Detective, here's the part you're dyin' for. Next, Doc grabbed my shoulders and shoved me backward onto the seat. He laid down and pulled me on top of him without giving me time to prepare. He was going after me extra hard, slammin' me so violently that I felt each thrust up in my throat. His sweaty fingers squeezed my breasts like they were melons in the market."

Zander cast his eyes downward as he listened.

"I yelled for him to stop, but he ignored me, and made my skin burn. He said, 'Tell me the pain makes you hot.' His voice was mean as his thighs tightened, and I could tell he was getting ready to come. I woulda said anything to get it over with, so I replied, 'Yeah, baby, I'm hot, baby. Keep going. Don't stop. Coco's gonna ride you like nobody else.' Then, Doc shuddered beneath me, and just when I thought he'd climaxed, he walloped me with the back of his hand, knockin' me off balance and sending me flying backward. My head smashed against the car window, and I seen white stars swirling in front of my eyes. I reached for the door handle to escape, but he shouted he wasn't done with me. I was terrified."

Jessie flinched as though she'd been the one receiving Doc's beating, and she scanned the room to gauge the reaction of the others. The rapt attention of Ebony, Zander, Hal, the chief, and the rest remained on Lissie. Jessie could only believe their criminal justice experience had jaded them, while her corporate training had ill-prepared her for the stark realities of mental and physical violence.

"My hands were shaking as I touched the lump on the back of my head. My fingers felt sticky, and I knew they were covered in blood. My ears were ringin' like crazy, and I screamed a bunch of stuff like I was done with him, and that he'd gotten what he'd paid for. And if he knew what was good for him, he wouldn't touch me like that again, ever." She paused and spoke to Hal. "I figured I could sic Kurt on him." Hal nodded politely in reply.

"Then everything blew up." Lissie's hands flew to her throat, as if acting out what was about to happen next. "Doc grabbed my throat and squeezed. He shouted, 'It's my dollar and I'll do what I want.' I tried to pry his fingers away, but I couldn't. I could barely breathe, and little white spots danced before my eyes as I gulped for air."

She paused. Her hands fell into her lap and her face drained of all color.

"Ms. Sexton," Hal said, "I know this is very upsetting. So if you'd like to take a break, please say the word."

His voice was gentle, as though he was comforting his young son, Tyler. Even under pressure, Hal's kindness never wavered. He never condescended and always treated people with respect. Even those who infuriated him like Jeremy Kaplan and Zander Pulaski. Jessie admired that about him.

"Maybe some water, please," Lissie replied. Hal jutted his chin toward Zander, and he disappeared as the videographer switched off the camera. The room fell silent. When he'd returned with a bottle of water, Lissie smiled weakly and took a long draw. "Thanks."

Zander grinned politely and resumed his place with his tail between his legs.

The room crackled with electricity in anticipation of the tale's resumption.

"Where was I?"

"Doc had you in his grip," Jessie prompted.

"Oh, yeah. Doc's grip relaxed, and then he dragged me back onto the greasy rear car seat and dove on top of me. He went at me hard, thrusting along with each word he shouted at me. I was in pain and things got fuzzy, but he said somethin' like, 'Here's-more-for-you-bitch. I'm-going-to-fuck-you-until-tomorrow.' At least he'd loosened up on my throat so I could breathe, but it scared me shitless." She shivered. "I'd had rough sex before, but there was somethin' different about Doc this time. It was like he didn't care whether he killed me or crushed the life outta me. I really thought I was gonna die and figured I was runnin' out of time."

Doc's violence on poor Lissie was becoming difficult for Jessie to hear. She wanted to run from the room, pretend that such abuse didn't exist, but she knew better. She'd experienced it at the hands of Ryan's older brother, Robbie, and she had to live with the brutal scars every day for the past ten years. Jessie reminded herself that she and Lissie were survivors. Lissie was alive, telling her story, yet her honesty didn't quell the knot of horror in Jessie's stomach. She wondered about the other nine missing women and whether they'd met the same fate.

"Doc's eyes were shut, and I could tell he was in his pleasure palace. I knew if I didn't do somethin', he'd kill me for sure." Lissie scanned the room. "My son's face kept popping into my head, and I knew I had to survive for him. So, I fumbled along the seat, the footwell, searching for somethin', anything, to use against Doc. My fingers fell into a small hole filled with soft, gritty ash, and I touched the metal edge of the cigarette lighter. I'm not religious, but I thank God for small favors. Then I pushed in the knob and counted to ten. As I did, Doc pumped away, his fingers yanking my hair from my head."

Jessie's eyes drifted to the shiny bald patch on Lissie's head, and her scalp ached in sympathy. It also registered that Lissie's DNA would be in Doc's garage, leaving evidence to seal their deal.

"The seconds seemed to last forever, and his fingernails dug into my throat again, making me gasp for breath. I thought the lighter was hot, and I pulled it out and jabbed it into Doc's flabby butt. The stink of burning flesh filled the car as he screamed, and rolled backwards, grabbing for my arm. 'You're going to be sorry you did that,' he yelled, but I didn't give a crap. I wiggled free from his hands, opened the car door, and scrambled out as Doc crawled across the seat after me. Before I could get all the way out, he grabbed my ankle."

Even the young videographer shuddered at the foiled escape attempt. The officer checked her equipment and was careful not to interrupt; she mouthed to Hal that they'd been rolling for thirty-five minutes. He jotted the time on his tablet without missing a beat of Lissie's statement.

"The garage was like a handyman's dream, and I seen a tool belt hanging above me on the pegboard wall. I snatched the screwdriver from it, and I can tell you I felt relief when I stabbed the rusty Phillips' head into the fleshy skin at the base of Doc's thumb and twisted it. 'Take that, you bastard,' I shouted, and when he tried to remove the screwdriver, I bit his arm.

"Luckily, Doc had turned me loose, and I ran away from him, but my sneakers slid around on the greasy garage floor. I fell backward through a plate glass mirror propped against the wall. It felt like a thousand tiny needles pricked my arms and legs."

Lissie spoke faster, and faster, swept up in the retelling of the events.

"As I told you, Doc is like a giant. I was surprised how easily he wormed his way out of the car door. He loomed over me, clenching and unclenching his bloody fist as his breath streamed from his nostrils like a cartoon bull. He reached down, grabbed my hair, and lifted me off my feet. I knew I was as good as dead. I seen it in his beady eyes. I was trapped in the garage with the devil, with no escape. He'd shut the garage door, the opener was outta reach, the breezeway door looked locked, and the windows were sealed tight."

Jessie's breath hitched. Her muscles were so tight they felt like they were going to snap.

"I was beat. I couldn't take it no more, and every muscle and bone ached. Every inch of my skin stung, and my crotch burned. I let my body go limp, prepared to be clobbered and to die in this dirty hellhole. I closed my eyes and told my son I loved him. We'd meet again someday, and I prayed he wouldn't forget me.

"My hand throbbed like nobody's business, and I realized that the sharp edges of a mirror spear were stuck in my palm. Fuck the pain, I thought. I squeezed it tight until my fingers grew numb and bloody. I felt jazzed, like I had one last shot. But then Doc drew his fist back and punched me in the eye. My head flew backward, and an electric zing traveled from my eye socket to my toes. He walloped me again, right underneath my jaw, knocking my head back onto the pointy hooks on the pegboard."

In her mind, Jessie could hear the silver hooks clink as though applauding Doc's brutality.

"My mouth tasted like copper and salt, and I figured what the fuck, and I spit in his face." Lissie ran her tongue across her teeth and took another sip of water. "Doc came at me again and smacked me. He looked at me like a crazy man, eyes bulging, tongue wagging, and I could tell he was about to screw me again. I didn't know what to do, but I knew this time it would be even worse than before. This time he'd kill me."

The interrogation room was silent, except for the air blowing through the vent. Everyone—Ebony, Zander, Hal, Jeremy, the videographer, the sketch artist, and Chief Shepardson—were as still as statues, waiting for Lissie's declaration.

"I reached up, and with all my strength I nailed him hard, right between his shoulder blades with the piece of mirror."

* * *

The hollow sound of a pen rolling off the table and onto the floor shattered the silence of the room.

Lizzie stopped and looked at the faces staring back at her. "The rest is a blur," she said, blinking back the tears. "I remember high-pitched screams. I didn't know if they were Doc's or mine. I grabbed my jeans and bag, smashed a garage window, climbed out, and ran like holy hell toward the sound of cars." Her voice hitched. "It was pourin' so hard I could barely see, but I didn't care. I had to get away from that monster before he killed me."

Chapter Forty-Five

"I came to you. I told you about him." A wet sheen of tears glistened on Lissie's cheeks as she glowered at Ebony with enough hostility to slay the worst of enemies.

Jessie reached out, and this time Lissie permitted her hand to linger. Lissie's rigid physique seemed to lose its resolve, and she melted into her chair as if on Jessie's command.

"It's always girls like me who get screwed, isn't it?" Lissie snorted at her pun.

Across the room, Hal leaned against the wall with his arms crossed over his chest. In this pose, he appeared larger than life, like Zeus on Mt. Olympus. He always seemed to recognize the exact moment to seize control, and Jessie's stomach fluttered at his impending domination of the room.

Hal nodded imperceptibly, barely dipping his chin at the video operator, and she shut off the camera. He arched his back, pushed away from the wall, and approached Lissie, capturing her gaze. "Ms. Sexton, you're absolutely right. We've failed you and those missing women miserably. But, thanks to you, Doc's days of cruising the streets are at an end. We'll get him, I promise." He sealed his promise with a winning smile, conveying he was a man true to his word. He'd fulfill his vow, even if his life depended on it.

Spellbound, Lissie beamed with the ardor of a rival for Hal's affections.

"Here's the plan," Hal said, laying out the assignments for the team. "Ms. Sexton, Jessie, and Jeremy will meet with our sketch artist, Officer Mancuso." He motioned toward the dark-haired uniformed officer, setting up the electronic tablet and laptop on the table. "Chief, in the interim, you'll dispatch Detectives Jones and Pulaski back to Smith Street to collect further evidence. And I'll secure the search warrant of Doc's premises after Detective Jones and Pulaski have confirmed the location of Ms. Sexton's assault." He paused. "Officer Mancuso, you ready for Ms. Sexton?"

The artist eagerly arranged his computerized sketchpad and stylus on the table, awaiting further instructions, while the videographer dismantled the tripod and loaded the camera equipment into a black nylon bag on the floor.

"I'll check back with you in an hour or two," Hal said.

"Hey, aren't you forgetting something?" Jessie cocked her head to the side and outstretched her arm with her palm upward.

He smirked, stepped out of the room, and shut the door behind him.

* * *

"Hey!" Jessie shouted, chasing Hal down the hallway. His stride, long and assertive from walking the golf courses, gave him an advantage, and she scrambled along the narrow corridor after him. She caught up with him, tagged his shoulder, and spun him around to face her. "We had a deal."

"We don't need a deal." His tone was flat, matter-of-fact.

She studied him, unsure whether to be confused or furious. Hal Samuels, the love of her life, couldn't possibly be screwing her over. Or was he? She'd stupidly permitted Lissie to testify with only a videotaped agreement rather than a formal court order, and he'd outplayed her. He'd pressured her to get what he needed, and now he was casting her aside.

How could she explain this to Lissie and Jeremy?

"We don't need an escrow agreement."

"But, you—" The frenzy of the police station interrupted Jessie; phones rang, voices announced police calls over the PA system, and somewhere in the distance, a police siren blared. Hal grabbed her by the wrists and tugged her into a dark corner of the hallway, away from the din. He held her so close his warm breath grazed the fists tucked beneath her chin.

She wriggled, struggling to free herself. "Hal, let me go."

"Will you calm down and let me finish, please?" His grip tightened and twisted, burning the skin on her wrists.

"After what I heard from Lissie, she's the real deal. I'll forward the immunity paperwork as soon as I'm back at the office." His grip loosened. "I couldn't mention it earlier because I didn't want it to appear as though you were receiving preferential treatment, because you're not. At least for this, anyway." He gave her a quick kiss and released her. "You've got to have a little more faith in me, babe," he called as walked away.

Dumbstruck, Jessie rubbed her achy arms and staggered back to Interrogation Room One to deliver the news to Lissie and Jeremy. The jagged grin blazing on Lissie's battered face convinced Jessie that, like everyone else, Lissie had fallen under Hal's magic spell.

Chapter Forty-Six

In the golden light of the afternoon, Lissie's apartment building on Smith Street appeared shabbier than Ebony remembered. Forest green shutters dangled from their hooks, posing a threat to passersby. The white paint had sun-blistered to gray, and last winter's debris tumbled down the hard clay driveway reminiscent of the Great Dust Bowl.

"What a dump," Ebony said, stubbing her toe on the uneven pavement. "Did it look this decrepit before?"

"I don't really remember. We were trying to find Sexton and ended up wrangling Hendricks," Zander replied.

Across the front door, the yellow crime scene tape billowed and shimmied like a stripper, beckoning them. They ducked beneath the barricade, entered the building, trod up the creaky wooden steps, and unlocked the apartment door. Once inside, darkness greeted them first, followed by the sour stench of rotting garbage. Exchanging disgusted glances, they tugged on their blue latex gloves and slipped white facemasks over their mouths and noses.

With the shades drawn, their eyes adjusted to the muted light of the waning sun. Zander searched the cracked plaster wall for the light switch with the flashlight on his phone. He flipped on the single bare bulb dangling from the ceiling. Forensics had been there, leaving their handiwork behind. Papers littered the soiled beige shag carpet, and dust outlined the former sites of the computer boxes, now in police custody. They had cut the cushions of the frayed yellow sofa and chair open, giving the impression that mad raccoons had ransacked the place.

Ebony and Zander were on a treasure hunt, and given the war zone condition of the place, it wouldn't be easy.

With Zander in the lead, they dodged the piles of trash constricting the narrow hallway leading toward the kitchen. Ebony dabbed the tears from her eyes and pinched her nose as the stench intensified. Her welling eyes sifted through the debris for the clues Lissie had promised lay hidden there.

In the kitchen, the cabinet doors and drawers stood wide open, their contents bare except for the crumbs, spider webs, and beer bottle caps. Black plastic garbage bags bursting with rotten food and debris, presumably the cabinet's contents, blocked the refrigerator's door. A rustle beneath the trash caught Ebony's attention, and her peripheral vision sensed movement, a blur. Perhaps it had been a mouse, or it could've been her imagination. Either way, the place was creepy.

Cautiously, they entered the sparsely furnished blue front room, which served as Lissie and Kurt's bedroom. A mattress, piled with soiled sheets and blankets, was shoved into the corner. As they'd witnessed before, clothing littered the floor as though dropped wherever it had been stripped off.

While Zander took the bedroom, Ebony searched the cubbyhole of a bathroom. Years of abuse were clear from the blue toothpaste coating the chipped enamel sink, the greasy tub ring and the drain clogged with dark hair. The door of the medicine cabinet stood ajar, and she gingerly pried it open with the end of a pencil, careful not to disturb its contents.

"Just the usual," she said. "Toothpaste, deodorant, Band-Aids, condoms, and a lot of expensive men's cologne." She selected a shiny amber bottle, unscrewed the top, and sniffed. Her eyes stung and welled up. "Phew, Z, this stuff's a real chick magnet."

"Eb, that's great, but I could use help in here."

Ebony joined him in the bedroom and discovered Zander on his knees, buried headfirst in the closet, scavenging in a canine fury.

"Check this out. Nothing's going to bite you."

She recalled the rustling of the rodent and shivered.

As Lissie had directed, a wicker laundry basket brimming with discarded clothing hid in the closet's rear. He dragged it out into the room, and swimming among the red patent leather stilettoes and over-the-knee platform boots, he located a high-top sneaker and sequined jacket caked in mud.

"I should've bet you she was legit," Ebony said. Zander flipped her his middle finger. "Nice. Here are the evidence bags, so stuff it." She pitched the plastic bags at his head, and he caught them before they'd made contact. "I'm going to take another look around, just in case we've missed anything. Hurry up and finish before my olfactory glands explode, will you?"

Ebony returned to the living room and scoured every inch of the messy room. She wasn't exactly sure what she sought, but her cop's intuition whispered about another clue waiting to be discovered.

* * *

Jessie had never witnessed anything like it. She couldn't draw a cat or dog or bird if her life depended on it, but Officer Mancuso was an artistic genius. He began by asking Lissie to describe everything she remembered about Doc's face—his eyes, chin, forehead, nose, cheeks, mouth, and hair—and introduced her to a series of generic portraits highlighting those features to see if any looked like Doc.

Then, he set his stylus on the tablet and drafted a sketch that appeared on a computer screen.

"No," Lissie said, "his nose is thinner and add longer hair. And his head's square like Frankenstein's and his eyes are small and beady."

Mancuso efficiently made the corrections, while Lissie contributed some final suggestions to the composite sketch.

"Make his ears smaller. Yeah, that's him. Sort of."

Over an hour had passed and Jessie's stomach growled with hunger. She glanced at her watch. It was almost dinnertime, and she fretted she'd be home late, so she texted her mother.

Should be home by 6. Please feed Lily and get her ready for bed. C U soon. Thnx. J

"That should do it," Mancuso said. "The facial recognition software has identified three suspects from our local mug shot database, so I'll run these photos up to the chief, along with the sketch. He'll take it from there." As he rose, the artist juggled a canvas tote full of drawing supplies and the computer. "We'll be in touch."

Jessie smiled at Officer Mancuso as he held the door open and the group piled out.

"I did the best I could, but I was pretty stoned," Lissie said. "I'd done Doc before, but a lot of guys look alike. In my line of work, it's not the faces that stick out." Lissie smirked and poked her elbow into Jessie's side.

"You did good," Jessie said. "Let's hope Ebony and Zander find your clothing for DNA samples. For now, though, let's get out of here. I think we've had enough of the station for today. Right, Gayle?"

Gayle jumped up from her chair and joined Jeremy as they walked toward the exit. "It's been a long day, and our boys are probably wondering where we are. I'll go get the van and text them we're on our way."

The van pulled up to the entrance as Jeremy, Jessie, and Lissie were engaged in conversation with a burly State Trooper, who Jeremy had introduced as Lissie's father, Captain Clinton Sexton. Gayle rolled down her window to beckon her husband, but hesitated, evidently not wanting to interrupt what appeared to be a serious discussion.

"Before you get all upset, hon, Matt Shepardson's an old friend. He thought you could use some family support, so he called me," Captain Sexton said. "He said you were terrific, brave even, taking on a suspected killer. Why didn't you mention all this when we came to the hospital?" The trooper swallowed hard, attempting to choke back his emotions. "Your momma and I thought that maybe you'd like to come home...." His tone was soft, yet it contained a knifelike edge. "For a visit."

"Clint, that's a wonderful offer," Jeremy said, clapping his hand on the man's shoulder, "but Gayle and I have invited Lissie to stay with us until she gets back on her feet."

"Maybe you could spend some time with Luke. He'll be so proud that his momma is a hero." Captain Sexton crushed the brim of his Smokey Bear hat.

"Can't I stay with you, Martin?" Lissie asked, half-jesting.

"You, me, and the DA? Cozy, but I don't think so."

Lissie's hazel eyes examined Jessie inquiringly.

"Sweetie, it's totally up to you," Gayle said. "You're welcome with us, but if you want to see your son, go for it. If it doesn't work out, call us and we'll come get you."

Lissie nodded at her father, who slipped his arm around his daughter's shoulder and guided her to his car, a white Cadillac convertible. She hesitated and turned around. "Thanks, guys. For lawyers, you guys don't suck. At least so far." She climbed inside and disappeared behind the tinted windows.

"Troopers must make some serious coin to drive such a sweet ride," Jessie muttered as Jeremy climbed into the passenger seat of his mini-van that reeked of grass cuttings, French fries, and teenage boy perspiration.

He saluted as he closed the door, and the van drove away.

Seconds later, a car horn blared in a long, interminable lament. Searching for the source of the racket, Jessie's eyes fell upon Jeremy's van straddling the traffic median leading from the parking lot. Apparently, others heard it too, because a team of officers joined her as she sprinted toward their vehicle. Her throat went dry and her pulse throbbed in her temples when she reached the van and threw open the door. Gayle wailed like a banshee, as Jeremy's dead weight had her pinned against the steering wheel.

Chapter Forty-Seven

The rusty refrigerator was the last place to search, and its motor rattled, urging Ebony to retreat. "You won't like what you find inside," it warned. Undaunted, she hauled aside the black mountain of plastic bags in her way, making a path forward. Once there, she leaned her shoulder against the door, tugged on the greasy handle, and pried open the mold-encrusted door.

She gagged at the sour stench of the bottles of orange juice skimmed with fungus, the furry green hotdogs, and the thick green slime of decomposing vegetables coating the fridge's shelves. Gripped with revulsion, Ebony slammed the door and stepped back for a breath of fresher air.

After a minute, she ventured into the freezer. Popsicle boxes, empty ice trays, potpies, and bagels hid beneath a winter wonderland of icy crystals. On a hunch, she plowed her blue gloves through the snow and tapped a slender, round canister frozen against the back wall. Her numb fingers clasped it and yanked it free.

It was a can of store-brand pink lemonade, and someone had cleverly resealed its metal ends. With her pocketknife, she carefully slit the can's rim and popped off the top. She'd found Lissie's treasure, and considering it might have friends, she plunged her hand back into the snow.

* * *

Hal set his horn-rimmed glasses upon the yellow legal pad covered in scribbles and rubbed his eyes. In a half-hour, the task force meeting would begin and the FBI, state, local and county authorities, along with Mayor Meriden and County Executive Ketchum, would appear in his conference room.

Before Sexton's revelations, he'd been staring at a blank page. Now he still couldn't believe that a hooker with a record as long as his arm would break the case wide open.

Chief Shepardson had phoned about the three leads, and he was on his way over with the details. The two-block walk from City Hall to the District Attorney's office along Market Street took about five minutes, and Hal needed the time to compose his thoughts.

He considered calling Jessie, who'd texted him about Jeremy's collapse, but it was probably too early for any news, anyway. He closed his eyes and whispered a silent prayer for his frenemy's recovery. It was the least he could do.

A light, rapid knock on the door aroused him from his meditation.

"Well, aren't you the lucky one? Catching a power nap on the job?"

He pinched the bridge of his nose, hoping Lauren Hollenbeck was a mirage. But no such luck. The good senator had a nasty habit of turning up when he least expected or least wanted her around. She never phoned before her pop-ins and strutted around the DA's annex as though she were still in charge, much to the chagrin of her former staff.

"This isn't a good time. I've got a meeting starting in a few minutes and I need to prepare." Hal hoped she'd take the hint, but Lauren settled herself into the worn captain's chair opposite his desk. She hiked up her pencil skirt to remind him of what he was missing.

"Were you channeling my spirit? After all, this is my old office, and you know people leave a little piece of them behind wherever they go. Just like you'll do when you're gone."

Her words were baiting. But he refused to nibble at the cheese in her game of cat and mouse. "Lauren, what do you want?"

"I wanted to give you a head's up, for old time's sake. I'm going to be announcing my run for office." She paused. "This office. I want it back."

Great. He played it like he couldn't give a crap. "Things aren't panning out in Albany?"

"With the governor clamping down on legislators' outside income, it's best if I collect my chips and come home. I live comfortably, but not enough to survive on a legislator's part-time salary." That was an understatement. Lauren was a walking mannequin for the latest runway trends. Armani. Ferragamo. Gucci. Dior. Louis Vuitton. She was too rich for his blood.

Lauren brushed her jet-black hair from her face and, narrowing her indigo eyes, she drummed her nails on his desktop. Waiting.

He let out a slow breath of relief when Chief Shepardson burst into the office, interrupting her feeble attempt at intimidation.

"Lauren, I appreciate the information, but I'm busy."

"I'll be looking for a Chief ADA. Interested in your old job?" she asked and rose to leave.

"Matt, pull up a chair and let me see what you've got," Hal said, ignoring Lauren's departure, but listening for her footsteps along the granite hallway. The hall was silent. "Do me a favor and shut the door, will you?"

The chief did as asked, but sloppily left the door ajar.

Shepardson explained Sexton had identified three suspects from the mug shot database. "The first, John Harrison Patrick, has a criminal history of assault and rape, and he's been connected to a murder in Springfield, Massachusetts. Ironically, Patrick's already in Dutchess County lockup for DWI and reckless driving. He's posted bail, so he's scheduled for release pending his preliminary hearing. My guys can intercept him at the jail and bring him in for questioning."

The chief informed him that suspect number two, Amir Hanann, had died of a heroin overdose two months ago, which predated Lissie's attack.

Shepardson continued. "The third suspect, Duvall Bennett, is clean. He appears to be a solid citizen, a military vet employed as a sonographer in a local obstetrician's group. However, six months ago, we questioned him on the complaint of Camila Cordoba." Hal's eyebrows shot up at the mention of one of the missing women, and a sometime informant. "She alleged he attempted to strangle her and he sexually abused her. No charges were filed because Cordoba never pursued the complaint, and she'd made the allegations weeks after the alleged attack. The department presumed that it was another sex worker gripe and dropped it."

"The Cordoba connection is worth pursuing, but it's dated and could be coincidental," Hal said. "Not to discount these two leads, let's see what the task force shakes up. We'll need flyers, billboards, social networking, questionnaires about violent johns, neighborhood canvassing, and area roadblocks. Pulaski and Jones will be the lead boots on the ground, and they'll interview other prostitutes who might have information about John Doe." He rubbed the back of his neck, thinking. "We'll have the state and federal agencies activate their canine units and helicopter surveillance, and I'll pursue the search warrants for Patrick and Bennett."

The chief nodded. "Sounds like you've got it under control."

The pent-up tension in Hal's neck and shoulders unexpectedly melted away. "Good, then we're ready to go." He pressed the intercom for Cindie's extension. "Run background checks on John Harrison Patrick and Duvall Bennett. The chief will fill you in. And do me a personal favor. Please tell Jess not to wait up."

Chapter Forty-Eight

Hal awoke with a start, soaked in perspiration. He sat up and dabbed his face with the hem of his tee-shirt. Next to him, Jessie twitched in her sleep, emitted a squeaky snort, and rolled onto her side, facing away from him.

He checked the bedside alarm clock. Three-thirty.

The nightmare was still fresh in his mind. The names of the nine missing women had been branded into the wood paneling in his office, with the letters spelling out their names bleeding bright crimson and dripping like slick candle wax down the wall to the carpet.

He shook his head to dispel the gruesome image, but yesterday's harsh reality replaced them. Early in the evening, he'd organized the troops, commanding them to fulfill their duties and report back to him. They were the best in their fields of surveillance, forensics, cyber, canine, and aerial reconnaissance, and possessed skills, which were foreign to him, yet integral to the hunt for the women and their killer.

Before the meeting, things hadn't proceeded as planned. Sexton had misidentified the location of the suspect's home. Luckily, the DMV records verified that Duvall Bennett lived within Brickyard Estates at 72, not 70, Limerick Circle, as Sexton had identified. The houses looked similar, making it an easy, but nearly catastrophic, mistake.

And the team's efforts to obtain the search warrant of the premises had been disastrous. He'd dispatched his law clerk to the court to process the documents, but the boy had returned flustered and empty-handed. Usually, the judges executed Hal's warrants on the spot, but a judicial conference in New York City had stripped the courthouse of its judges. The kid had been told to return in the morning unless he wanted to trot over to a neighboring county. The irony hadn't been lost on Hal. Every regional judge was *incommunicado* in the Big Apple.

Hal wasn't used to waiting, and in this case, the timing stunk. Cindie had prematurely issued a press release announcing the task force, and they'd planned to have Bennett and Patrick in custody before the news hit the media.

Worst of all, the publicity would certainly tip off the killer that they were closing in on him.

Hal lay back on the pillows, watching the ceiling fan whirl slowly overhead, trying to relax. But he couldn't. The investigation wasn't his only nightmare. He worried about discovering more cold cases now that the word was out, and about the killer fleeing the area to continue his butchery elsewhere.

Plus, the files stacked downstairs on the den's coffee table taunted him. He'd reviewed the dossiers a dozen times, and each backstory differed from the next. Kiara was four months pregnant. Eve's parents had been searching for her for two years. Rebecca, Jessie's friend, was a tattoo artist from a respected family. They were all loners with common denominators of drug addiction, sex trafficking, and minor arrests tethering them together.

Each disappearance had occurred within the past two years, and sadly, in each instance, the local departments had dropped the ball. His stomach soured at the realization that he had, too. He'd been the Assistant District Attorney, head of Major Crimes, focusing on violent felony offenders, yet unaware of the Missing Persons reports. Hal scolded himself for his complacency. He should've known. It was his job to know. This brutal failure gnawed at his gut, his conscience, like the hull of an icebreaker biting into the frozen Hudson River.

In an exhausted haze, he rose from bed, careful not to wake Jessie. He wandered barefoot down the hallway, pausing in the doorway to watch Lily sleep. The moon bathed her in a heavenly silvery glow, and a universe of stars twinkled overhead. The image soothed him, erasing his blood-soaked nightmare.

"Rough night?" Jessie whispered, creeping up behind him.

"Sorry, I didn't mean to disturb you." He turned to her and slipped his arms around her, hugging her tight and never wanting to let go. Through the thin cotton nightgown which smelled fresh like spring rain, her skin felt warm, reassuring. He wanted to cry, to bare his soul to her and release the guilt chewing him up inside. Yet, he didn't know how or where to begin.

She entwined her fingers in his damp locks and pulled his head down to her shoulder, saying everything without uttering a word. In the darkness, her body swayed to an inaudible tune playing to banish his demons. The tension in his shoulders eased, and he joined in the dance to the rhythms of their heartbeats.

* * *

Hal stood in the empty kitchen, sipping his first coffee of the day. Jessie had left early for a yoga class and to drop Lily off at Lena and Ed's. In the driveway, the raindrops pelted the blue plastic wrapper of the *Poughkeepsie Journal*, half-submerged in a puddle.

For the past week, gray clouds had socked in the Hudson Valley, bringing intermittent deluges. Hal didn't mind springtime showers because the golf greens and fairways grew lush in their aftermath. But he was a frontline guy, and the thought of conducting a manhunt with wind-driven rain pelting his face and body was unwelcome.

On the counter next to his briefcase and rain slicker, his charging cell phone buzzed incessantly. Hal ignored it, enjoying the peace before the storm. As he sipped on his coffee, his brain connected the waterlogged newspaper and the phone calls. He grabbed an umbrella and dashed outside to retrieve the paper.

Within seconds, he was back inside the kitchen, shaking off the excess water. He stripped off the blue sheath and flattened the soggy news on the butcher-block island. The runny ink made the print almost illegible. However, the headline remained crystal clear.

MISSING WOMEN SEARCH BEGINS–FAMILIES IRATE AT POLICE DELAYS.

Shit.

He'd hoped the task force would have had more lead-time to produce results before the media blitz, and that the premature announcement wouldn't jeopardize their mission.

Shit. Now the pressure was on.

Perhaps, he could flip the situation by establishing a Tips Hotline to engage the public with a call to action. He'd get Cindie on it ASAP.

He eyed his jitterbugging phone.

Shit.

* * *

By the time Hal stepped into his office, the mist shrouding the Mid-Hudson Bridge had lifted. The sky had brightened, although his mood remained dark and gloomy.

The blinking light on his voicemail goaded him, as Cindie popped her head into his office. "I know," he said brusquely, stopping her before she could speak.

"No, no, you don't." She shook her head. "We've received calls from the victim's families asking why the hell we didn't get on this sooner. And your constituents are also calling." Cindie hesitated, twisting her mouth in contemplation. "How can I put this? Um, to demand your resignation."

"What?"

"Your immediate resignation." Her tortured expression conveyed her sympathy. "And it's all over the news websites and social media. Here, check out these Twitter feeds." She handed him her cellphone.

@SweetAnnabel–*How can the DA sleep at night?* #OustSamuelsNow

@msilverman–*I bet that if his wife, sister or mother disappeared, he'd be searching for them pretty damn quick.* #DADeadGirls.

@TBaker–*The DA has let us down. Time for him to go.* #SamuelsIsPro-Pho-bic.

@cwooden–*Lock up your children. The streets aren't safe.* #PokSerialKiller AtLarge.

"That's not all," she said. "There's an outcry for your resignation on our Facebook page. Hal, what are we going to do?"

"This is absurd. We can't let it distract us. We have to proceed and get the job done." Hal swiveled his chair away from her and stared out the window at the sun peeking through the fog.

His face grew hot with anger at the unwarranted attacks. He'd dedicated his life to the public service. First, in the Teach for America corps, next for the City of New York, and now as DA he'd committed his blood, sweat, and tears to solving these crimes. As soon as the evidence had pointed to a potential serial killer, he'd jumped on it. There'd been no delay, no expense spared. He'd enlisted the foremost criminal justice experts in the state to help locate these women and their alleged killer. And he'd located a live, reliable witness, and a narrow list of suspects. Hal was so close he could taste it. He was on the verge of an arrest and just needed a little more time.

Hal ran his index finger along the rim of the moist shirt collar, constricting his neck like a boa. He loosened his tie and unbuttoned the top button. Reaching into his pocket for his phone, he scrolled through his recent voicemails, halting at County Executive Ketchum's.

He replayed the message.

"We need to talk," Dan Ketchum said, his voice tight.

At first thought, the message hadn't seemed ominous. However, considering the public lynching on social media, he sensed a veiled threat in those four words.

"Screw this. I'm going to put this issue to rest, once and for all." He punched the call-back button.

Chapter Forty-Nine

In the center of Reservoir Square Park, a Civil War Monument dedicated to the New York 128th Infantry Division, lorded over the contemporary landscape of drugs and sex. One block away, Ebony's unmarked SUV parked facing westward toward the monument of a Union soldier guarding the American flag. She occupied the passenger seat, and Zander sat behind the wheel.

"It's been a while since we've been on a stakeout," Zander said, shoving a stick of gum into his mouth. He offered her one, but she declined.

"Yeah, there's a reason for that. It's a lousy waste of time. And what's the deal with white Toyotas? Don't they make them in any other color?"

It was ten in the morning and they'd been babysitting the park since the yellow and blue streaks of dawn had faded away. During their surveillance, a dozen white Toyotas had scooted around the park, but none had been their target. The boredom made Ebony so frustrated she wanted to punch something. Instead, she crumbled the wrapper of her blueberry muffin and pitched it into the heap of water bottles and fast-food bags accumulating on the back seat.

"Don't get pissy with me because you and lover boy are fighting." He threw her an annoyed expression. "And you're cleaning this car after our shift."

Her problems with Drew were none of his business. Last night, they'd had a knockdown, drag-out fight. Their competitive personalities had turned a quibble about not putting the dishes in the dishwasher into a battle about work, sex, and her meds. Drew had stormed out of the apartment to his truck and texted her.

"Sorry, Suga. Gone to the firehouse. Need some space. Drew."

Coward.

Lately, work had stressed them out. For the past two months, Drew's schedule had been the opposite of hers. He worked mostly nights and she worked mostly days, leaving them minimal time together. When they were together, they stomped on each other's nerves, unless they were having sex. Soon, next month, Drew would be back on the day shift, and life would return to normal. It always did, but maybe not this time. Love shouldn't be hard. Relationships shouldn't be hard.

She'd had it with all men, from Drew to Zander to Duvall Bennett.

"I've had enough of this. We should hit the street, not sit here ingesting carbs." Ebony glanced at the composite drawing of Doc taped to the computer console. She wondered how many guys looked as bizarre as their suspect with his large Frankenstein head, beady eyes, Carmel-colored skin, and freckles. She prayed they'd be able to nab him before he struck again.

Zander shot off another look of exasperation. "Okay, in a half-hour we'll take a ride. A short one."

"Or maybe now's a good time." Ebony gestured toward two white Toyotas cruising past them. The first continued northward, while the second slowly rounded the park. They glimpsed the nine stars on the license plate. It was a vanity plate with an Army Reserve insignia, and the letters WAZUPDC matched the DMV record for Duvall Bennett.

"There's no warrant, so we need to take this slow."

"Slow is relative," she replied.

The Toyota leisurely circled Reservoir Square three more times, and on the third pass, Zander blended into the traffic, two cars behind their prey. They followed him northward past Mansion Square Park, and past the Dutchess County jail complex toward College Hill Park. The Toyota's red directional signal blinked on and he turned into the park's entrance, making a quick left into the lower lot near the basketball and tennis courts. They waited curbside as the car performed a U-turn and pulled back onto the street. Once more, they blended into the traffic, stalking their quarry to Main Street along the strip of fast-food joints, beer warehouses, and gas stations, and then back to Reservoir Square.

"Do you think he's playing with us? Maybe he knows we're following him?" Zander asked.

"Nah, he's trawling, but there's no talent."

The Toyota jumped onto the eastbound arterial, driving toward Brickyard Hill, and they shadowed him to 72 Limerick Circle. His home. They lagged a block away, watching the driver exit his car. The black man, built like a linebacker, glanced around suspiciously as he dragged a garbage can from the curb to the house. He opened the garage door, pulled the car inside, and the door slid closed.

"Come on, that's him," Ebony urged, looking at the composite sketch. "Let's pick Bennett up on Lissie's complaint, or maybe on traffic. He sailed through a stop sign back there."

"Are you nuts? We need to wait for the warrant. How many times do I have to tell you to cool your jets?"

"I can't stand this. Doing nothing."

"We're not. We tailed him and he's done nothing wrong." Zander's eyes fixed on her, steady. "We've confirmed his residence, so we'll wait for the warrant."

Ebony shrank back into the seat, resenting her partner's righteousness and obstinacy. Mr. WAZUPDC was clearly up to something fishy. Just like Drew and Zander. The lot of crazy, selfish bastards made her sick, and she wished they'd leave her alone. Let her do her thing and make the arrest.

Or maybe she should split and leave the lot of them behind. Drew, Zander, the chief, and Hal. She could take the cool thirty grand she'd found in Lissie's freezer, score some heavy-duty painkillers, and hit the beaches of Cancun.

She stared out the car's window and huffed. Who was she kidding? As much as she wanted the fantasy, she wanted Bennett more.

The dashboard radio crackled to life. "Car 25, return to base. Report to the chief immediately. Do you copy?"

* * *

The duty sergeant intercepted Zander and Ebony as they passed the on-duty desk. "Chief's gone, but he left you this." He handed them a note on the official department stationary.

"There's a present for you in Number 2," Shepardson's message said.

Ebony shoved the door open to Interrogation Room Two, where a nervous rookie guarded a burly black man with a scruffy beard who was handcuffed to the table. The kid thrust the file folder at Zander and sprinted past him.

"Who do we have here?" Zander asked, thumbing through the file and before passing it to Ebony. "John Harrison Patrick."

"You can't hold me. I'm free on bail. If you've got nothing else on me, you have to cut me loose." Patrick combed his fingers through frizzy shoulder-length hair tinged with silver.

"Nice duds," Zander said, mocking the suspect's camouflage shirt and pants embroidered with patches glorifying America and the NRA. "John Harrison Patrick," he repeated, clucking his tongue on the K in a threatening tone. "All the infamous murderers have three names. John Wilkes Booth. Mark David Chapman. Lee Harvey Oswald."

"Are you screwing with me or are you going to tell me what you want?" Patrick rolled up his sleeves to display his iron man biceps. He relaxed back in his chair and crossed his outstretched legs at the ankle as though he could handle anything they could throw at him.

"Mr. Patrick, the report states that you were arrested on April 30th for reckless driving, reckless endangerment, and DWI." Ebony's stomach soured as she studied the details of the arrest report and returned it to Zander. "You ran a red light and collided with another vehicle on the arterial highway. You must have been in quite a hurry."

"No comment," Patrick replied.

"How does a scumbag like you make bail?"

Ebony kicked Zander under the table and glared at him. She couldn't have him going off half-cocked on another case. This was their shot to identify him as John Doe. "Mr. Patrick, we're not here to discuss the accident. We'd like to ask you about some women whose whereabouts are unaccounted for."

"I don't know what you're talking about." Patrick's reply was a bit too quick, too glib.

She slapped the composite drawing onto the table. "This sure looks a lot like you, doesn't it?"

His eyes shifted to the sketch, and then rapidly back to her. "That's not me. No way."

Without a doubt, their two suspects, Patrick and Duvall Bennett, bore a striking resemblance to the sketch and to each other. Both men exceeded six feet in height, possessed broad, athletic shoulders, and the muscular build of a grizzly. Either of them could snap a woman's neck with little effort, especially one as petite as Lissie Sexton.

Ebony hadn't gotten close enough to Bennett's Toyota to steal a good look at his face, but Patrick's was weathered, mid-forties, with cigarette wrinkles around his mouth and nicotine-stained teeth. He bore the appearance of a middle-aged stoner, more anarchist than rapist or murderer. From the body odor, Patrick didn't appear interested in his personal hygiene and looked like a guy who'd have to pay for sex. And his uniform was camo, not scrubs.

Ebony studied him as he awkwardly crossed and uncrossed his arms. "You like women, don't you, Mr. Patrick?"

"I can take them or leave them. They get in the way when you're living off the land."

After some prodding, Patrick revealed himself to be a shiftless wanderer, moving around the country from odd job to odd job, chasing the sun. "I'm camped out at the Boy Scout Campground, Camp Nooteeming, up north in Salt Point. My cousin oversees the place and lets me crash there. The terrain's rough, but the hard ground's thawed enough to set up a campsite. For now." He rested his hands behind his head.

She'd recently read about the troubles plaguing the Boys Scouts of America and their campgound in the Hudson Valley. Camp Nooteeming was being sold to help compensate the thousands of victims who'd claimed their scout leaders had sexually assaulted them. It was a strange coincidence that Patrick was living there.

"We need your cousin's contact information to verify your story," Ebony said. "Can you tell us where you've lived during the past two years?"

"You've got the report, it says in there."

This freeloader was giving Ebony a headache right behind her left eye, and if Patrick didn't watch it, he'd be getting another free night at the City Hall Hilton just for pissing her off.

"We want to hear it from your mouth, Mr. Patrick," Zander said, twirling a pencil in his fingers like a baton.

"I've been in Nevada, New Mexico, Texas, Utah, Oregon, Colorado, and Florida."

"What about Massachusetts?" Zander asked.

"I've passed through there."

They were finally getting somewhere.

"Weren't you questioned in connection with the rape and murder of a sixteen-year-old girl in Springfield last year?" Ebony asked, tapping on the rap sheet in front of her.

"I suppose if the report says so, it must be true," Patrick replied with a hint of sarcasm.

She and Zander exchanged glances.

"We're done for now, Mr. Patrick. But we're going to detain you for further questioning."

They exchanged glances again. Lissie needed to come back in for questioning and a lineup.

Chapter Fifty

Having John Harrison Patrick in custody should have satisfied Ebony, but it didn't. Patrick may physically resemble the John Doe sketch, but he didn't feel like their killer. From their brief interview, he'd revealed himself as a nomad with a penchant for guns. The charges pending against him also pegged him as a drunk, not the sadistic, over-sexed attacker Lissie had described.

"Z, I don't think Patrick's our guy," she said.

"We'll know more after the raid, so sit tight."

She itched for immediate confirmation, yet the next phase of the investigation was beyond her grasp. The chief had locked them out of the New York State Police's raid on Patrick's campsite, leaving them sidelined like two rookies.

Arguing with Chief Shepardson had proven fruitless.

"I've told you, no," the chief said. "You're staying put to wait for the Bennett warrant." He sat behind his desk, jabbing at his teeth with a toothpick, and then spitting into the trashcan. "I don't want you and Pulaski traipsing around in the woods with the state troopers. Their maneuvers up in Salt Point may only be a half-hour away, but they're outside our jurisdiction. It's going to be your job to bust Bennett once the warrant hits. Do you copy?"

Ebony felt useless, watching and waiting for the action to unfold. She was tempted to assert her seniority on the task force, but opted to accept her defeat with grace. After all, Shepardson was the boss, with the ultimate power over this investigation and her career.

An hour later, the chief summoned them to the dingy training room in the bowels of City Hall.

"Ah, the sweet smell of success," Zander said. The savory, smoky bite of the fifty pounds of pot confiscated from Kurt Hendricks' apartment filtered into the training facility from the evidence room next door.

Ebony playfully elbowed his ribs as the chief motioned for them to take chairs facing the blackboard-sized flat-screen mounted to the far wall.

"Any moment," Shepardson explained, "we'll receive the trooper's live body-cam feed. Their Millbrook unit has just arrived at Lake Nooteeming and is preparing for the raid on Patrick's lodgings and the campground."

"Sergeant Ken Toomey here, sir," said a deep, bodiless voice.

The screen blinked to life with a shot panning the area's parking lot. This time of year, Nooteeming was usually a ghost town, but an army of gray uniforms had swarmed the site and the adjacent muddy playing fields.

"Chief Shepardson, hold on, sir," Toomey said, as the picture faded to snow. "We seem to have lost visuals. Can you hear me, sir? We're on the move."

"Affirmative, Sergeant."

The sharp edge of Ebony's chair cut into her thighs as she heard the pounding of men's boots slogging through mud and tramping through fields of high grass. Snapping twigs and brush accompanied Toomey's heavy breathing as she envisioned his ground unit searching for Patrick's makeshift encampment. The approaching thunder of whirling propellers drowned out the distant baying of bloodhounds, and she imagined the choppers hovering overhead, searching for signs of life or death.

"Apparently Troop K spared no expense. It costs a small fortune to dispatch the choppers from Stewart Airport," the chief said, "but it's the only way to comb the three hundred acres for signs of life or freshly turned earth in the dense foliage."

A crackling sound filled the room, and then a distant shout.

"Sir, the target has been located two hundred yards to the left. Right where the suspect indicated," a garbled voice reported. The sound of running footsteps followed.

"Sir," Toomey said, "we've found a tent site two hundred yards out at ten o'clock on the southern end of the lake, close to the ranger's station. A black fiberglass canoe, presumably the suspect's, is resting on the lakeshore, and his laundry—jeans, camo shirts, and boxers—is strung on a rope between two trees."

The image on the screen flickered to life as Toomey's gloved hands peeled back the flap of an army surplus tent, creased with wear. "I believe we're back online. Do you read me?"

"Yes, Sergeant, proceed," the chief replied.

The camera broadcast Patrick's stark accommodations; a sleeping bag, a few tin pots and pans, a portable camping stove, and a Coleman lantern perched on a collection of older *Playboy* magazines from when the girls still got naked. Toomey opened the lid of a white cooler and examined the milk, eggs, orange juice, and bread inside. In the corner sat an empty luggable loo, a necessity since the camp's restrooms had been winterized.

"No alcohol or drugs are visible on the premises," Toomey reported, "only bottled water."

The grizzled face of the troop's commander, Captain Lawrence Worthy, appeared on the screen. He pushed his sunglasses up on his forehead. "Shep, there's no sign of the girls or foul play up here at the camp, but we've confiscated a modest arsenal from the storage unit inside the bed of Patrick's truck."

"What's the haul?" Shepardson asked.

"He'd concealed two Remington custom hunting rifles and a semi-automatic varmint rifle in a blanket along with a round wheel hunting bow, an ultra-light crossbow with a scope, arrows, a fishing pole, a variety of hunting knives, and a jungle machete. There's no ammo, and none of the guns appear to have been fired recently."

Captain Worthy's bravado in itemizing Patrick's arsenal hadn't been lost on Ebony. She was about to speak, but the commander continued as though reading her mind.

"There's nothing illegal about the weapons stash, but this guy fashions himself as a one-man militia." Worthy hesitated for a moment while Toomey

272

whispered into his ear. He frowned, and when he continued, his manner had turned hard, angry. "Two of my men are down with minor injuries from his booby traps, constructed of ropes and netting concealed around the complex. Fortunately, the hounds uncovered the rusty bear traps buried in the leaves outside the tent's entrance before they'd injured anyone."

"Sir, we're collecting the evidence, and forensics is on its way, but there's not much here. Just a loner living off the grid," Toomey said.

"I'll inform Samuels," the commander said curtly.

"Over and out," Toomey said. The chief thanked him and the screen faded to black.

Ebony had been gnawing on her fingernails, contemplating their next move. They were narrowing the possibilities to one name. Duvall Bennett.

"Aren't you glad you didn't waste your time?" the chief asked.

Her teeth nipped at a hangnail, drawing blood.

"Jones?"

His voice, like her thoughts, was a million miles away.

John Harrison Patrick. He was downstairs, waiting for her.

Duvall Bennett. He was out there waiting for her.

They'd detained Patrick for over twelve hours, and she calculated that time was running out. Under the law, they could hold him until tomorrow at the latest, and then they'd have to either charge him or cut him loose. Lissie, who'd sounded pleased and relieved to hear from Ebony, was en route to Poughkeepsie for a lineup later in the afternoon. If Bennett and Patrick both appeared in the line-up, and Lissie identified one of them, they'd have their killer.

A soft nudge to her shin drew her attention to the training room. "Chief?" Zander asked, covering for her.

"You're both dismissed. I'll let you know when the warrant arrives."

* * *

Ebony's heart raced as she clutched the folded white paper. It was their ticket to hunt a killer. Zander leaned back in his chair with his pointy black boots up on his desk. When he spied her approaching, he quickly hung up his cellphone and snuck it into his pocket. He lowered his eyes as if she'd caught him red-handed at the cookie jar.

She had. The department discouraged personal calls during duty hours, but she really didn't care. His love life was his business, and she pitied the girl on the other end of the phone.

Ebony smacked his shoulder with the paper. "Chief says we're good to go. Come on."

Zander sprang from his chair and followed her like a stray pup. He'd asked no questions because, like her, waiting made him bored and fidgety. He preferred to wrap up cases quickly and move on to the next challenge, as he did with his conga line of girlfriends.

They drove in silence to Limerick Circle and parked across the street from Duvall Bennett's drab gray split-level. The glassy-eyed mailman raced down the front walk toward them, clasping a handkerchief over his nose and mouth. Upon reaching the street, he coughed and gulped at the air.

This response seemed odd, but upon exiting their car, the stench slapped Ebony's face like a cold rag. An acrid, rotten egg smell caught in the back of her throat, making her gag.

Zander, whose senses were unusually tolerant, wrinkled his nose, reached into his pocket, and plastered his handkerchief against his face. "Are we downwind from a sewage plant?"

They stood in the street and surveyed the sad-looking house with its sun-bleached black shutters and its lawn choked by weeds. The place was an embarrassment to the neighborhood of modest, neatly maintained homes.

"Maybe the odor is coming from over there." Ebony gestured toward the driveway where a mountain of black plastic garbage bags, broken lawn furniture, mattresses, and flat-screen televisions lay. "Whatever it is, we've got to check this out. Come on, let's go."

Moments later, they knocked on the front door and waited.

The door slowly opened, and the oily scent of Pine-Sol spilled out of the house. The toxic combination of rotten eggs and tar rolled around on her tongue and stung her eyes. Through her glassy vision, she spied a face

274

peeking out from the slender opening secured by a brass chain. A petite woman with dewy, sepia skin and silver hair straightened into a short bob scrutinized them as though they'd arrived from Mars. Judging from the royal blue shirt draped over her shoulder serape-style and her flowered apron, they'd interrupted her housekeeping chores.

"Is Mr. Bennett at home?" Zander asked. They flashed their shiny badges and sparkling smiles. "We'd like to speak with him."

"Mr. Bennett?" the woman replied, confused. "Why, he's not here. Can you tell me what this is about?"

"When will he return?" Ebony asked, disappointed their prey had eluded them.

"I'm afraid my husband's at work and he won't be back until dinnertime. Perhaps you'd like to return then." Her manner was dignified, but her tone was riddled with distress.

"We'd like to speak to Duvall Bennett," Ebony said, correcting the confusion.

"You want to speak to my son, Dewey?" Mrs. Bennett pivoted away from them and bellowed. "Dooo-wweeee." There was no reply to her call. "He was here a few minutes ago. Let me check to see where he is."

The creaking of springs and the clunking of a motorized garage door drew their attention away from the front door. Ebony and Zander raced toward the driveway, where the garage doors strained open to reveal a white Toyota. An ogre of a man was preparing to get into the driver's seat, however, upon seeing them he appeared to panic. With the power of a pro wrestler, he charged toward them, swatting Zander aside as though he were a mosquito.

Ebony planted her legs firmly on the blacktop, ready to thwart Bennett as he hurtled toward her. "Stop, police!" she shouted, her hand slipping to her holster. He wasn't nimble, but she felt the power of the two hundred fifty-pound freight train barreling toward her. Her hand gripped her weapon. "Stop!"

Duvall Bennett failed to heed her warnings. As the distance between them shrank to a car length, Ebony raised her gun, aimed, and pulled the trigger, counting to five. They were the longest five seconds of her life.

The Taser darts flew straight and fast, penetrating Bennett's thin t-shirt. He yelped as the electrical probes attached to his chest, tethering him to her gun. Like a marionette, he danced as fifty thousand volts of electricity surged through him, overriding his muscles, and causing him to collapse onto the driveway.

Ebony stood over their suspect as he convulsed and curled into the fetal position. In stark contrast to his mother, Duvall Bennett's complexion was a creamy caramel with cocoa freckles. Up close, there was something freakishly cartoonish about Bennett; the kinky black hair slicked back into a ponytail accentuated the blockhead topping his muscular body.

"Mr. Bennett, we're taking you in for questioning in connection with the assault of Elisabeth Sexton," Zander said, kneeling over the man. He detached the handcuffs from his belt and snapped them on Bennett's wrists.

"What have you done to my son? There must be some mistake," Mrs. Bennett screamed, racing to her son's side. "Is he all right?"

"He'll be fine in a few minutes."

Zander heaved their stunned suspect to his feet and led him toward their car.

Mrs. Bennett clasped her hand over her mouth, blinking back the tears. "Oh, Dewey," she cried.

This had been too easy, Ebony thought. Perhaps Bennett was another red herring, and Lissie had fingered the wrong guy. She'd admitted she'd been high during the attack and had serviced a lot of men. Maybe she'd confused him with someone else. Or she'd lied. But why would she? Were they back at ground zero?

Ebony's eyes settled on the distraught mother watching her son shuffle toward their Explorer. The breeze picked up, ruffled the shirt on Mrs. Bennett's shoulder, and sent it fluttering to the ground. The name, "D. Bennett," was embroidered in white script across the heart of the royal blue scrub top.

* * *

Walking Bennett along the cinderblock passageway leading into the station, Ebony thought about the crisp, white moment of silence following a catastrophe when time appeared to stand still. The split second when, after the twisted wreckage settles onto the asphalt, disbelief becomes reality. When bystanders can't fathom the horror before their eyes, and try as they may, they can't banish the images of rubble, blood, and dirt.

Such silence and awe greeted them as she and Zander escorted the giant, Duvall Bennett, through the police department's central booking area into Interrogation Room Two, and slammed the door behind them.

Zander unlocked the cuffs and hooked them back on his belt.

Duvall Bennett smirked and rubbed the red welts on his wrists. "Carpal Tunnel. Sometimes it aches so bad, I can't sleep."

"Mr. Bennett, we've brought you in because we're investigating an assault and battery complaint. Do you know Elisabeth Sexton? Lissie Sexton? Coco?"

"Can't say." He shifted his gaze to avoid their probing, but she'd already glimpsed his charcoal eyes. They were deep-set, like buttons on his doughy features, which bore a resemblance to Mancuso's sketch. She'd recognize the lethal demon lurking behind Bennett's eyes anywhere.

"Or won't say?" Ebony asked, catching the brief spark of recognition on his face. She'd dealt with criminals like him before. He wasn't the sharpest pencil in the box, but he was a cunning killer with a plan.

"I meet lots of people in my line of work."

"You're an ultrasound technician? With which group?" Zander asked.

"I'm a floater with River Valley Health Services. I travel throughout their network."

"They're based in six counties up and down the Hudson Valley, correct?"

"Western Connecticut and the Berkshires, too." Bennett rolled up his shirtsleeves, and he appeared to notice Zander studying his forearm. Small purplish dots formed a crescent on his skin, and a square flesh-colored bandage covered the back of his hand. "I cover a lot of territory. I'm a busy guy and I meet lots of people."

"How did you get those marks?" Zander asked.

"Carpal tunnel." Bennett rolled down his sleeves and thrust his hands into his lap, out of sight. "I don't know what this woman said, but I didn't touch anyone inappropriately."

"Mr. Bennett, we've had several complaints about you from different women." Ebony paused. "They've stated you roughed them up pretty good." Over the past six months, the department had received two other complaints about Bennett, or a man fitting his description, which they hadn't investigated. He'd walked free and the girls, Kiara Taylor and Camila Cordoba, were now missing. The injustice made her nauseous.

If only.

"Think what you want. I've done nothing wrong," Bennett scoffed. A flicker of violence charged his eyes, and he glowered at Ebony as though the roles had been reversed; Bennett was the accuser, and she was the accused.

Her fingers fondled the handle of her gun in its holster and squeezed it.

Like hell, you didn't. But I've got you now, Duvall Bennett, and I'm not letting go.

Chapter Fifty-One

Fear juiced Jessie's heart. This was her first lineup, and the cops had sequestered her and Lissie in the police observation booth, which wasn't much bigger than a utility closet. As she waited for the proceedings to begin, her chest felt as though it was going to explode because only a slender pane of one-way glass separated them from a serial killer.

Before entering the booth with Officer Wyatt, the blind administrator of the lineup, Ebony and Zander had explained the procedures. And as per the regulations, Lissie had signed the instruction sheet. They'd also warned them that to make the identification admissible in court, it was essential for Lissie to adhere to the rules. This was nearly impossible for Lissie Sexton, and Jessie knew her presence was necessary to temper Lissie's volatility.

Even as a bystander, Jessie couldn't dodge the attack of nerves, because the appearance of the serial killer, John Doe, was imminent. She'd come face-to-face with a murderer before. Her mentor, Terrence Butterfield. As she waited for the latest killer to arrive, Terrence's name stabbed her heart, both for his betrayal of her and his revenge against her.

John Doe was different. He'd sexually assaulted Lissie Sexton and, perhaps, countless other women who'd never be coming home to their families, friends, or lovers. Lissie had been the lucky one.

"The person who attacked you may or may not be in the lineup," Zander had explained.

"Then what's the point? Why did you drag me back here?" Lissie asked.

"Remember," Ebony said, hooking her thumbs through her belt loops,

279

"it's just as important to clear an innocent person as it is to identify a guilty one."

Bull. They all knew that line was a crock. They all wanted to catch a killer.

The atmosphere inside the tiny viewing booth grew tense as the lights lowered, setting the stage for the show taking place on the opposite side of the viewing window. So far, the identification process had been unlike the cases Jessie had studied in law school or had seen on television or in the movies. Each of the six participants, including a cast of fillers who resembled Lissie's description of John Doe, would be paraded separately in the participation room for Lissie's inspection. There'd be no melodramatic chorus line marched before a height chart on the wall.

Standing beside Jessie, Lissie gouged her neon green nails into the window frame and she pressed her forehead against the glass, leaving an oily smudge on the surface. The glaring light streaming into the booth through the glass reflected Lissie's unmistakable anguish. It was Jessie's job to be the strong one, the rational one, so she assumed an air of confidence to disguise her own fears.

"Are you sure they can't see me?" Lissie asked, nervously shifting from one foot to the other.

The officer cleared his throat. He'd remained so quiet, Jessie had forgotten he was there. "Miss, they only see their own reflection in the mirror. They know someone is watching them, but they don't know who it is. Are you ready?"

"Uh, huh?"

Jessie glanced at Lissie, who stared straight ahead through the glass. Her mind rattled off the description of the man who'd attacked Lissie and who'd be among the group they were about to observe. Black. Tall. Long, dark hair. Muscular. Dark Eyes. Flat Nose. Wide Lips. Broad Forehead. Close-set eyes. Two hundred fifty-pounds.

Lissie's breath remained even and calm as the first two men strode by. They were both dark-skinned and strapping, as Lissie had described, and Lissie watched them in silence. When the third entered the room, she cocked her head to one side, appearing to focus on the blackened fingernails gripping the "NUMBER 3" sign pressed against his undershirt. He was slightly taller than his predecessors, more rugged with a grizzly beard, and muscular enough to dislocate a woman's jaw with one slap. His wolf grey eyes exuded smugness, as though he were above the law.

Lissie's hands flew to her neck, absentmindedly stroking the dots on her throat, which had faded from amethyst to jade. Seeming to realize what she was doing, she dropped them limply to her sides. After he'd left, she quietly asked to see him again.

"You must inspect all the participants first before we can run through them all again," Officer Wyatt replied, and they continued on until the last man entered the participation room.

Lissie smiled weakly and slipped her hand into Jessie's. It was cold and clammy.

On the opposite side of the one-way mirror, a beast of a man with thick fingers grasping a sign stating "NUMBER 6," lumbered into the lineup room. Stripped down to his white undershirt and slacks, he pivoted and faced the mirror. Jessie watched him. He looked familiar, but she couldn't figure out how she knew him. Then it dawned on her.

No, she thought, it couldn't be the tech from Dr. S's office. The sonographer. Maybe he was the filler Ebony had mentioned, the person they used to smoke out the actual suspect.

Jessie squeezed her eyes shut and tried to picture the tech's face. The room had been dimly lit so he could read the monitor, and his features had been shadowy, ominous. He'd had a square eraser head that was too small for his linebacker's body, and when he'd smirked at her, his teeth had been the color of corn kernels.

She slowly reopened her eyes. The tech stood before her holding the "NUMBER 6," with the corner of his lip curled in arrogance. Number Six's arm twitched, and Jessie's eyes fell to the flesh-colored bandage on his caramel-colored skin. A sinking feeling grabbed her. The room seemed to shift, and she swayed slightly, giving way at her knees.

A squeal emanated from Lissie's direction, and the damp hand clutching

Jessie's squeezed. Even in the darkness, Jessie could read the horror of recognition on Lissie's face.

Images of this animal's brutal hands flashed before her eyes. First, squeezing Lissie's neck, making her gasp for air, and then stabbing his wand inside Jessie's own body. "Tell me the pain makes you hot," he'd said to Lissie. He'd tortured the poor girl to the brink of death. And with a sadistic sneer, he'd left Jessie's gut blazing with blood trickling between her thighs.

Now, viewing John Doe in the bright light, she would never forget his dark, threatening eyes. In an instant, Number Six had become the glue binding her to Lissie, and Jessie swore she was going to make him pay for his abuse.

"That's him. That's Doc," Lissie shouted angrily. "He's the asshole who beat me up. Let me at him. I want him to pay."

Jessie's mind raced. She needed to get Ebony. Now. She needed to tell Hal what Number Six had done to Lissie and the other women. And what he'd had done to her.

She opened her mouth to speak, but the full force of Lissie's body slammed into her, shoving her aside. Jessie's jaw snapped shut as her temple smacked the cold, hard surface of the window with an echoing thud. White pain ricocheted within her skull, and she slid to the ground, cradling her head in her trembling hands.

"Miss, please calm yourself," Officer Wyatt shouted, struggling to subdue Lissie. He tilted his head away to avoid the onslaught of whirling neon green claws. "Don't make me cuff you, miss."

"Let me at him," Lissie hollered, trying to wriggle free from the officer's hold.

Jessie scrambled to her feet, and without hesitation, lunged at Lissie from behind. Her arms encircled Lissie's waist, and she tucked her throbbing head between Lissie's tense shoulders, riding the twisting, bucking body. Surprised at the strength packed into the woman's slender form, she toughened her grip and yanked to disentangle Lissie from the officer.

"Lissie!"

"Screw you. Whose side are you on?" Lissie arched her back, continuing to wrestle with the officer.

"Lissie, stop," Jessie shouted. "Use your head."

As if by magic, Lissie stopped resisting. Her muscles slackened. A long moment passed, and no one spoke or stirred. Jessie listened to the thrumming of her pulse as she, Lissie, and the officer stood in a tangle of arms and legs, each waiting for the other to make the next move.

"Come on. Are you good? Can he release you?" Jessie asked finally, letting her hands slip away.

Once freed, Lissie rushed toward the total darkness of the far corner of the room. A mixture of heavy breathing and stifled sobs filled the air.

"Why do you make everything so difficult?" Jessie asked.

"Because life's hard. Maybe not your life, but mine is damn hard." Lissie's tone was flat, yet venomous.

"So, make it easy. Tell Ebony and Zander so they can nail his ass to the wall."

Chapter Fifty-Two

Bang!

The clatter of chairs crashing, muffled shouts, and loud thumps sent Ebony and Zander flying toward the observation booth. The worried expression on Zander's face mirrored Ebony's own concern. *Lissie.*

Ebony grasped the doorknob, ready to turn it, but the tumult subsided. Officer Wyatt, his hair ruffled and his plump cheeks as red as pomegranates, flung open the door from the inside and flicked on the overhead lights inside the room. Ebony and Zander rushed in, and in astonishment, they surveyed the upended tables, tipped over chairs, and papers littering the floor.

"Is everyone okay? Jessie? Lissie?" she asked.

From the corner, Lissie eyed her, then the exit, with the uneasiness of a convict plotting her escape. The woman began inching her way toward the door.

Jessie's cheeks flushed, and her eyes shifted to the floor. Her curly hair was an untamed frizz, her silk blouse had lost several buttons, and her blazer hung off one shoulder. One of her feet was bare, and the missing high heel lay hidden among the rubble. She nursed a bump on her forehead as though she'd gone a few rounds in the ring, and it was no mystery who her sparring partner had been. The question was why.

Wyatt shouldered his way past them into the hallway, slapping the clipboard against Zander's chest. "Good luck. The short one's got claws like a polecat." He flicked his head toward Lissie, who responded by flipping him the bird.

"What happened in here?" Zander asked. He stepped in front of Lissie, blocking her path. "No, you don't. Hold up. You're not done yet."

"Are you sure you're all right? Do you need me to call the paramedics?" Ebony asked Jessie.

Jessie shook her head and dabbed her split lip with a tissue. "I'll live."

"Lissie, would you like to explain—" Ebony began, but Jessie interrupted her.

"She's upset. She recognized—"

Ebony leaned in, studied the clipboard over Zander's shoulder, and pivoted toward Lissie. "Are you sure? Number Six? He's your guy?"

"Do ya think I'm lying?" Lissie asked.

"You said you were high on the night of the attack?" Ebony eyed her suspiciously. She'd dealt with her share of unreliable witnesses. Liars and cheats who would incriminate their best friends for no good reason. Ebony knew that if Lissie was correct, she was staring down the barrel of a major bust, and her own credibility and career depended upon this woman's trustworthiness. She needed to be certain. She'd press a few buttons to see whether Lissie squirmed.

"Hey, I wasn't so stupid high I wouldn't recognize the guy who beat the crap outta me."

Taking the cue, Zander flipped back through the paperwork. "You're sure? Maybe you'd like to sit in the tank and think about it for a while." His tone was cool, detached.

"You've done nothing but bully Lissie since you stopped us across the river. I'd think you'd be more appreciative of a witness who put her life in danger to help you. We, she, didn't have to cooperate, but she did, so show a little respect, will you? She could have made it more difficult for you to nail Number Six," Jessie said.

"Yeah. What more do ya want from me, blood?" Lissie snorted. "I already gave ya mine."

"We know how to get in touch with you, so scram," Zander said, waving the clipboard dismissively.

"I'm done? Don't I get to tell that shithead how bad he messed me up?" Lissie's face fell in disappointment.

"You've done your part by identifying Doc and by giving us your statement," Ebony said. "We'll fact check the evidence and if he's our guy, we'll prosecute him to the fullest extent of the law. Trust us, we'll take it from here."

"Trust you? You want me to trust you, even though ya think I'm some lying ho? And what about the money he owes me? Them hospital bills ain't gonna pay themselves. And for my pain and suffering? Look at me." She tugged on a tuft of fuzzy hair around the red, bald spot. "It'll be months before this grows back. My son told me I look like a monster. And he's right. I'm nasty lookin'." Lissie's eyes grew hard, cold. "Nobody's gonna wanna pay me for nothin'."

Ebony glanced over at Jessie, who seemed distracted by something other than the bump on her head. At last, Jessie grimaced and hobbled over to Lissie. "Once Doc goes to trial, you'll testify in court and ask for restitution. The time to tell your story will come, but it's not right now," she whispered with a slight catch in her voice.

"I know how these things work. It'll take months, years, before Doc gets what's comin' to him. And if he gets a good lawyer, he could go free."

"Lissie, remember you're one of several women Number Six attacked. Let Ebony and Zander do their jobs. In the end, you'll get your chance, and maybe even a thank you for your service, so be patient."

"Patient? What'em I supposed to do N-O-W? I got no job, no money, no home. I got nothin'," Lissie shouted. Tears garbled her words, but her expression was a combination of fire and ice. Her crimson face contorted with anger, and her frigid stare appeared to frighten Jessie, who stumbled backward and guarded her face against another vicious attack. "You all got what ya wanted, and you're done with me."

To Ebony's surprise, the tension between Jessie and Lissie had rapidly escalated. Her idea of pushing Lissie's buttons seemed to work, but better yet, it was Jessie taking the heat, not her. While she felt guilty watching the attack, she couldn't help it if Jessie was off her game. Their entire case hinged upon Lissie's identification of Doc, so she would willingly let the scene play out. Unless Lissie was a brilliant actress, the rawness and spontaneity of her reactions would reveal whether the girl was lying or telling the truth.

"First, you've got your son, and your parents, and us. I'm not...we're not...going to abandon you. We'll help you. Just give us some time." Jessie let out a deep breath, apparently gathering her thoughts.

"I don't need charity. I'll manage, I always have." Lissie reached into her satchel and withdrew the red flannel shirt she'd worn at Abe's. She balled it up and pitched it at Jessie's head, catching her off guard. It deflected off Jessie's cheeks and fell to the floor. "Here, now ya got everything ya want." The prostitute stalked off toward the entrance, muttering to herself.

"Wait, Lissie, wait," Jessie called after her, and moved to pursue her. Ebony snagged her friend's elbow and dragged her down the hallway, away from Zander's earshot.

She leaned in close to her friend and tenderly brushed the curls from Jessie's face. Ebony had wanted to share the secret of Lissie's stash and make her feel better, but she couldn't. Not yet. She needed Jessie to trust her a while longer. "Let her go. I may be able to help."

"No, you can't."

"What do you mean?" The bone-chilling horror in Jessie's eyes signaled something more pressing was wrong, causing a wave of helplessness to capture her. "Jess, please, tell me what's happened."

"I know him," Jessie whispered in a choked voice. "I know John Doe."

Chapter Fifty-Three

E bony. Zander. Duvall Bennett. Ebony's world, her universe, had shrunk down to the three people suspiciously eyeing each other inside the interrogation room.

She opened up a manila folder, selected two eight-by-ten color glossies, and dealt them face up on the table. In the first photo, Lissie Sexton, her wild, black hair artificially tamed by pink barrettes, glared dead-on into the camera, looking like a hostage forced to hold up a newspaper.

Lissie's second headshot still made Ebony cringe. It recalled their first encounter in the emergency room; Lissie covered in blood and bruised beyond recognition, and her raspy voice begging for help. Lissie's blackened eye was swollen shut, a skullcap bandage covered her partially-shaved head, and deep scratches and scrapes crosshatched her cheeks. Her slim neck was the color of eggplant.

"Mr. Bennett, we're asking you again. Do you know a prostitute named Elisabeth Sexton?" Ebony asked. There was an odor in the room, the sour smell of armpits, onions, and boiled cabbage unsuccessfully masked by heavy aftershave.

Duvall Bennett crossed his legs, folded his arms across his chest, and shifted uneasily in the metal desk chair. Watching his elephantine body crammed in between the narrow chair arms was almost comical, but Bennett's defiance was not.

"I don't believe so," Bennett said, picking up the photos, examining them, and flinging them back onto the table. They landed face down and he made no move to flip them right side up. "I don't know what she told you, but I didn't do this to her."

Ebony glanced at her notes on his intake sheet. Bennett had no RAP sheet. The US Army had issued him an Honorable Discharge seven years ago, and he'd married and divorced while stationed in Hawaii. He'd lived a quiet life as a sonogram technician until six months ago when the department had started receiving complaints about him. They had interviewed him twice, with no charges issued.

"So you know her." She couldn't shake what Jessie had said about Bennett, about knowing him, too.

"We've met. In her line of work, I'd expect that getting mugged goes with the territory. Some girls even enjoy it." He smiled a perfect, practiced smile. His teeth glowed an unnatural, pearlescent yellow in the fluorescent overhead lighting.

At first sight, she'd despised his freakish blockhead, his callousness, and his dismissal of Lissie as if she was yesterday's trash. Duvall Bennett was a classic American psycho; an empty vessel capable of maiming and killing without remorse.

Her gut told her Bennett's massive paws had beaten Lissie to a pulp, and he bore responsibility for the disappearance of the other women, as surely as her name was Detective Ebony Jones. He might have been cunning enough to plot a series of murders over a two-year period and cover his tracks. However, he wasn't the smartest man. Fortunately, she was smarter and crazier than him.

Nobody could kill and maim nine women, and attack another, without leaving clues behind. Nobody. It was her job to find Bennett's mistakes and nail him.

"What about the others?" she asked. Ebony imagined his mighty hands wrapped around Lissie's throat, squeezing her soft flesh and making her eyes bulge with the fear she'd taken in her last breath. Had he strangled the others as well?

Bennett caught her studying his hands and smirked.

"Mr. Bennett, what about the other girls?" Zander didn't hide the annoyance in his voice.

No answer.

Ebony took a fresh approach. "You work in women's health care, correct?"

"Why, yes. Are you referring to my female patients? The ones who come into the office for sonograms?" Bennett's tone was jovial, tinged with hubris.

Before she could clarify her question, Bennett spoke. "There's a difference between the rich women and the poor ones. The rich ones drive fancy cars, have beautiful homes, and are meticulous about their personal hygiene. They spare no expense for Brazilian waxing." He chuckled at the brazenness of his remark. "They strut into the office, dressed to the nines, carrying Gucci, Chanel, Michael Kors, and LV. A vaginal infection sends them into weeks of therapy...years, if it's endometriosis or ovarian cysts or infertility."

His eyes turned dark and stormy. His nostrils flared, and the muscles along his jawline twitched. "Poor women don't care who they screw and don't use protection. They're the breeding ground for unwanted pregnancies, and disease means nothing to them. They're walking Petri dishes teeming with bacteria, spreading germs around like mayonnaise on a turkey club. These women are death machines and don't give a damn as long as they get paid."

"Mr. Bennett, isn't your opinion contrary to someone in your occupation?" Ebony treaded lightly, making an inquiry, not an accusation. She longed to accuse the bastard of being a misogynistic sociopath who shouldn't be allowed within a hundred miles of any woman, rich or poor.

"From my position between the stirrups, I consider all women to be whores." He fidgeted in his chair and drummed his long, thick fingers along the table's metal edge. "It's always about fucking."

"If you feel that way, shouldn't you be applying your medical talents elsewhere?" Zander asked.

Ebony grimaced at the thought of him touching her. Or any woman. Or Jessie.

"Just because I think they're amoral—" He paused, shifting his attention to her. He spread his knees apart, flexed his wide hips, and presented his wares, a remarkably abundant bulge beneath the fly of his slacks. He caught her eye and smirked. "It doesn't mean I dislike women. Quite the opposite. They provide me with great pleasure, and I'd like to believe it's reciprocal." He sniggered. "Don't forget, I'm a healer. I detect cancer, cysts, or pregnancy complications..." His voice trailed off.

Her cheeks flushed with anger at the pleasure and pain Bennett could inflict upon women and the other dangers he presented. Every day, his job placed him in an intimate environment with vulnerable patients over whom he could exert physical and psychological control. His unbridled access to medications, sedatives, and rape drugs rendered these women even more defenseless. Finally, as a floater, he traveled from practice to practice, providing the perfect setup for a rapist or a killer.

Jessie's words rang in her ears, "I know him." What had she meant? Had Bennett drugged and raped her?

Had he molested other patients? Had he raped the rich ones and murdered the poor ones? Was Bennett a human Petri dish spreading disease?

Her detective's mind meandered through these dark, crooked alleys, leading her to a horrific conclusion. Bennett's crop of potential victims had blanketed the Hudson Valley, from one River Valley Health Office to the next. From Newburgh to Beacon to Red Hook to Millbrook, no woman was safe, especially those who lived on the streets like Lissie.

For the time being, Ebony's focus returned to the reality. Her assignment was to prove Duvall Bennett had assaulted and raped Lissie, and thanks to Lissie, she had him by the scruff of the neck and wasn't letting go. She wanted to shake him hard to force him to admit the killings and lead her to the bodies.

While Jessie meant more to her than almost anyone, digressing to pursue her claim, or those of other River Valley patients, might be overwhelming. She needed to stay focused. Once they'd charged Bennett with attacking Lissie, she'd make sure he received punishment for all of his sins.

Once again, Bennett caught her eye, making her nerves tingle. He flashed his corrupt smile as though reading her thoughts. There was a piece of lettuce wedged between his incisor and canine teeth. Instinctively, she ran her tongue across her own teeth, feeling for the intruder.

"Mr. Bennett, we're holding you under suspicion of the assault and battery of Elisabeth Sexton," Ebony said.

"Detective, am I under arrest?"

"You're being detained," Zander confirmed. He unsnapped the handcuffs dangling from his belt and slapped them on the suspect, struggling to latch them around Bennett's thick wrists. He sniffed at the aura of boiled cabbage enveloping the suspect and wrinkled his nose.

"It's going to be her word against mine, and who are you going to believe? Me or a whore?" Bennett said.

Screw you, Bennett. We'll see who's really the whore.

Chapter Fifty-Four

E bony stretched and stifled a yawn. It was well past midnight, and the task force had been meeting in the DA's conference room since the delivery of the search warrant of Bennett's home, around dinnertime. For the past five hours, the team had been reviewing its fine print, weighing the options, and developing an operational timeline down to the second.

"With our suspect in lockup, Judge Coppola has us on a short leash. We've got to execute on the warrant before ten a.m. tomorrow or we're done," Hal said, crushing a paper coffee cup and pitching it into the trash in frustration.

"What can I say? It's an election year and there are lots of eyeballs on this case." Dan Ketchum shrugged and bit into a powdered donut that outlined his thin lips with white sugar.

"Jones, you and Pulaski will be the operational team leaders with backup from the town, county, state, and fed squads," Hal announced to the team. "Captain Worthy, commander of the ground search of Camp Nooteeming, and Town of Poughkeepsie Police Chief Holt will serve as Chief Communications Officer and Executive Officer, respectively, to assist you and create the after-action report. It'll be crucial to our prosecution of Duvall Bennett."

Ketchum nodded, and a murmur of approval trickled through the group.

"Yes, sir," she and Zander replied in unison. Like her, her partner's body tensed with excitement.

"Zero hour is set for seven a.m., so let's regroup here at five to gear up," Hal said. "Go on home and get some rest, if you can." He rolled his shoulders, stretching out the stiffness of the long night.

"Come on, Z," Ebony said, "you can crash at my place. It's just Wrangler and me, and I'm sure he'll share the couch with you." The offer made sense since her place was only two blocks away in the downtown Historic District, but there was a queer, uncomfortable twitch in Zander's eye. After a few moments' hesitation, he agreed, and they left.

At five, they returned to the station as a pinkish glow bathed the Catskills hinting at sunrise. At precisely seven o'clock, the task force tactical team invaded the quiet neighborhood of tidy houses like mud wasps around a nest. An imposing fleet of black, white and gold cruisers, emblazoned with law enforcement insignias, assembled outside the Bennett residence, and waited.

"It looks like we're ready," Ebony said.

Zander scanned the group and maneuvered their Explorer next to the Bureau of Criminal Investigation's mobile unit command center, parked alongside the Bennetts' driveway. The command center was a state-of-the-art RV on steroids with satellite dishes, camera masts, cameras, and a weather station mounted on top. Ebony imagined the fancy tech inside the vehicle and itched to catch a glimpse before they'd completed the operation.

On the other side of them was an ambulance. While there was hope they'd discover someone alive to be taken to the hospital, it was more likely they'd be transporting bodies to the morgue.

They exited their vehicle, slipped on blue bomber jackets with POLICE printed in large white letters across the back, and snapped their respirator masks over their noses and mouths to the amusement of their colleagues.

"What's the story?" asked a beefy State Trooper, the squad leader deployed from the Millbrook barracks.

"You'll find out," Zander replied.

"The smell's enough to knock a buzzard off a manure wagon," Ebony said. "There's a box of masks in our back seat if you're interested,"

"Naw, we're good." The trooper puffed out his chest, adjusted his hat, and rejoined his squad. A short distance away, he huddled with his troops and motioned in their direction. A few laughed and shook their heads.

What idiots. They'll be sorry, she thought, tightening the elastic band of her mask.

"You ready to go?" Hal asked. Ebony started at the sound of his voice and the sight of a Glock handle peeking out from beneath the hem of his police jacket. "A little jumpy, aren't we? Eb, this is a critical operation, so don't screw it up." He must have read the horror in her eyes, because he smiled and nudged her shoulder with his. "Just kidding, Detective Jones." Suddenly, he furrowed his brows, and his manner turned serious. "We have the probable cause, so bring me the evidence to put Bennett away. Remember, this guy's former military, so we can't rule out weapons and explosives. We don't know who or what you'll encounter inside his home, so be alert and stay safe." He glanced at his watch and nodded. "Zero hour."

"Move out," she said, pressing the walkie-talkie button clipped on her collar. Her call to arms crackled to life on the team's communication network and "Copy" echoed in reply.

The air sizzled with electricity, prickling the fine hairs on her arms. Trying to curb her impatience, she swallowed hard as she, Zander, and six uniformed officers marched toward the front door. Support squads fanned out around the house to secure the perimeter, while a third team lagged behind the yellow barricades to control the crowd of on-lookers and to record the show.

With each step up the sidewalk, Ebony grew more keenly aware of Hal's spying on her through his binoculars. She fought her self-consciousness by focusing on the inky smell of rotting newspapers, the chipped terracotta pots containing decayed plants, and the frayed welcome mat outside the Bennetts' front door. Her brain documented every detail, noting that even the most insignificant observation might mean the difference between life and death.

Despite her insecurities, she took pride in her importance to the task force. It wasn't every day that she and Zander orchestrated a major bust. It wasn't every day that their colleagues deployed from the state's Bureau of Criminal Investigation and other neighboring towns followed their commands. It wasn't every day that the District Attorney observed them in action and relied upon them to complete a sanctioned mission.

Last night, Hal had established a clear mandate, which she'd taken to heart. "Until further notice, it's search-and-rescue. Determine whether Kiki, Becky, Sharone, Justine, Vanessa, Camila, Jacqueline, Angela, and Eve are still alive and free them."

Hal had been optimistic about the mission, while she and Zander were the realists. There was no predicting what they might discover inside Bennett's house of horrors. The FBI had warned them about serial killers and how they coveted mementos of their kills. Bennett could have stashed gruesome trinkets like teeth, fingernails, jewelry, or underwear anywhere on the property. If anything or anyone were there, they'd find them. They'd scour Bennett's home from the basement to the rafters, including the garage and the storage sheds. They'd detain anyone found on the premises and uncover any shred of evidence linking Duvall Bennett to Lissie and the missing women.

They rang the bell, and seconds later, the door opened. A bloodshot eye blinked at them through the slender crack secured by the security chain. Ebony quickly computed the strength of the chain and the force necessary to bust the door down. In the background, the television played, and even through the respirator mask, she smelled the sour essence of Duvall Bennett.

"Mrs. Bennett, we're from the City of Poughkeepsie police and we've got a warrant to search the premises. Please open the door and let us in," Zander demanded. He spoke loudly to compensate for the mask covering his mouth, but his words were clear and serious. He slid a copy of the warrant through the crack.

"Come back later, my husband's not home." Mrs. Bennett's voice sounded clipped and tense. "You already have my son. What else do you want?"

"It's your choice whether to cooperate. We're coming in."

"No one's here but me. He wouldn't like me letting you in."

"We're giving you to the count of three to open the door, then we're coming in." Zander slowly counted. "One...two..."

The seconds dragged on like hours.

CHAPTER FIFTY-FOUR

"Three."

The door slammed shut.

Chapter Fifty-Five

"Mrs. Bennett wasn't very hospitable, was she?" Ebony remarked.

At the end of the driveway, a SWAT officer, dressed in black protective gear, waited for her signal. She spun toward the curb and waved. He flipped down his helmet's visor and strode toward her, gripping the handles of a black battering ram.

Before he'd reached her, a metallic jingle returned Ebony's attention to the front door as it slowly creaked open. A blast of acrid smoke saturated her respirator mask, stinging her nose and eyes.

Her teary eyes settled on a trembling Mrs. Bennett, then traveled past her into the living room-dining room area.

"Mrs. Bennett, please step aside," Zander barked. The woman refused to move. "Officer Thomas, please take Mrs. Bennett into custody," he ordered the officer at his side.

Without waiting for a response, their team rushed past Mrs. Bennett and burst into the house. They stopped dead in their tracks and gazed around at the clutter in disbelief and disgust.

Yellow sunlight filtered through the stained sheets tacked up over the windows, creating a muted, suffocating atmosphere. A flat-screen television, bolstered by shoulder-high stacks of magazines and newspapers, played a cooking show. The earsplitting volume competed with the high-pitched whining of the window air conditioner blowing at high speed.

Piles of laundry intermingling with pyramids of cereal boxes and unopened Christmas boxes smothered the wooden dining table, where a tower of books had replaced a missing table leg. Black plastic garbage bags, bulging to the point of explosion, reclined like guests on the dining table chairs, while junk mail littered the floor beneath their feet.

"Holy crap," Ebony muttered, wondering how they were going to uncover any clues hidden in this trash before the ten o'clock deadline.

Evidently jolted into action by their quandary, Zander hurried down the hallway, while the uniformed officers retreated into the kitchen. Ebony entered the living room, scurrying through the empty plastic milk jugs, takeout food containers, rag bags, and unopened cardboard boxes dumped haphazardly on the sofa, chairs, and the threadbare carpet.

She paused to study a silver-framed photo of a young, fresh-faced Duvall Bennett in his stiff Army uniform displayed on an end table. Posed on a veranda overlooking the ocean, he hugged a beautiful Asian woman dressed in a crisp, white suit. Cradling a wedding bouquet, his bride's face exuded serenity. She appeared happy to be tucked against her giant of a husband. The golden sunset lit their faces and the flower leis around their necks, and they beamed with the promise of love. There was a chip in the frame, and a crack in the shape of a spider's web had defaced the bride. She worried about the fate of the stunning Mrs. Bennett and whether she was alive today.

"Eb, down here," Zander called from the far end of the house.

Ebony followed his voice down a narrow hallway, lined with thigh-high mounds of moldy books. She passed a bathroom whose tub and sink overflowed with refuse and peeked into the room across the corridor.

Zander stood in an uncluttered bedroom, which appeared to be Bennett's; its decor frozen in time to the 1990s. Michael Jordan, Scottie Pippen, Shaq, and Charles Barclay posters covered the sky blue walls. There was a shrine to Bennett's high school glory days on the bookcase headboard of the tidy single bed. Below a maroon and gold Arlington High School banner, a varsity football letter leaned against a gallery of photos and sports trophies.

"Baseball. Basketball," Zander said. "Football, MVP, 1992. Check out this team photo."

In the center of the front row, Bennett kneeled on one knee, balancing his helmet. Even as a teen, he towered over his teammates, being almost a foot taller than the rest.

Inside the sliding door closet on the far wall, Bennett's clothes hung equally spaced apart along the top and bottom rods. On one side, he'd organized his blue scrubs, tops above their bottoms, and on the other, he'd coordinated his street shirts and slacks by color. On the closet floor, a dozen pairs of shoes buffed to a high polish lay regimented with military precision.

"Who is this guy?" Zander asked.

He was right. The room was perfect. Creepy perfect. Serial Killer perfect.

Ebony snapped on her blue gloves and withdrew a pen from her jacket pocket. She opened the desk drawer and poked the pen's tip through the markers, pencils, rubber bands, and postcards to uncover another torn wedding photo containing only Bennett's portrait. "Look, this one's got friends." In other photos, he'd decapitated his bride, or she was missing entirely.

"I guess their marriage didn't end well," Zander said. Ebony threw him an offended frown. "Oh, sorry for the poor choice of words."

"Let's hope the ex is still alive. Later, we'll try to locate her," she said, tapping her watch. "Come on, move on. Forensics can tear up this room later."

The sun vanished behind a cloud, darkening the room. Ebony flipped on the wall switch, but no lights came on. She whipped out her flashlight, focusing its beam on the ceiling light. The bulbs inside the milky glass fixture were as dead as the moths lining its bowl.

Zander, too, turned on his flashlight and cast the beam upward. The circle of light danced across the ceiling and reflected off a quarter-sized brass ring recessed into the sheetrock.

"Look, there's a hatch up there," she said, directing her light overhead. Their beams crossed and slowly traced the barely detectable outline of a hidden door. The ceiling was approximately nine feet high, and she could reach it with Zander's help. "Here, give me a boost."

He bent over, knitted his fingers together, and she stepped into his hands.

She reached up, hooked her finger through the brass ring, and tugged. Unsteadiness seized her knees, and she felt herself losing her balance. She released the ring and tumbled back to earth, landing flat-footed on the floor. Upon impact, a burst of disorienting pain shot from the ball of her left foot, up her leg, and into her hip. "Shit."

"Feels like you've put on some weight from all Drew's southern cooking. Maybe you'd better give me a leg up."

"Shut up. The door's stuck. Just come here and help me, will you?" Again, Ebony stepped into his hands, reached up, and this time, she hooked two fingers around the ring.

"Got it?"

"I think so." She groaned and yanked with all of her strength. The sound of scraping wood and creaking hinges gave way to the panel loosening and swinging wide open. Ebony jumped down, ducking before it could smack her in the head.

The opening revealed a second recessed door leading to the attic. Zander snagged the thick, white rope dangling from the door and tugged. A set of folding wooden stairs attached to the door led the way into the dark space above them.

Ebony pressed the button on her walkie-talkie. "Chief, there's a hatch into the attic, and we're going up. Do you copy?"

Chapter Fifty-Six

Before Hal's eyes, a gray curtain of storm clouds hid the sun, robbing the light from the sky. He squinted at his watch in the dreary light. It was nine o'clock. Only sixty minutes remained before the deadline. The chief smiled at him wearily, acknowledging that time was draining away.

He reached into his pocket and nervously squeezed the search warrant. Ever since Ebony's message a half-hour ago, there had been no word from her. What were they doing in there? Had they found anything?

Neither the approaching storm nor the sudden dampness seemed to discourage the curious neighbors from gathering at the scene. Minute-by-minute, the throng swelled. Hal expected even more gawkers if they found survivors or bodies. The social media posts about his search-and-rescue mission had gone viral, which was in nobody's best interest. Especially the victim's families and his task force.

A murmur rippled through the crowd as house lights blinked on along Limerick Circle, a hopeful symbol of normalcy when nothing was normal.

"I was thinking about how difficult it is to get any police work done with our limited funds for body-cams, car repairs, or even hiring more officers, but cellphone cameras are everywhere." The chief shrugged at the crowd.

"And don't forget about the press," Hal said. As if on cue, the news trucks and vans rolled toward them and flashed their bright lights. His hands flew up, protecting his eyes from the glare, and he sighed in disgust at the disembarking newscasters armed with cameras, lighting, and microphones, searching for prime-time sound bites. "They're like ants at a picnic."

"You're not talking about me, are you?" a female voice asked.

Startled, Hal pivoted to discover Jessie standing behind him, laden with espresso and Italian pastries.

"Here, let me grab those. You're a sight for sore eyes, especially since you've brought caffeine and sugar."

"Any news?" she asked.

"None, but Ebony—" The walkie-talkie snapped to life, interrupting him.

* * *

Except for the muted light from the entrance hatch, the attic was pitch black. Ebony could neither see the fingers she wiggled before her face nor detect Zander's presence beside her. Her eyes adjusted to the darkness, and even with the full-face respirator mask, Ebony noticed the attic's pungent scent. She'd smelled the musty fecal odor before. It was something she never got used to—the smell of death.

Like the darkness, the stench engulfed the attic, swallowing her up. Her breath grew labored, and the lens fogged, trapping her face inside the rubber mask. Ebony's heart raced in a claustrophobic panic, and she stripped off the protective gear defeated by the invisible foe. Her lungs screamed for fresh air, and she gulped hard to expel the tart taste in her mouth.

Zander wheezed and coughed convulsively.

"You okay?" she asked.

"Uh, huh?" Zander doubled over, trying to catch his breath. "You smell it too, right? It's like an open sewer after a rainstorm."

"More like rotten cabbage, eggs, and manure. But the smell is worse with the masks on. Come on, let's see what's up here."

Their flashlight beams bounced around the walls, joists, and floor as frenzied as fireflies. Zander alighted on a naked bulb suspended from the rafters on a thin wire and he yanked the tin chain, creating a dull circle of light, which offered no real escape from the gloom.

The far recesses of the space, where the roof's pitch line met the exterior walls, remained inky black. Ebony scanned the skeletons of broken chairs, bureaus and bookshelves, and the shadowy graveyard of boxes, crates, and trunks.

"There must be fifty, sixty, boxes up here." Zander tapped his watch. "It's nine, and we'll never get through them all in time."

"If we call for backup, we risk contamination, so we'd better book it if we're going to beat the warrant."

"Let's revisit calling in backup in a half-hour, but for now, just watch your step." Zander pointed his light toward the makeshift floor. Someone had installed loose sheets of plywood across the floor beams, covering a thick layer of pink blown-in insulation. At first impression, the floor appeared solid, but upon closer inspection, sizeable gaps separated the sheets from one another, and in spots, the plywood was missing altogether.

The cotton candy insulation looked pretty, but it was deadly. Last year, she and Zander had chased a suspect through another unfinished attic. The loose batting had sucked them into its depths, and they'd plummeted through the sheetrock ceiling into the bedroom below. The suspect had escaped and Ebony had re-injured her hip, so this time she'd proceed with caution.

Zander had vanished. The room was quiet, except for the groaning of the floorboards beneath their weight. In the dark seclusion, Ebony crept toward what she believed was the back of the building. The beam from her flashlight bounced off the rickety flooring and the walls of boxes arranged in a helter-skelter maze. Her fingers grazed their smooth cardboard surfaces, which led her deeper into the recesses of the attic. With each step, the air grew heavier and the musty taste of rotting paper rolled around on her tongue.

As the minutes ticked by, the humidity became tomb-like. A thin layer of perspiration glued Ebony's body armor to her torso, squeezing her chest. Her throat tightened, sealing off oxygen into her lungs, and she rocked her head to dispel the white spots of lightheadedness dancing before her eyes.

She stopped and listened for Zander or any sign she wasn't alone. She'd been on her own before, but not when so much had been at stake. In the distance, she heard Zander trip and curse. The tension in her neck relaxed, and she plodded onward, alert for any evidence linking Bennett to the missing women.

Ebony rounded a corner, and as if reaching the labyrinth's center, the boxes fell away, revealing a small clearing occupied by an overstuffed chair with ratty arms. Against her better judgment, she collapsed into the dusty seat, allowing her pulse to slow and her wits to return. Across from the chair, she spied a neatly organized row of boxes. Rather than displaying store and brand names like the others in the attic, the Bennetts had marked each of these with a red *X*.

"Zander," Ebony yelled, springing to her feet and racing toward the boxes. "Zander!" Her voice fell flat, as though trapped within the towers of cardboard.

She inserted the flashlight handle between her teeth, and rattled and rocked the boxes, testing their integrity and contents. Estimating their weight at about sixty pounds, Ebony wondered whether they were large enough to conceal a body or dismembered body parts. Were there any suspicious signs of moisture, urine, or blood? Sniffing the musty containers, it was hard to pinpoint the source of the attic's stench given the pervasiveness of the odor.

Zander still hadn't appeared. As the countdown timer ticked away inside her head, Ebony tore back the packing tape and opened a box. To her disappointment, it contained junk; wadded newsprint, magazines, clothing, shredded towels, stained blankets, and soiled baby clothing. She resealed the carton and moved on to the next ones. There were new and used coffee makers, bread machines, stand mixers, gelato makers, panini machines, food processors, humidifiers, irons, and laser printers inside. But there were no clues to the missing women.

Ebony's body tensed. She'd wasted valuable time uncovering crap, when the women were here, buried in the attic. They could be anywhere in these mountains of junk. They had to be, but where?

A loud crash, the tinkling of breaking glass, and a yowl interrupted her search.

"Shit. Eb, need a little help here," Zander howled. "I'm over here."

"Hold on. I'm coming!" she replied, dashing toward his cries at the far end of the attic.

She found him sprawled on his back, buried beneath a pair of eight-foot artificial Christmas trees. Zander's feet protruded from beneath a Frazier fir decorated in the Americana regalia of flags, red-white-and-blue ornaments, and figurines and portraits of the U.S. presidents, with an American eagle topper. Washington. Jefferson. Lincoln. Roosevelt. Reagan. Obama. Biden. They were all there. A second shiny white tree, dressed like a snowman with a black hat, a red scarf, plastic carrot nose, and coal eyes had toppled as well. Ebony bit her tongue to keep from laughing at his predicament.

"Be careful. There's glass all over the place," he said, embarrassed.

"Are you all right?" Ebony hoisted aside the Frazier fir, and the FDR and Obama ornaments skittered across the floor. Glass crunched beneath her foot, and she flashed her beam upon the remnants of the White House.

"I told you to be careful," Zander said, "and before you ask, I tripped over the kid's chair." A few feet away, a pint-size chair rocked as though hosting a ghost.

Zander tossed aside the snowman tree, rose, and brushed off the tinsel and sparkles clinging to his clothing. After stacking the trees against the wall, they began collecting the presidents assassinated during the disaster.

"Crap, a few rolled into the insulation." Zander crouched beneath the low eaves, shining his flashlight over the edge of the plywood into feathery tufts of pink fiberglass. A JFK ornament and a decapitated bust of Bill Clinton appeared within the light's beam.

Ebony reached into the fluff to retrieve them, and her gloved fingers grazed something soft and spongy. Startled, she recoiled and fixed her flashlight on the bare spot in the insulation. The ray of bright light reflected off a shiny plastic surface. "Are you seeing this? Did you bring your brush?"

Blood rushed to her head as she and Zander stared down into the fiberglass. Zander, who fancied himself the good Boy Scout, always prepared for any situation, dug deep into the arsenal of double-duty objects—safety pins, bobby pins, scissors, wire, and glass cutter—stashed in his pockets. He retrieved a toothbrush, leaned over, and gently brushed away the insulation. The outline of a foot wrapped in heavy-duty clear plastic sheeting poked through the surface. The toenails, painted in maroon polish, were unmistakable.

"Holy shit," she muttered, afraid of waking the dead. Ebony swung the beam toward Zander and her terror melted away at the sight of his fist-pumping and stamping his feet.

"Gotcha, you sick bastard!" he shouted gleefully.

Ebony's trembling fingers pressed the button on her microphone. "Chief, we've found a Jane Doe. Do you copy?"

Chapter Fifty-Seven

Someone had left open the windows in Jeremy's office. Overnight, green pollen had floated in, dusting the library's windowsills, bookshelves, conference table, and the tower of cardboard boxes in a powdery coat. Jessie had wiped down her workspace and computer before settling in, but even sipping on her water failed to dispel the gritty taste lingering on her tongue.

Down the hall, Mo was clearing her throat, and when the honking grew louder, Jessie glanced up to discover Mo lollygagging in the doorway.

"You didn't have to come in today. With Jeremy in the hospital, there's nothing for you to do around here," Mo said.

"Lily's with my mom and Hal's been tied up with the investigation, so I figured I'd come in. Just in case Gayle needed anything. Do you have any word on Jeremy's condition?"

"I've called the ICU twice and the nurses would only tell me he's stable, so that's good, I guess. He's a tough, old bird, so he'll be fine." The fake cheer in Mo's voice failed to hide her heartfelt concern for the man she'd safeguarded for decades.

"I'm sure he will, but I'll keep positive thoughts for him." Better to change the subject before Mo got teary, Jessie thought. "Any word from the Douglases about Becky? I haven't heard from Hal about her so I'm hoping for the best." She'd received a few brief texts from Hal, but with the discovery of the first body inside Bennett's house, he was engrossed in the recovery phase of the investigation. It was too soon for an ID, so there was always the possibility of horrible news.

"No, I haven't. So like I said, no news is good news all around." Mo blew her nose and then grinned suspiciously. "I have a favor to ask. Can you help me carry those boxes out to my car? I have a bad back."

"The white cartons over there?" Jessie looked at the stack against the wall next to the bookshelf. "Sure. Where do they go?"

"In the back of my car. We're transferring Butterfield's files over to the State's Office of Mental Health. After sentencing, Butterfield became a ward of New York State and the OMH will supervise his care, treatment, and legal representation. Let the OMH deal with Terrence Butterfield. I've had enough of his badgering for a lifetime." A flush of pink flashed over Mo's face. She had never mentioned Terrence's name to Jessie before, and Jessie understood the discomfort of dredging up their unpleasant memories. "Thanks," Mo said, tossing the car keys to Jessie.

Hmm, she thought, snatching the keys in mid-air. Mo was delivering Terrence's legal files to his new attorney.

For months, Terrence's harassment had frayed Jessie's nerves. Calling when she least expected it. Imagining him monitoring her every move. All along, Terrence's evil essence had been festering in the library, within reach. It was as though he'd been lurking in the room.

Jessie shivered. Now that she knew, the sooner she disposed of the files, the better.

"I'll meet you upstairs."

Jessie slipped Mo's keys into her pocket and grabbed the first box with a manila envelope addressed to "Kevin Bryant, Esq." taped on top. It was as heavy as Lily, but manageable, and she toted the carton upstairs and hoisted it into the hatchback of Mo's BMW. She resisted the temptation to open the letter and read its contents. Instead, Jessie snapped a photo of the box and slammed the trunk.

At Curtis and McMann, Jessie had specialized in real estate and corporations, and her experience with governmental agencies had taught her that the state had rules and regulations for everything. Therefore, the state's mental health department must have an administrative code, procedure, or policy governing the use and abuse of personal phone calls by a patient in a forensic psychiatric hospital.

She'd speak with Mr. Bryant at the OMH and tell him about Terrence's persistent phone calls. Perhaps, after hearing her story, he could put a stop to them. Providing evidence was no problem. Her phone records would substantiate Terrence's abuse of his phone privileges, and once she informed Mr. Bryant of the situation, the OMH would have a responsibility to take action.

Armed with this new ammunition, it was time to call Terrence out and make him leave her alone. She refused to permit him to manipulate any patient "Bill of Rights" the state hospital system afforded him. She had rights, too, and living free from Terrence's harassment was one of them.

* * *

After Lily was asleep, Jessie propped her feet up on the den's ottoman with her laptop poised for action. She logged on to her phone carrier's website and began collecting her evidence against Terrence.

Locating the cellphone records proved to be easier than she'd expected. Within minutes, Jessie had accessed her bill, tracked her usage, and gathered the data, text, and talk logs for the past year. Digging deeper, Jessie downloaded the incoming and outgoing phone logs dating back to the time of Terrence's hospitalization.

Her tongue grew as dry as sandpaper as she printed out the documents and studied the pages. Terence's calls began ten months ago, two weeks after his commitment to the Mid-Hudson Forensic Psychiatric Center in New Hampton, N.Y. According to the carrier, he'd accessed over fifty phone numbers at the exchange dedicated to the psychiatric center. There'd been no pattern, except for the timing between 9 a.m. and 4 p.m. weekdays.

A sudden coldness hit her core when she counted the incoming calls. There had been one hundred seventy-two calls.

A tidal wave of fear, anxiety, and rage flooded back in recognition that Jessie's own weaknesses had let Terrence infiltrate her life.

But no longer.

After redacting the unrelated personal calls from the logs, Jessie composed an email to Kevin Bryant outlining her case against Terrence, including the history of their relationship, and every detail of his threats, his manipulations, and his relentless stalking. She held nothing back. She had nothing to lose, but everything to gain.

Jessie uploaded the phone records into a file named "Harassing Calls from T. Butterfield," attached it to the email, and hit "send."

This wasn't a quest for revenge against Terrence. This was a quest for justice. And a step toward reclaiming her life.

Chapter Fifty-Eight

H al had unzipped his white Hazmat suit to his waist, and his respiration mask dangled below his chin like a turkey's wattle. He cradled a paper cup of stiff, black coffee within his hands, blew on the rising steam, and pressed his palms against the cup's warmth to ward off the chill in his bones.

His aching back felt every minute of the endless night, but he was certain it had seemed even longer to the team. For the past eighteen hours, CSI and forensics had scoured the Bennetts' home, processing the crime scene and recovering the body they believed to be the first of many hidden inside this house of death. It was a tedious job, and Hal didn't envy them. The laborious tasks of photographing, videoing, fingerprinting, bagging, collecting, and cataloging the piles of junk in the attic had to be completed before dismantling the plywood floor to reach Jane Doe #1.

Around dinnertime, he'd shot off a text to Jessie, promising to call her with details no matter the hour, but time had slipped away. It was 1 a.m., Hal thought with frustration. They were no farther along in the investigation than when they'd spoken in the morning, except they'd secured the scene and Jane Doe #1 was safely in their hands. Once the ME determined the cause of death, Hal could formally charge Duvall Bennett with a crime. However, the charges were up in the air, too.

At least his mind was at ease about the collection and preservation of the evidence. This wasn't his team's first rodeo, plus he was on site, and would remain there as long as necessary to ensure they'd accomplished their mission. To convict Duvall Bennett of murder, procedures had to be followed to the letter, and the case had to be bulletproof.

A radio newscaster from WPDH leaned over the barricade and thrust a microphone in Hal's face, jostling his cup and spilling coffee down the front of his jumpsuit.

"Hey, man. Watch out, will you?" Hal said.

"Sorry. Come on, Mr. Samuels. You've been stringing us along all day. We saw the body, so what's the story?" the reporter asked.

Like it or not, the time had come for him to issue a formal statement. Hal's "no comments" were wearing thin, but he despised speaking off the cuff. It left room for errors, misquotes, and unplanned hesitations, which made him look stupid or ill-prepared. Hal preferred the security of an outline, as when selling a case to the jury. With the discovery of Jane Doe #1, there had been little time for preparation, and he'd fended off questions long enough.

The families of the missing women had become anxious. They were demanding transparency and bombarding him with questions.

"Have you found my daughter?" "—my sister?" "—my friend?"

"Why did you wait so long to investigate her disappearance?"

"When will we know who they've found?"

"What happened inside that house?" their fearful voices pleaded.

He owed them answers, but the interminable, worrisome events had fried his brain and left his body limp with exhaustion.

A text message vibrated on the cellphone tucked inside his jacket pocket, and the dead weight of his hand collected the phone.

The message read: *I've been up all night following your progress on Facebook. Here are some talking points. Go get 'em, Chief. C.*

Hal took a swig of coffee and shut his bleary eyes.

God bless you, Cindie Tarrico.

* * *

Inside the mobile command center, Ebony stretched her stiff back. Their mission was far from over, and she tried to blink away the sandy feeling irritating her eyelids. It was a useless gesture. While her body longed for sleep, her mind remained alert; her eyes glued to the live stream on the monitors showing the team tirelessly burrowing through the attic's insulation. The space was so crammed with junk it might take days to locate Jane Doe's missing companions. But her instincts predicted the others were there, too.

Ebony stifled a yawn as Zander debriefed the task force commanders.

"You should see the place, sirs. It's a dump with garbage stacked up to the rafters. If you'll pardon my language, it was a bitch to sort through the mess. The overwhelming smell drew me up into the attic and to the corpse." Feigning humility, Zander raced through an embroidered version of their discovery to prevent Ebony from interrupting. "But that's how I uncovered the body. I'd been trapped beneath a pile of debris and was pulling myself out when a Christmas ornament slipped through a crack in the floor and landed on the insulation. I brushed the insulation aside, and there she was."

Ebony's eyes widened in shock. He was showboating, acting like she hadn't even been present at the scene. She opened her mouth to protest, but rage struck her mute. She'd never felt so blindsided, so betrayed.

As usual, Ebony had considered the discovery of Jane Doe to be a joint effort. For god's sake, they were partners and had been for five years. They were supposed to cover each other's back. Share the guts and the glory.

No doubt Zander was ambitious. Ebony admired the trait in him. But he wasn't only grandstanding; he was suffocating her in a pool of pink insulation.

Ebony shook her head, gathering her wits. Two could play at this game.

"Sir, Bennett had buried the victim beneath the floorboards in the insulation and my flashlight caught the toe's nail polish at just the right angle, attracting our attention. It was a clever, but poorly executed grave." The words escaping her lips rang hollow and desperate.

"Good job, Pulaski," Shepardson said, clapping Zander on the back. "Write up the report, and we'll talk later. Go back to the station and follow up with the suspect."

"Thank you, sir." Zander turned to her. "You heard the chief, let's go."

It was too late. Ebony drew in slow, steady breaths as she felt her promotion slip away.

* * *

Upon entering the interrogation room, Ebony and Zander found Bennett sitting at the metal table. He bucked the flimsy plastic chair, attempting to wrench his shackled hands free from the large ring welded to the table's leg. Bennett's beady eyes, puffy with sleep deprivation, spotted them and he stopped yanking. Bennett looked bedraggled; his long loose hair was matted into a greasy ball on one side, his clothes were wrinkled and unkempt, and a day's worth of stubble cloaked his chin in a sinister shadow.

"Mr. Bennett, as you may recall, we're Detectives Pulaski and Jones."

"Yeah, I remember."

"Good. Our investigation of the assault and battery of Elisabeth Sexton has expanded into a task force to locate several women missing here in the Hudson Valley," Zander said. He leaned against the wall, digging at his fingernails with a penknife.

"What's that got to do with me?" Bennett's eyes focused on them as intense as a bird of prey.

"We've just returned from your home," Zander said.

Zander's earlier boasting still bristled, and even now he positioned himself to lead the interview. Ebony watched and listened. She knew his modus operandi, an aggressive start with a passive finish, so she'd let him ramble on, waiting for her opportunity to squeeze the admission out of their suspect.

"How's my mother?" Bennett asked, quietly. "Is she all right?"

"Is there anything you'd like to tell us?" Zander asked.

"About what?"

Ebony couldn't resist. She had to jump in. "Don't you mean, about who?"

"You need to tell me, please, how's my mother?"

Bennett's polite concern surprised Ebony. She'd expected this sociopath to have a depraved indifference for human life, not to say "please" and "thank you," or worry about his mother's welfare. His sentimentality was the chink in his armor, which she could exploit to break him.

"We found a body in your attic, so how do you think she is?" Ebony asked. Her eyes never left his doughy face. "How's she's going to feel after we tear up her house? What else, or who else, are we going to find there?" She let the accusation sink in. "If I were your mother, I'd give you up for lost. Write you off completely. Even if you were my only child." Bennett remained stoic while lightning flashed in his eyes. "Why don't you tell us about the dead woman before we have to ask your mother about her?"

"No, please don't," he said.

There was no need to tell Bennett that his mother was in the next room being questioned by other members of the team. They'd find out quick enough whether Mrs. Bennett was an accomplice to the crime or whether she was aware of her son's activities, especially with the stench in the house.

Bennett exhaled, and his eyes skittered around the room until they finally settled on Ebony. "Which woman?"

Which woman? His words confirmed what she'd believed all along. There were more victims entombed in the Bennetts' graveyard.

"In the attic, wrapped in a plastic drop cloth. Dark hair. White skin. Mole between her eyes. Can you tell us how she got there?" she asked.

"I loved the Army, and I was good at my job in the medic's corps," Bennett said matter-of-factly. "Once I contracted HIV in Thailand, it was only a matter of time before they discharged me, or worse. I saw them disgrace infected soldiers like they were criminals, prosecuting them for willful disobedience, conduct unbecoming an officer, and reckless endangerment."

"I was next. I felt it. The brass was going to punish me for the crime of having unsafe sex." He paused, wrenching his hands. "After my discharge, I got medical treatment, but my life's not normal." Bennett lowered his head, resting it in his palms. "I follow the health law and the regulations. I'm not a risk to my patients, but I'm still persecuted by the health care system.

A chill raced up Ebony's tailbone to her neck, and she shivered. Once again, Bennett's humanity, or the concern for his patients, contradicted the grisly corpse buried in his home.

"My life is worth nothing because of those whores. Their poison has spread through my veins and I'll never be free as long as I live. Besides, what have I got to live for? Nothing. So, you know what? I'm taking as many as I can to hell with me. And I don't give a shit. At least I got pleasure from those miserable bitches before they died."

The puzzle of Bennett's existence snapped together like Legos. A seedy motel in Southeast Asia. A newly divorced, lonely serviceman on leave. To prove his machismo, he engaged in unprotected sex with an exotic prostitute, or two or three. Twenty-five years ago, a diagnosis of HIV would have meant a slow, torturous death sentence. Today, the prognosis was different, but Bennett was unconvinced. Despite the success of antiretroviral therapy and medical studies proving he'd live as long as any other person, Bennett believed he was a dead man walking. The virus's poison had corrupted him and robbed him of his moral compass. Angry at the world, he intended to leave a trail of blood and death as his legacy. Duvall Bennett was correct. He had nothing to lose.

"Did you strangle her?" Ebony asked.

"That whore was just like all the others. She deserved it."

"Are there others in the house? The yard? The garage?" Zander interrupted.

No answer.

Zander pushed away from the wall and stood behind Bennett, whispering in his ear. "Mr. Bennett, how many others have you killed?"

No answer. A beat passed. Bennett swiveled his head from Zander to Ebony in confusion, not knowing whom to address. "I want a lawyer," he demanded, as though it was a threat.

Lawyering up wouldn't help Bennett. Premeditated, cold-blooded murder meant life without parole. If Bennett craved a death sentence, the criminal justice system wouldn't be fulfilling his wishes.

* * *

By sunrise, the crowds gathering across from Bennett's home had swelled into a sea of onlookers, excited to view a true crime unfolding in their neighborhood. Flanked by Sheriff Stone and Chief Shepardson, Hal approached the yellow barricade, mentally reviewing the talking points prepared by Cindie. The television cameras and microphones sprang to life, and a hush settled over Limerick Road.

Hal looked past the blinding camera lights toward the teams working in Bennett's house and cleared his throat.

"Ladies and Gentleman. I have sad news to report. The Missing Women's Task Force has recovered the body of an unidentified white female in her thirties from inside the house at 72 Limerick Circle. At present, the cause of death is unknown. Since this is an ongoing investigation, I'm unable to provide any further details at this time. However, we have a suspect in custody, pending formal charges.

We will release more details as events develop. In the meantime, I ask for the patience and cooperation of the victim's families and ask that you allow us to continue to do our jobs. Thank you."

He swiveled away from the press corps and strode toward the Command Center.

A text buzzed on his phone.

You look terrible. XXX Lauren.

Chapter Fifty-Nine

Hal couldn't shake the dread that Bennett had buried more bodies inside his home. He'd been inside. He'd witnessed the tomb reeking of death and hidden tragedy. And he didn't need poor Jane Doe #1 to confirm Bennett being one sick mother.

He wanted justice for Bennett's crimes and wouldn't abandon the distraught families. He prayed for any information to end their misery. But when the forensic team extracted the sixth body, he despaired at informing them about another brutal discovery. Hal knew the news summoned a deeper, more personal question for each next of kin, "Is she mine?"

Sadly, Hal couldn't respond. Not until the ME identified the remains. However, he took solace that each family was closer to knowing the destiny of their loved one. In return, they'd embraced him. Over the hours of endless vigil, they'd shared their home-cooked lasagna, chicken casseroles, and apple pies, along with their memories about their lost mothers, daughters, sisters, and aunts.

Although the hour was early, he called Jessie. He needed to hear her voice.

"Jess?" His voice was hoarse from the cold and lack of sleep as he told her about the progress of the search-and-recovery mission. Sadly, their rescue had become a recovery of fatalities.

"Hal," she said in a mixture of sleepiness, relief, and sympathy. "Honey, you've been at this non-stop for more than a day. You need to come home for a break. Your being there isn't making the search proceed any quicker. All it's doing is running you down."

"I can't leave. The families are relying on me."

"I know, but this isn't healthy. Don't you see it's killing you?"

She was right. The pungent odor of death had permeated his skin, hair, and clothing, repulsing him. "Okay, just a quick shower, shave, and nap. Then I'm coming back until this is over," Hal agreed reluctantly.

"You'll be as good as new, and I'm sure the team will call you if anything dramatic occurs."

He'd meant to keep his promise, but the clean cotton bed linens were as seductive as a lover's embrace. Around dinnertime, he awoke to the buzzing of a text. It read:

Found and extracted the eighth and last body. Sent her off to ME. Details to follow. Great job and we'll talk later. Matt

The ordeal was over, but he felt numb.

Hal stepped into the shower and scrubbed away the residue of the crimes. Afterwards, he draped a towel around his waist and was vigorously toweling his hair when a warm kiss on his shoulder interrupted him.

"I didn't have the heart to wake you, so I let you sleep. You were snoring up a storm, so obviously, you needed the rest," Jessie said.

Glimpsing himself in the bathroom mirror, he couldn't argue with her. Even now, his eyes were bloodshot and his otherwise robust complexion was pale and pasty. He leaned closer to the mirror and stroked his new copper stubble in admiration. The buzzing razor vibrated in his hand, hovering dangerously close to his neck. "What do you think?"

"Oh, yeah. It's a keeper," Jessie replied, caressing Hal's face like a new pet. "There's something about a man with facial hair."

Hal snapped off the razor and pulled her into his arms. "We'll give it a trial, but I don't want to hear any complaints." He smiled mischievously and rubbed his bristles against her soft cheek.

Jessie slid her arms around his damp waist and nestled her head against his heart. Her hair was warm and smelled of lavender. He tightened his embrace. After what he'd witnessed, he wanted her to make him forget the unforgettable. He wanted to cling to Jessie forever inside a cocoon where only they existed.

"We don't have to talk about them, you know. Not if you don't want to."

Reflexively, his grip loosened. Jessie had been so inextricably immersed in Duvall Bennett's killing spree that there was no way to shield her from the truth. But he'd tried. "You don't understand, Jess. I saw them. And I'll never forget it. I don't want to put you through the horror." She placed a hand on his chest and nodded, urging him to continue. Hal exhaled a long breath. He closed his eyes, recalling the details branded into his memory.

"Bennett had sealed them in human-sized plastic bags. He'd posed them all exactly the same way. Naked. Their eyelids held shut with pennies and their hands cupped over their breasts. It was bizarre, like they were a collection of shrink-wrapped sleeping angel dolls." He paused. "Bennett planned the killings. Maybe not these exact victims, but he had a vendetta. It was just a matter of time and opportunity." Hal's voice cracked. He couldn't begin to describe the bodies in various stages of decay, and how on some only the bones, hair, ligaments and cartilage remained. He'd already revealed too much.

Jessie squeezed him in reassurance. "Have you identified any of them?"

"Only one so far. Kiara Taylor."

She stepped back, slipping from his arms. Her face filled with shock. "Kiki? Lissie's friend? No, it can't be."

He shook his damp head. "I'm sorry, but the dentals matched."

"What about the other girls? Was Becky among them? You'd know her instantly. She's covered from head-to-toe in tattoos."

"We've collected DNA from the families and we're processing the specimens for matches. From what I saw, Becky's not there. But don't get your hopes up."

The brightness in Jessie's eyes dimmed slightly. He'd had that effect on people during the last few days after disclosing they'd recovered more women. The denial, anger, bargaining, sadness, and acceptance; the five stages of grief rolled up into one second. Now he saw those emotions in Jessie's eyes, and it tore him up.

"I hope you hold the bastard responsible for everything he's done... for the lives he's ruined and the lives he's stolen."

She'd tossed the ball back into his court. He'd been responsible for the missing persons investigation, and he'd handle the prosecution of Duvall Bennett, making sure Bennett paid for his crimes and never saw freedom again. While it would be small consolation to the victims' families, it was the best he could do. But he'd always carry the burden of knowing he could have prevented this tragedy.

Hal embraced her again; thinking about how easily he and Lily could've lost Jessie. "Thank god Bennett didn't get you."

* * *

The next morning, Hal opened his office window and inhaled the fresh air, stroking his new beard. Outside, the late morning fog was lifting, but the clouds still hovered like apparitions on the murky surface of the Hudson. He preferred those ghosts to the demons possessing his desk.

The task force had fast-tracked the preliminary findings and the two-inch black binder brimming with photos, charts, evidence lists, and reports waited for his perusal. He needn't read it, though; he already knew the gist of its contents.

Two days.

Eight female bodies.

Four had been hidden in the attic - one in the insulation, two folded up like pretzels and stuffed inside steamer trunks, and one crammed into a worm-eaten wardrobe.

Four buried four-feet deep in the dirt crawlspace below the kitchen.

Bennett had acted alone in his crimes, and had encouraged his parents to hoard to cover his dark secret. He'd lied to them about the smell, claiming that rabid, dead raccoons were the culprits, and he'd threatened to abandon them if they contacted a pest exterminator about the problem. He was their only child and his parents doted on him, but his bouts of anger intimidated them. They'd relented rather than lose him.

Also, a cookie tin extracted from the basement contained a vacuum-sealed bag of panties, jewelry, trinkets, and locks of hair tied in ribbons. They'd found a vacuum sealer with Bennett's DNA in the attic.

Bennett had carefully enshrouded each fully intact body in a custom-made plastic bag, but they were all in different stages of decomposition.

Boxes of women's soiled, used clothing, and gallons of what appeared to be embalming fluid, hypodermic needles, syringes, and tubes had been seized from the garage and transmitted for DNA sampling and analysis.

The ME had identified the first victim, the freshest kill, as Kiara Taylor from her DNA and dental records. She'd been three months pregnant and had last been seen three weeks ago. The preliminary report ruled her death as "death by strangulation," pending the autopsy.

The remaining souls were still awaiting identification.

With the hunt concluded, the task force was wrapping up their work. The FBI had returned to New York City, but the state forensics experts would continue to comb Bennett's home for evidence. Judging from the condition of the house, it might take a month before forensics concluded their work. Then, he'd have more details about the deaths and enough evidence to put Bennett away for multiple lifetimes.

Hal's team was just beginning their mission, starting with impaneling the grand jury. So far, in connection with the death of Kiara Taylor, they'd seek to indict Duvall Bennett for one count of murder in the first degree, which carried a sentence of life without parole. For his violence against Lissie Sexton, they'd charge Bennett with first-degree assault, rape, sexual abuse, unlawful imprisonment and patronizing a prostitute, and second-degree strangulation. As soon as the medical examiner determined the causes of death of the other victims, they'd amend the indictment to include additional charges.

Settling into his chair, he noticed a sheet of yellow legal paper left on his desk. Someone had folded it in half and marked "For Your Eyes Only." He opened it. In neat cursive, Cindie had composed a list of the staff attorneys she'd lead into battle against Bennett's defense lawyers. Dragging his finger down the names, he confirmed she'd selected the best prosecutors for the task, seven in all. He'd supervise the team, but his hands-on work was complete. This was Cindie's game now. With the evidence gathered by the task force, Ebony, Zander, and Jessie, he was sure they'd convict Bennett and obtain justice for the victims.

Chapter Sixty

Jeremy's collapse had hit Jessie hard. For the past few nights, she'd slept little since receiving a text from Gayle that Jeremy had been rushed into emergency heart valve replacement surgery. Jessie checked her cellphone obsessively, desperate for a call or text about Jeremy's condition, but none came. Nor had Mo or the Kaplans returned her calls.

Their silence was a clear sign. The Kaplans believed that Jessie's going rogue and swiping Lissie's information to hunt her down had fueled Jeremy's illness. She'd become a persona non grata, so there was only one honorable thing to do.

Early the next morning, Jessie slinked past Mo's desk toward the library. Since Mo simultaneously sipped on her extra-large diet cola, while organizing the files, the clients, and the phone calls, she rarely acknowledged Jessie's coming and goings. Jessie had hoped to grab her belongings from the library and elude the busybody secretary.

Jessie was tossing a navy sweater, a family photo, and a thermal mug into a canvas tote when she sensed movement out of the corner of her eye. She jerked around to discover Mo scrutinizing her over the rims of her magenta reading glasses and blocking the library's exit.

"I'm surprised to see *you* here," Mo said.

"How's Jeremy?" Jessie resumed her packing, stuffing a pair of sneakers into the bag.

"What do you think you're doing? Stealing away like a thief in the night?"

"Nobody's bothered to call me. I know when I'm not wanted." She glowered at Mo as though she were a hostile witness on cross-examination.

"I'm not stupid."

Mo made a slight *pfft* sound and shook her head in apparent disgust.

"I think it's best for everyone if I left," Jessie said. "Just give me a few minutes and I'll clear out the rest of my stuff and be out of your hair forever. It's what you've wanted all along, isn't it?"

"You're being ridiculous. I've left several messages on your home phone. And frankly, I was concerned when I didn't hear from you."

"What?" Jessie never checked the phone machine's messages anymore. In fact, she'd meant to throw the damn thing out. It was a constant reminder of her fears about Terrence and her tensions with Kyle. Mo still hadn't told her about Jeremy, and she sensed Mo's reticence. "Please tell me how Jeremy's doing?"

"You have such a flair for theatrics. If you'd listened to your messages, you would know Jeremy's recuperating nicely. The surgery was a success. He'll be in the cardiac ICU for a week or two. Then, bed rest for another month. He's not allowed visitors at present, just so you know. And don't go blaming yourself. It was the cigars and booze that almost killed him, not your silly scavenger hunt for Ms. Sexton." Mo paused. "And the Douglases called to let us know Becky contacted them. She's honeymooning in Las Vegas at a tattoo convention. Apparently, she and her boyfriend reconciled and eloped. They sounded happy to hear from her, and hope her new hubby will be a stabilizing influence on her, but who knows."

"I'm relieved to hear she turned up. When they didn't find Becky in Bennett's house, I was still worried about her. With a killer on the loose, all of us—Mr. and Mrs. Douglas, you, me, Jeremy, Hal, and Ebony—could only assume the worse. And without leads, it was like Becky had vanished. Her running off may have been irresponsible, but at least the Douglases now know she's safe."

"It's more than irresponsible considering what she subjected her poor parents to. I'll never understand some people."

Had Becky been running away from her parents or running toward someone or something? It would remain Becky's secret, but thankfully, she was unharmed.

326

"All we can do is wish her well," Jessie said.

"I suppose you're right. And since we're clearing the air, I know you rifled through Lissie's file."

The accusation wounded her as badly as a slap across Jessie's face. Sharp, unexpected, and stinging.

"Now, I'm going to tell you what you don't know. Over the years, Jeremy has made friends in high and low places, who he cultivates as informants. Lissie's father Clint is one of them. He's a cyber-security specialist, and that's all I'm going to say."

Jessie stowed away the juicy tidbit into her mental filing cabinet for future use. It might come in handy should Terrence reappear, or if Kyle challenged Lily's custody.

"In exchange, Jeremy watches over Lissie. He gets her out of jams, and slips her a few bucks now and then... And by the way, Lissie doesn't know about the arrangement, so let's keep it between us. Do you hear me?" She glared at Jessie. Mo approached the Rolling Stones photos mounted on the library's wall and tapped her purple nails on a man with a dark, flowing ponytail and a handlebar moustache, hugging Keith Richards and Ronnie Wood. "Do you see this guy? It's Abe Delameter. Abe grew up with Jeremy's oldest brother, and they've been friends forever. In the 1990s, Abe was the tour manager for the Stones, and Jeremy performed legal work for the band, if you catch my drift."

This was their first genuine conversation, and to Jessie's surprise, Mo wasn't the bitch she appeared to be. Aside from Mo's snarky attitude, which was probably to protect Jeremy, Mo was nice. Sort of.

Jessie's cheeks warmed at her own stupidity. She'd believed she could read people, but lately, she'd misread so many it was mind-blowing—Jeremy, Gayle, Lissie, Ebony, Kyle, Mo and, of course, Terrence.

"I'm sorry. I shouldn't have interfered in Jeremy's plan to hide Lissie. It wasn't my place, but there were lives at stake. I had to help."

"Think about it for a minute. Jeremy knew you were smart and took initiative. He couldn't take out a billboard announcing Lissie's hiding place, so he did the next best thing. He left a sticky note. Jeremy knew you'd figure it out."

No way. Jeremy had played her. He'd wanted her to locate Lissie and convince her to cooperate with Ebony, Zander, and Hal. She'd fallen for it hook, line and sinker. It had been a novice's move and one she'd never make again.

"Why didn't he just tell me where she was?"

"What would be the fun of that?" Mo smirked. "Lissie can be as vicious and stubborn as a mule, but Jeremy thought she'd listen to you. He wanted to see if, and how, you'd worked together. I'd say pretty well. You caught a serial killer." She paused and handed Jessie an envelope. "I found this on my desk this morning. It's for you."

Jeremy had scrawled *Jessica Grace Martin* on the envelope in his scratchy hand. However, this wasn't a stock white envelope. The embossed black letters announced "LAST WILL AND TESTAMENT."

"Don't look at me, Jessie. I'm as surprised as you."

A ghoulish shiver slithered up her spine, as if Jeremy had been predicting his death.

"Why would Jeremy be giving me his Will?"

"There's no explaining anything he does. And who'd want to? The crazy man's baffled me for twenty years. See these gray hairs?" The secretary parted her hair to reveal a silver forest sprouting among the henna roots. "Stop over-thinking it and open the damn letter, will you?"

Jessie tore open the envelope, and the contents tumbled out, scattering like dry leaves in the autumn wind. She collected the papers and examined the first page. It contained a note from Jeremy, dated prior to the line-up and his collapse, when she'd barely seen him around the office.

That seemed like a lifetime ago. Yet, only days had passed. So much had happened to Lissie, Ebony, Duvall Bennett, Hal, and the Task Force. Events which had irrevocably altered her life.

She motioned for Mo to join her at the table, knowing the secretary was going to breathe down her neck, anyway.

Jessie read the letter aloud:

My Dear Jessie:

I realize that I've left you in countless difficult situations over the past year, and I hope to make amends to you for my—

"Boy, his penmanship's awful. What's this word?" Jessie asked, pointing at the page.

"Trans-something."

"Transgressions, that's it."

"No worse than doctor's notes, but I've gotten used to it over the years." Mo laughed at her joke. "For a while, he tried typing out his memos, but it was a disaster. I had to type everything over again."

—transgressions. First, I made false accusations against you on behalf of our mutual friend, Terrence Butterfield, and now I've left you in the lurch.

In seeking you out, Gayle's intentions were pure, so she bears no blame in this situation and neither does Mo. This is my fault. I hired you to assist me, and because of my declining health, you were stuck handling the caseload of two attorneys. I placed you in an untenable situation, and for that, I apologize. I know it hasn't been easy, especially when you found yourself involved with Lissie Sexton. Again, this was my fault. And please believe me, I never meant to place your life in danger.

She read on, periodically seeking clarification from Mo.

But Jessie, I've known you since you were in high school, and even back then, I saw something special in you. You never missed the opportunity to rise to the occasion, and your talent remains clear. You never shirked your responsibilities and handled each obstacle with the professionalism of an officer of the court. I'm proud to think I helped train you to become the lawyer you are today.

She turned the page and wiped away a tear staining her cheek.

Despite what Gayle believes, I'm not in denial about my health. For some time, I've known the extent of my illness, but I didn't know the restrictions it would place upon my life.

Gayle and I have spoken at length about our future. We don't know where life will take us, or how much time I have left in this world. I don't mean to be morose. I'm being practical. I would be remiss to my family and to you if I didn't prepare for the inevitable.

Damn, this was his will, she thought.

On behalf of Gayle and myself, I thank you for picking up the slack. Without you, we would have been lost, emotionally and financially.

In consideration of these factors, I, we, want to express our appreciation, and sincerely hope you'll consider making our business arrangement more permanent.

I don't mean as an associate, but as a partner of the firm.

She paused for a second, rereading the last sentence.

I would be proud to display your name on the shingle with mine. You've more than proven your talent, intelligence, dedication and, most of all, honor to my family and me. I know you'll accomplish great things in the future, and I'd like to share the experience with you.

I sincerely hope you'll join my legal family.

Sincerely, Jeremy

P.S. Glad you could read my handwriting on the sticky note.

"Wow, I knew nothing about this. I swear," Mo said, glancing at Jessie in astonishment. "But the wrapping is true to Jeremy's morbid sense of humor."

"That sneaky bastard." Jessie turned the page and discovered a ten-page contract entitled *"Partnership Agreement between Jeremy Kaplan and Jessica G. Martin."*

Adrenaline surged through her, accelerating her heart. Her hands trembled and her mind zoomed as she attempted to absorb the ramifications of the agreement. She'd immediately become a forty percent partner in the law firm, with an additional ten percent vesting in two years. There was no capital contribution required. In the event of Jeremy's death, the firm would be Jessie's at a price to be negotiated with his estate.

This unexpected gift had left her dumbstruck.

"Congratulations," Mo said. "Are you all right, dear? You look like you're going to keel over."

"I never expected this. I've got no criminal experience."

"Stop it. Give yourself some credit. Jeremy wouldn't have offered you half of his practice if you hadn't earned it or weren't capable. Too bad there's no champagne, we need to celebrate." The secretary hesitated. "Hold on." Mo rose and disappeared from the library, returning moments later with two mugs and a bottle of Macallan Scotch. She set the cups down between them on the table and poured four fingers' worth. "I know where he keeps his stash."

They raised and clinked their mugs together. "To Jeremy."

"Sláinte chugat, Jessica G. Martin. May the good Lord be with you," Mo said.

"I guess I'd better unpack." Jessie took a healthy slug of whiskey, and as the fire seared her throat, she knew she'd need more than the good Lord's blessing when she told Hal about the partnership. He made no secret of his hatred of Jeremy. Hal loathed the false accusations Jeremy had levied against her, Jeremy's disrepute, his brusqueness, the low-life clientele, and his cavalier attitude toward the law.

Hal was only being protective. He didn't want Jeremy's dubious reputation to tarnish her. However, in the short time she'd worked for Jeremy, he'd been compassionate toward Lissie and had been a dedicated husband, friend, and counselor. He'd made retribution for the harm he'd caused her, and the partnership offer was tangible proof of his remorse. Jessie felt honored to be mentored by a colleague whose clients meant almost as much to him as his family.

Chapter Sixty-One

The brilliant spring sunshine did little to lighten Hal's mood. His mind felt fuzzy, and his body ached as though he was fighting the flu during a January blizzard. He kept reminding himself that OPERATION JUST CAUSE had been a success. Duvall Bennett was behind bars. They'd found the missing women, were identifying them, and soon they'd be returning them to their families. Everyone, including Dan Ketchum, had hailed him as a hero for leading the charge. But he remained unconvinced. His own troubling malfeasance had contributed to the tragedy, but he'd be forever grateful to Ebony, Zander, and Jessie for compelling him to do his duty as District Attorney.

They had also accounted for the two other missing women, who luckily were unrelated to Bennett's crime spree. According to Jessie, Becky Douglas a/k/a Epiphany Rivers had gotten hitched in Vegas. And Ed Martin had reported that his missing student had become a pawn in her parents' divorce. When her folks had shacked up with their new partners, they'd left the teen to fend for herself, and she'd run away to live with her cousins in the Bronx.

It was tough to be a young adult these days. Even worse, if your parents emotionally or physically abandoned you. Or disowned you. Hal should know.

Hal hoped a caffeine detour might jolt him out of his funk. The trip would take him a few minutes out of his way, but he could spare the time before heading into the office. The thought of the rich Ethiopian coffee featured only at the Krafted Cup Café near Vassar College made his mouth water. Its dark roast was a million times better than the slop served at the diner across the street from his office.

"Hey, I'm kind of in a hurry," Hal said, checking his watch and tapping his oxford's toe on the café's wooden floor. It had been a simple order, a Grande Dark Roast with soymilk, but he'd had to repeat it to the barista at least five times. For some odd reason, Hal always got stuck with this hipster, who was way too old to be wearing a gray knitted beanie, and never remembered his selection. Maybe Hal was getting too old for the college hangout, and it was time to settle for a watered-down brew like the other lawyers in town.

He removed the cup's white plastic top, savored the robust scented steam, and strolled outside into the spring morning, beckoning him to play hooky. Screw it, he thought, sitting at a café table to watch the world pass by.

His cellphone buzzed. The caller id simply read "Unknown." Annoyed at the intrusion, he answered it, determined to tell the caller to go to take a hike.

"Hal, Steve Hutchins here."

"Oh, hey, Steve-o. What's up?" Hal's prickliness vanished at the sound of his buddy on the other end of the line.

"Hope you don't mind me calling you so early, but there's a sensitive matter I need to discuss with you."

"Sure, Steve. How can I help?"

"I've been asked to explore whether you're interested in moving up?"

"What do you mean? Moving up? To Albany. Hell no. You know I'm running for re-election."

"We're aware of your campaign, but suppose another opportunity arose? Are you open?"

We. Steve's words evoked the halls of power in the state capitol. While intrigued, Lauren's dilemma in the State Senate popped into his mind. "Legislative or judicial?"

"Don't sound so suspicious. We're not talking about animal control." They laughed. "The latter."

Without thinking, Hal responded. "Go ahead. I'm listening." Rather than dipping his pinky toe into the pool, he'd jump in headfirst.

"Governor Assento's appointing Perry Hamilton to the Court of Claims, of course, subject to senate confirmation. We're vetting his replacement in the County Court. The term starts in September."

As Steve spoke, a rusted green sanitation truck rattled by, screeching its air brake at the yield sign on the corner. Hal pressed the phone to his ear. "Come again?" The Attorney General repeated the sentence.

Dutchess County Court Judge, he thought. Interesting. The judgeship presided over all criminal matters in the county, and minor civil matters seeking less than $25,000 in damages. Given the civil docket overload, he'd also be an Acting Supreme Court Judge. However, he'd be exchanging the world of advocacy for the decision-making power of the bench. And his suit and tie for a black robe. As a public servant, there would be no greater honor than to serve all New Yorkers, not only those in need of criminal justice. He'd be making the law, not merely enforcing it.

The offer was heady, indeed.

"Hamilton's got a flawless track record, so we don't foresee any hurdles to his confirmation, but these things take time, and there's no certainty."

"So I'd complete his term and then run for the seat." He calculated Hamilton was halfway through his ten-year term.

Lauren popped into his mind again. Their relationship was complicated, even more so now.

"We need an answer immediately, Hal." He paused a beat. "As your old friend, I can confide that you're our first choice, and you'd have to be crazy to refuse. This is just the first door about to open for you, but I don't have to tell you how these things work. Do I?"

There was a long silence at the end of the phone as he considered the scenarios. If he lost his DA re-election bid to Lauren, she'd never appoint him as her assistant. There wasn't any bad blood, but politically, she'd be unlikely to rehire her Chief from the opposing party, regardless of his skill and experience. If the offered judgeship didn't materialize, he'd be screwed with two families to support.

If he refused the judgeship, and won re-election as the polls predicted, nothing would change. Lauren would be forced to seek greener pastures, but he'd be stuck at the end of his political line. District Attorney was not an awful place to be stuck.

However, if he continued to run and won, and then received the appointment, he'd be sitting pretty, and Lauren would be out on the street. And his assistant, Cindie, was more than qualified to assume the reins as his successor.

No doubt the offer flattered Hal. It provided more prestige and opportunity than compensation, since the judge's salary would be comparable to his current one. The urgency in Steve's voice suggested another motive.

"Come on Steve, there's something else going on here, isn't there?"

"The timing is coincidental. But you just apprehended New York's most notorious serial killer. Your success certainly didn't hurt."

What difference did it make if the Governor benefitted from his appointment? He'd earned it.

"All right. I'm in, as long as I'm the only candidate." Hal's tone was confident, but his stomach lurched at his overt cockiness. He should have discussed the promotion with Jessie, but Steve had put him on the spot. He'd sworn never to betray Jessie's trust again, but his snap decision stunk of the same duplicity as Emory's. Luckily, their relationship was rock solid, and they'd stay put here in Poughkeepsie. She'd understand the time pressure, and he'd consider not only his career but also their future.

"You are now. And until it's firm, don't withdraw from the ballot."

Honorable Harold Samuels III, Dutchess County Court Judge. He liked the ring of it. Hal pictured himself being sworn in with his hand on a faded leather bible with Jessie by his side. He flashed forward to the bailiff shouting into the crowded courtroom, demanding silence. "Please rise for the Honorable Harold Samuels III."

Yeah, he liked the ring of the title a lot.

Chapter Sixty-Two

The police bullpen buzzed with a frenzy fueled by nicotine, donuts, and caffeine. When the chief's summons arrived, Ebony welcomed the distraction from the overdue paperwork on her desk, but she worried about what would happen next. It would be the first time she'd seen Zander since Bennett's arraignment. He'd been dodging her for days, as though she still exuded the stink of Bennett's attic. His shunning her had been surprising and unsettling. For five years, they'd been more than partners, more like conjoined twins who couldn't survive without each other. He'd left her off balance, like her yin was missing its yang.

She arrived at the chief's office just as the heavy door swung open, almost smacking her in the face. Zander exited with his eyes downcast, pushing past her as though she was invisible.

"Hey, Z," she called after him. To her dismay, he ignored her. She called out again. But he acted deaf, dumb, and blind as he made a beeline through the hive.

The chief sat behind his desk, massaging his graying temples in a manner suggesting a headache. "Jones, get in here and close the door behind you." His gruffness implied her job was on the line, and she wondered what secrets Zander had divulged. Had Zander become a turncoat, or was he still her partner?

Before Ebony could be seated, the chief started in on her. "Jones, I don't like being manipulated or misled by my officers."

She froze.

"Goddammit. I'm the commanding officer and your antics could've

337

jeopardized not only the task force's investigation, but Bennett's arrest."
His face glowed tomato red and a purple vein bulged on his forehead.

Definitely, turncoat, she thought.

Had Zander blabbed about the phony search warrant, or rather the blank
sheet of paper she'd waved at him in pretense? Had Zander figured out that
she'd nicked certain items during their search of Lissie's apartment?

"I could have your badge for this—" The chief raised a clenched fist and
caught himself before he slammed the desk. He examined her, inhaling
deeply and exhaling loudly to control his erupting anger. "Jones, you must
have some goddamn guardian angel."

Ebony watched him in silence.

"I'm a bit confused and maybe you can clarify some points for me." He
sighed. "You and Pulaski arrived at Bennett's house at four p.m., correct?"
She nodded. "But, apparently, no one bothered to contact either me or
DA Samuels when Judge Hamilton had executed the warrant on the prior
afternoon. Therefore, can you explain how, if neither Samuels nor I had
the warrant, you had it? It really baffles me how you—" his voice trailed off.

Her tightening chest felt as though he'd reached inside her body and
squeezed her heart. Shepardson wasn't outright accusing her of misconduct,
but he was toying with her. She understood the insinuation. How could
she have obtained the signed search warrant when the Judge had locked it
away in her chambers overnight? That the signed document existed at all
when she and Zander had visited Bennett's house had saved their careers.

"You're one goddamn lucky—" Shepardson rose from his desk and walked
around it toward her. He stood so close she could observe the tiny veins in
his eyes and the broken capillaries on his broad nose. Ebony edged back,
flattening her spine against the door. "Do you know why I'm tough on
you?"

Ebony blinked as his spit sprayed her cheeks.

Another one of his rhetorical questions. Great.

"Because it makes you tough. And you need to be tough in this business,
tougher than your Kevlar bulletproof vest. Especially if you're going to be
a Detective Sergeant in my department."

Over the galloping pulse throbbing in her ears, his words were slow to register.

"Jones, without you and Pulaski, Bennett would still be terrorizing the streets. Or at least the Governor and the DA believe so."

"Thank you, sir." Her voice quavered and the din in her ears subsided.

"Don't thank me. Governor Assento recommended you both for commendations, and she's requested we place your name on the eligible list for the Detective Sergeant's exam this fall. So, you have plenty of time to bone up." He pursed his lips, failing to hide the grin slowly spreading across his face. "You meet all the qualifications as long as you follow the rules."

"Thank you, sir." The cards were in her favor, so she went for broke.

"I hope Detective Pulaski's also eligible."

"Pulaski? He's eligible, too. But he's opted to sit for the Deputy Sheriff Sergeant's exam instead."

"What?" The screeching white noise inside her head returned.

"He's requested a transfer to County." The chief returned to his desk and fiddled with a stack of papers, avoiding eye contact with her.

"Sir? That's impossible. There must be some mistake." Zander? The Sheriff's Office? Not telling her? She suddenly realized she'd been gaping at the chief and shook off the confusion and despair.

"I suggest you speak with Pulaski. I informed him that there's only one opening in this department, and he argued that you're the better city cop and deserved the promotion. Because of Bennett's case, he recognized how the lack of communication between the local communities has been thwarting arrests, and the need for a systematic overhaul. He mentioned the county had approached him about developing a regional investigative network, or maybe it was the other way around. Like I said, you'd better speak with Pulaski."

"I guess he's been itchy for a change," she muttered.

"If we can speak honestly, you're both ready to move on. I'm glad I get to keep one of you. As Pulaski said, you're the better cop. Also, the bigger pain in the ass." The chief's rare smile faded, and then he waved his hands, shooing her away. "Now, take care of your leg before it becomes a real problem and get out of here."

* * *

The elevator seemed to take forever, Ebony thought, repeatedly punching the down button. She imagined Zander's face on the red plastic button, absorbing her unbridled anger.

She'd been mad at Zander before. They'd had plenty of disagreements over the years; the way she trashed the interior of their car, his occasional reckless driving, her forgetting to submit their incident reports. Just trivial stuff. Not a massive, cataclysmic betrayal of their partnership, their friendship.

Ebony clenched her fist, preparing to wallop the button again, but stopped herself as the door slid open. She stepped into the elevator, rubbing her sore knuckles, and wondered whether she was misdirecting her anger at herself toward Zander. If she thought about it, she'd been a walking time bomb lately. She'd lied to him, withheld critical information from him, and had treated him like crap. She had to admit that ever since Lissie had entered her life, she'd gone off half-cocked chasing after the big bust, without considering the impact on his career. No wonder Zander wanted to transfer and get away from her.

But her career had motivated her selfishness, her drive to succeed. She'd had to overcome obstacles and prejudices to become a cop and a detective. It hadn't been easy for a bi-racial woman to thrive in these ranks, let alone achieve her goals in a swamp populated by men who seemed to hassle her intentionally. She'd harnessed her insecurities as motivation, but maybe this time she'd gone too far.

Zander wasn't like the rest of the guys. He got her. He understood her moods, her idiosyncrasies, and her dedication to making their community a safe place. They balanced each other personally and professionally. He was the last person she wanted to alienate, but she'd done a damn good job of it if he wanted to transfer to another department. They had always had each other's backs, but who would have his now? Or hers?

She shook off the chill of self-rebuke as the doors slid shut. This time she tapped the button for P-2 for the cops' locker room. She'd already searched the entire first floor–Interrogation, Booking, Break, and Processing rooms and the hive, but Zander was nowhere to be found.

He couldn't have left, she thought. The time stamped on his timecard showed he'd logged in and hadn't logged out, and their car keys jangled from her belt loop.

She shoved open the unisex locker room door with her shoulder, and the essence of testosterone, male perspiration, and surreptitiously smoked cigarettes urged her to retreat, but she plowed ahead. Like the other five females on the force, she infrequently visited this male domain. It always seemed easier to shower at her apartment down the street, and more convenient to stash her stuff in the bottom drawer of her desk, her messenger bag, or in the back seat of their car.

At present, the locker room was dark, oozing with the creepiness of a teenage horror movie. As Ebony entered, she scanned the labyrinth of the ninety-five gunmetal grey lockers, one for each cop on the force, and heard the soft whoosh echoing from the back of the locker room.

She snaked her way through the rows toward the showers, which had suddenly become silent. Since Zander's locker was next to hers along the wall next to the showers, she hoped to find him there, but was unprepared for the sight of Zander standing naked before his open locker. His back was toward her, so he hadn't seen her approach. His dark hair was slicked back from the shower and he casually toweled off the rivers of water streaming down his spine. He reached between his thighs and patted himself dry.

In all of their years together, she'd never seen him au naturel. Ebony tried not to stare, but the subdued lighting cast sensuous shadows across his body. She shifted her eyes away, but the image of Zander's taut pecs, six-pack abs, and gluteus maximus as round as ripe apples had burned straight through her retinas into her brain.

"Zander?" Ebony's voice squeaked. Her well of anger seemed to melt away, and she struggled for words. Her cheeks grew hot, and she felt grateful for the darkness of the damp locker room.

"Eb, you scared me," Zander said. He pivoted around, quickly wrapping the towel around his waist in one graceful movement. He raked a hand through his wet locks. "What are you doing here?"

"When were you going to tell me?" Ebony stammered, regaining her composure. Her words echoed off the plaster ceilings and tile walls.

"Do you really want to get into this right now?" He gestured, emphasizing his state of undress.

She reached past him into his locker, snatched his slacks, and pitched them at him. "Get dressed. We need to talk."

Ebony turned and stomped out of the locker room, hoping that he'd follow her. With no destination in mind, and blind to everyone and everything except her rekindled anger, she burst out of the police station, slamming the glass door behind her. She tilted her face upward, soaking in the sun, and inhaled the fresh air to calm her nerves.

Too much had happened today. Good and bad. She'd gained a commendation and entrance to the sergeant's exam, but had lost a part of herself. Maybe the best part.

She climbed onto the picnic table next to the parking lot and collapsed on its rough surface. Crouching forward, she cradled her head between her knees and tried to control the thoughts whizzing through her head at hyper-speed.

Anger, disappointment, disbelief, and fear had seized her by the shoulders and shaken her. In her desolation, Ebony questioned everything she'd believed and trusted about their relationship over the past five years. Zander's imminent departure had sucked the joy out of her successes, their successes. Bennett's arrest.

But even though she was partially responsible, Ebony couldn't deny that Zander was a traitor, a deserter, and a liar. He'd played her like a pinball machine, pushing the right buttons to make her believe they were the best of friends. And he'd tricked her into confiding in him, telling him secrets she'd told no one. Not her sister, not her parents, not Jessie, not even Drew.

Mostly, she felt stupid for undervaluing Zander's importance in her life.

"It's not what you think," Zander said, quietly. She hadn't heard him approach, and he stood before her, his features twisted in visible pain.

"What do I think? I think you hate me because I'm a shitty partner."

His lips parted as his jaw dropped open. "Come on Eb. You know that's not true."

"If it's not the case, then what's going on?"

"Eb, you're the best detective I've ever met." His steel-blue eyes locked onto hers. "Sometimes your methods are really out there, you know. Unconventional, but your heart is always in the right place. You want to save lives and help people." He joined her on the picnic table and grew quiet, as though searching for the right words. "But, it's hard to live in your shadow."

"We're partners, Z. I never meant to hurt you."

He clasped her hands in his and whispered. "When you're a sergeant, you won't need a partner anymore. You'll pass the exam with flying colors the first time around, and I don't want to compete with you for the job. You deserve it, and you've earned it."

Ebony gazed toward the rush hour traffic speeding toward the Mid-Hudson Bridge. She tried to quell the tears welling in her eyes, concentrating on the squeaking of brakes rounding the bend of highway.

"Besides," Zander said, "the sheriff's office is creating a new county-wide network for reporting and investigating major crimes. They've recruited me to take the sergeant's exam and oversee the program. The opportunity never would have happened if we hadn't cracked the Bennett case." She understood him to mean if she hadn't cracked the case, but he'd never admit it to her. "So, I'm getting a promotion, too."

Her fury abated as she considered the inequities Zander would suffer if he remained in the department. The chief had mentioned there was only one sergeant's slot. So, if she passed the exam, Zander would report to her. They'd always been equals, and neither one of them could handle being subordinate to the other. It wouldn't be fair. With Zander transferring to the sheriff's office, they'd hold comparable ranks in two different departments.

While Ebony understood, she wondered whether she'd continue to be as good a cop without him. She relied upon his intuition, his fastidiousness, and his ability to rein in her crazies. However, it would be unethical to manipulate him into staying to ease her insecurities. She knew that the transfer was the best move for Zander. As much as she'd miss him, she had to suck it up for his sake.

"I don't want to lose you, lose us," she admitted, "but I respect your decision. You'll show those deputies how proper police work gets done."

Zander nudged her shoulder. "Hey, none of this is happening tomorrow. We still have plenty of time to get on each other's nerves." When she half-smiled at his joke, he nudged her again. "Come on, Eb. We'll work together again. I promise. After all, you're my point person on serial killers."

It was May, and the thought that they still had time together before the fall exams lightened her spirits. But their inevitable separation would loom over them until their last day as partners.

"We'd better, Pulaski."

* * *

Ebony returned to Interrogation Room One for a final examination of the Missing Persons Investigation Board. Someone had shoved it into the corner, abandoned like the women on the whiteboard had been. They'd lined up the eight photographs as though they depicted travelers waiting for a bus or train. Or a pickup, which reminded Ebony of Reservoir Square Park where their tragic one-way journeys had begun, and its ironic nickname—"Hooker Avenue."

One by one, she dismantled the charts, maps, reports, and photographs, and set them inside the cardboard box as evidence for the prosecution's case. The heaviness in her chest reminded her that Kiki, Angela, Eve, and the rest had become victims of the most gruesome killing spree in county history, but she was proud to have helped secure justice for them and their families. Perhaps Zander's new project would prevent the criminal justice system from neglecting additional missing, vulnerable women, and their cold trails. She could only hope.

The chief stuck his head in the door. "Jones, I thought I'd find you here. I followed up on Bennett's ex, Bianca. She's alive, remarried, and practicing pediatrics in Honolulu."

Ebony smiled. At least the former Mrs. Duvall Bennett had found a happy ending.

Her thoughts wandered to Jessie and their flagging friendship. She partially blamed her own ambition, but Duvall Bennett had exacerbated their rift. In their common pursuit of Lissie's attacker, he'd brought them back together, but then polarized them even worse than before. He'd condemned them to opposite sides of the legal fence—the system versus the individual—and she hoped someday there'd be no wall dividing them.

Chapter Sixty-Three

J essie parked her Jeep in the busy lot at Adam's Farm Stand and sighed. Her hands gripped the steering wheel, and she stared sightlessly out the windshield at the baskets of begonias, petunias, geraniums, and impatiens for sale. This was her first trip to the farmstand since the fateful evening when she'd saved Lissie during the thunderstorm. The surrealism of the past few weeks was fading as her new reality sank in.

A law partnership.

Terrence's calls had ceased, and hopefully, she, Hal, and Lily's future together would continue to blossom like the flowers on display.

Her eyes focused on the red geraniums, and they reminded her about the chores waiting in her garden. She'd add some hanging baskets to her grocery list to brighten her spirits and the front porch.

She didn't know how long she'd been sitting when a car horn honked, interrupting her daydream. In her rearview mirror, she spied a blue Honda idling with its directional signaling dibs for her space.

Jessie shook her head and leaned over to grab her purse from the passenger seat. She started at the sudden, fierce rapping on the driver's window.

"I said no. I'm not leaving right away." She turned toward the pounding and discovered a young woman hugging a terracotta planter of Tiger Lilies, their orange buds swaying in the breeze.

"Martin, don't ya recognize me?" the woman asked. Her dark hair was shorn short into a pixie cut and oversized Jackie O-style sunglasses obscured her tiny face.

"Lissie?" Jessie opened the door and got out. "You look terrific!"

Lissie's facial scars, swelling, and bruises had faded, revealing a fine bone structure with cupid lips. A new ensemble of a stylish motorcycle jacket, pressed denim jeans, and white designer silk blouse completed her makeover.

"I just visited Mr. Jay at the hospital, and he said he was comin' home next week. He looks pretty good for an old dude." Lissie awkwardly thrust the pot at Jessie. Her crooked smile displayed new dental work. "I was on my way over to see ya. Here, this is for you. Your daughter's name is Lily, right?"

"Yes. Thanks. This was very thoughtful." Touched by the gesture, Jessie blinked away the tears as she stowed the plant in the back seat of her Jeep. She'd display it in a place of honor in her yard. "It looks like things are going well. I'm happy for you." She meant it. She hoped Lissie had finally reconciled with her state trooper, cyber-expert father.

"I gotta long way to go, but I'm goin' to community college in the fall. I wanna take my son, Luke, and get an apartment, but my dad says I gotta earn it. He's right, I guess, 'cos I really messed up my life. But that's not all my fault. At least my therapist and NA sponsors are helpin' me to straighten my life out. Those jerks better be right."

She was pleased to hear about Lissie getting help for her issues. And she was pleased to see that despite her polished veneer, Lissie hadn't lost her spunk.

"I'm thinking about accounting. I did a pretty good job cooking Kurt's books, and it was pretty cool."

Ebony had mentioned how Lissie's key-code to Kurt's ledger of illegal drug and stolen property operations had busted the trafficking ring wide open. It had also helped incentivize Hal to expunge Lissie's records, giving her a fresh start. One thing was for sure, Lissie had the talent to become one creative accountant.

"Have you seen Detective Jonesy lately?" Lissie asked.

"No, I haven't, but I heard she'll be taking her sergeant's exam soon." The mention of Ebony made her anxious. Their close relationship seemed to have unraveled like their moth-eaten high school varsity sweaters.

"If you talk to her, please tell her I said thanks. She'll know why." Lissie averted her eyes as though keeping a secret from Jessie.

Considering the acrimony between Lissie and Ebony, Lissie's warm greeting was odd. Jessie could have pressed her about the change of heart, but she recalled Lissie mentioning a stash she'd left behind in her apartment, her "freedom money" as she'd called it. Ebony must have retrieved the cash for Lissie, and from the head-to-toe makeover, it must have been a pretty penny.

"Why don't you tell Ebony yourself?"

"Maybe I'll call her one of these days," Lissie said. "I gotta split. I'll stop by the office when Mr. Jay returns, and I'm sure I'll see ya around." She hesitated, appearing as though she had more on her mind. "Martin, I know you double-crossed Mr. Jay by comin' to find me at Abe's. He also told me you were the one who fished me out of the ditch. That makes three times you saved my butt. It's like you're my guardian angel or somethin'. I want ya to know I appreciate it." She looked Jessie straight in the eye. "My folks brought me up to say please and thank you. So, Jessie. Thank you. I mean it."

A tear slid down Jessie's cheek and kissed the corner of her mouth, and she motioned to Lissie to come closer. "I know it. I'm proud of you. You were very brave to come forward and if you ever need anything, you let me know."

Deep inside, Jessie cherished how much she, Lissie, and Ebony had transformed each other's lives for the better. They'd begun their journeys from different places, but had become unified by the hunt for a killer. Because of their adventure, Ebony had helmed a major law enforcement operation, which had resulted in arrests for murder, racketeering, drugs, and larceny, and had received accolades and a potential promotion.

While she'd received no commendations, Jessie felt content. Without her convincing Lissie to identify Duvall Bennett, the missing persons investigation would have grown old and musty, like the case files belonging to Eve Greenberg, Vanessa Leone, Sharone Standly, Justine Harp, Angela

Gibbons, Camila Cordoba, and Jacqueline Randall. Hal would ensure that Bennett paid for his crimes against them, and that he'd never abuse another woman again. With multiple sentences of life without parole, Bennett would rot behind bars.

As shoppers scurried around the parking lot and cars jockeyed for spots, Jessie and Lissie clung to each other, shedding well-earned tears of joy. Jessie sensed a newly discovered happiness within Lissie and believed that she'd forsaken tragedy to embrace new opportunities. This was yet another takeaway from her misadventures with the recovering drug addict, alcoholic, and hooker.

Jessie felt gratified that she'd helped jumpstart Lissie's new life, but the ultimate reward had been that three women—an attorney, a cop, and a prostitute—had brought Duvall Bennett to justice.

Chapter Sixty-Four

After work, Hal dashed up the front porch steps two at a time and rang Jessie's doorbell. His house keys jangled in his pocket, but he'd wanted his entrance, and his apology, to be dramatic. Behind his back, he clenched a bouquet of red roses. He held them gingerly, careful to silence the crackling cellophane threatening to ruin his surprise.

He had news to share, but tonight he had one mission in mind. Hal wanted everything to be perfect, but the flower's dizzying scents made his head spin. He grew more intoxicated with every breath, more anxious with each step, and more self-conscious of the Tiffany box pressing against his wildly beating heart.

Hal worried Jessie might refuse his impromptu dinner invitation and send him packing. After their fight last night, he'd spent a sleepless evening at his condo, examining why he'd overreacted to Jessie's revelations about Terence Butterfield's menacing calls. It was undeniable that he'd felt wounded about her not confiding in him.

She'd always been independent and strong-willed, but he trusted her judgment. She'd helped apprehend Duvall Bennett and convict Terrence Butterfield, but sometimes she went overboard in keeping her problems private, like those with Terrence.

They'd been sitting outside on the patio enjoying the twilight when Jessie had broken the news about Terrence's phone calls. Regrettably, he'd laid into her long and hard about trust, their relationship, and betrayal.

"Not telling me about Butterfield's call is like Kyle not telling you about his new job," Hal had said, his voice agitated. "It's a sin of omission and in my book, it's as good as a lie."

"Aren't you over-reacting? This isn't about you, it's about me. And it was my problem."

"Yeah, a dangerous problem you hid from me."

"I'm a big girl, and I handled Terrence in my own time and in my own way." She paused, staring at him with her mossy green eyes shimmering with tears. "I researched the law, and I knew what had to be done. Once I discovered that the Office of Mental Health's Mental Hygiene Legal Services represented Terrence, I made my case with them. I outlined Terrence's harassment in an email to his attorney and I attached my phone logs as proof. It didn't take long, maybe a week, before the director of the Mid-Hudson Forensic Psychiatric Hospital contacted me and took action. They terminated Terrence's telephone access indefinitely, so the matter's resolved. Can you please forget about it?"

"How can I forget? Butterfield is a psycho, and he's set on making your life hell. You should have told me." He couldn't seem to control his rising temper or his bitterness. "And while we're on the subject, what about Jeremy Kaplan?"

"Hold on a minute. I know how you feel about Jeremy, but you're wrong about him. Accepting his partnership is my decision, and you need to accept it. It's up to you whether you can get over it." Her lower lip trembled.

"I can't believe that you're tying your professional future to Kaplan. He's a lousy lawyer and a first-rate asshole." The moment he'd finished, he'd wished he'd eased up on his allegations. At least about Kaplan. At Kaplan's encouragement, Jessie had assumed the lead with Lissie Sexton, serving her client and the community without crossing the line. Perhaps the old shyster was mellowing in his infirmity, but he still didn't completely trust the guy. He knew he shouldn't be imposing his opinions on Jessie, but his emotions were getting in the way. "I don't want you to get hurt."

"Don't worry about me. Worry about yourself."

There was no use responding. Every word seemed to dig a deeper hole.

Toward the pink light of dawn, he'd realized he'd been trying to protect their relationship. He'd spurned Jessie once before when he'd married Erin.

His marriage had been a sham, and all the while, his love for Jessie had endured. He'd sworn to himself he'd never run from her love again as he had because of Erin. Yet, last night, he'd run for the hills.

And he'd been hypocritical by accusing Jessie of withholding information about Terrence's calls. He'd practically accepted the judgeship without discussing it with her. But his was good news, not like hers about some lunatic stalking her. In the end, he knew they'd discuss his opportunity and together they'd decide about their future.

More than anything else, though, it bothered him that Jessie needn't have suffered alone. He was there for her, and always would be. Hal thought he'd made his feelings clear to her, but perhaps he'd been mistaken. He'd have to trust that one spat wouldn't destroy the life they'd sacrificed so much to achieve.

Jessie opened the door and smiled wryly, interrupting his reflections.

"Forget your key?" She cocked her head, swaying back and forth. Jessie's fresh, pink skin glowed like a teenager's, although fine worry lines were developing on her forehead.

Dressed in faded jeans and a gray tee-shirt slouching off one shoulder past her bra strap, and her hair pulled back into a ponytail, she looked amazing. A gooey orange handprint tattooed her heart. Lily, smothered in the telltale-pureed carrots, squirmed in Jessie's arms, and she shifted the baby onto her right hip. Even covered in baby food and holding a kid, Jessie looked sexy. God, how lucky he was.

His mind cleared, but his words became choked somewhere between his brain and his tongue. "These are for you." He thrust out the red blooms, and she stared blankly at him.

"I thought you'd still be pissed off at me. The way you stormed out of here after I told you about Jeremy's offer and Terence, I didn't expect to hear from you again."

"Well, I was angry." He realized her arms were full so she couldn't accept the bouquet. Hal entered the house and placed it on the front hall table next to the mail. "Can you blame me? For all those months, a killer was calling you and you never said a word. I could have stopped it with one phone call. Like that." He snapped his fingers.

"You're missing the point. I needed to solve the problem myself, but I appreciate your concern." Jessie handed him Lily, who leaned in and gave him a slimy open-mouthed kiss. Lily's attention returned to Jessie, and she threw herself into Jessie's waiting arms. "Terrence is out of my life forever, so let's move on."

"I'm sorry. You were right, I was wrong. And I won't do it again." Hal justified their argument as playing into his plans. His tantrum had thrown her off course, making tonight's surprise even sweeter. It was kismet.

"Good, I'm glad you've realized the errors of your ways."

"I'm happy, too." His cheek muscles burned from grinning back at her like a teenager in love. "I'm here to take you out on a make-up date."

"Right now? I can't drop everything." She sputtered her words. "What about Lily?"

Behind him, tires crunched across the gravel driveway and halted next to his Volvo. Phase two of his master plan had begun. Lena and Ed had arrived to babysit.

"Bob-bob-bob," the baby squealed, pumping her legs and reaching her chubby hands toward her grandparent's car. "Daaa."

"You've got no excuses. You look beautiful, as usual, but we're going out so it's up to you whether you'd like to change." He raised an eyebrow questioningly and curled one corner of his lip into a half smile. "Our reservation is for six-thirty, so you have twenty minutes to shower and dress for dinner." He knew she couldn't resist the invitation, so he left her no room to waffle. "Get going!"

While Jessie got ready, Hal sprang into action. He had fifteen minutes to accomplish his mission. Just as Lena and Ed whisked Lily away for the night, the caterers arrived. Hal directed them to the back patio where they set an intimate table for two, complete with white linens, crystal candleholders, bone china, and polished silverware. Then they retreated to their van parked around the corner to await further instructions.

There was one last touch to be added to set the mood of romantic mystery. Fairy lights. When he'd finished stringing them across the patio, he flicked on the switch and surveyed his handiwork. Not bad. On cue, the birds chirped, the table and lights sparkled, and the sun waned, spreading its golden warmth over the backyard, like a scene in a movie.

He was pleased, and he hoped Jessie would be, too. Tonight would be the night their futures merged forever.

* * *

Jessie peered down at Hal waiting for her at the bottom of the staircase. He watched her descend, his eyes gleaming, almost misty. He'd dropped no clues about their reservations, so she'd slipped on one of her favorite dresses, a clingy, low-cut black silk wrap dress sprinkled with red flowers. She figured that since he'd apparently choreographed a special evening, she could dress the part. She'd opted for wedges, not stilettos, just in case he wanted to go salsa dancing. With Hal, you never knew.

When she reached him, Hal firmly knitted his fingers in hers and guided her out the front door. They strolled toward his Volvo, but confusion settled over her when they bypassed his car and proceeded toward the backyard.

They rounded the corner of the house and the soft, husky strains of Diana Krall welcomed them out of the shadows and onto the path leading to the bluestone patio. Strings of twinkling fairy lights festooned the yard, and although it was still light out, they looked like fireflies dancing above the most beautiful setting she'd ever seen.

A burgundy Oriental rug spread before her like a runway. Pitched upon it, a white tent sheltered a dining table exquisitely set for two with crisp white linens, an orchid centerpiece, and polished silver domes covering fine bone china. Crystal glasses glinted in the late afternoon sun, and within a silver stand, a bottle of champagne rested askew in a tiny igloo. A chef in a white coat embroidered with the green logo of the Culinary Institute of America waited at attention as Hal guided her past the tent.

"Thanks, Andre," Hal said to the chef, who bowed in acknowledgment. Then, as if by magic, the cook disappeared as they strolled across the lawn.

A slight breeze tousled her hair and billowed her flowered skirt. "This is amazing. You've transformed our yard into an oasis. I don't know where to look first."

"I know where to look." He gave her a knowing smile and slipped his arms around her waist. Their eyes met, and he raised her hand to his lips. She shivered at his kiss. "Cold?"

"Not at all. Just overwhelmed. At this. By you."

Everything she'd ever desired stood in front of her. Hal. Their home together. And Lily. And if there was one thing she'd learned, it was to hold on tightly to people she loved and never let go. She'd been an idiot, keeping Hal at arm's length and denying happiness because of the past. This was the present. Hal was her future, and she wanted it to start now.

"Let's get married," she blurted.

Hal grew quiet, and his eyes widened. "You really know how to steal a guy's thunder." He hesitated. "I wanted this to be a special night. One you'd always remember. I guess it will be."

Jessie's pulse quickened as she realized she'd beaten him to the punch. The principal motive behind his secrecy, the fancy meal, and the romantic setting became as clear as the love shining in his eyes. "Well? Do you want to?"

He chuckled. "You've got to let me do this, Jess. I've been practicing my speech for months."

"Do what?" she replied, mocking him.

Hal dropped to one knee and cleared his throat.

"I've waited, we've waited, a lifetime to be together. And I won't let anyone or anything come between us again." He reached into his blazer pocket and withdrew a robin's egg blue box. He opened it. A diamond solitaire ring rested on a white satin pillow. "Jessica Grace Martin, will you marry me?"

Jessie studied his boyish face, lined by years of fighting for justice against perpetrators of crimes and misdemeanors, and the silver sprinkled through his copper hair. Time had chiseled him from a boy, intimidated by a brutish, domineering father, into a man who stood firm in his convictions. He'd grown from the boy she'd adored into the man she loved.

When he'd married Erin, she'd believed that Hal had vanished from her life, creating a void that no man could fill. She'd tried to make it work with Kyle, but her heart had always belonged to Hal Samuels. She'd known, and ultimately, Kyle had, too. After so many years, she and Hal were together in the most beautiful place in the world, their home, and they were going to get married.

So much had changed in a year. Ryan Paige's murder had thrown her and Hal together, and as tragic as his death was, she'd be forever grateful for their extraordinary reunion. They'd suffered through separation, betrayal, and misunderstandings, to find their way back to each other. To this moment.

"Hey," she said. "I asked you first."

His golden eyes sparkled, pleading for an answer.

"Yes, I'll marry you. I want to spend the rest of my life with you, Harold Samuels III." She lifted her eyes brows inquisitively.

"Yes, Jessica Grace Martin, I will marry you, too."

Jessie's knees turned to rubber, and unable to prevent her legs from buckling, she collapsed onto the grass beside him. Hal slipped his hands around her waist, pulled her to him and squeezed he so tightly she felt his racing heart.

"I love you," he murmured.

"I love you, too."

Their lips met, sealing their fates, their future, and their love.

She never wanted the kiss to end.

Chapter Sixty-Five

The rest of the summer passed in a blur, leaving Jessie with a sense of wellbeing and the sense that life had settled into a routine. She sat at her desk in her den, staring at the computer screen and thinking about how proud she'd been at Hal's swearing-in as Dutchess County Court Judge. Year-old Lily was walking and babbling nonstop. And Jessie and Kyle had finally made peace. They were signing their custody and support agreement next week.

She sighed in relief and tugged her sweater around her shoulders. September had ushered in abrupt changes in the weather. The days were still warm, but the nights were cool, tinting the leaves red and yellow.

Her partnership with Jeremy was working out fine. He was on the mend, and considering taking on an unusual, challenging case, so she was busy researching the rise in hate crimes in the Hudson Valley.

Jessie had been so absorbed in her thoughts she hadn't heard Hal enter the room, and she jumped when his lips touched the back of her neck.

"What are you working on?" he whispered in her ear.

She quickly minimized her research, leaving up a spreadsheet of their wedding guests.

"Who wants to know? Judge Harold Samuels III or my fiancé?" He struck a playful judicial pose with his shoulders squared and his hands clasping the collar of his imaginary robe.

"The latter, of course." He kissed her again, this time on the lips, and leaned over to review the list. "Wedding stuff, huh? Isn't it a bit early to be preparing for something next summer?"

"No, June will be here before you know it, and my mother is nagging me for the invitation list. You know how she is." Her mother's attitude toward Hal had shifted one hundred eighty degrees, and sometimes Lena seemed more excited about the wedding than they were. Her father had also succumbed to wedding fever, blubbering like a fool with happy tears every time he came over to their house.

"Oh, I do, and I see Ebony's included with a plus one. Have you spoken to her lately?"

"The jury is still out on whether she makes the final cut, and no, I haven't spoken to her since Bennett's arraignment. She acted distant toward me, but apparently, she and Lissie are buddies now. At least's according to Lissie."

"Ah, the notorious Ms. Sexton and Ebony Jones. Now there's an odd couple."

Jessie chuckled. His expression grew stern, and she braced herself for a lecture.

"Ebony's your oldest friend. You really don't want to throw her away, do you? You should call her and find out what's going on."

"You're right. I should, but I've been busy with the wedding, the job, Lily, and finalizing the settlement with Kyle."

"Those sound like excuses to me, but it's your life." He shrugged. "I'll leave you to whatever you're doing, but we shouldn't waste this beautiful afternoon."

"You're right. I'll call Ebony this week. Let me save my work and we'll go apple picking across the river in Highland. We have plenty of time since Kyle won't be bringing Lily home from their visit together until after dinner."

"It's a relief that you and he have worked things out. Makes our lives a lot easier."

She knew he meant it. Tensions had eased between Kyle and Hal, and between herself and Kyle. And Kyle seemed to accept their impending nuptials.

Hal gave her a peck. "Let me grab a sweatshirt."

"I'll be ready in a few minutes," Jessie called after him.

Jessie glanced at her phone to check the time—noon—and her messages. Even though Terrence's calls had stopped, checking her phone had become a habit, reassuring her that the nightmare with him was over. She noticed a message from Fedex saying that the leather jacket she'd ordered for Hal's birthday was out for delivery and would arrive that afternoon.

The doorbell rang, and Jessie shut down her computer and ran to answer the door.

Acknowledgements

As I keep telling my family, my books don't write themselves. With that truism in mind, I would like to thank my family, friends and associates, all of whom contributed to the growth and development of *Hooker Avenue*.

Foremost, all my love and thanks to my incredible family. During the pandemic lockdown my husband, Mike, our younger son, Ben, and my older son Max, his wife, Aleigha, and their baby, Wade, and I were all hunkered together in our Hudson Valley home. While we all pitched in to keep our family, including my mother, safe during those scary, dark months, my family gave me the space to complete this manuscript. Many thanks to them for letting me shut my office door and for honoring the "Do Not Disturb – Novel in Progress" sign. I couldn't have finished this book without their support.

I want to thank my amazing friends Maureen Cockburn, Jackie Beltrani, Joy Dyson, Margaret King, Dave Lowrie, Nalaini Sriskandarajah, and Rajan Sriskandarajah for rising to the call as Beta Readers. Their honesty, insightful remarks and questions helped me fill in the plot holes and streamline the manuscript. Sometimes, I couldn't see the forest for the trees, or the typos, and they helped me navigate through the woods.

For almost five years, I've been working with the amazing Laurie Sanders and her Yellow Highlighter Workshops. Over that time, Laurie has reread *HOOKER AVENUE* almost as many times as I have. I am grateful for her patience, her eagle eye and keen editing skills, which helped me chisel away at this block of marble and turn it into the polished manuscript you are reading.

Sometimes, you never know when someone special will enter your life. That is the case with Jess Taylor, who began as my editor at Revizion.net, but became a friend and a trusted advisor on my journey along *Hooker Avenue*. Jess's encouragement and wry humor helped me put my writing into perspective, and make Ebony a kick-ass, yet sentimental, cop.

While I was researching this novel, I called upon my friend, Ron Hicks, Asst. Dutchess County Executive with questions about the Dutchess County 911 Emergency Response Center. I would like to thank Ron, Commissioner Dana Smith and their staff for the insightful information on their procedures and for the essential lifesaving services they render to our community. Also, special thanks to Stacey Madoff, MD for providing her OB-GYN expertise so I could accurately portray Jessie's adventures in the shadowy ultrasound room. And thanks to Dave Warshaw, Esq. at the New York State Mental Hygiene Legal Services, for sharing his expertise on patient's rights.

This is my second go-around with the amazing publicity team at Meryl Moss Media. Deb Zipf and Meryl have been my tireless partners in scheduling podcasts, print, television and media interviews, and book tours, which have brought attention to my novels and "The Writers Law School" lecture series. As usual, they have gone above and beyond for me, and many thanks again. I'd like to give a special shout-out to Jim Alkon and Cynthia Conrad at Booktrib.com. When I'm not writing my own books, I'm having a blast reading and reviewing other writers' works.

To the Dames of Detection - Shawn Reilly Simmons, Verena Rose, and especially my editor, Harriette Sackler. Thanks for inviting me to join the talented "Besties," and supporting me through my writing journey and bringing *HOOKER AVENUE* into the world. Joining Level Best Books was like coming home to a welcoming community of thriller, mystery and crime writers.

Special tips of the hat go to my terrific graphic artist, Kelsy O'Shea, who's always available to help me create my brand and seems to read my mind, and to the Poughkeepsie Public Library District for assisting in my research of the history behind the real "Hooker Avenue" and their support of local authors. And thanks to my writer friends who graciously wrote blurbs for this book. I'm grateful to belong to such a giving community.

A brief note of thanks goes out to the Crime Bake 2019 Master Classes with Hallie Ephron and Ann Cleeves. Hallie helped me realize Ebony needed a personal stake in the outcome of case, and Ann helped me elevate the Hudson Valley into a crucial participant in the crimes.

Finally, thanks to all the wonderful writers organizations: Sisters In Crime, Guppies-Sisters in Crime, RWA Kiss of Death, International Thriller Writers, OIRWA, Mystery Writers of America, Authors Guild, and Women's Fiction Writers Association, who have provided and continue to provide education, support and networking for writers in this lonely business during these challenging times.

To sign up for my newsletter, view my events calendar, and discover the true crime behind the story, please visit my website, www.jodemillman.com.

About the Author

Jodé Millman is the acclaimed author of *The Midnight Call*, which won the Independent Press, American Fiction, and Independent Publisher Bronze IPPY Awards for Legal Thriller. She's an attorney, a reviewer for Booktrib.com, the host/producer of *The Backstage with the Bardavon* podcast, and creator of The Writer's Law School. Jodé lives with her family in the Hudson Valley, where she is at work on the next installment of her "Queen City Crimes" series—novels inspired by true crimes in the region she calls home. Discover more about Jodé, her work and sign up for her newsletter at www.jodemillman.com.

SOCIAL MEDIA HANDLES:
  Facebook: @JodeSusanMillmanAuthor
  Instagram: @Jodewrites
  Twitter: @worldseats

AUTHOR WEBSITE:
  http://www.jodemillman.com

Also by Jodé Millman

The Midnight Call (2019, Immortal Works)

Seats: New York - 180 Seating Plans to New York Metro Concert Halls and Sports Stadiums (2nd & 3rd Edition) (2002, 2008 Applause Theatre and Cinema Books)

Seats: Chicago - 120 Seating Plans to Chicago and Milwaukee Metro Area Theatres, Concert Halls and Sport Stadiums (2004, Applause Theatre and Cinema Books)

CPSIA information can be obtained
at www.ICGtesting.com
Printed in the USA
BVHW032043250422
635297BV00010B/35